IN AT THE DEEP END

Kate Davies was born and brought up in north-west London. She studied English at Oxford University before becoming a writer and editor of children's books. She's also a screenwriter, and had a short-lived career as a burlesque dancer that ended when she was booed off stage at a Conservative club while dressed as a bingo ball. Kate lives in East London with her wife. *In at the Deep End* is her first novel.

Praise for *In at the Deep End*:

'Without a doubt, *In at the Deep End*, by Kate Davies, is the afterparty book for anyone looking to extend their *Fleabag* fun ... Davies' book is **raucous, sexy, poignant and smart**, and is definitely the most **fun** you will have with lesbian BDSM short of doing it yourself' Hadley Freeman, *Guardian*

'*Fleabag*-level dirty jokes, *Eleanor Oliphant*-levels of empathy and a heroine who feels like your best mate spilling the gossip after two glasses drunk a little too quickly. **Fresh, funny** and **filthy**' *Grazia*

'**Raucous and raunchy** tale of coming out, of good sex with bad people ... **a rip-roaring read** that's also painfully honest about what it means to be a sexually active woman of any orientation' *DIVA Magazine*

'**Brilliant**! The best thing I've read in AGES. I can't remember the last time a book made me laugh so hard, while also making me think about life, relationships and what makes us who we are' Gill Sims, author of *Why Mummy Drinks*

'A frank, very **funny** and, at times, filthy exploration of sex, love and self-understanding ... **brilliant**' Francesca Brown, *Stylist*

IN AT THE DEEP END

Kate Davies

THE BOROUGH PRESS

The Borough Press
An imprint of HarperCollins*Publishers* Ltd
1 London Bridge Street
London SE1 9GF

www.harpercollins.co.uk

HarperCollins*Publishers*
1st Floor, Watermarque Building, Ringsend Road
Dublin 4, Ireland

First published by HarperCollins*Publishers* 2019
4

A catalogue record for this book is available from the British Library

ISBN: 978-0-00-831138-4

Set in Perpetua Std by Palimpsest Book Production Ltd,
Falkirk, Stirlingshire

Printed and bound in the UK by CPI Group (UK) Ltd, Croydon CR0 4YY

MIX
Paper from
responsible sources
FSC
www.fsc.org
FSC™ C007454

To my one true Spud

1. SEX NOISES

One Saturday morning last January, Alice pointed out that I hadn't had sex in three years. I knew I'd been going through a dry patch – I'd been getting through vibrator batteries incredibly fast, and a few days previously I'd Googled *penis* just to remind myself what one looked like – but the full force of how much time I'd wasted not having sex hadn't hit me till then.

The last time I'd had sex was nothing to write home about either, let me tell you. He was a twenty-one-year-old editorial assistant from Alice's office with an unusually large forehead, and it happened after a terrible house party that left our flat stinking of pastis. I tried to take him to my room, but a couple were already in there, dry-humping on top of the duvet, so we did it on the fake leather sofa in the living room. I kept getting stuck to the sofa, sweat pooling in the gap beneath my lower back. I don't think he'd ever fucked anyone before, so it was a bit awkward and thrusty, and he cried and hugged me for too long afterwards. It comes back to me in flashes all the time – I could be boarding a bus, washing my hair, or sitting on a particularly squeaky sofa when suddenly I see his clenched red face or his sweaty pubic hair and flinch involuntarily. Enough to put anyone off sex for, say, three years.

To be honest, I'd always preferred the idea of sex to sex itself. In my imagination, I was experimental, confident, uninhibited, a biter of

1

shoulders, a user of words like 'pussy'. I could think about sex in the filthiest terms and speak frankly about it to friends – but when it came to actually doing it, or talking to someone I might do it *with*, I clammed up. I struggled to think of myself as sexy when I was with another person. I struggled to say sexy things with a straight face. It all felt performative to me, ridiculous, too far removed from the way I behaved in a non-sexy context, like I was playing a part in a porn film, and playing it badly. I couldn't even flirt convincingly, certainly not when I was sober. Which might go some way towards explaining why it had been so long since I'd fucked anyone.

Alice and Dave, on the other hand, did have sex. A surprising amount of it, actually, considering they'd been going out for five years. The Friday night before that Saturday morning, I was alone in the living room, trying to ignore the sex noises coming from their bedroom. Our flat had incredibly thin walls, so it was almost as if I were there with them. How can something that is so much fun when you're doing it (though not always – see previous note about sweaty sofa sex) be so repulsive when overheard? I didn't mind living with a couple; having three people in the flat brought the rent down. Also, Dave had several Ottolenghi cookbooks and some very tasteful mid-century furniture, so we were better fed and more stylish than we would have been without him. But sex-noise-wise, I'd had enough.

The next morning, I heard Alice walk Dave to the door. They whispered to each other revoltingly and kissed wetly. I sat on my bed, picking the dry skin on my fingers, practising my speech in my head.

Alice walked into my room without knocking; people tend to do that when there's no risk you'll be shagging. She sat on my bed, her hair rumpled, a post-coital smile on her face. 'Do you fancy brunch?' she said. 'I'm starving.'

'I'm not surprised,' I said, which wasn't how I'd intended to broach the subject.

'What?'

'Nothing.'

'Why aren't you surprised? What do you mean?'

'Well – you and Dave sounded like you had fun last night.'

'You listened to us having sex?'

'I didn't listen. I *heard*. It wasn't an active choice.'

'We weren't that loud,' said Alice, as though asking for reassurance.

'You asked him to—'

'To what?'

I looked away. 'You know what you asked him to do.'

'How do I know if you won't say?'

'Fine. You asked him to stick a finger up your arse.'

'Julia!'

'You're the one that said it!'

'That's private!'

'So keep your voices down!'

Alice's cheeks were pink.

There was an unpleasant silence.

'Did you really hear us?'

'Yes! I always hear you!'

'You can't always hear us. We don't even have sex that often any more—'

'Three times a week isn't often?'

'Not for us.'

'Well. I'm very happy for you.'

Another silence.

'You wouldn't care so much if you had a boyfriend too.'

'I don't want a boyfriend, thank you.'

'Sex, then.'

'I have sex.'

'No, you don't,' she said. And that's when she pointed it out, about the three years.

I went back to bed after that, and stayed there for most of the

3

day, eating cheese and trying to remember what sex was like. I'd never had really, really good sex, the kind that resulted in the sort of noises I heard Alice and Dave making. Oral always felt a bit like someone was wiping a wet flannel over my nether regions, and having a man on top of me made me feel quite claustrophobic.

The thing is, sex had never been particularly high on my list of priorities. In my teens, I was too obsessed with becoming a dancer to worry about having a relationship. I did manage to lose my virginity after my first year at ballet school, though; my friend Cat took me to Jamaica to stay with her grandparents, and I did it on the beach with a boy named Derrick, who had terrible acne and a bottle of cheap rum, which is what led to the sex. We didn't use a condom; the sheer terror I'd felt afterwards at the prospect of being pregnant and the mechanics of trying to procure a morning after pill without Cat's grandparents finding out had put me off sex for years after that. I still can't drink daiquiris. But I was pleased to have got it over with – I felt more sophisticated than the other girls in my year, enjoyed muttering wisely, 'Don't do what I did. Wait until you're ready,' whenever we talked about sex at sleepovers.

Then there was Leon. I met him during a Freshers' Week toga party at Warwick. He'd looked very fetching in his white sheet, and it was only later that I realized he wore corduroy trousers every day. Nevertheless, we stayed together, right up until he dumped me just after graduation because he wanted to 'travel the world' and be 'free of ties'. He moved to Peckham three months later and started a graduate training scheme in management consultancy.

Leon and I had quite fun sex in the early days – we tried out the reverse cowgirl, did it standing up in the shower, things like that – but by the end of the relationship he could only get in the mood by listening to the 'Late Night Love' playlist on Spotify, and I knew exactly where his hands would be at which point in each track, so it was a bit like an obscene, horizontal line dance. The boring sex was bad for both of us, self-esteem-wise, I think. After we broke up I decided to have a bit of a sex break, and the longer I left it, the scarier sex seemed, like crossing a big, naked Rubicon. I had a couple of drunken one-night stands – including the sofa sex – but most of the time going home alone seemed like a much more sensible, less humiliating option, and far less likely to lead to stubble rash.

I masturbated, though – I had a couple of reliable vibrators, a Rampant Rabbit and a small bullet-shaped one that I took on holiday with me. The only thing I didn't have was someone to grab my breasts. I tried to do it to myself sometimes, but it wasn't the same.

Dave made us roast beef that Wednesday night. As he was cooking, I sat on the sofa imagining myself fucking him – something I swear I'd never done before – and I found my heart speeding up a bit. Dave is objectively a very good-looking man, despite his massive beard. I found myself staring at the beard, wondering whether it got in the way during oral sex, and looking at his knuckles, imagining what they'd feel like inside me. I couldn't look him in the eye for a little while after that. I didn't really want Dave's fingers inside me, honestly. But I did want *something* inside me. Something live and warm and moving and not made of pink latex.

I was more awkward than usual during dinner that night, which isn't that surprising, really. Dave did most of the heavy lifting, conversation-wise, asking me lots of questions about work in his lovely northern accent and pretending to be interested in my answers, even though I was a civil servant at the Department of Health and Social Care, answering letters from members of the public about foster care and NHS waiting times and other things I'd rather not think about, and he was a graphic designer, which is both cooler and less depressing.

He passed me the horseradish and asked, 'Get any good letters this week?'

People don't usually send letters to the government unless they are very angry and very old. But there are exceptions.

5

'Got another one from Eric,' I said.

'The Bomber Command vet?'

I nodded. 'He's upset about the cuts to social care.'

'Didn't he write to you about that last month?' Alice asked, through a mouthful of beef.

'Last month it was the standard of hospital meals.'

'Getting old's a bastard, isn't it?' Dave said, but his eyes were fixed on Alice, and I could tell he was playing footsie with her under the table. I stared down and concentrated on the steam curling up from my potatoes, but the footsie continued.

There was a pause in the foot fondling while Alice cleared the table and served our dessert (Ben & Jerry's), but then it started up again, and it put me off my ice cream – no easy feat. So I ate it as quickly as I could, then pushed my chair back.

'Thanks for cooking, Dave,' I said.

'No worries,' he said, smiling at Alice.

Alice looked up at me. 'Stay and hang out with us,' she said. 'There's that Benedict Cumberbatch thing on tonight.'

'I'm not really into Cumberbatch,' I said. 'And I've got a bit of a headache.'

I went to my room and switched on my TV. I tried to watch a cooking show, but Alice and Dave were soon snogging so loudly that I could hear them above the shouty presenter. So I opened my laptop and put my headphones on, and then I switched on private browsing and searched for *real couples* on Pornhub.

There's something comforting about watching ordinary people having sex; I always think I'd probably do it better than them. Maybe that's not the point of porn, but I don't care – their incompetence turns me on. I clicked on a video and watched a thin, pale man adjust his shaky video camera and walk over to the bed where an overweight woman was waiting for him. I pulled my trousers down to my ankles and started to wank as the pale man slapped himself arrhythmically into his partner. That'll show the patriarchy,

I thought. I'm going to give myself an amazing orgasm in about two minutes, because I know how to push my own buttons – I don't need a man to do it for me.

But then it was over, and I felt hollow and desperate to come again. The video ended, and an ad for *Hot local sluts* popped up. I flinched and clicked on it to make it go away, but I accidentally clicked on the ad instead, and a woman with huge, spherical breasts filled my screen, panting and rubbing her nipples. I tried to shut it down, but hundreds of windows had popped up, each one filled with hot blondes, or dirty Russians, or naughty teens, like endless mirrors reflected in mirrors. Looking at them turned me on, and that made me feel sordid again, so I slapped down the lid of my laptop and hugged my pillow. It didn't hug me back.

I told Nicky about my unsatisfying wank. Bringing it up was a bit awkward; it was only my third session and I wasn't that comfortable with her yet. I wasn't that comfortable with the idea of being in therapy at all; I never thought I'd have a shrink at 26, even a semi-amateur one. A therapist feels like the sort of thing only glamorous New Yorkers should have, the kind who can afford to buy olives from Dean & DeLuca and who say things like 'My ob-gyn told me to eat less wheat.' This is how it happened: I'd been suffering from constant, low-level anxiety, the sort of feeling you get when you realize you've forgotten to turn the hob off, but all the time. Then one day I had a panic attack in the middle of a team meeting about letterheads at work, probably triggered by the fact that I have a job which involves team meetings about letterheads. Nobody noticed – it was a subtle panic attack – but that evening I burst into tears in the middle of the Sainsbury's frozen-food aisle, holding a packet of fishcakes. So I went to the GP.

'Would you say that you've been excessively worried, more days than not, for over six months?' the GP asked, looking down at a checklist.

'I don't know if I'd say *excessively* worried.'

'What sort of things are you worried about?'

'Just – everything, really.'

'Probably excessive then.' She smiled at me. 'Do you think the world is an innately good or evil place?'

'Definitely good,' I said, pleased, because I knew that was the correct answer.

'And you haven't thought about hurting yourself? You don't have suicidal thoughts?'

'Never.'

'Do you feel like you can't cope with everyday things?'

'No.'

'Do you have trouble making decisions?'

'Not really.'

'And do you often find yourself crying for no reason?'

'No. I mean – I cry quite a lot, but I usually have a reason.'

'OK,' said the GP. 'It's unlikely that you have clinical depression.'

'Hooray!' I said, giving myself a little cheer.

The GP smiled again – a patient smile, I now realize, looking back on it. 'You appear to have what we call Generalized Anxiety Disorder,' she told me.

I was very excited to have an actual disorder.

'I'll refer you for talking therapy,' she said. 'But it might be better to go private – the NHS waiting list is nine months long.'

'I know,' I said. 'The Department of Health and Social Care gets a lot of letters complaining about that.'

I felt calmer than I had in ages. I went home and Googled *cheap counsellor north London anxiety*, and Nicky's name came up. She was still training to be a therapist, which is why I could afford her, and she had an un-therapist-like way of voicing her very strong opinions on almost every topic. When I told her about the anxiety, and about feeling lost and directionless in life, she said it was no wonder I was anxious, and that my job sounded so dull they should 'prescribe it to insomniacs'.

Anyway, I told Nicky about the wank. I could feel myself sinking deeper and deeper into the armchair as I spoke, as though it was recoiling from me. She didn't recoil, though. She wanted to know all about it.

'What did the couple look like?'

'Does that matter?'

'I don't know until you tell me.'

'She was overweight and black. He was skinny and white.'

'Aha.' She nodded in a therapist-like way.

'What?'

'Nothing.' She scribbled something in her notebook and underlined it several times.

'Do you often masturbate thinking about Alice?' she continued.

'I wasn't thinking about her!'

'But you said you were wanking out of resentment.'

'I was pissed off with them for having such loud sex, that's all.'

'Because you're not getting any?' She gazed at me, unblinking.

'Look, I'm not repressed, all right? I'd have sex if anyone wanted to have sex with me, but no one has for ages.'

'So you're just waiting for someone to offer it to you on a plate.'

'Well, no—'

'That's what it sounds like to me. It's just like your career. You've just decided to sit back and stay in this dead-end temp job—'

'I'm a contractor, actually, not a temp. And I might apply for the Fast Stream this year,' I said.

'Why didn't you apply last year?'

I hadn't applied because that would mean saying 'I'm a civil servant' when people at parties asked, 'What do you do?' and then having to answer a lot of questions about NHS funding and whether I approve of the government. I hate it when people ask, 'What do you do?' I assume everyone does, even if the answer is 'I'm a novelist,' or 'I'm a surgeon specialising in babies' hands,' because even then you know someone will say, 'Will you show my book to your agent?' or 'Can you look at this lump on my finger?' I missed being able to say, 'I'm a dancer.'

I looked at the floor. There was some sort of stain on the carpet – ketchup, possibly.

'You need to make an effort with your career,' Nicky said. 'It's the same as your love life. You're not prepared to put yourself out there.'

'I'm not going to go looking for a relationship. I don't need one to make me complete. I'm independent.'

She put down her notebook. '*Are* you independent?' she asked. 'Or are you really, really sad?'

I maintained a dignified silence.

'It's OK to cry,' she said.

'I'm not *that* sad,' I said.

'Just let it out.'

'I'm not crying,' I said, which wasn't strictly true.

She handed me the tissue box triumphantly.

I called Cat on my way home from Nicky's. I didn't want to be alone with my thoughts, and I could always rely on Cat to tell me an anecdote about her terrible career to put my problems in perspective.

'Do you fancy a drink?' I asked, when she picked up the phone.

'I wish,' she said. 'I'm in Birmingham. Doing the life cycle of the frog again.' She sounded a little out of breath. She'd probably been having energetic sex too.

'When are you back?' I asked, sidestepping a puddle.

'Not for ages,' she said. 'It's a UK tour.'

'Ooh!'

'Of primary schools.'

'Oh.'

'I'm probably going to get nits again. Or impetigo.'

Cat couldn't get work as a dancer after school – every company she auditioned for said, 'You have the wrong body type,' which is the legal way of saying 'You're black.' But instead of doing what I did when my dance career ended – moving back in with my parents and swearing never to perform again, except to sing my signature version of 'I Wanna Dance with Somebody' at karaoke nights – she retrained as an actor. Now she earned most of her money performing in Theatre in Education shows, playing roles like 'frog' and 'plastic bottle that won't disintegrate' and 'uncomfortably warm polar bear'. I think we probably stayed close over the years because neither of us could stand our other friends from dance school, with their *OMG I just got cast in Birmingham Royal Ballet's Swan Lake! #Blessed* Instagram posts. I did feel envious of Cat sometimes, though. She still got to experience the thrill of applause, even though the people applauding sometimes pulled each other's hair and had to be sent to the naughty corner.

'Lacey's playing the frogspawn,' Cat continued, 'and she won't stop going on about the musical she's writing about periods.'

'I bet that's actually going to be really successful,' I said.

'It is, isn't it? Oh God . . .'

I heard a muffled sort of stretching sound on the other end of the line.

'Are you taking your tadpole costume off?' I asked her. 'Go on, sing me the tadpole song again.'

'I'm the frog this time. Fucking green leotard is a size too small.'

'You've been promoted!'

'Very funny,' said Cat. 'One of the kids came up to me today and said, "You're not a real frog. You're too big." I swear six-year-olds are getting stupider.' More stretching and shuffling, and then a grunt of effort. 'Got it off.'

'So now you're naked.'

'Yep. This is basically phone sex,' she said.

'This is the closest I've come to a shag in three years.' I gave myself a mental pat on the back. At least I could joke about it.

'I thought I had it bad,' Cat said. 'Lacey's been shagging Steve, the new tadpole, all tour, and I've been feeling like a total third wheel.'

'You're best off out of that,' I said. 'Tadpoles shagging frogspawn is all wrong. Sort of like incest.' I tucked my phone under my chin and unlocked the front door.

'How are you anyway? How's work?' asked Cat.

'Too boring to talk about.'

'You need a creative outlet outside work.'

'No thanks,' I said. All I wanted to do was watch TV without listening to people have sex. I sat on the sofa, coat still on, and felt around between the cushions for the remote. *Come Dine with Me* was on, and Alice and Dave were out. This was shaping up to be a good evening.

2. NO-MAN'S-LAND

I was a little late to work the next day, so my usual desk was taken. I waved at Owen, who I usually sit with, across the grey no-man's-land of desks and chairs. I could feel other people looking up at me from the trenches, so I ducked down into the nearest seat, next to Stan, one of the press officers. I usually try to avoid Stan, because he breathes loudly and eats crisps all day. An unsociable combination. This morning he'd gone for salt and vinegar rather than cheese and onion, which was a blessing.

I couldn't concentrate on logging the new emails and letters – my session with Nicky was still playing on my mind – so I pulled out the latest letter from Eric, the Bomber Command vet, written on thin, yellowing lined paper in shaky blue biro, and started drafting my reply.

You're not supposed to draft a stock response to government correspondence – you're supposed to treat each letter writer as an individual. There are guidelines that tell you how to address a Baroness ('Baroness Jones, not Lady Jones; it's important to distinguish Baronesses from women who become Ladies when their husbands become Sirs') and how to refuse an invitation to a Minister ('Unfortunately, pressures on her diary are so great that she must regretfully decline'). Sometimes you take letters to the Minister for their signature. Sometimes, if the letter isn't addressed to the

Minister, you sign it yourself. Some people write back over and over again, so working on the correspondence team is a bit like having lots of self-righteous pen pals. Eric, the Bomber Command veteran, wasn't self-righteous, though.

> *The care home staff are under so much pressure that they don't have as much time to spend with us as they used to. I think the cuts to social care are a crying shame. Older people are an easy target, because once we reach a certain age, we're hidden away out of sight.*
>
> *Most of the old dears at my care home don't get any visitors at all. That just breaks my heart. I'm lucky – I have a daughter who comes and sees me twice a week. She's very good. But it's very lonely getting older. I miss Eve, my wife, more than I can tell you. She died four years ago. Have I told you about her already?*

Lovely Eric. He reminded me of my granddad, who I missed every day. When I was at university, Granddad had written to me every month or so, in wobbly, old-fashioned handwriting, telling me stories about his allotment and his cats, always slipping a ten-pound note into the envelope. I had usually been too busy getting drunk to write back. So I took extra care with my letters to Eric. I typed out the old lines about difficult choices and austerity, and then I asked him to tell me more about his wife, because I knew what it was like to be lonely. I caught myself thinking: At least he had a wife. And then I realized that being envious of a bereaved care home resident was taking self-pity too far, and decided to pull myself together.

I finished my letter and I was wrangling with the printer – usually you have to put the headed notepaper in face down, with the letterhead closest to the printer, but someone had fiddled with the settings – when I saw Owen heading to the kitchen for a coffee. I decided to corner him.

I glanced into the hallway to check that no one was about to interrupt our conversation and asked, 'How long has it been since you had sex?'

Owen spends most nights gaming, and most of his lunch breaks reading comic books, and not a lot of time with members of the opposite sex. So I thought his response to my question would make me feel better. I was wrong.

He glanced at his watch. 'Two and a half hours.'

'You had sex this morning?'

'That's right.' Owen crossed his arms and smirked.

'No need to be so smug about it.'

'But I am smug!' said Owen. 'Do you know how long it had been before I met Laura? Four years.' He grabbed my arm and gave it a little shake. 'Over four years. I hadn't had a shag since I was twenty-four!'

I felt slightly better after that. 'I haven't had sex in three years.'

I could see Owen trying to arrange his face into an expression of sympathy. 'Poor you,' he said.

'So. Who's Laura?'

He shrugged. 'We've been seeing each other for a few weeks.'

'Great.' I nodded and smiled, as convincingly as I could.

'She does roller derby. She has tattoos all over her thighs.'

'I don't think I need to hear about her thighs,' I said, lowering my voice as a group of Fast Streamers walked past the kitchen, speaking to each other in low voices as if they knew something we didn't, which they undoubtedly did.

'Sex is great,' he said, smiling to himself in a way that let me know he was thinking about Laura's thighs. Or what was between them. Grim. 'I'd forgotten how good it is.'

'All right,' I said. 'Don't rub it in.'

The sex chat made us late to our team meeting. Owen and I huffed into the glass-walled meeting room, breathless, saying, 'Sorry, sorry,' as we sat down.

Tom didn't look up. He had a very passive aggressive management style – that's what I'd have liked to say in the annual Staff Engagement Survey, but our team was so small I thought he'd trace the feedback to me and passive-aggressively punish me for it. Probably by making me answer all the correspondence about Brexit.

There were three of us on our immediate team besides Tom: me, Owen and Uzo, who was smiling up at me kindly now. Uzo was always smiling at me kindly. She'd been working on the correspondence team for twenty years and had the least ambition of anyone I'd ever met. Whenever I messed up, she'd say things like, 'Don't worry, girl. You won't care when you've worked here as long as me,' and I'd go and quietly hyperventilate in the toilets. She did have a lovely collection of statement necklaces, though.

'As I was about to say,' said Tom, still not looking up, 'they're bringing in a new Grade Six.'

Owen and I looked at each other.

'What, another senior manager?' said Owen.

'Yes, Owen,' said Tom, smiling his tight smile.

'Above you?' said Owen.

'Yes,' said Tom, his smile tighter still. 'Above me.'

'But we thought you were going to be promoted,' said Owen.

'Yes, well. So did I,' said Tom. He fiddled with his tie.

'Fuck,' said Uzo, which, to be fair, was what the rest of us were thinking.

'And I have it on good authority that the new Grade Six is hard-line on swearing in the workplace.'

'Shit,' said Uzo.

'That was a joke,' said Tom.

'What's his name?' asked Uzo.

'*Her* name,' said Tom, 'is Smriti Laghari. I'm pleased to see you were paying attention during unconscious bias training.' Sarcasm was another of Tom's management techniques.

Owen took out his phone and started Googling Smriti. 'She's

with Private Office at the moment. Used to be a banker.'

Groans from around the table. Former bankers were the worst for trying to make the Civil Service more efficient, which often meant getting rid of people and cutting 'luxuries' such as having enough desks for people to sit at.

'According to LinkedIn, her interests include Cardiff University, Pineapple Dance Studios and the London Amateur Violinists' Network,' continued Owen.

'I can play the cello,' said Uzo. 'Maybe we could form a quartet. Ha!'

Tom closed his eyes a moment, as though trying to gather his strength. 'It's fine,' he said. 'We just need to cut down on the backlog before she gets here. Let's show her what a brilliant, efficient team we are. Shall we?'

We stared at him. He had never used the words 'brilliant' or 'efficient' to describe us before. Nor, it's safe to say, had anyone else.

It was dark by the time I left work. I called my mother as I walked down Victoria Street to the Tube, trying not to slip on the lethal rotten leaves that covered the pavement.

'It's me,' she said, as she picked up.

'I know,' I said. 'I called you.'

'Oh, sorry. I'm a bit distracted. I'm on the computer, doing the Sainsbury's shop. They have a very good offer on olive oil, if you need any.'

'Thanks, Mum,' I said, imagining her in the lovely warm kitchen in leafy North Oxford, my dad at the table next to her, reading his undergraduates' essays and grumbling about how badly academics are paid these days. I suddenly wanted to be there with them. 'How are you?'

'Awful, if you must know,' she said. 'The neighbours are digging out the basement *and* doing a loft conversion.'

'Is that a bad thing?'

'A nightmare. Nothing but dust and banging. And the mess in the street. They've thrown away the Victorian doors!'

'Not the original features!' I said.

'Sarcasm doesn't suit you, Julia,' she said. 'The house is going to look ridiculous. And it's not as if they need more space. There are only four of them! They're knocking down all the walls downstairs to build an *entertainment centre*.'

I was approaching a new tower block on the corner of Vauxhall Bridge Road. It looked like a middle finger, mocking me.

'Sorry, darling,' said Mum. 'You caught me at a bad time. They just came round for a chat about the party wall and called our kitchen "quaint". What can I do for you, anyway?'

'Nothing,' I said. 'I'm about to get on the Tube.'

'Wait, darling. What were you calling to tell me?'

'Nothing much. Just a new Grade Six joining our unit.'

'Oh,' said Mum. 'What does that mean?'

'She's going to be in charge of our department. It sounds like she might want to make things more efficient.'

'I'm sure you're very efficient, darling.'

'No, I'm not. And I'm a contractor, so I'm easy to get rid of.'

'No one has said anything about you losing your job yet. Have they?'

'No.'

'Well then. Anyway, it's not as though you're the Health Secretary.'

'Thanks, Mum.'

'Come on, darling. You know what I mean. You're selling yourself short, staying in that job.'

'I'm not qualified for anything else!'

'Rubbish! You could train to become a Pilates teacher. Or an osteopath.'

'You think osteopaths are quacks!'

'Fine. A barrister then!'

18

'Be serious.'

'You could! You could go to law school!'

'Who's going to pay for that?' I said.

'Or edit books, like Alice does. You have exactly the same qualifications as her.'

'Yeah, because that's a great way to make money. She's been doing it for five years and she still has "assistant" in her job title.'

I heard her sigh.

'I miss dancing, Mum,' I said.

'Of course you do,' she said. 'But I did warn you.'

That felt like a low blow, but it was true. Mum had been a ballerina too, and had done all right for herself – a stint at the Royal Ballet, dancing as soloist in a couple of Kenneth MacMillan productions – but it's hard to have children and keep dancing, so she retired soon after meeting my dad. 'You'll be washed up at thirty,' she had told me, when I got into ballet school. 'You'll feel guilty every time you eat a potato. And you'll never meet a man who isn't a homosexual.' But I was sixteen, and when you're sixteen thirty is ancient, and anyway, being washed up is sort of glamorous, the way being addicted to painkillers is glamorous. I didn't think I'd be over the hill at nineteen, though. The summer after I graduated – after, against the odds, I'd been hired by the English National Ballet for their production of *The Nutcracker* – I broke my ankle turning a pirouette on a sticky floor during class and that was the end of that.

I think it was Martha Graham who said that a dancer dies twice and that the first death – the one that comes when you stop dancing – is the most painful. I didn't know what I was, if I wasn't a dancer. I didn't know who I was, either. I felt like the only good and interesting thing about me had been taken away. I still felt like that, sometimes.

'Look, darling,' said Mum, 'I know it's hard. But I find a lot of satisfaction in doing walking tours. It appeals to the performer in me. You could come home for a while and try it out, see if you like it.'

'That's never going to happen,' I said.

'Well. The option's there if you need it.'

I didn't say anything. The idea of moving home and working at my mother's walking-tour company made me want to die.

'I'm not leaving London. All my friends live in London,' I said, really wallowing in it now. 'Not that it matters. They're basically all in relationships. Everyone has someone except me.' My voice rose to a squeak. 'I thought I was independent. But I'm just really sad.'

'Your therapist told you that, didn't she?'

'She's very intuitive.'

'You're just feeling sorry for yourself. If you want to meet someone, go online! Isn't that what everyone else is doing these days?'

'Last time I went on a Tinder date, the bloke talked for half an hour about why Dysons are the only vacuum cleaners worth buying. And he made fun of how quickly I eat.'

'Well, darling, you *do* tend to bolt food down—'

'Plus I kept getting—'

'What?'

'It doesn't matter. Just – horrible messages.'

Mum whispered, 'Dick pics?'

'Yes,' I said. And then: 'How do you know about dick pics?'

'They were talking about them on *Woman's Hour*,' she said. 'Repulsive!'

'Exactly.'

'Still, darling. You can't complain until you've really put yourself out there.'

'That's what my therapist said.'

'Maybe she's not completely hopeless then.' She sighed again. 'Listen, I have to go. If I don't pay for this shop in two minutes I lose my delivery slot. Do you want to come up for dinner tonight?'

'No thanks, I'm OK,' I said.

'All right. But you're coming for Dad's birthday?'

'Yes.'

'He wants a nice shirt or a biography of Hitler.'

'OK.'

'Take up gardening. It'll do wonders for your anxiety levels.'

'I don't have a garden.'

'You can always come over and help me with the pruning.'

'Thanks, Mum.'

'Are you feeling better?'

It took me a moment to reply. 'A little bit.'

'Remember, being alone isn't the same as being lonely. Believe me, being single is a damn sight better than being with someone who makes you miserable.'

In the background, my father muttered, 'I heard that, Jenny.'

So I gave in, and that Friday, I 'put myself out there' for the first time. I'd been watching a lot of US box sets on Netflix, which led me to believe that sitting alone at a bar knocking back shots was acceptable, even attractive, behaviour; it always seemed to lead to handsome strangers saying 'I'll have what she's having,' and whisking you upstairs for well-lit sex. But it didn't quite happen like that for me.

I live in Manor House, which is convenient if you like the Piccadilly line and Finsbury Park and kebab shops, but not if you're looking for a 'putting yourself out there' location. I decided to walk down to the Rose and Crown in Stokey; I'd seen Jarvis Cocker there once, and I've always found him attractive, despite the age difference. Apparently he used to live in Paris, and I thought his voice would sound sexy saying '*Voulez-vous coucher avec moi?*' or perhaps something slightly smoother. Not that I expected him to do all the chatting up.

I felt quite powerful when I was getting ready to go out. I'd never been to a pub on my own before. It seemed like the sort of thing a grown-up, sexy, independent person might do – I could see myself swishing in, stilettos clacking, leather skirt squeaking erotically, as I signalled authoritatively to the barman for a shot of vodka. Now, I didn't own a leather skirt, and I always find it hard to get a barman's attention, but whatever. I was a good-looking woman taking charge of her own destiny! Maybe I'd find someone I sparked with. Or someone who didn't laugh when I did my 'sexy' face – I'd settle for that at this point.

I put on my good pair of underpants (not as faded as the others) just in case I got lucky, and my most flattering jeans. I didn't have a clean bra, but hopefully the lighting would be low if I got to the point of taking my top off. I considered wearing heels, then remembered that I'd once bruised my coccyx dancing the 'Macarena' in a pair of wedges, so I went for trainers instead. I brushed my hair and nodded to myself in the mirror. 'Looking good, Julia,' I said out loud, panicking momentarily before I remembered that Alice was out at a book launch and wouldn't hear me chatting myself up. (A low point.)

I left our flat and marched down Green Lanes towards the pub listening to the 'Young, Wild and Free' playlist on Spotify, my heart beating louder than the music, my breath white in the cold night air. I was alive! Anything could happen!

And then I was at the Rose and Crown and the whole thing suddenly seemed like a terrible idea. The windows were steamed up with the breath of everyone having a lovely time inside without me. But I wouldn't have been able to live with myself if I'd turned back.

I pushed the door open and did my best to swish my way to the bar. It wasn't easy – the pub was packed with tight-knit groups of friends, laughing at in-jokes, not looking particularly open to being chatted up by lone women. There was no sign of Jarvis anywhere.

I sat at the bar and drank a large glass of house red incredibly quickly, trying to catch someone's eye, but I was hemmed in by tall men leaning over me to order drinks, knocking into me with their rucksacks.

One man did notice me – an old bald man with a very red nose at the other end of the bar. As he raised his pint to me, I looked away, and then realized that I probably looked just like him – a lonely borderline alcoholic, albeit younger and with more hair.

I rummaged around in my bag for a bit after that, trying to look purposeful, a 'Where are my paracetamol?' expression on my face – and then my phone buzzed with a text from Alice: *Where are you, Jules? Me and Dave going to a party with some of his friends, want to come?*

I ran all the way home, my vision jarring as my feet pounded the pavement in that fun way it does when you've had some wine and you're about to have a lot more.

3. THOSE AREN'T MY TITS

The party was at a warehouse in Hackney Wick, which was quite exciting – the sort of place trendy people who have lots of sex might go on a Friday night, I thought. As we walked up the concrete stairs, edging past a couple in his-and-hers fur coats drinking rum straight from the bottle, my body began to pulse with possibility. Who knew what was on the other side of that door?

'So my friend Jane lives here with about six other artists,' said Dave, knocking on the door. 'She's a conceptual painter. Her work is kind of confrontational – you'll see what I mean in a minute.'

The door swung open and we edged our way into the warehouse, past a DJ playing electro on actual decks. The walls were covered in canvases splashed with phrases like *You're a cunt* and *What are you looking at?*

I stopped in front of a huge blue square bearing the words *No one likes you*.

'Sell a lot of these, does she?' I said to Dave, but he was standing at the makeshift bar with his arm around Alice, pouring vodka into two plastic cups.

I looked back at the painting. I was beginning to take it personally.

'What do you think?' A woman had sidled up next to me and was standing with her arms crossed. She had a blunt bob and was

24

wearing high-waisted trousers; she looked just like I do in the daydreams where I'm a bohemian novelist (and part-time detective) living in Berlin.

'They give a lovely homely feel to the place,' I said.

'Ha!' she said, and turned to face me. 'I like that. You're funny.' She held my gaze for longer than was comfortable.

'You painted them, didn't you?' I said.

'Yep.'

I opened my mouth to say something, but my humiliation had slowed down my thought process a bit.

She waved away my embarrassment with her hand. 'To be fair, I was going through a bad break-up at the time,' she said. 'My new stuff's much softer. I'll show you some of it.' She caught me by the hand and pulled me through the fog of sweaty, dancing bodies to the far end of the warehouse.

'Here,' she said. She pointed to a pink canvas with curving purple script that read *Your cunt tastes delicious*. 'What does this one make you feel?'

I considered the painting. 'Flattered? Sort of?'

She raised her eyebrows.

I turned back to the canvas. 'Violated' was the honest answer, so I said that out loud, and she seemed pleased. 'Are these all things someone has said to you?'

'They're things I've wanted to say to people but never worked up the nerve.' She looked me in the eye again. Not smiling any more.

'Right,' I said, focusing on the painting while I thought of something to say. Was she hitting on me? 'I guess you're going out with someone you like now, then.' I said.

'Nah,' she said, shrugging. 'It was a one-time thing.'

'Right,' I said again.

'You seeing anyone?' she asked. I could feel her eyes on me.

'Not right now,' I said, still not looking at her.

'You ever been with a woman?' she asked.

'No,' I said, flicking my gaze at her and away again straight away. I wasn't drunk enough for that level of intense eye contact.

'You should try it,' she said.

'Maybe I will!' I said, in an Enid Blyton sort of voice. I started nodding and didn't seem to be able to stop. 'Do you need another drink?'

'Nah, it's all right,' she said. 'I'm on the K. Want some?' She held out a wrap.

I looked at the wrap. It was made of a flyer for a club night that I'd never been to; the photos on Facebook were full of trendy genderqueer people and I'd always assumed I was too boring to get in. This was my chance to be cool, to be young and spontaneous.

I'd always vaguely wondered what it would be like to be with a woman; I had occasionally masturbated while thinking about Beyoncé, and I'd even half-heartedly come out as bi to Cat when we were 17. We'd talked about it in whispers, and hugged melodramatically, and then somehow I just sort of . . . forgot about it. Maybe I should seize the moment, have a line of ketamine and a little light lesbian sex. But I'd just read an article in the *Guardian* about ketamine damaging your bladder, and I can't even handle cystitis without wanting to scratch my insides out. Besides, I wasn't sure I wanted Jane to taste my cunt. Apart from anything else, she was obviously a cunt connoisseur, and I wasn't sure mine would be up to standard. I couldn't think of anything worse than being the subject of a painting that said something like *You need to trim your pubic hair*, or *Your cunt did not taste as good as that other cunt*.

So I shook my head.

'Another time then,' she said, already on her way to the toilets.

I looked around for Alice and Dave, but they were dancing in a corner, foreheads together, grinding into each other like a pestle and mortar. I needed wine, a pint of red wine, preferably. There was none in the bar area so I walked around the edge of the room, picking up every bottle I came across. They were all empty or dark with cigarette ash, the butts floating on the surface like drowned flies.

I took out my phone and texted Cat. *At a party with Alice and Dave. They are basically having sex on dance floor. Help.*

She replied straight away: *If you can't beat em join em, mate.* And she put a wink emoji at the end. She knows I hate the wink emoji.

Eventually I found a half-full bottle of vodka on a windowsill and took a swig. It was like a delicious slap in the face, if there can be such a thing. I stood there for a while, drinking and watching the people on the dance floor. Almost everyone was in a couple – a relatively recent one, judging by the level of groping that was going on. I turned and looked out of the window, over rows of graffitied brick walls towards the glow of the Olympic Park, the party behind me reflected in the glass. Fuck this, I thought to myself, drinking a bit more vodka. I was not going to stand there staring mournfully out of a window like a Jane Austen heroine. I too could have a casual fuck. I'd turned over a sexy new leaf. Conceptual artists wanted to have lesbian sex with me. I would find a man and I would snog him. Maybe I'd even bang him if the snog got me in the mood.

I took another swig from the bottle – a longer one this time, till my gag reflex kicked in and my body started to buzz – and then I walked with purpose into the thick of the party, giving what I thought were sultry come-hither looks to the men I passed.

Everything is a little bit blurry after that. Or soft-focus – let's go with soft-focus. I remember dancing for a while, standing in a big circle, opposite an angular woman in dungarees who was waving her cigarette around above her head, the tip striping the air with fire. Out of the corner of my eye, I saw Jane emerge from the toilets.

She felt her way around the room, her hands against the wall, clearly not trusting herself not to fall over. I looked down at my vodka bottle and was surprised to find it almost empty.

I don't remember how I met him. The first thing I remember is pushing him out of the circle towards the fire escape, both of my hands on his back, the two of us stumbling and laughing. And the next thing I remember is being pressed up against him, him stroking my face and murmuring to me in his sexy Irish voice. He had green-brown eyes and very red lips, and stubble. He smelled a bit like he hadn't washed in a few days, but there was something appealing about that, something raw and masculine and unconventional.

I kissed him first. I'm proud of myself for that. He kissed back and pushed me against the fire escape railing so it dug into my back. I closed my eyes and let my hands wander over his arse, using his body to turn myself on. I'd bloody done it. I was touching another human being. I'd broken the bloody spell.

'Come home with me, like.' He breathed into my ear, hot and damp. 'I want to see what's underneath that T-shirt.'

It occurred to me that the answer to that question was 'an old M&S multi-pack bra'.

'I don't know . . .' It was so fucking nice to feel the warmth of another human being, but the world was beginning to tilt and lurch, and the vodka was threatening to reappear.

'Your tits are so firm,' he said, running a hand over the pointy edges of my ribcage.

'Those aren't my tits,' I said, picking up his hand and moving it upwards.

He laughed. 'Thank fuck for that. Come to the toilets with me.'

That's when Alice's face appeared over his shoulder. She gave me two thumbs up and ducked away.

I pulled away from him and called to Alice. 'Wait!' I began to walk back into the warehouse.

He grabbed my hand. 'What, you're not going, are you?'

'Yeah. Sorry. Thanks, though.'

'Swap numbers then?'

'Sure.' He gave me his phone and I typed in my number with the slow deliberation of the extremely drunk.

My phone buzzed in the taxi on the way home. *Gonna dream about you tonight ;) Finn x*

I smiled to myself. I'm going to have sex with you, Finn, I thought. And if you're lucky, I'll let you have sex with me back.

I couldn't quite believe how bad my hangover was the next morning. I could practically feel my brain knocking against the sides of my skull when I moved. I lay on my back, as still as possible. What had happened to me last night? Why did I feel like I'd been rubbing a cheese grater against my cheek?

I had a sudden vision of an empty bottle of vodka and a fire escape and a hand fondling my ribcage. Finn. Finn and his stubble. I'd snogged Finn.

Even though I was concentrating very hard on breathing in and out and not vomiting, I felt very pleased with myself. I had kissed an actual man – I had not forgotten how. And although I couldn't imagine enjoying anything at all at that particular moment, I had a feeling I'd really enjoyed the kiss, too.

Not only that, but I had been about two units of alcohol away from fucking him on a ketamine-covered toilet cistern in Hackney Wick. I closed my eyes and thanked the universe that I hadn't had sex for the first time in years while in a vodka coma. I wanted to remember such a momentous occasion.

I was woken again by Alice opening my door, which was a little awkward, as I wasn't wearing any clothes. She handed me a cup of tea; as I took it, I had to clutch the duvet with my chin so she didn't get a flash of nipple.

'Feeling rough?' she said cheerfully.

'Yes,' I said. 'Do we have any Haribo, or crisps or anything?' I took a sip of tea. It seemed to curdle in my mouth.

'I'll get you some later. Tell me about the guy you snogged!' Her arms were crossed. She was far too excited about it.

'I don't really remember . . .'

'He had great hair. Reddish.'

'Did he?' I said, putting my tea down and delicately lowering myself onto my back again.

'Yes! I couldn't really see his face, though, the angle you were at.'

'He definitely smelled quite masculine,' I said, closing my eyes. I could hear birds singing and the pounding of the blood in my head.

Alice took the hint. She padded out of the room, ostentatiously quietly, and returned clutching a pack of Haribo Starmix.

'Thank you,' I said, and she sat there, smiling at me indulgently, as I piled the sweets into my mouth, one after the other.

I had a mouth full of cola bottles when my phone started to ring. I reached out for it, swallowing hastily and narrowing my eyes against the glare of the screen.

It was Finn.

I waved Alice out of the room. She went as slowly as she could, clearly trying to overhear as much of our conversation as possible.

'I feel like shit this morning,' said Finn. His voice was deeper than I remembered, a lazy drawl.

'I literally think I'm about to die,' I said.

'Not because of me, I hope,' he said.

'No,' I said, trying to ignore Alice, who was standing in the doorway, grinning at me.

'Cool,' he said. 'So, like – do you want to go for a drink some-time then?' He sounded like he wasn't arsed either way, and yet he obviously was arsed, because here he was calling me the morning after we'd met. 'Next Friday maybe?'

'Sounds good,' I said. He must actually like me, I thought. This could genuinely lead to sex. I wasn't sure I could remember how to do it. What if I couldn't – what's the female equivalent of 'get it up'?

4. UNSEXY SEX

I thought about sex on Sunday and did an emergency underwear wash. I hung my black bra to dry on the radiator in my bedroom, so that it would be ready for my date. I thought about sex on Monday on the packed Piccadilly line, my face pressed up against someone else's armpit, and then I stopped thinking about sex because I had a sudden vision of what it would be like to shag the owner of the armpit and started to feel queasy. As I walked to the Victoria line platform, I allowed myself to check out the other commuters. I hadn't done that in years – it felt pointless and liable to lead to disappointment, like window shopping in Knightsbridge. That man has hands, I thought to myself. What a lovely smile. (I was a bit out of practice.)

Once I arrived at the office, all thoughts of sex fled from my mind, as if they'd been chased away by a very unsexy person. In a way, I suppose, they had; Tom followed me into the lift.

'Ready?' he asked, looking straight ahead, as the lift carried us up to our floor.

'For what?'

'Smriti. It's her first day.'

There was an atmosphere in the office. I'd never known there to be an atmosphere in the office before, apart from a general sense of ennui. Owen was wearing a tie. Uzo was sitting up straighter at her

32

desk than usual and, worryingly, wasn't checking her mobile phone every five minutes. In fact, her phone seemed to be *in her bag.*

The lift opened with an ominous bing! and there, all of a sudden, was Smriti Laghari, our new Grade Six.

We pretended to work for about ten minutes, our attention very much focused on where Smriti was in the office, our bodies turning slightly to face her, like sunflowers following the sun. Smriti *was* a little bit like the sun – she was shiny, or at least her teeth were. Her hair too. Looking at her made me feel a bit unwashed, though I'd had a shower that morning and shampooed my hair twice by accident.

After about a quarter of an hour, Smriti walked into the middle of the office – next to the cupboard where we keep our biscuits – and said, 'Hey guys!' Even her voice was sunny. Everyone swivelled towards her. 'I just wanted to introduce myself.'

'She shouldn't have said "just",' I whispered to Owen. 'It weakens her message.'

'This is my first role outside private office, so I hope you'll be patient with me as I get up to speed. I'm psyched to be working with you guys!'

'She shouldn't have said "psyched", either,' muttered Owen. 'No one should say "psyched".'

There was an awkward silence – people didn't usually make speeches on their first day in a new job – and then a half-hearted round of applause, because she seemed to expect one. I could see people on other teams looking round to see if it was a birthday or a leaving party, and whether there might be cake.

'She didn't mention restructuring,' said Owen.

'Would have been a bit bold to lead with that, wouldn't it?' I said.

'She didn't even say "streamlining". I think we're going to be OK.'

We watched Smriti walk, smiling at everyone she passed, into her new glass-walled office, followed by Tom. Uzo gave Tom a thumbs up. Tom looked straight ahead, like a child in a school play pretending not to see his parents.

Once Smriti's office door was shut, the rest of us relaxed a little. Uzo took her phone out and started texting. Owen offered to make a tea round. Across the office, I saw Stan open a bag of ready salted.

'I already wish it was Friday,' said Uzo, eyes on her phone.

'Me too,' I said.

'Doing anything exciting this weekend?' Uzo asked.

'Not really,' I said, casual as anything. 'Just going on a date.'

'A DATE?' boomed Uzo. 'Owen. Owen, man. Did you hear that?'

Owen put the mugs down in a hurry, spilling a little tea on the pile of correspondence on my desk. 'What?' he asked. 'What have you heard?'

'Nothing about work,' I said. 'Uzo's just excited because I'm going on a date on Friday night.'

'Oh! Who with?' asked Owen.

'No one,' I said. 'Just a guy I met at a party.'

I sipped my tea and logged the latest letters and emails in the system. I had to draft replies to several urgent emails from the Treasury, but I had another letter from Eric, the Bomber Command vet, so I read that first.

I'll always remember the day I met Eve – 9 October 1943, in the sergeants' mess at RAF White Waltham. She was a First Officer in the Air Transport Auxiliary and she could fly a Spitfire like the best of them! I liked the look of her, so I went to say hello, and she smiled at me, and that was that. She had beautiful blue eyes – right up until she died, they were the bluest eyes I've ever seen. We were married for seventy years. I've got the telegram from the Queen framed here in my room at the home; I'm looking at it now, as I write to you. I don't know why she had to die first. But I'm very lucky to have had her as long as I did, I suppose. Here's a photo of us on our wedding day. (I photocopied it at my local library. Aren't libraries smashing?)

I'll let you go now, my dear. I'm sure you have much better things to do than read any more of my drivel!

Yours (as ever),

Eric Beecham

P.S. — Are you married? Or do you have a fellow?

Not yet, Eric, I thought. The 'yet' shows you how optimistic I was about my date. I looked at the grainy black-and-white picture of the young couple outside a church, squinting in the sunlight. They were arm in arm, beaming, Eve in a white dress and Eric in his RAF uniform, his ears sticking out beneath his Brylcreemed hair. They looked so young and happy. I tucked the picture into my wallet, so I could look at it when I needed a dose of Forties optimism.

My impending date was the talk of the correspondence team for the rest of the week. On Wednesday, Uzo sent me a link to an article about depilation and advised me not to use expensive new face products in the run-up to the date in case they irritated my skin. 'I'm not going to make that much of an effort,' I told her. 'I'm not desperate.' Uzo gave me a look that clearly meant, 'You should be.'

And as I was getting ready to leave on Friday, Owen decided to give me some first date advice. 'Ask him which three bands sum up his taste in music,' he said. 'Or what his childhood nickname was. If you get him to talk about himself, he'll think you're a good listener.'

'You Googled "conversation starters" before your first date with Laura, didn't you?' I asked.

'No!' he said. 'I just happened to read an article about them in *Men's Health*.'

The idea of Owen reading *Men's Health* made Uzo snort so loudly that Smriti came out of her office to see if anything was wrong.

'Text us and let us know how it's going, yeah?' said Uzo, as I shut down my computer.

'I am not going to text you in the middle of my date,' I said. 'Unless it's really bad and I need someone to come and rescue me.'

'I hope you don't,' said Owen.

'Me too,' I said. 'Me too.'

I met Finn outside the BFI. It was my idea to go there; if he turned out to be incredibly unattractive or boring, at least I'd have seen one more Derek Jarman film, which would give me something to talk to my dad about.

I stood at the entrance, eavesdropping on a conversation between two women smoking at an outdoor table, coats clutched close against the cold.

'Michelle did it with Joe last night.'

'She never!'

'I know! Apparently he asked her to piss on him.'

I felt a bit sick all of a sudden. Maybe the rules of sex had changed since my encounter with the twenty-one-year-old. What if Finn wanted me to piss on him, but I had performance anxiety or an empty bladder?

I took out my book, a collection of essays by Nora Ephron, but I couldn't concentrate. I read the same sentence three or four times: *Never marry a man you wouldn't want to be divorced from.*

I glanced up, looking for Finn. Would he recognize me? I was pretty certain I'd have no idea who he was. I tried to remember if he had any distinguishing characteristics. Nice reddish hair, according to Alice. Abrasive stubble. A distinctive unwashed smell.

I looked back down at my book. *Never marry a man you wouldn't want to be divorced from*, I read again. I was getting a bit ahead of myself.

And then there he was, calling to me.

'Julia!'

It felt like he was giving me a compliment just by saying my name in his malty, barrel-aged voice. He walked towards me, hands in his pockets, hips thrust forward, smiling. He leaned in to kiss me; he was wearing cologne. He'd made an effort. This was promising.

'How are you, then?' I said.

'Not bad, not bad,' he said, looking at me and smiling. 'I've been thinking about you all week.'

'Me too. You, I mean.' I really was very bad at this.

He didn't reply. He just grabbed my hand and led me into the cinema. It was so nice to feel that I belonged to someone.

We sat right at the back with our knees pressed up against the seats in front, like teenagers on the bus to school. I'd smuggled in a bag of Maltesers and he had a hip flask full of whisky – a delicious combination.

The film seemed to go on forever. I couldn't follow the plot, which might have been because there wasn't one, but I'm going to give Jarman the benefit of the doubt here. I couldn't concentrate on anything except the fact that I was on a date with a man, a man who was sitting next to me, a man who had his actual hand on my actual knee. I've never been much good at mindfulness but I was fully present in that moment. I remember the way the seat fabric felt through my trousers; the sound of Finn's breathing, so close to me; the musty, sweet smell of popcorn and other people's perfume. My body seemed to be one throbbing nerve ending.

After about an hour, Finn looked across at me and said, 'Is it me, like, or is this film a load of shite?'

'I don't think it's you,' I said. I smiled to myself: we agreed about something. We had something in common already.

Finn put his arm around me and pulled me closer. I put my head on his shoulder as an experiment. He put his head on mine. I began to get a crick in my neck. The film wasn't any better from a ninety-degree angle.

On the screen, some punks were getting beaten up by the police, which was probably the most exciting bit of the whole film. I'm not sure, though, because by this point I was looking into Finn's eyes, and he was staring into mine. His eyes were green when the light from the screen flashed bright across them, then brown. And then he closed them and I closed mine and we were all over each other, hands up each other's T-shirts, leaning over the armrests to get closer, ignoring stares and disapproving tuts from the other cinemagoers.

We pulled apart and grinned at each other. 'Want to get out of here?' Finn said.

We practically ran back to the Tube station and stood all the way to Leyton, kissing messily. I felt reckless for the first time in ages – reckless, at least, in a way that didn't just involve spending the last of my overdraft on two bottles of corner-shop wine and drinking them both myself.

The teenagers opposite us laughed at us openly. 'Ooooh, you're going to fuck. You haven't fucked yet, have you?'

The youth of today are very observant, I thought. And yes, I fucking well hope I'm fucking going to fuck. I felt like I might explode. Nothing seemed to matter any more except coming, coming in the presence of another human being, being made to come by someone else.

We nearly missed our stop. We lurched out of the Tube carriage onto the platform and the abrupt change from warmth to cold made me self-conscious all of a sudden. It felt like coming down from MDMA and realizing you're sitting in a cat basket, stroking a stranger's face.

'How far is it to yours?' I asked, as we tapped our Oyster cards on the exit gates.

'About fifteen minutes,' he said.

I nodded. 'Cool,' I said.

He nodded back.

As we walked, I became increasingly aware of the echoing of our feet on the pavement and of Finn's hand in mine, large, dry, unfamiliar. Increasingly aware that I knew nothing about this man other than his first name and that he had unpredictable grooming habits. I considered texting Alice to let her know where the police should look for me if I didn't arrive home the next day, but I didn't want to break what remained of the pre-sex atmosphere with the light from the screen. At last he slowed, stopping in front of an unremarkable Victorian terraced house.

'This is it,' he said, fumbling with the key. 'I think my flatmates are in, so be quiet, yeah?'

The flat smelled of mildew. There were T-shirts drying on the radiators and a curling *Clockwork Orange* poster Blu-Tacked to the wallpaper. 'My room's up here,' he said, running up the stairs two at a time.

He opened his bedroom door and ushered me through. 'Welcome to my spacious abode,' he said, shutting the door behind us and leaning against it.

'Great,' I said.

'Great,' he said. 'You need the toilet or anything?'

'No, it's OK.'

There was a silence.

'Nice room,' I said.

'No, it's not,' he said.

'Yeah, all right, it's not.' The room was barely big enough for both of us to stand in. It was entirely taken up with a single bed and a clothes rail, crammed with jumpers and jeans in shades of brown, green and grey. The only attempts at decoration were a few moody photos of arm creases, knees and foreheads pinned to the walls.

He sat on the bed, grabbed my hand and pulled me down next to him.

'Did you take those photos?' I said.

He nodded, looking me in the eye now, still holding my hand.

I looked away, back at the photos again. 'So is that what you are, then? A photographer?'

And then he licked his lips, which made them look sausagey and wet all of a sudden, and I wasn't sure I wanted to be there any more.

'Julia,' he said, stroking my face. 'You're beautiful.'

I felt the urge to push him away; I was fully sober now and very aware of him entering my personal space. But I managed to pull myself together and stared meaningfully back at him. He leaned in slowly and kissed me. I closed my eyes and tried to enjoy the sensation, but kissing felt ridiculous all of a sudden; someone breathing all over your face, licking the inside of your mouth. Why do we do it?

I'm kissing a man, I thought to myself. He is kissing me. This is sexy.

He drew back and looked at me in a way that made me feel very aware of my own face, not necessarily in a good way.

Then he started to kiss my neck and leaned in to pull my cardigan off. I had to shrug to help him. Neither of us spoke. I became aware of some kind of gurgling noise coming from the pipes. I wished he'd put some mood music on; I was nostalgic now for the 'Late Night Love' playlist my ex-boyfriend used to play. At least that had helped me get into character as a person who enjoyed sex.

He started with my bra, and then pushed me back on the single duvet and pulled off my jeans, then my underpants. I was naked. Do not cross your arms, I said to myself. It is not sexy to cross your arms. It was really cold in his flat, though. At least that meant my nipples were erect.

Help, I thought – am I supposed to undress him now? I've never been good with buckles.

I knelt up and pulled his T-shirt over his head. It got stuck for a bit, and then when he pulled his head free, his face was slightly purple.

He clearly decided I was no clothes removal expert, because he hurriedly took off his own jeans while I lay back on the duvet, the colour and stiffness of a corpse at this point, probably.

He wasn't wearing boxers. His penis was there, erect, waving from side to side as though it was greeting me. I'd forgotten how hideous-looking penises are. Penis is not a sexy word, I thought. But was cock better? I didn't know. I had been out of the game too long. I prayed I wouldn't have to say either word, or, in fact, anything else.

He was lying on top of me now, rubbing himself against me. 'Talk dirty to me,' he said.

Fuck. 'Mmm,' I said.

'Tell me what you like.'

'This is really nice.'

'What do you want me to do? Do you want my big cock in your—'

Right. So he said cock.

'Yeah,' I said.

'I'm going to fuck you good,' he said. 'Is that what you want?'

'Yeah,' I said.

'Go on. Ask me to fuck you.'

'Just – do it.'

I had turned into a human Nike advert.

He stood up to get a condom. It took him ages to rip the packet open. He looked so proud of himself as he rolled it on.

And then he clambered back onto the bed. The mattress shifted as he positioned himself above me. Staring into my eyes, he went to push himself into me. He missed.

'Jesus. That's never happened before,' he said. He picked up his penis and guided himself in, frowning as though he was trying to assemble a particularly tricky piece of IKEA furniture.

He started to thrust, thwacking against me in the horrible silence of the room.

'Yeah?' he asked, looking at me again now, smiling, nodding.

'Mmm,' I said.

I tried to clench my pelvic floor muscles so I could feel him inside me – he was no Rampant Rabbit, let's put it that way.

I looked past him, staring over his shoulder at the ceiling. Spider webs hung in the corners and there was a dark brown smear on the ceiling just above me. A dead fly, maybe. I wonder if he'd thrown a book up there to kill it and not wiped it off.

He moved faster, then slower, without any discernible rhythm. A bead of sweat fell from his forehead to my neck.

'Have you come yet?' He was slowing down now, breathing hard, or maybe out of breath – I couldn't tell.

'Just about to,' I said, closing my eyes, trying to imagine I was somewhere else. But I couldn't think of anything else, anything at all.

Panting, that's what's needed, I thought. 'Uh, yeah, that's good,' I tried.

'Yeah?' he said, encouraged, speeding up.

'Yeah!' I said. 'Oh! That's right!'

'Yeah? You like it hard, you dirty bitch?'

I had a lot of feminist problems with that question, but I didn't think this was the time to get into them.

'Mmm!' I said, breathing faster now. I panted out a pained 'Oh!' and then sighed, slowing down my breathing, opening my eyes.

'Was that it?' he said, unimpressed.

'Yeah,' I said, anxious now. Was that not a convincing orgasm? Was I too quick? I couldn't really remember how long it usually took when another person was involved.

He clambered off me and lay there, looking straight up at the ceiling. He was still hard. 'I can't come,' he said, pulling off the condom and flicking it into the bin. 'Will you sort me out?'

I should have said no. I see that now – I should have stood up, told him I'd had a nice time but that it wasn't really working for me, and walked out. But that seemed impolite.

As I've said, he didn't smell as though he washed very often. I wished he'd kept the condom on. But I thought I could get the whole thing over with quickly. I had faith in my blow job abilities. I'd practised on a fair few blokes at university and they'd never complained.

I did my best, taking his dick (I'm going with dick) as deep into my throat as I could, eyes closed, willing him to come.

'What are you doing?' he said. 'That's not how you do it.'

I stopped and said, 'Yes, it is.'

'No, it's not,' he said. 'You're being too mechanical.'

I tried to process the insult. 'What do you want me to do, then?'

'Nothing,' he said. 'I don't know what's wrong. I always come, like.'

I just looked at him.

'Are you going to wank me off, or what?'

Saying no seemed too difficult, somehow.

I knelt by the bed and gave him a hand job, trying to put some feeling into it, trying to vary the pressure, but I felt as though I were pumping a particularly resistant bicycle tyre. Finn lay there, silent. I could feel him growing flaccid in my hand.

'This has never happened to me before,' he said. 'I think you've broken my penis.'

He pushed my hand away and tried to get the job done himself, his face clenched with the effort.

I knelt there, wondering what to do. Should I just leave? Should I join in somehow? Or did he just want to be left alone to enjoy himself in peace? He didn't say. It seemed rude to leave without saying goodbye, and I didn't really want to interrupt, so I stayed there on my knees while he kept wanking. I looked up at the clock above the window. It was one in the morning now.

At 1.16, he switched hands and carried on.

At 1.34, he paused for a few seconds to catch his breath, eyes still tight shut.

At two, I began to feel like I was hallucinating. I had never known time to pass so slowly. I had never been so viscerally aware of every sensation, every sound. It felt like punishment for every time I'd felt like life was rushing past me and I'd willed it to slow down.

He wanked for over an hour. And I just knelt by the bed and watched him, hypnotized by his broken penis.

And then, at 2.05, he grabbed my hand and wrapped it around his dick, pumping it up and down, eyes still closed. This was it. The home straight. The end of the hellish marathon.

At long, long last he came, all over my hand and his horrible pale chest. He breathed out, apparently as relieved as I was that it was all over. I discreetly wiped my hand on the side of his mattress.

And then he turned to me, and said, 'Thanks, yeah, but I think it would be better if we were just friends.'

'Yes,' I said. 'I agree.'

I got dressed as quickly as I could, stumbling as I pulled up my jeans, while he lay there on his back with his eyes closed. I picked up my shoes and walked as quietly as I could out of the room, down the stairs and into the street, sitting on the doorstep to pull them on. And then I ran and ran, to find a night bus that would take me as far away from him and my humiliation as possible.

As I sat at the bus stop, eyes down to avoid the attention of two teenage boys, shouting at each other with 3-a.m. rage, I made a resolution: I was done with sex. It was disgusting, unnatural, inexplicable. And I never, never wanted to see a penis, dick, cock, whatever you want to call it, ever again.

5. NEVER SAY NEVER

I went straight into the bathroom when I got home. I turned up the shower as high as I could bear, hot enough to turn my skin red, till I could see steam evaporating from my body. My knees were still dimpled with the texture of Finn's carpet, and I couldn't seem to rub them smooth. The smell of his cum clung to my fingers. I washed my hands – both of them, just to be safe – till they were pink and tender, scrubbing beneath my nails with Alice's nailbrush.

'Julia? Are you OK?' The shower must have woken Alice up.

I didn't answer. I was concentrating on making my mind as blank as possible, but I couldn't keep the sex flashbacks at bay:

Kneeling by his bed.

His thigh slapping against mine.

The dead fly on the ceiling.

'You've broken my penis.'

Why did I let him get away with saying that to me? Why didn't I just walk out of there? How fucking *dare* he blame me because he didn't come? I hadn't fucking come either, but at least I'd had the decency to fake an orgasm.

I spent the following week going to work, coming home, and going straight to bed. I watched comforting old TV shows on repeat and imagined myself back to a purer time; a time when the thing I wanted most in the world was berry-coloured lipstick from The Body Shop and the furthest I'd got with a boy was when Phil Green kissed me on the cheek after his Bar Mitzvah.

Alice tried to comfort me by telling me about the time that her ex-boyfriend Joe tried to prove he could give himself a blow job; he'd thrown his legs over his head in the yoga plough position but he hadn't been able to reach, and then he pulled a muscle in his neck and screamed in pain till she helped him lie flat on his back again. That did make me feel slightly better. Not better enough to want to have sex with anyone ever again, though.

Work was a distraction of sorts, but I wasn't behaving normally, I knew that; I chose the desk next to Stan every day, to avoid my team and their questions about the date. Uzo cornered me one lunchtime and said, 'So? How was the hot date?' but I just said, 'Fine, thanks,' and then Tom called her into his office to tell her off for buying stuff from ASOS during work hours.

Luckily there was a new sense of purpose in the office, everyone bustling around trying to impress the new Grade Six, not as much small talk. I couldn't really look anyone in the eye, least of all Owen – he'd probably want to tell me how fantastically it was going with Laura and compare date stories, and I didn't think I'd deal with his happiness well. But I couldn't avoid him forever, and on Wednesday he insisted on taking me to Pret for lunch.

'Are you all right?' he asked me, as we finished off our chicken and avocado sandwiches. 'Did something happen on your date?'

I nodded. 'I had sex,' I said, and to my horror I felt my eyes filling with tears.

'I hope Laura doesn't cry when she tells people that,' he said.

'I'm guessing you're not as bad in bed as Finn was,' I said, still crying, but laughing a bit too.

Owen frowned. 'He didn't— he didn't hurt you—'

'No . . .'

He put on what he obviously thought was a caring face. 'You can tell me.'

'He masturbated for an hour, and I just sat there.'

'Wow. What a wanker.'

'Literally,' I said, nodding.

He patted my arm. 'Do you need some company tonight? We could go to the cinema or something, if you like.'

'Thanks,' I said, 'but Cat's got a few days off between shows, so I'm going to meet her for dinner.'

'I haven't met Cat yet,' Owen said.

'Sorry, Owen,' I said. 'You're not invited.'

Cat took me for a curry in Brick Lane. We sat at a tiny corner table in the windowless downstairs room, next to a tank full of fluorescent fish.

'At least you banged someone. You needed to get that out of the way,' Cat said, ladling dhal onto my plate.

'I'm never going to do it again,' I said. I bit into a samosa, hoping that was the end of the conversation.

'Never say never,' Cat said. 'Remember how I was feeling like a third wheel with Lacey and Steve, the new tadpole?'

I nodded.

'I fucked someone last night. A year-five teacher.'

'Is that ethical?'

'Why wouldn't it be? I'm not a student. I'm a pretend frog.'

'I wasn't sure where the line was drawn.'

'The point is, it wasn't the best sex, but it's not going to put me off forever. You wouldn't stop drinking just because you got one bad hangover, would you?'

'This is different,' I said. 'I broke his penis.'

'I wish you actually had broken his penis,' she said. 'Then he wouldn't be able to inflict shitty sex on anyone else.'

*　　*　　*

But here's the thing – the next morning I was writing a letter to a man who was very, very angry about the cost of prescriptions when I felt an unmistakable hollowness within me, a deep ache between my legs. I was turned on – turned on and bored, a very common combination for me – and I knew I wouldn't be able to concentrate till I came, silent and hard, in the disabled toilets.

There was no point in trying to resist it. I locked myself into the cubicle, sat on the closed lid, pulled down my trousers and Googled *Women's erotica* on my iPhone. I wasn't in the mood to be fussy, so I scrolled quickly through the worst of it, looking for a story about two consenting adults fucking anonymously, preferably somewhere they could be caught. The words *handcuffs* and *dripping pussy* caught my eye – I like directness – and I wanked, leaning forward into my hand, rocking as I came, my face a wordless scream.

Maybe I needed to give sex one final chance.

6. A SEXY, WORDLESS
TONGUE CONVERSATION

So when Alice and Dave invited me to a house party in Dalston at the beginning of February, I said yes. It was hosted by another of Dave's arty friends – a designer who embellished H&M vest tops with sequins and sold them for huge amounts of money on Etsy.

'You're sure Finn won't be there?' I asked Dave, as we walked along Kingsland Road.

'I checked,' he said. 'He's home in Ireland for the weekend.'

The party was sedate compared to the one in Hackney Wick. There was no DJ, just a Spotify playlist, and the flat was lit by IKEA standard lamps rather than industrial strip lighting. The place was rammed, people pressed up against one another like rush-hour commuters. I went straight to the kitchen, poured three glasses of red wine and carried them carefully back to Alice and Dave, who had somehow found space on a sofa. They edged closer together to make room for me.

But soon they were arguing about a wedding they'd been invited to, that way couples do when they've been together for a few years and have stopped pretending to like each other's friends.

'We've *got* to go. She's the editorial director. It's flattering that she's invited me at all.'

'No. *You've* got to go.'

'You're coming. I've RSVPd for both of us.'

'But I won't know anyone.'

'I'm sure she'll sit us next to each other at dinner.'

'Everyone will talk about books and wanky authors and I won't know what to say.'

I looked around for someone else to talk to but I was hemmed in by a sea of legs. Legs in jeans; legs in dresses; legs that obviously spent more time in the gym than mine did. I drank my wine steadily, for something to do.

'Do I have to wear a suit?'

'I don't think so. It's not a traditional wedding. She got a tattoo instead of an engagement ring.'

'Nice.'

I pushed myself up off the sofa and carried my wine glass to the toilet queue that was already taking up half the living room. I looked around; I vaguely recognized a few people from the Hackney Wick party – the couple in matching fur coats, and a bloke with an undercut who I remembered being a bit of a liability on the dance floor.

And then, in that mysterious way you often can, I felt someone looking at me. I glanced over towards the kitchen and there, framed in the doorway, was Jane, the conceptual artist. A woman with long dark hair was leaning towards her, gesturing and chatting away intently, but Jane was staring straight at me, as direct as one of her paintings. She raised her hand and smiled at me. I smiled back – but then two men stumbled out of the toilet, rubbing their noses, holding hands, and it was my turn.

I sat on the toilet staring at my fingers, the harsh halogen light throwing up every wrinkle, every nibbled nail. I decided to take myself home; I didn't have anyone to talk to, and I was being stared at by a sexually confident lesbian. I had a feeling that something would happen if I stayed.

As I was putting on my coat, I felt someone walk up to me.

'You're not going yet, are you?' said Jane.

'I'm not feeling great,' I said, trying to sound casual, though

I could feel my heart speeding up. 'Not in a sociable mood.'

'Nor am I,' she said. 'But I'd make an exception for you.'

She looked at me till I had to look away.

'Go on,' she said. 'Stay and have a drink with me.'

There was something compelling about her. My body began to throb with the promise of something I didn't even know if I wanted.

'All right,' I said.

One of the many lessons I learned from the seminal classic *Sliding Doors* is that the most insignificant-seeming things can change your life. If Gwyneth Paltrow had caught that Tube, she wouldn't have ended up with such a terrible haircut. And if Jane had poured me a glass of red wine or a beer, I might not have— but I'm getting ahead of myself. The point is, I can't handle vodka. And that's why everything that happened, happened.

Jane was sitting on the kitchen work top, pouring Smirnoff into two tumblers.

'Let's do shots,' she said, handing one to me. 'Down it in one.'

We clacked our glasses together and tilted our heads back. I managed to dribble half my vodka down my chin.

'That's cheating!' she said. 'You have to do it again now.'

She twisted the lid off another bottle of Smirnoff.

A new song came on, with a bored-sounding female vocalist.

'Come on,' she said. 'Dance with me.'

She jumped down from the work surface and put her arms around my waist. I put mine around her neck, feeling self-conscious, like a girl at a prom in a teen movie, only not, obviously. She moved her hips against mine in time to the bass line. I tried to focus on her face, but it seemed to flicker. The vodka was buzzing in me, and I couldn't tell if we were swaying, or the room was, or both, but it didn't matter.

Jane looked up at me through her fringe. 'I'm going to kiss you now,' she said. 'Stop me if you don't want me to.'

51

I didn't stop her. I closed my eyes instead.

I'd never kissed a woman before, except once during spin the bottle at university. That kiss was just for play, though, not so much a lesbian kiss as an impression of one – lips barely touching, tongues waggling around outside our mouths, wet in every sense of the word. Kissing Jane wasn't like that at all. Her mouth was hard one minute, soft the next. I felt as though we were having a sexy, wordless tongue conversation. She pushed herself into me until I was leaning against the hob. I accidentally pressed the ignition with my bum. I could hear it sparking behind me, like an unsubtle metaphor.

A man came into the room and immediately backed out again, saying 'Shit, sorry,' shutting the door quietly behind him. I heard him say, 'There are two women kissing in there.'

The door opened again as someone peered in to see for themselves. It must have been Alice, because a moment later I heard her voice in the corridor: 'Julia's in there! Kissing Jane!'

'You're joking.' It was Dave. 'Isn't she straight?'

Jane and I stopped kissing for a moment and looked at each other.

'You don't seem very straight to me,' she said.

I shrugged and pulled her to me again, feeling powerful and young and spontaneous.

'Come back to mine,' Jane said.

But I shook my head. 'I can't tonight,' I said. I hadn't sufficiently recovered from the Finn incident to have drunken sex with a stranger again.

On the night bus home, Dave turned around from the seat in front and smiled, leerily. 'That was hot,' he said, breathing beer on me. Not that I could talk; I could barely feel my mouth, I'd drunk so much vodka.

'You're disgusting,' said Alice, hitting his arm.

'Well, it was,' he said, scratching his beard. 'I could have watched that for hours.'

'Don't be such a misogynist,' said Alice. But she turned to me and said, 'Do you fancy her? She's sort of dangerous seeming.'

'Jane's not dangerous,' said Dave. 'She just knows how to get what she wants.' He was still looking at me, unsteadily. 'Are you bi, then, or what?'

'I don't know,' I said. 'I'm pissed.' I didn't know what I was, or how I felt, except that I was excited.

Alice moved to the seat next to mine and leaned close to me. 'I don't think you can really know if you're gay or whatever until you've – you know.'

'Until I've gone down on a woman.'

'Exactly. It might be disgusting! Like licking a snail.'

'But blow jobs are disgusting,' I said.

'What? No, they're not,' said Alice.

'Yes, they are,' I said. 'Who would actually want to put a penis in their mouth?'

'Not me,' said Dave.

'Maybe you *are* a lesbian!' said Alice. She seemed very excited by the idea.

'Maybe *I'm* a lesbian,' said Dave.

'Can we stop talking about it now, please?' I said.

We swung off the bus into the February air. I let Alice and Dave walk ahead of me, casting one long shadow in the streetlights. I wanted to be on my own for a moment to think about Jane, and to remember the kiss.

7. LICKING THE SNAIL

I was nearly fifteen minutes late for my session with Nicky that week. I arrived at her door panting and sweaty, despite the cold, and as soon as I was waist-deep in the terrible armchair, she asked me, 'Why were you late?'

'Sorry,' I said, still breathing too quickly. I hate being told off. 'I lost my keys—'

'No,' she said, holding up her palm to me. 'No, no, no.'

I frowned. 'What do you mean, no?'

'I mean why were you *really* late?'

'Honestly,' I said, ready to get angry, 'I must have dropped them in the kitchen—'

'When we are late for things,' Nicky said to me in a sing-song voice, 'it's because somewhere inside us we really don't want to go to them. Which reminds me. I had a dream about you last night.'

'Are you supposed to tell me that?' I asked. 'What was I doing?'

'We're not really here to discuss *my* dreams, Julia. Why didn't you want to come here today?'

'I did want to come.'

She seemed disappointed. 'Fine,' she said. 'What would you like to talk about?'

'I'd quite like to talk about your dream.'

'Why don't we talk about what you did at the weekend?'

I was a bit thrown. 'I didn't do much,' I said. 'I went to a party.'

She looked at me for a long time. I could feel myself reddening. 'What happened at the party?'

I frowned. 'What?' I said, my face getting hotter.

'Something happened, and you're a tiny bit embarrassed about it.' She looked at me with her head on one side.

'Well, yes,' I said, 'but that's true every weekend, pretty much.'

'You had bad sex again.'

'No!' I said. 'I just kissed someone.'

She nodded and started writing in her notebook. 'Knew I'd get it out of you,' she said.

'You didn't "get it out" of me,' I said. 'I'm supposed to tell you things.'

She stopped writing and looked at me again. 'But you didn't want to tell me. So you must have kissed someone . . . unusual. Was it a relative?'

'What? No!'

'Look, I'm not here to judge.'

'Seriously?'

'My grandparents are first cousins.' She shrugged.

'I did not kiss my cousin. All my cousins are teenagers. I kissed a woman.'

She leaned back and crossed her legs. 'A woman.' She held my gaze and nodded. 'That makes a lot of sense.'

'What—'

'Was it good?'

I let myself remember the kiss. 'It was really good.'

'So. Are you going to see her again?'

'I don't think so.'

'Why not?' she asked. 'Did you fancy her?'

I thought about it. 'Yes. But I'd had a lot of vodka.'

'So?'

'So I don't think I actually want to go on a date with her. I don't have anything in common with her.'

'Have you fancied women before?'

I felt I was losing my grip on the conversation. 'Well, I mean – I had crushes on girls at school—'

'Have you ever considered that you might be gay? Or bi, at least? Do you think that might be where some of your anxiety is coming from? Not acknowledging who you really are?'

'Just because I kissed a woman, doesn't mean I'm gay,' I said.

'Answer the question.'

I breathed out. 'Yes. I've thought I could be.'

'But you've never done anything about it before.'

'. . . No.'

'Why's that? Why haven't you ever dated a woman? And don't tell me it's because no one's ever asked you.'

'But no one *has* ever asked me!'

She stared me down. I picked at the cuticle on my thumb.

'Maybe I'm scared,' I said.

'Of dating a woman.'

'Yes.'

'Right.' Nicky made a few more notes. I tried to read what she'd written. I was sure I could see the word 'passive' underlined.

It's fair to say I was pretty het up by the time I left Nicky's house. I went for a walk in Clissold Park to calm myself down. I bought a hot chocolate from the café – I don't like hot chocolate, but I wasn't thinking properly – and walked past the skate park, down the slope, around the pond and back up the hill, over and over again, my brain a blur.

Sure, I had questioned my sexuality as a teenager, but I hadn't thought about it much since then. I'd had a horrible, painful crush on Louise from my musical theatre class when I was 16. She'd loved Andrew Lloyd Webber, so I pretended I loved Andrew Lloyd Webber too; I bought a black leotard to match hers, and I stuck pictures of bands she liked on my locker, hoping she'd notice. She never did. I hadn't fancied her, though. I'd wanted to be her, to be her best friend, to move like she did onstage, to be close to her. But I never had sexy thoughts about her. The way I felt about her had seemed much more real, more intense, than any crush I'd had on a boy. Less trivial.

Which, to be fair, does sound pretty gay.

And yes, I had told Cat that I was bi when I was 17 – but as a teenager, the idea that I might fancy other girls made me feel predatory, like my friends might not trust me, as though I would be a danger at sleepovers. It just seemed easier not to.

Now, though – now being queer seemed positively aspirational. The world felt very different from the one I'd lived in as a teenager. Then, same-sex couples couldn't marry, and teachers had failed to step in when kids called each other 'fag' and 'dyke' in the back rows of classrooms, and when people came out, they'd labelled themselves: gay, lesbian, bi. Everything felt more fluid now. Plenty of people slept with men, and then women, and then men again without feeling the need to make a big deal out of it.

'Excuse me, miss?' said a park warden. 'I have to shut the park now.'

I nodded, blinking, and walked out onto the street. I hadn't even noticed the sun going down.

I thought about what Nicky had said all that week. At night, the idea of sleeping with a woman seemed bigger, filling my thoughts and my bedroom, keeping me awake until the sun came up and the streetlights blinked out. Could I do it? What would it mean? What if I hated it? What if I *loved* it? What would my parents say? In the morning, I'd wake with my heart racing, wondering whether I should try to make it happen – and how I could make it happen. I was a virgin again, essentially. Would that put women off? What if I was shit in bed, lesbian-wise? There was only one way to find out.

As the days passed, I felt more comfortable with the idea, less nervous, more excited — and angrier, too, with Nicky, for calling me passive. Fuck her. I wasn't too scared to go out with women.

During quiet moments at work — fewer and fewer these days, because Smriti had a habit of popping up behind people's desks and saying, 'Just run me through what you're doing!' — I Googled the Civil Service Rainbow Alliance. They organized meet-ups. They even marched in Pride. But the next drinks night wasn't for a couple of weeks, and I was worried I might lose my nerve before then.

So that Friday night, when Jane texted me, asking *What are you doing later?*, I decided to seize the moment. I was meant to be meeting Alice in Dalston for Turkish food, but I called her to put her off.

'I'm going to have sex with Jane,' I explained.

There was a silence.

'What?'

'Jane. I'm going to have sex with her.'

'But do you even fancy women?'

'I don't know until I've licked the snail.'

'Are you sure? Come on, just come and have Turkish food with me. We can rent *Tipping the Velvet* or something if you need to get it out of your system.'

'No. I'll text you if I'm not coming home.'

'But what about the *Your cunt tastes delicious* paintings?'

'See you later.'

I finished the call and stopped in the middle of the pavement to reply to Jane before I could change my mind. *Not much*, I texted. *What are you doing?*

My phone buzzed in my hand a few seconds later.

You? ;)

I had a pretty thorough bath when I got home. I moisturised more than usual. As I was getting dressed, I searched *lesbian* on Pornhub to see what I might be getting myself into, but the women didn't seem into it; they were rubbing each other's nipples pointlessly and staring off camera as though seeking some anonymous third person's approval.

My hands felt shaky as I did my make-up. I poured myself a large glass of wine to steady myself. I couldn't back out now. I had to go through with it.

I rang Jane's doorbell, feeling sick. I couldn't work out how to stand naturally, or how to smile. What the fuck was I doing here?

But then the door opened, and the situation was out of my hands. Jane didn't even say hello. She grabbed my hand, pulled me towards her and kissed me. She kicked the door shut behind us and kept kissing me as we stumbled to her bedroom. She turned away from me for a second to light a candle, and then she joined me on her bed and started kissing me again.

This was really happening. I was kissing a woman. We were almost certainly going to fuck. And I really, really wanted us to fuck. So much that I forgot to feel nervous, or self-conscious, or anything other than completely and utterly turned on.

I reached up and stroked Jane's face, so smooth compared to a man's. She mirrored me, touching my cheek. I have discovered sexual equality, I thought. I have discovered feminist sex.

'I'm going to take your top off now, if that's OK,' she said.

'That's OK,' I said, holding up my arms. She was asking for my consent and I was giving it. This was what adults did in bed.

Jane pulled my T-shirt over my head as she clearly had with tens – hundreds? – of other women. She didn't paw me or grope me; she knew exactly what she wanted her hands to do. She was precise, which doesn't sound hot but it honestly was. She knew exactly where to touch me, and what it would do. And when she fucked me, oh my GOD I finally understood what all the fuss was about. I went down on her too, which was easier than I expected, probably because I'm a clitoris owner myself. I didn't fuck her, though. I couldn't quite get the nerve up.

I learned a lot that night. That hands are a lot more versatile, and reliable, than penises. That women know how to use their tongues. That touching another woman's breasts can transport you to a place of unexpected ecstasy. And that women are amazing at sex.

You know when you wake up after something awful has happened to you, and everything seems fine and normal for a moment before reality smacks you in the stomach? The morning after I had sex with Jane was exactly the opposite of that. I lay on my back, smiling stupidly at the memory of the best sex I'd ever had in my life. The best sex anyone had ever had, possibly – sex so technically excellent that I thought anyone would have enjoyed it, regardless of their sexuality. It hadn't been perfect, obviously – she'd leaned on my hair as she fucked me, and she'd interpreted my yelp of pain as pleasure; I'd been pretty tentative about going down on her, and my tongue had got a bit tired about halfway through, and it had taken her a while to come. But she had come. And I'd felt sexy. I'd licked the snail, and I'd loved it. I'd felt like an equal partner in the whole thing. I felt, more than anything, a huge sense of relief.

Jane's side of the bed was empty. Through the curtainless window I could see a man in the warehouse opposite brushing his teeth. Which meant that he could see me; I was lying on top of the duvet, completely naked, my legs glowing pastily in the sunlight. I scanned the room for my underpants and found them folded on a chair with the rest of my clothes. As I picked them up, I felt hot with horror for a moment – the crotch was as stiff as a board. I had obviously been quite turned on.

And then I smiled again. I had been totally turned on. Possibly for the first time in my life.

I got dressed and walked out into the main warehouse to find Jane. She was standing where the DJ had been at her party, barefoot, her blunt bob swinging as she painted a canvas red. I stood and watched her for a moment, trying to decide on my opening gambit. Frankly, I just wanted to thank her for the amazing sex, but I didn't think that would be very cool.

She turned and noticed me watching her. 'All right?' she said. 'How you feeling this morning?'

'Great, thank you.' Smiling stupidly. Standing there awkwardly.

'Coffee's in that pot on the hob if you want it.'

I nodded and poured myself a cup, grateful to have something to do.

'You were great last night,' she said, eyes still on her painting. 'I'd never have known it was your first time with a woman. Guess I'll be getting another toaster!'

She turned to look at me and laughed as if we were sharing a joke, so I laughed along, but I can't have done it very convincingly, because then she said, 'You've got no idea what I'm talking about, have you?'

'Not really.'

'You've got a lot to learn, girl. Google it.'

As we said goodbye, I asked her, 'Do you want to do this again sometime?'

'No offence,' she said, rubbing my arm, 'but once is usually enough for me. Have fun exploring the ladies, though.'

I wasn't offended. I practically bounced out of the warehouse, laughing my way through the streets of Hackney Wick, people staring as I ran past. The reds and blues and yellows and pinks of the street art felt like they'd been painted just for me, a riot of rainbow against the grey sky. I hadn't felt so at home in my stupid body since I'd stopped dancing. I'd never felt so alive. I wasn't weird or bad at sex. I wasn't an outsider.

Definitely a lesbian, I texted Alice.
A full one?
Enough of one.
You did the deed?
Fucking loved it.
!!!!!!!

Gay clubs were my clubs now. Carhartt trousers, rainbows, team sports, *But I'm a Cheerleader*, *RuPaul's Drag Race*, Pride parades, *Moonlight*, the Pet Shop Boys, vegetarian food, *Oranges Are Not the Only Fruit*, *Orange Is the New Black*, Old Compton Street, San Francisco, the colour pink, k.d. lang, Ellen, Dusty Springfield, Brighton, musical theatre, Tegan and Sara, lip-synching – some of the best things in the world belonged to me. Lucky, lucky, lucky me.

8. WELCOME TO THE FAMILY

'But are you *sure* you're a lesbian?'

Alice and I were shopping for vintage clothes in Stoke Newington. She was looking for a fake-fur coat. I was hoping to find some tweed trousers that didn't smell of funerals. I wanted to wear more tweed, now that I was gay.

'Yes,' I said. 'You'd understand if you'd been there during the sex.'

'I'm very glad I wasn't.'

'So am I.'

'Maybe Jane was just really good at sex, though,' said Alice. 'That doesn't mean you should rule men out altogether.'

'I think it does,' I said. Since my night with Jane, I had thought back to every sexual experience I'd had with a man – to the grunting, and the chest hair, and the noises I'd feigned. I used to think I just wasn't very expressive during sex, and I'd always made a conscious effort to look like I was having fun, because staying silent when someone's fucking you is a bit like not laughing during a stand-up set (very bad for the performer's morale). But I hadn't needed to make an effort with Jane. Now that I had something to compare it to, sex with a man seemed like a dodgy imitation of the real thing, like instant coffee, or frozen yoghurt, or the Miley Cyrus cover of 'Smells Like Teen Spirit'. Since I'd realized I was probably a lesbian,

63

I had started seeing attractive women everywhere, a bit like the way you see a word everywhere as soon as you've learned what it means.

Alice picked up a pair of gold clip-on earrings and said, 'I promise I won't make fun of you if you start dating men again.'

'I'm not going to,' I said.

'Did you know an ex-lesbian is called a "hasbian"?'

'Stop it.'

I turned up to my next session with Nicky with an uncharacteristic smile on my face. Nicky had dyed her hair black since I'd last seen her. She was wearing bright-red lipstick, too – essentially, she was one bowler hat away from being Liza Minnelli in *Cabaret*.

'So you're officially a dyke,' she said.

'Yes,' I said. 'I prefer the word lesbian, though.'

'You have problems with the word dyke.'

'It just sounds a bit weird, hearing you say it.'

'How do you feel about homosexual?'

'It's fine.'

'Or queer?'

'That's fine too.'

'Gay?'

'Any of those words are completely fine,' I said.

'But not dyke,' she said. 'Does the word dyke have bad connotations for you?'

'It's not the sort of word you expect your therapist to use. It's pretty pejorative.'

'Ooh,' she said. 'Pejorative. Nice big word.' She wrote it down. 'You're wrong, though. Dyke isn't a pejorative word any more. It's been reappropriated.'

'It's been reappropriated by lesbians. So only lesbians can use it, surely.'

'You're making assumptions about me,' said Nicky, wagging her pen at me.

'What,' I said, 'are you gay?'

Nicky shook her head. 'I keep telling you, Julia. These sessions are about you, not me. So. Why the need to label yourself?'

'Because I've figured out who I am, and I'm not ashamed about it.'

'Are you seeing Jane again, then?' she said.

'No.'

'Are you seeing anyone else?'

'Not right now.'

'OK, so, off the record? Just go on Tinder, or whatever. The Internet. That's where all the dykes meet each other now. Even the cool ones.'

'Right.'

'That's what I've heard.'

'OK.' I shifted in my seat. 'I've been wondering about telling my parents,' I said. 'I'm going to see them for my dad's birthday on Wednesday.'

'I feel as though you're rushing things a bit,' said Nicky. 'Are you coming out so soon to stop yourself chickening out of dating women?'

'No . . .'

She tilted her head on one side.

'. . . maybe.'

'Would you like to role-play coming out to your parents?'

'No, thank you.'

'Come on. I'll be your mother.'

'It's OK, I'll be fine.'

But Nicky was already saying, 'Hello, Julia!' in a snooty accent.

'She's not that posh,' I said.

'Just go with it,' Nicky said.

'OK.' I tried to get comfortable in the chair. 'Mum,' I said, 'I have something to tell you.'

'Can't you think of a more original opener?'

'I don't want to be original – I want her to know what's coming,' I said. 'It's like saying, "We need to talk" to your boyfriend.'

'Or girlfriend,' said Nicky.

'Or girlfriend,' I agreed.

'OK,' said Nicky. 'Give me your line again.'

'Mum, I have something to tell you,' I said.

'Oh God, darling!' said Nicky, in the snooty voice. 'What is it? Are you dying?'

'I really don't think she's going to say that.'

Nicky shrugged. 'We'll have to see, won't we?'

So far, being a lesbian was pretty much the same as not being a lesbian. My alarm clock went off at 7.30 a.m. just like it always did. I snoozed it till 8 a.m., as usual. I put on the same tights with the holes in the toe, spooned down a bowl of Alpen and felt out of breath running for the bus just as I had before. I'd have thought I'd imagined the whole thing if I didn't still feel bruised and sore between my legs.

I called Cat to tell her my big news, but she didn't seem particularly surprised. 'You made me go and see *Les Misérables* three times because that girl Louise was in it,' she pointed out. 'By the third time I couldn't wait for her to get shot.'

'She wasn't exactly a triple threat, was she?'

'She was shit,' said Cat. And then: 'Hey! This means we're both minorities! You're a bit less privileged now!'

'You're right!' I said. I looked forward to being a lot more self-righteous on social media, now that I was a lesbian.

I felt a secret sense of achievement that helped me stand a little taller as I walked into the Department of Health and Social Care building and swiped my pass on the security gate. I felt like I belonged, at last, in the world of the sexually fulfilled. Now I had a sense of purpose. I was going to find someone to be a lesbian with – a girlfriend, someone I respected and who respected me, someone I could fall completely in love with. She'd be funny and creative; she'd have a better job than me, probably, and she'd inspire me to figure out what I really wanted to do with my life. She'd identify as a feminist and drink at least as much as me and we would go on dates to immersive theatre shows and classical concerts. She would be my best friend. We would have a truly equal relationship. I wasn't going to be lonely any more. I couldn't wait.

Tom, Smriti and the other managers were out at an all-day meeting, so I took the opportunity to look for lesbians on the Internet. I couldn't bring myself to go back on Tinder; I knew there was a much lower chance of dick pics, now that I was dating women, but I hated the idea of swiping past thousands of nameless people, knowing they were doing the same to me. I thought it might be nice to meet someone in real life. I found gay vegan meet-ups and a lesbian volleyball team and a stressful-sounding lesbian architecture appreciation society, none of which really appealed to me. And then I saw an ad for something called Stepping Out:

*QUEER SWING DANCE CLASSES Fun, friendly, suitable for beginners
and more experienced dancers. All LGBTQ+ people welcome.
Sundays, Upstairs at the Kings, £7 a class.*

I felt Owen walk up behind me. I minimized the screen.

'Are you going to go to that?' he asked.

'Might do,' I said, glancing back at him to gauge his reaction.

Owen raised his eyebrows and nodded. 'Cool,' he said. And then, 'My sister's gay.'

'Good for her,' I said, and I turned back to my screen and started clicking through my emails.

'Are you gay?' he asked.

'Shh.' I nodded across to Uzo; I didn't want her to know – not yet, anyway. She had a habit of 'whispering' secrets extremely loudly in the kitchen, for everyone to hear. Plus I'd heard her say 'What a waste' once, when we were talking about Sir Ian McKellen being gay (she had a thing for white-haired white men). I wasn't sure she'd react brilliantly to my news.

'Sorry,' Owen said, crouching by my desk. 'Are you, though?'

'Might be.' I felt like a bit of a fraud, to be honest. I wasn't sure one (highly enjoyable) episode of lesbian sex was enough to qualify me.

'That's cool,' he said again. 'So's Catwoman.'

'As in – the comic-book character?'

Owen nodded. 'She's thinking of having a baby with her girlfriend,' he said.

'Catwoman?'

'No, Carys. My sister.'

'Oh, right,' I said. 'I'm not at that stage yet.' I went back to my emails.

Owen didn't. 'Do you want me to come with you?'

'To what?'

'To the gay dance thing.'

A thought struck me, and I looked up at him. 'Are *you* gay, Owen?'

'No! No. No. Not that there's anything wrong with it.'

'Right.'

'I'm going out with Laura, remember?'

'Of course.'

'I just like gay people,' he said.

'All of them?'

'No, you know. Like Cara Delevingne. And Ellen Page.'

'You mean, you fancy lesbians.'

'No! Well – only the hot ones.'

I looked at the Stepping Out website when I got home. There was a video of the Friends of Dorothy, their Solo Jazz group, competing at the London Swing Dance Festival in sequinned hot pants (surprisingly flattering). They had won first prize. Watching the video, I felt the potent combination of nostalgia, envy and self-pity that comes whenever I watch people perform. I had gone cold turkey on dance after my ballet career ended. I thought it would be too painful to teach, or to try contemporary, or move into administration or anything; I even found Zumba classes a bit triggering. Maybe going to a swing dance class would be like opening an old wound. Maybe it wouldn't, though. Avoiding dance hadn't made me miss it any less. I decided to give it a go.

I made the most of the time before the first class by practising telling people I was gay. I announced it via WhatsApp to my school friends, none of whom seemed particularly surprised, and when I got my legs waxed, I told the beauty therapist that I was going to a queer dance class. 'So I'll be dancing with other women, because I'm gay, which means I fancy women, because of being gay,' I told her.

'Right,' she said. 'Can you turn over for me?'

I also did a fair bit of lesbian Internet research. I discovered that the toaster thing was a hilarious lesbian in-joke – when a woman 'converts' another woman to lesbianism, she's supposedly given a toaster as a thank-you from the lesbian community.

One click led to another, and I found myself reading a dictionary of lesbian slang. Apparently if I noticed a fellow lesbian walking down the street, say, I was supposed to say 'She's family' to whomever I was with. It seemed there was a whole lesbian language I knew nothing about, but I liked that; I felt I was being invited to join a secret club. I liked the idea of being part of a family.

I found a wikiHow article called *How to be a lesbian*, illustrated with pictures of women in pastel clothes, smiling at each other like the couples in the erectile dysfunction ads you see on the Tube. 'You can't make yourself a lesbian if you aren't one already,' it told me. You can't make yourself a straight, either, I thought. Yes, I'd had the odd Jarvis Cocker fantasy. I'd enjoyed the occasional fumble on a single bed. But I'd never really got the point of sex till now. *Touch your partner like you touch yourself*, said wikiHow. *A come-hither motion always works*. All right, I thought, I'll give that a try. When I've found someone to be a lesbian with.

I took my time over getting ready. I changed into my best jeans and flossed my teeth, and I tried to ignore my stomach, which was making all sorts of unsociable noises.

'I think you're really brave,' said Alice, standing in my doorway, watching as I put my make-up on.

'Don't be patronizing,' I said. I looked in the mirror. 'Do I look like a lesbian?'

Alice considered the question. 'Now you mention it, yes. It's your hair.'

'No – it's my shirt.' A tartan one, buttoned to the very top.

'Do you want to borrow one of Dave's ties, too? You know, ram the point home?'

'No thanks,' I said. I stood with both hands on my hips, which makes you feel more confident apparently, according to a TED Talk I'd seen. It didn't really work. 'I'm off. See you later.'

'Unless you get lucky!' said Alice, as I edged past her to the front door. Now she'd got used to the idea, she really was very excited about the prospect of my new lesbian sex life. Come to think of it, I hadn't heard so much of her and Dave recently.

'At a dance class? I think everyone will be able to contain themselves.'

'You never know.' She gave me a kiss on the cheek. 'Promise you won't make any friends you like better than me?'

'Promise,' I said.

The class was in a pub just off Clerkenwell Green, in a pretty, Dickensian corner of the city. I felt immediately at home, as the walls were the same shade of dark red that I'd painted my teenage bedroom. The tables were crowded with thirty-something men drinking pints. There wasn't a queer dancer to be seen. The barman saw me looking around and jerked his head towards the stairs. 'They're up there.'

'Right!' I said cheerily, pleased to have been identified as a lesbian, and walked up the creaking staircase, wondering what I'd find at the top.

I hesitated in the doorway of a large, loft-like room. Women and a few men were standing around, some chatting in twos and threes, some on their own, leaning against the radiators for warmth, arms and legs crossed for comfort. A woman wearing purple lipstick was sitting on a table at the front of the room, swinging her legs back and forth. 'Can everyone pay me now, please!' she called. 'There are labels here for you to write your name on.' I wrote *JULIA* on a label in thick black marker, stuck it to my shirt and walked to the edge of the room, next to a woman with short brown hair, who was wearing bright-red braces and, amazingly, a bow tie. Her clothes were intimidatingly trendy, but she moved awkwardly, as though she didn't realize how long her arms and legs were, and that made her seem more approachable.

'Hello!' I said, waving at close range, the way I do when I'm nervous. I pointed to my name tag and said, 'Julia.'

'Hello!' she said back, and pointed at her name tag. 'Ella!' She grinned at me, like she was delighted to see me. I liked her immediately.

The woman wearing purple lipstick clapped her hands and walked to the middle of the room. 'I'm Zhu,' she said. 'Great to see so many new faces here today! Obviously, this is a queer dance class, so we're gender neutral – it doesn't matter whether you're a man or a woman or outside the binary. If you want to try leading, you lead, if you want to follow, you follow.'

I decided to lead. I hadn't been leading enough in my life lately. Ella, it turned out, was a follower.

'Shall we?' I said, holding out my hands, and we learned to do a rock step.

From the moment Zhu turned on the music – Ella Fitzgerald singing 'Tain't What You Do (It's The Way That You Do It)' – I was in heaven. I hadn't danced for so long, and when I had danced it had been my job, tied up with my self-esteem and my body image and whether Cat was going to get picked for a solo over me. I had forgotten what it was like to dance for fun, to be in sync with your partner, with the music. I'd forgotten how free it made me feel. Everyone had their own way of dancing – we switched partners every time we learned a new part of the routine, and I danced with a girl named Annie, who was quite stiff and awkward, and a guy named Ollie, whose arms were loose, like skipping ropes – but everyone, everyone had broad smiles across their faces. You couldn't not smile when you were swing dancing, it seemed. I hadn't been so purely happy in years.

'You're really good at this,' said Ella when we came full circle and danced together again at the end of the class. Ella was my favourite partner. She flailed her arms and kept kicking with her left leg instead of her right, but she seemed so delighted to be dancing that none of that mattered.

Some of us went downstairs for a drink after the lesson. I sat with Zhu and Ella and a woman named Rebecca – dark brown hair, a lot of earnest opinions on almost every subject – who had her arm around Bo, very smiley, round glasses, wearing a badge reading *They/Them*. In fact, all of my new swing dance friends smiled a lot, which was relaxing. I had been worried I'd have to hang out with intimidating people like Jane, now that I was a lesbian.

'Rebecca's my girlfriend,' said Bo, unnecessarily. I remember thinking how wonderful it would be to have someone who was that proud of going out with you.

Bo, it turned out, was a freelance coder, which was appropriate, because they moved in a slightly robotic way. Rebecca worked in social media for Greenpeace.

'She met Gillian Anderson for work the other week,' Bo said, hand on Rebecca's knee.

'Such a waste,' Zhu said. 'She doesn't even fancy her.'

'She's a bit too femme for me,' Rebecca said, shrugging.

It was wonderful to be surrounded by queer people, casually throwing words like 'femme' into the conversation.

'What do you do?' I asked Ella.

'I'm a dentist.' She fiddled with her bow tie.

I stared at her for a moment. 'Wow.'

'I know.'

'Was that like . . . a vocation?'

'Not really,' said Ella. 'But the money's good, and I have lots of time to do fun things outside work.'

'Look at her teeth,' said Bo.

Ella opened her mouth for me to inspect them, like a horse. They were flawless.

I started gabbling away about the class, talking too fast and too loudly, about how much I had loved it.

'Own up,' Zhu said in her teacherly voice. 'You've done swing before.'

'I haven't,' I said, but I explained how I used to be a dancer.

Rebecca leaned towards me. 'How did you feel about that? Working in such a heteronormative world?'

'I didn't really think about it at the time,' I shrugged. 'I wasn't a lesbian then.'

'Are you a new recruit?' asked Zhu.

'Very new,' I said, because I'd had some beer.

'So,' said Zhu, 'does that mean you're single?'

'Zhu,' said Ella, shaking her head at me, apologizing silently.

'What?' said Zhu. 'Fresh meat!'

I swapped numbers with everyone before I left. Ella hugged me – a really tight hug – and said, 'Welcome to the family!'

I felt the loveliest, warmest feeling of belonging.

*

As I was walking home from the Tube, I got a message from Ella. *Great hanging out with you! Are you coming next week?* I was about to text her back to say yes, I was definitely coming next week, when my phone buzzed with another message.

Come at seven next Friday. Dad's joined a wine club so there'll be lots of booze. Don't tease him about being nearly sixty or about his thread veins, belly, liver spots etc. He's feeling a bit delicate.

9. SCARY LESBIAN EYES

I caught the coach to Oxford straight after work the following Friday. I wrapped the Hitler biography and wrote a card as we rumbled through West London, hoping Dad wouldn't mind the wobbly handwriting. I felt sick; I knew I didn't *have* to come out to my parents yet, but I wanted to get it out of the way. I've never liked uncertainty, and I hated the idea of sitting at the dinner table, listening to Mum talking about party wall agreements and Dad gossiping about his graduate students, wondering how they'd react when they found out. In a way, I wished I didn't have to do it. Telling them I enjoyed fucking women felt a bit like telling them I liked it from behind.

My mother answered the door wearing a draped sheet-type dress, the sort of thing they sell in Hampstead Bazaar for about a thousand pounds. She'd cut her hair since I'd last seen her – it was cropped close to her head and was greyer than I remembered it being. She looked strange but good, like a national treasure.

'Julia, darling,' she said, doing a little twirl. 'Do you like my outfit?'

'Yes,' I said. 'Very bohemian.'

'I had to stop wearing pencil skirts when I cut my hair. I looked all wrong, like a human Heads, Bodies and Legs.' She leaned towards me and whispered, 'Have you seen what they're doing next door?'

I glanced over to the house next to theirs, currently hidden from view by chipboard and scaffolding.

75

'Isn't it hideous?'

'I don't think that's the final look they're going for, Mum.'

Mum shook her head and ushered me into the hall. 'You're no fun to moan to,' she said. 'You're supposed to agree with me and say how awful it is.'

Dad was at the kitchen table, flicking through the *Radio Times* and ranting on about how one of his colleagues had become a media don and was presenting a documentary about the Victorians on the BBC. Dad has always wanted to present documentaries, but he has a slight lisp, which puts the commissioners off a bit, I think.

'Just look at his face,' said Dad, pushing the magazine towards me.

I looked down at the photo of Geoffrey, a fellow English lecturer at Oxford Brookes, standing in front of some stately home or other with his arms crossed.

'He looks pretty smug,' I said.

'Yes,' said Dad, sipping his wine. 'And unnaturally smooth. Like an alien. Never trust a man with a smooth face. Just look at Stalin.'

'I don't think Stalin's face was that smooth, Dad,' I said. 'He did have quite a prominent moustache.'

'Yes, but underneath the moustache, he was extremely smooth, I promise you. Same with Hitler, Napoleon, Cliff Richard . . .'

I took that as my cue to give him the Hitler biography. We opened the book to the glossy photograph pages and argued about the smoothness or otherwise of Hitler's skin until Mum came in with the dinner.

'Now,' said Mum, as we were all tucking into our roast chicken, 'have you got over your loneliness?'

'What?' said Dad, glancing up.

'Julia was feeling lonely the other week. I told her to get out there and meet people on the Internet.'

'And I did,' I said.

'See?' said Mum, smiling a self-congratulatory smile. 'And?'

Dad sat up suddenly and pointed to the radio. Radio 4 was babbling in the background. 'Is that that Portia de Rossi woman?'

I listened. 'Yes,' I said.

'She has lovely hair,' said Dad, taking another forkful of chicken.

Mum turned to me. 'Your father has been rather passive aggressive since I cut my hair. He keeps drawing my attention to celebrities with nice hair.'

'That's not true, Jenny,' said Dad. 'Your hair is very becoming. It was an innocent comment: I like Portia de Rossi's hair. That's all.'

'Fine.' My mother speared a roast potato.

'You needn't feel threatened,' said Dad. 'It's not as though I fancy Portia de Rossi.'

'Dad,' I said, 'please don't say the word "fancy" in my presence again.'

'Well, I don't. She's an odd woman. Is she Australian? Is she American? Who can tell? And she's married to Ellen DeGeneres. Very nice hair, though, nevertheless.'

I looked up at Dad. 'By "odd", do you mean "gay"?'

'No, Julia,' he said. 'I have no problem with alternative sexualities.'

'Good,' I said, preparing myself.

Mum frowned. 'You aren't about to tell us that *you're* a lesbian, are you?'

I was a bit taken aback. 'Well,' I said. 'Yes, actually.'

'Really?' she said, eyebrows raised.

'Yes, really,' I said.

'Oh,' she said. And then: 'Good for you. Later in life lesbians are quite the thing these days, aren't they?'

'I'm not later in life, Mum,' I pointed out.

'No, I suppose not,' she said, 'but it must be comforting to know you're on trend.'

'Thanks, Mum,' I said. I felt a bit deflated. I'd expected a little bit more of a reaction from her.

I looked at Dad. He seemed to be trying very hard to settle on the appropriate facial expression.

'Are you OK?' I asked him.

'Of course I am.'

'You're not,' I said. 'What's wrong?'

'Nothing! Nothing,' he said, cutting a potato into unnecessarily small pieces. 'I just think you're being silly. You're not really gay, are you?'

'Why would I say I was gay if I wasn't?'

'Have you got a friend, then?' asked Dad, much more blustery and starchy than usual.

'I have lots of friends.'

'No, a *friend* friend. A lover.'

'Not right now,' I said.

'Then you're not a lesbian,' said Dad, wiping his mouth with his napkin. 'You can't just decide to be a homosexual. You have to try it out.' He stood up and took some mustard from the fridge, as if the conversation was over.

I wasn't really sure what to say. I opened my mouth, but I shut it again, because I felt as though I might be about to cry. I hate crying in front of my parents, and I do it surprisingly often.

'*Martin*,' my mother said, in her cold, telling-off voice.

'What?' Dad said.

'Don't listen to your father,' she said to me. 'He's being ridiculous.'

'I'm *not* being ridiculous,' said Dad. 'I'm just stating the facts. You have to actually have homosexual sex to be a homosexual.'

'Well, if you must know—' I started, but Dad put his hands over his ears like a 5-year-old and sang, 'Lalalalalalalalala!'

'You are such a hypocrite,' Mum said. 'Do you have no memories of the Seventies whatsoever? What about that time you and

I had a threesome with James? And that other time, with Melinda?'

'Oh God,' I said, closing my eyes to block out the mental images. James was my dad's best friend. He looked like David Attenborough. He used to take me to the park and push me on the swings.

'That was different,' said Dad. 'That was what everyone was doing then.'

Which gave me an interesting insight into life in the Seventies. I thought everyone was wearing flares and using typewriters and walking around in the dark because of power cuts. But they were also having threesomes, it turns out, left, right and centre.

It gave me an interesting insight into my parents' sex life, too. Clearly they were more sexually adventurous than me. I resolved to change that.

'Well,' said Mum, while I sat twitching at the kitchen table, 'I'm delighted you're a lesbian, Julia. All I've ever wanted is for you to be interesting. And now you really are.'

Not as interesting as my bloody parents, though.

I texted Cat on the way back to London to tell her I'd come out. *Well done, mate!* she texted back. *Let's go lesbian dancing to celebrate. Tomorrow?? PS do you think I have a German aura? My agent thinks I do.*

I texted Ella, too, because I wanted to tell someone who would appreciate the importance of what I'd just done and who wouldn't immediately change the subject to make it all about them.

Hooray!! So brave!!!! she replied. *Please can I buy you a drink to celebrate? Some swing dance people are going out in Dalston tomorrow night, if you'd like to come.*

I said yes. For the first time in ages, my life was moving forward, and not in a depressing, hurtling-towards-the-grave way.

* * *

I was a bit nervous about going out in Dalston; I hadn't been clubbing in months, partly because I was always skint and partly because the last time I'd been clubbing I'd taken too much ecstasy and ended the night by cutting my eyebrows off with a pair of scissors. I was fairly sure I'd learned my lesson since then, though. My eyebrows were probably safe.

Alice was a bit suspicious of my new friends. 'It's a bit weird, isn't it? You barely know them,' she said as we pushed our trolley around Sainsbury's. She paused in front of the milk. 'Don't you think we should switch to whole milk for tea? It really makes a difference to the taste.'

'Sure,' I said, about the milk. And then: 'I think the rules are different with queers. If you find people you like, you hang onto them.'

She didn't look convinced.

'You should come out with us,' I said, putting some yoghurt in the trolley.

She cheered up a bit at that. 'OK then,' she said.

'Cat's coming too.'

'Oh!' said Alice, trying and failing to sound pleased. Alice and Cat pretend to like each other for my sake, but I know they don't really. We have a three-way WhatsApp group that only I send messages to. 'How long is she back?' Alice asked now.

'Just for a week. She's got an audition.'

'What for?'

'An ad for a German supermarket. Her agent says her aura appeals to Germans.'

Alice started laughing and didn't stop until we'd reached the cheese section, where we had a minor argument about mature versus extra mature cheddar.

By the time we arrived at the club that night, the queue was snaking around the block. A power-drunk doorman wearing a fascinator with a flamingo on it was walking up and down the queue, picking out people wearing particularly exciting outfits and hustling them inside before everyone else. Cat, Alice and I were not chosen.

'What if he doesn't let us in?' Alice asked, hugging herself against the cold.

'He will,' said Cat, smiling at the doorman. He ignored her. 'Dickhead,' she muttered.

Ten minutes passed. I began to feel hot and impatient, anxious to get inside. I texted Ella: *Sorry. Stuck outside.*

Eventually the trendy people ran out and we made it to the front of the queue. But the doorman dropped his arm in front of us like a camp portcullis.

'You know this is a gay club?' he said.

'Yes,' I said. 'I'm gay.'

'You don't look it,' he said.

'Why?' said Cat. 'What does a gay person look like?'

'Even if you are,' he said, 'I can't just let *every* gay person in London in.'

Bo appeared in the doorway of the club. 'Hey!' they called to us. 'You coming in?'

'If we're allowed to,' I said. I gave the doorman what I hoped was a cold, hard stare.

He swivelled around to look at Bo. The flamingo on his fascinator bobbed in the breeze.

'Hey, Orson,' said Bo.

'They with you?' asked Orson.

'Yeah. Can you let them in?' Bo gave him a golden smile. He didn't stand a chance.

'Sorry,' said Orson. 'I didn't realize.' He stood aside. 'Have a great night.'

We hurried inside, before he could change his mind.

'That was really cool,' Alice said to Bo, in a really uncool way.

'He was in my year at uni,' said Bo, shrugging. 'His real name's Tim.'

*   *   *

Bo led us to the corner of the dance floor where Ella and Rebecca were dancing, their coats in a pile on the floor between them. Ella was dressed eccentrically again, in a jumpsuit that looked like a tuxedo. I was nervous introducing them to Cat and Alice, but I needn't have been. The heat and darkness of the club made everyone stand closer together than they otherwise would have done, shouting into each other's ears like deaf old friends. Soon we were on our second bottle of house red, and Rebecca was talking to Alice – I couldn't hear what they were saying, but there was a lot of intense nodding – and Ella was teasing Cat about her advert audition.

'Why are they auditioning British people?'

'Maybe no one in Germany wants the job,' Cat said.

'Are you fluent in German?'

'Do I look like I'm fluent in German? It's a non-speaking role,' Cat said. 'I just have to look enthusiastic about sausages in a German way.'

Ella laughed again, throwing her head back, showing her perfect teeth. 'She's brilliant!' she said to me.

'She is,' I said, and I gave Cat a hug.

The music seemed to get louder and the club hazier, though it's possible it just seemed that way because of all the wine. People started dancing and we joined in, eyes closed, hands in the air. Bo and Rebecca were dancing together, trying out some lindy hop moves to the EDM.

'We should go out more!' Cat shouted in my ear, over a dance tune I didn't know.

'Yeah!' said Alice. 'I love lesbians!'

'Me too!' I said, draining my glass and trying to refill it, then realizing we had run out of wine. 'I'm just going to the bar,' I shouted.

'What?' Alice shouted back.

'The bar!' I did a drink mime.

I pushed my way through the sweaty, smelly bodies, looking over my shoulder at my oldest friends dancing with my newest friends, feeling a surge of happiness and gratitude.

I ordered another bottle of house red and was waiting, half dancing, when I noticed a woman at the other end of the bar, long curly hair, leather jacket, staring at me – a 'What the fuck are you doing here?' sort of stare.

I looked away, a bit put out, but when I looked back she was still staring, still apparently hating me for no reason. When she caught my eye, she tapped her friend on the shoulder and whispered something in her ear. Her friend turned and then started walking towards me, looking me up and down, like we were in a Western and were about to have a shoot-out. I clutched my glass of wine in what I hoped was a threatening manner.

'All right?' she said, raising her chin to me.

'Yes,' I said.

'My friend – the one with the curly hair? Yeah – she thinks you're hot. Are you single?'

I turned the woman down – the staring put me off – and went to tell the others what had happened.

'Don't you know about that yet?' said Ella, taking charge of the bottle and refilling everyone's glasses.

'About what?' I asked.

'About the scary lesbian eyes. It's a thing,' said Ella. 'If you fancy someone in a lesbian bar, you have to stare at her like you want her dead. And she stares back like she wants you dead.'

'And then what?'

'Then you have sex,' said Rebecca, shrugging.

I looked at Cat and Alice. They seemed as fascinated as me. 'Without speaking to each other?' I asked.

'Sometimes,' said Bo.

'But how does that work?' I asked. 'How do you go from death stares to kissing?'

'You just do,' said Ella. 'Although I've never got past the staring stage, personally.'

'Try it,' Cat said to me. 'Pick someone. See if it works.'

I scanned the room. Several of the lesbians were wearing baseball caps at a jaunty angle. I noticed more than one undercut. I felt out of my depth. And then I saw a woman standing next to the DJ booth who seemed more sure of herself than anyone else in the room. She was probably in her late twenties, tall and angular, with golden skin and short, dark hair, curly on top and shaved at the sides. She was standing up, shoulders back, surveying the room like she owned it, which made her seem even taller; her posture was the first thing I noticed about her. The second thing I noticed was that I found her incredibly attractive.

I looked at Cat. 'Do it!' she said.

'She's too cool for me,' I said.

'She's not,' said Ella.

'She's looking away now, anyway,' I said.

'Go on!' Alice said.

So I stared at the woman until she looked away from the woman she was talking to and looked back at me. I kept staring. The others sniggered and turned their backs, but they were obviously still half watching us, because I heard Ella say, 'She's coming over!'

The attractive woman walked up to me and leaned towards me, so close that I could tell she was wearing men's cologne, to introduce herself over the music.

'Sam,' she shouted.

'Julia,' I shouted back, and as we shook hands, I noticed the muscles in her forearm tense. They were pretty well developed, and I had a sudden vision of that forearm having sex with me.

Sam smiled a half-smile like she knew what I was thinking, holding my gaze. Her eyes were a very dark brown. 'I like your jumper,' she said.

'I like your face,' I said.

Sam laughed. I felt very pleased with myself. Maybe I wasn't so bad at flirting, after all.

'I've seen you somewhere before, haven't I?' she asked, one arm against the wall, blocking my view of my friends.

'I don't know,' I said. But there was something vaguely familiar about her.

'Are you an artist too?' she asked.

'No,' I said, but then I realized. 'You know Jane, don't you? Did you go to a party at her warehouse in Hackney Wick a few months ago?'

She gave me another half-smile. '*That's* where I saw you. She was trying to chat you up but you weren't having any of it.'

I started to contradict her – I was pretty proud of the lesbian sex I'd had – but Sam was looking at her phone.

'Listen,' she said, glancing up, 'I'm meant to be meeting a friend now – but I'd love to buy you a drink sometime, if you like.'

'Great,' I said.

'Have you got your phone? I'll give you my number.'

I was collecting numbers wherever I went these days. I hardly knew myself.

I looked around Sam as she typed her number into my phone, wanting the others to notice that she had chosen me. Me!

I drop called her and we said goodbye, and then I just sort of stood there for a minute, everything brighter and louder and more exciting suddenly. And then the others ran up to me, practically rubbing their hands together.

'Did I just see you give Sam your number?' Rebecca asked.

'Yeah,' I said, as casually as I could.

Cat shook her head, apparently very proud of me. 'Mate,' she said. 'You fucking did it.'

'You're going to have fun,' said Rebecca.

'What?' I said.

'With Sam,' she said.

'Have you . . .?' I raised my eyebrows.

'When I first came out,' said Rebecca. 'She's really good.'

'Oi,' said Bo, who had been listening to our conversation.

'What?' said Rebecca. 'She is!'

You might think I'd have been put off by Rebecca's revelation, but I wasn't. I hoped Sam would fuck me, teach me all about lesbian sex and send me on my way a seasoned lesbian, capable of discussing my past conquests in Dalston clubs with people I'd only just met.

Sam texted me that night as I was getting into bed. *Sleep tight, beautiful Julia . . . I'm free next weekend if you are. Sam x*

I crafted a reply that was neutral and noncommittal but open to sex: *Yeah sure. Maybe next Saturday? Julia x*

She texted back straight away: *Brilliant, babes. I'll think of somewhere good to take you and let you know. Looking forward to it . . . will be thinking about it all week.* She put a kiss emoji at the end of the text, which gave me a bit of a thrill.

I closed my eyes and said a silent thank you to the universe. When I'd been sleeping with men, theoretically at least, I'd gone three years without so much as a bit of half-hearted fingering, and here I was, about to have sex with my second woman in as many months.

10. A SEX-CUPBOARD STAPLE

That March was the rainiest on record, and there was a leak in our terrible flat's terrible skylight, but my swing dance classes and my new friends and the prospect of a date with Sam made the world seem sunny and the flat seem like a luxury apartment designed for Chinese investors. The Monday after I met Sam, I cheerfully put a washing-up bowl underneath the skylight and left for work, smiling at people as I walked to the Tube. My anxiety had a purpose now; it was excitement making my heart race, not nameless dread. But by Thursday, I still hadn't heard from her. She had told me she'd be in touch, so I didn't want to text her first. I spent my days listening out for her text, snatching up my phone whenever it buzzed in my pocket, keeping it in front of my computer screen at work so I wouldn't miss anything. The only texts I got were PPI spam, or Alice telling me to buy milk, or Ella asking *What's happening?? When's the date????*

Then on Friday, during a briefing about the new measures to tackle childhood obesity, my phone lit up with a text from Sam. Tom's eyes flicked towards it. I pulled it under the table before he could read it.

Still up for meeting? What's your address? I'll pick you up at eight tomorrow.

I had never been picked up at eight before.

Smriti was saying something impressive about 'horizons of expectations' and everyone was nodding, so I nodded too. Owen looked at me and raised his eyebrows in a question.

'Sam,' I mouthed. 'My date.'

'Nice,' he mouthed back.

'Everything OK, Owen?' Tom asked. 'Anything you wanted to share with the group?'

'No,' he said. 'Just – I agree with Smriti, really.'

'About . . .?'

'About what she was just saying.'

I was nervous about the date, mostly for sex reasons. Jane had done much of the doing when we'd banged, and we hadn't used any accoutrements. I had started watching *The L Word* as research, and from what I'd seen, I was worried that lesbian sex might be quite accoutrement-heavy. I was hoping that things like dildos were for advanced-level shagging – not the sort of thing you'd whip out on a first meeting – but I didn't want to expose myself as a beginner. I decided to text Ella for advice.

Do you think Sam will expect me to have a strap-on? The Internet says it's a sex-cupboard staple. I need some lesbian sex help.

She replied straight away, with three laughy-cry-face emojis. *I am NOT a sex expert but I'll do my best. What are you doing on Saturday during the day? Want to go to a sex shop?!*

I'd never been to a sex shop before – hadn't needed to. You can get everything you need for straight sex in Boots or in a vending machine in the pub toilets, if push comes to shove.

'Where is it?' Alice asked that morning as I was getting ready to go out. She was putting on her foundation, staring at her reflection in the mirror.

'Shoreditch,' I said. I edged around her to pick up my toothbrush. 'Can I get to the sink for a minute?'

Alice sighed and stepped back to let me in. 'You could have asked me to come.'

I looked at her. 'Why would you want to come to a sex shop?'

'I have sex!'

'It's a women-only sex shop.'

'I'm a woman!'

'I'm going to be buying a dildo.'

'Maybe I need a dildo.'

'To use on Dave?' I whispered.

She shrugged. 'Might spice things up a bit,' she said, voice quieter now.

'I can get you one,' I said.

Alice looked as though she was about to argue and then she shut her eyes for a moment and said, 'Sorry. I'm being an idiot.'

'Only a bit of an idiot,' I said. The truth is, I liked Alice being jealous of me. I'd felt the same when she'd got together with Dave, all those years ago; suddenly the person I was used to doing everything with had someone else to do everything with. I'd hated it. But now Alice was going to have to get used to doing without me.

The sex shop Ella took me to was called Sh!. 'Everyone comes here,' she told me. 'It's a rite of passage.' As is the way with most things designed for women, it was decorated in various shades of pink and red and purple, so walking in felt like entering a large, latex-scented vagina. There were shelves full of sex toys and feminist porn, but I went straight for the books and cards. You know where you are with a book or a card. They might have nipples on them, but the nipples are non-threatening, two-dimensional nipples and no one will expect you to attach clamps to them or anything like that. But Ella wasn't having any of it. She put her hand on my back and steered me towards the shelves of dildos, saying, 'We did not come here to buy cards.'

I glanced up at the dildos and glanced away again. I found them terrifying, frankly. I'd never been a big fan of penises, and I'd certainly never aspired to wield one myself. What if I was no good at thrusting?

I scanned the shelves for an unintimidating cock. There were black ones and blue ones and purple ones, some as small as an index finger, some as thick as an arm.

'What do you like the look of?' Ella asked. She was studying me curiously and I had a feeling she was thinking about the size of my cunt.

'I don't think we know each other well enough for this,' I said.

'Just pick one.'

I was baffled by all the choice. 'Is this for someone else to use on me?' I asked her. 'Or for me to use on someone else?'

'Both,' she said. 'Or you could buy several?'

'I'm a junior civil servant,' I pointed out. 'Buying one massive latex penis is a luxury as it is.'

'OK,' said Ella, 'first of all, don't call it a penis. There's no man in this equation.'

'Good point.'

'Second of all, this isn't a luxury. It's a lesbian essential. Once you're properly seeing someone, you'll come back and pick out a cock together. So think of this as your fall-back cock.'

'My emergency cock.'

'Exactly!'

A shop assistant wandered up to us. 'Can I help you?'

'Not sure,' I said. 'Just looking, really.'

'Have you bought a cock before?'

'She hasn't,' Ella said, before I could answer.

She nodded. 'Are you into girth? Or, like, length?'

I wasn't sure, to be honest. I was used to taking what I was given when it came to cocks – having to choose my own felt like picking out a personality for myself. I ruled out the massive black ones as they seemed like the equivalent of a Ferrari – promising too much up front. I also ruled out the little thin glittery ones because really, what was the point? You might as well just use your fingers.

'I like girth, I think,' I said. 'But I was thinking of something quite . . . all purpose.'

'Got it,' said the sales assistant. She reached up to a high shelf and took down a medium-sized dildo with ridges along its length. 'This one's good for beginners,' she said. Which was embarrassing; a bit like someone at a pharmacy saying, 'Good condoms for virgins, those.'

'That looks great,' I said, reaching for it, just wanting to get out of there as quickly as possible.

'Ribbed for your pleasure,' she said as she handed it over.

'Lovely.'

'Easy to aim, if you know what I mean.'

'Great.'

I walked over to the till, but the shop assistant didn't follow. 'You'll need a harness, too,' she said, running her fingers over the display. 'Leather is more traditional. Or you could try the underpants. They're easier to get on and off, but they're not as sexy.' She picked up what looked like a pair of Y-fronts with a hole in them and stretched them to demonstrate their elasticity.

There was an apple sticker stuck to the floor. I scuffed it with my foot.

'The stretchy pants are easier,' said Ella.

'Don't get them,' said the shop assistant. 'You need a real harness. It's part of the ritual.'

Ella laughed. 'Yes, the ritual of having to stop in the middle of foreplay to strap yourself into a medieval torture device, and then you realize you've put your leg through the bum hole, and then you have to take it off again, except you're stuck, and whoever you're having sex with has to help you get out of it, and the moment's totally gone—'

'You get used to it,' said the shop assistant. 'If you do it often enough.'

Ella rolled her eyes. 'Try on a harness, then,' she said.

The shop assistant tossed me one.

Working out how to put on the harness was like doing kinky cat's cradle. I stepped into one of the holes, but Ella was right – it turned out to be the wrong one. She had to help me figure out how to put it on. She pulled on the straps to tighten it.

'Now you put the cock in,' said the sales assistant, handing it to me. I pushed it through the cock ring and there it was, standing up proudly in front of me, ready to pleasure the ladies. I felt completely ridiculous.

'I'm telling you,' said Ella. 'The pants are much easier.'

'But much less sexy,' said the shop assistant, shrugging.

I bought the leather harness.

There was a display of mini-vibrators at the till point. I picked up a blue one and handed it to the shop assistant. 'This too, please,' I said. I'd give it to Alice, to make up for having new friends.

'Now you're a proper dyke!' said Ella, as we left the shop.

'Hooray!'

'What are you doing now?' said Ella. 'Want to come to a vintage fair in Bethnal Green?'

'I'd better not,' I said. 'I have to go home and get ready for my date.'

'Of course,' she said. 'Your date!'

I felt a little ripple of foreboding.

11. WHIPS ARE VERY TWENTY-FIRST CENTURY

I spent an unusual amount of time washing when I got home. I took the shower head and sprayed it inside my vagina. I wanted to make sure Sam wouldn't have any complaints if I ended up going home with her. Or would she expect to come back to mine? In which case should I change the bed sheets? Should I trim my pubes? Or should I leave them unshaven so I couldn't take my underpants off, taking that decision out of my hands? And did wanting to trim my pubes make me a bad feminist?

Sam rang the doorbell at eight exactly. I opened the door, trying to block the view of the piles of shoes and coats in the un-Hoovered hallway, my arms crossed self-consciously; I was wearing Alice's push-up bra. Here she was, an actual woman who actually wanted to take me on a date. And she was sexy, too, in slouchy black trousers and a black silk shirt.

I felt sick with excitement. Or was it fear? I felt sick, either way.

'You look gorgeous,' she said, leaning over to kiss me on the cheek.

I made an involuntary noise. I felt like I might not make it through the evening without yelping through pure pent-up sexual frustration.

'You too,' I said.

I smiled the smile of a woman who was totally used to going on dates with other women, no big deal. But as I unhooked my

93

coat from the peg, I brought four other coats down with me, including Alice's mad, oversized leopard-print rug of a jacket. I managed to hang the others back up, but the leopard-print rug slumped off the peg every time, collapsing at my feet, and I was growing frantic.

Sam came up behind me and gently took the coat from my hand. She examined the neckline calmly, finding the fabric loop and slipping it over the peg. 'Happens to me all the time,' she said. She picked my coat up from the floor and held it out for me to slip my arms into, the sort of thing a receptionist at an expensive hairdresser might do.

'Shall we?' she said, offering me her arm.

The light was fading and the windows of the houses opposite glowed yellow. A large part of me wanted to go back inside and curl up on the sofa with a bar of Green & Black's, but Sam was leading me towards her car. She owned a car; I'd never been on a date with someone who owned a car before. It was a shit car, but so shit that it was trendy – an old Volvo painted brown on top and orange on the sides. Inside it smelled vaguely of cigarettes. Maybe she smoked. I didn't know if I wanted to date someone who smoked.

'The place we're going is round the corner from my flat,' she told me, as she turned the key in the ignition.

'You didn't have to come all the way out here to get me!'

'Don't be silly. I'm old-fashioned. In some ways. I know how to treat a lady on a first date.' I winced – I do not like being called a lady – but then she squeezed my knee and the vibrations travelled up my leg to my cunt and I was tempted to pull the handbrake and beg her to fuck me right there in the car in the middle of Green Lanes.

I didn't, though, obviously. Instead, I asked, 'What's the restaurant called?'

'Butter. Have you heard of it?'

I had indeed heard of Butter; I'd seen endless photos of their dishes on Instagram. It wasn't the sort of place badly paid public-sector employees went for dinner; even the bread basket was out of my price range. Would Sam be paying for the meal, as she'd asked me out and chosen the restaurant? But where would she get that kind of money? She was an artist, possibly the only job that paid worse than mine. And if she paid, would she think I owed her something – i.e. weird sex? No, I told myself. That is not how sex works. You never owe anyone sex.

We walked up one of those recently posh East London streets to the restaurant, which glowed with the promise of expensive food. Sam helped me off with my coat and pulled my chair out. She was really, really chivalrous; there's no other word for it. She seemed determined to be a gentleman, and I'd decided not to go out with gentlemen any more. But she wasn't a man, clearly. She looked nothing like a man, and sounded nothing like a man; she just had an incredible energy about her – feminine and masculine at the same time. Somehow she made me feel more female than I ever had in my whole life.

I ordered asparagus to start.

'We won't be doing water sports tonight then,' she said, ripping a piece of bread in half and taking a bite.

'Sorry?'

'I don't really like the taste of asparagus piss. This is the stuff, though,' she said, chinking her glass to mine. 'Prosecco's perfect if you're about to get kinky.'

'Not champagne?'

'Depends how often you want to do it. It can get expensive.'

That set the tone for the evening. Sam brought everything back to sex, which, needless to say, wouldn't have been my specialist subject on *Mastermind*. She asked me what I liked to do in bed in such a frank, disarming way that I almost answered. The only reason I didn't was that I didn't know what I liked to do in bed yet.

There was no use pretending – I came clean and told her I'd only slept with one woman.

'You shagged Jane? That night at the party?'

'After a different party.'

'Fuck!' Sam nodded, eyebrows raised, impressed. 'Well done. She's hot. She's a twat, though. But still – hot.'

'Why is she a twat?'

'I used to go out with one of her friends. She was a total dick about it, turned her against me. I think she was just jealous. Anyway, tell me more. Did she let you fuck her? And I hear she's good with her tongue.'

She wanted to know literally every detail of the encounter, and hearing me talk about it seemed to turn her on, which turned me on. I was so far out of my comfort zone I felt like I was pretending to be someone else; I was telling her things I'd barely let myself think before, let alone say.

'Sex is my hobby,' Sam told me, once we'd exhausted my sexual history (which took approximately three minutes). 'It's the number-one thing I love to do. I met most of my friends through the SM scene. We go to sex conventions together, things like that.'

'Sex conventions.'

'Yes.'

'Do you have to wear a lanyard to get into those?'

'A really kinky black one.'

'Right.' I concentrated on my food while I tried to work out what to say next. 'And SM – that's the same as S and M?'

Sam nodded. 'People in the scene don't tend to use the "and", though,' she said.

'Right,' I said again.

Sam looked at me and smiled. 'Don't be scared,' she said.

'I'm not scared,' I said, looking her in the eye. Which was a lie, but never mind – I was definitely more turned on than terrified.

'The SM community is really friendly,' Sam said. 'And no one would ever make you do anything you didn't want to do. Consent is a big deal.'

'So you wouldn't get a whip out on a first date or anything,' I said.

'Is that a request?'

After we'd eaten, Sam took me for a walk through the streets of Hackney, towards her flat. She stopped at a bench and lit a cigarette.

'You smoke,' I said unnecessarily.

She made a face. 'I tried to give up, but I have an addictive personality.' There was something sexy about the way she smoked, even though I knew there shouldn't be. She noticed me looking at her and held out the cigarette for me.

Why not? I thought. I felt reckless with Sam, as though the rules I usually lived by didn't apply. I took a drag. It was weirdly delicious, much nicer than I remembered cigarettes being.

We walked on, past a poster for the BFI, and I had a momentary flashback to my night with Finn; I already felt like a different person from the one who had been on that date. We paused outside Homerton station and Sam put her hands on my shoulders, and turned me to face her, and kissed me. It was a gorgeous kiss – soft and stubble-free.

Women were definitely, definitely better kissers than men.

Sam was getting really into it, but I was holding back slightly. You can do this, I told myself. You can totally have sex with her in her dungeon. You are an open-minded, sex-positive woman. Whips are very twenty-first century.

But she must have tasted my fear because she pulled away.

'Let's get you home,' she said, as though she was a kind uncle who'd taken me for a day at the zoo. Not, just to be clear, that any of my uncles has ever kissed me like that.

'I don't have to go home,' I said, leaning into her now that she was distancing herself.

'Not tonight,' she said, laughing, 'Good things come to those who wait.' And she walked towards the entrance of the Overground, leaving me to follow behind.

She sat with me till the Overground came, and told me more about her art.

'I did an MFA in New York,' she told me. 'Figurative painting is big over there, but most people here are still obsessed with fucking installation art.' She kicked a chocolate wrapper away from the bench we were sitting on.

'So you paint portraits?'

She nodded. 'Of women. From the point of view of the queer female gaze instead of the male gaze.'

'Do you paint full time?'

She nodded, then shrugged. 'I'm doing pretty well at the moment, but mostly in the States. I'm represented by this gallery in LA, the Night Gallery?'

I made an impressed noise, though I'd never heard of it.

'I had a painting in the BP Portrait Award, though, so people here are starting to hear about me. Ingvild Goetz bought one of my paintings. She's an important German collector,' she explained, seeing my blank look. 'Still not represented by a UK gallery, though.' That, judging by her facial expression, was a sore point.

'Can I see your work?'

'I'm having my first solo show in London soon, so you can see it then. If you play your cards right.' She nudged me with her hip. 'Anyway, what about you? Did you always want to work at the Civil Service?'

I laughed. 'Has anyone always wanted to work in the Civil Service?'

'Maybe,' she said. 'They have good pension schemes, don't they?'

'Not any more,' I said. 'I used to be a dancer. I broke my ankle and had to give up.'

She looked me in the eye and said, 'I'm so sorry.' As though she really meant it. 'I can't imagine how I'd feel if I couldn't paint.'

She understood. I felt a rush of gratitude towards her.

She put her arm around me. A man with a Fitness First rucksack a little further down the platform looked at us, as though trying to work out our relationship.

'It must be amazing,' I said, 'making money from the thing you love to do.'

'I thought it would be,' she said, 'but I'm always comparing myself to other people. Like, Jane – she's represented by this Hackney gallery, Revolution. And her work is such bollocks.'

'It is bollocks.'

'But bollocks is what people care about at the moment.'

'People don't want bollocks in their houses.'

'I know *you* don't, at least,' she said. 'Not literal bollocks anyway.' She winked at me.

And then, too soon, the train pulled into the platform.

'I'll be thinking of you all night,' she said, as the door closed between us.

I didn't try winking back; my winking technique is a bit hit and miss. I watched her waving as the train pulled away, my heart pounding, my head rushing.

She was so fucking sexy.

My bed felt empty that night. I lay awake, too turned on to sleep, wishing I'd gone home with her. So I unwrapped my dildo and tried it out, imagining Sam using it on me, slamming it into myself with the palm of my hand. It was pretty good; I kept at it till I felt myself getting sore. But I didn't come.

I couldn't get to sleep afterwards. I watched YouTube for a while, trying to soothe my racing mind with make-up tutorials, but I felt more awake than ever. Fuck it, I thought. I'll text her – just to say thanks, and that I'd had a nice time.

She texted straight back. *Any time babes. It was a pleasure to have such a delicious woman on my arm. Hopefully next time you'll come back to mine to check out my sketchbook.*

I wasn't sure I could go out with someone who wrote text messages like that. But I could definitely have sex with them.

12. A SALTY RIM

I called Cat the next morning as I lay in bed, to tell her about my date. I could hear loud mariachi music in the background when she picked up the phone.

'Where are you?' I asked.

'Wolverhampton,' she said. 'Having some tacos with the company.' She laughed.

'What?'

'Oh, nothing,' she said. 'Lacey was just saying something about the period musical. We're rehearsing in the evenings.'

'You're going to be in it?'

'Yep. We're applying for funding.'

'Great!' I felt a flash of envy. 'I had a date with Sam last night,' I said, to remind myself that there were all sorts of good things in my life now.

'Great!' Cat said, in the same enthusiastic/envious voice. Maybe it was all over with the year-five teacher. 'Did you bang?'

'No. We kissed, though.'

'Tongues?'

'Tongues.'

There was a pause, and then Cat said, 'Yuck.'

'Excuse me?'

101

'Oh, not you,' she said. 'I've just tasted my margarita and it has a salty rim.'

I was almost an hour early to work that Monday, which was a very strange and wonderful experience. I had my pick of the desks. I didn't have to offer anyone else a drink, because no one else was there; no one except Tom, that is, who was in Smriti's office. I felt a sense of smugness as I sipped my tea and read calmly through my inbox. I had been on a very sexy date. I looked through my latest letters and found another one from lovely Eric. I settled back in my chair to read it.

I was a teenager when I joined the RAF, just after the Blitz. I wanted to give the Germans a taste of their own medicine! My mother was beside herself when she found out, and she was right to be; I was the only one of my mates that made it back alive. But she couldn't have stopped me; you don't listen to sense when you're young, do you? I had no idea what I was getting myself into——

Owen walked in and stopped still when he saw me. 'Am I late?'
'No,' I said, putting Eric's letter down. 'I'm early!'
'Oh! Right! Wow!' he said, taking off his bag and sitting down. The 'wow' didn't make me feel brilliant. 'You look happy,' he said.
'I am,' I said.
'Have a good weekend?'
'Yes,' I said, mysteriously.
'What did you get up to?'
'Nothing much.' But I smiled to let him know I was lying.
'Me and Laura went to Highgate Cemetery. She's a big fan of Douglas Adams, and he's buried there. So's George Eliot. She likes her too.'
'Eclectic taste,' I said.
'Good taste,' he said. 'Highgate Cemetery's lovely, really. Nice and peaceful. Good for a date.'

In at the Deep End

'Apart from all the dead people.'

'No, *because* of all the dead people,' Owen said. 'Makes you feel better about dying, I think. And it's romantic, seeing the couples buried together.'

Owen sat down at his desk and I went back to my letter from Eric.

Sorry – this letter's all doom and gloom, isn't it? I'm going to make a cup of tea and listen to the wireless to cheer myself up. There's a lovely 1940s radio station that one of my carers found for me on the Web. It's marvellous, and it makes a change from Classic FM (can't bear all those adverts!). Give it a try, next time you need a bit of a lift.

    Yours,

    Eric

Poor Eric. I thought about his smiling face in the wedding photograph – smiling even though he knew he'd be back in a Lancaster bomber the following day, flying away from his new wife, towards flak and shells and almost certain death. I felt a rush of affection for him. I knew what it was like to feel young and invincible. I didn't feel like that any more, though. Except when I was with Sam. I typed out a reply to Eric, thanking him for the radio recommendation and telling him that I'd taken up swing dancing. I considered telling him about the Friends of Dorothy – I thought he'd get a kick out of the fact they were named after a Forties euphemism for homosexuals – but I decided against it. He seemed like a liberal man, with his love of the NHS and libraries and public services in general, but he might stop writing to me if he knew I was a friend of Dorothy's. He was in his nineties, after all.

Spring had finally turned up in London, fashionably late and a bit reluctant, like a teenager meeting its parents for dinner. I went for a walk in Finsbury Park after work; the birds were singing and the cherry trees were frothy with blossom, far too pretty for the streets of N4. The trees looked like pompoms; they were cheering me on, I decided, in my new lesbian life.

I took out my phone to Instagram the blossom and realized I'd missed a call from Mum. She had left me a voicemail: 'Julia, it's your mother, hi. I'm coming to London on Wednesday for the Blue Badge Guides conference. It's at that big conference place in Westminster, so near your office. If you can get there for one, I can buy you lunch.'

I called her back, but Dad picked up the phone.

'Oh,' he said, when I said hello. 'Let me go and get your mum.'

Dad always did this. He wasn't a fan of phone conversations.

'Wait, Dad. How are you?'

He was silent for a minute. 'Why?'

'I'm just making conversation,' I said.

'Oh!' he said. 'Right! Well, in that case: I'm fine.'

'Great.'

'How are you?'

'Great.'

'Actually, your mother said I should call you.'

'Why?'

'I wanted to call anyway.'

'OK.'

'I don't want you to think I'm homophobic.'

'I don't.'

'Bloody Catholic upbringing. You think you've shaken it and it comes out at weird times.'

'Don't worry, Dad.'

'And I've got a lot on at the moment. Your mother has gone completely mad about the neighbours and their basement, and Geoff has been made head of department, and he's making life difficult—'

'Really, it's fine.'

'OK,' he said. 'Good.' A pause. 'Still—'

'A lesbian?'

'That's not what I was going to say. I was going to ask if you're still keen on Stella Gibbons. I saw a lovely edition of one of her early novels the other day and I thought I might get it for you.'

'Oh! Yes, I still like her.'

'Right. I'll get it, then.'

'Thanks, Dad. You don't need to do that.'

'Oh, well. You know. I go to a lot of bookshops.'

Another silence. 'Mum said she was coming to London on Wednesday,' I said at last.

Dad sighed. 'I *knew* you were just calling to speak to your mother,' he said. 'Jenny!' he called. 'Your daughter on the phone!'

Mum and I had a sandwich in a pub full of grey-haired men in suits drinking pints. I wondered what they did, to be able to drink on a Wednesday lunchtime. They were probably civil servants too, I realized. The rules were just different for them.

'I can't tell you how glad I am to be out of Oxford for a day,' Mum said, picking the tomato out of her club sandwich. 'Want to hear the latest about the neighbours?'

'Not particularly.'

'Well. They've hired a landscape gardener who is ripping all the trees out of their garden. There was a pear tree that must have been at least thirty years old. Gone!'

'Terrible,' I said, taking a bite of my cheese ploughman's.

'And your father has actually decided to befriend them. The woman turns out to be a fellow at Magdalen – specializes in William Blake. So he keeps inviting her round for tea to talk about socialism in bloody Romantic poetry. The only good thing is, she was round in the kitchen the other day and she could hear how loud the drilling is, and she apologized and promised to make sure they didn't start before eight in the morning any more.'

'What does the man do?'

'He's a lawyer in the City. Hence all the money for landscape gardeners.'

'Right.'

'But you'll like this – they have a gay son! His name is Harry and he watches a lot of YouTube.'

'Good for Harry.'

Mum took a sip of her tap water and folded her hands in her lap. 'How's that going for you, then?'

'What?'

'Being gay.' She smiled at me encouragingly.

'Quite well,' I said. 'I went on a date with a woman called Sam the other day. We're going out again at the weekend.'

'Wonderful!' Mum said, though she looked a little taken aback. Maybe she preferred theoretical lesbianism to actual lesbianism.

13. AUBERGINE EMOJI

A second date is a bit like a difficult second album, or novel, I always think. If the first date was good enough to get you to the second, you're desperately trying to recapture whatever magic you had, and in my experience, 'magic' is usually just another word for 'drunkenness'. Second dates should, like all good sequels, be bigger and better than the first, with higher stakes. So I texted Sam to ask whether she'd like to meet me in a pop-up bar in a Hackney car park. Drinking on an empty stomach in the open air seemed like a stakes upgrade to me.

But Sam had other ideas. *There's a drag king contest on in Dalston. Fancy it?*

Sure, I replied. I'd always been a big fan of drag queens, but I'd never seen a king before.

I WhatsApped Cat and Alice to update them. Cat replied first: *Get in!*

I texted Ella, too. She sent me an aubergine emoji and wrote: *That's a dildo, not a dick!*

As I was trying to think of a witty reply, my phone pinged with another message from Sam: *We don't have to stay for the whole thing. I can think of a few things we could do afterwards . . .*

I decided to borrow Alice's push-up bra again.

*   *   *

The drag king show was in a dark, cosy, queer pub called The Glory, on Kingsland Road. By the time I arrived, the place was rammed with trendy-looking lesbians and gay men and genderqueer people, chatting excitedly, calling out to each other across the bar. The silver tinsel curtain at the back of the stage shimmered and rippled as unseen figures behind it moved around. The show was about to start.

'Julia!'

Sam was sitting at a quiet table at the back. She stood up as I walked towards her, grinning, hands in her pockets.

I found her almost unbearably attractive.

'What are you drinking?' I asked.

'I'm buying,' she said, in a voice that I couldn't argue with. 'Beer?'

'Some kind of lager,' I said. 'Thank you.'

She edged around me to the bar, stooping to kiss my cheek as she passed.

Sam was still at the bar when the house lights went down and the crowd began to stamp and cheer in anticipation. A man in his forties, who I guessed was the host of the club, took to the stage with a drag king in a leather jacket. They began to sing 'Under Pressure', the drag king taking the Freddie Mercury part. He wasn't wearing anything beneath the jacket; his nipples were covered in plasters, and he had a six-pack contoured onto his stomach. His stubble was quite convincing. He moved like a man.

Sam came back with two pints and a packet of crisps clenched in her teeth. 'Good, aren't they?' she said, nodding up at the stage.

'Hot, too,' I said.

'What, Butch Cassidy?'

'That's the drag king?'

Sam nodded. 'Out of drag, her name's Josie Cassidy. Went on a date with her once. But we both wanted to be in charge, so it didn't really work.'

I turned back to the stage. Butch Cassidy was kneeling now, flirting with the women in the front row, reaching down to touch their hands.

Sam leaned forward to open the packet of crisps, and offered me the bag. She put her arm around me, and I smiled at her. The silence between us seemed very loud, suddenly.

'So,' I said. 'You said you had a solo show soon?'

'It's at a gallery in Clapton, in this really raw-looking space—' and then she paused with a crisp on the way to her mouth.

She was staring at my chest.

'Sorry to be crude,' she said, eyes flicking up to meet mine for a moment, then back down. 'But your tits look fantastic in that top.'

'Thank you,' I said, crunching a crisp in slow motion, very aware of the shape of my mouth.

Sam took a swig of her pint, her eyes still on my chest. She put her glass down, leaned towards me and whispered, 'I really want to fuck you. Now.'

'Oh,' I said. 'Right.'

'Like, right now,' she said, pushing back her chair. 'Let me take you back to my lair. Let's get an Uber.'

'We can just get the Overground—'

'No,' Sam said. 'We're getting an Uber.'

Sam lit a cigarette while we were waiting, smoking it quickly, checking her app for the car's progress. When it arrived, she threw her butt in the gutter and opened the door for me.

'So chivalrous,' I said, sliding in.

'Always,' she said.

She stared out of the window as Hackney streaked past us, stroking my hand. I sneaked my phone onto my knee and texted Alice and Cat: *Going back to Sam's. Will report back on dungeon ASAP.*

Sam's lair turned out to be a studio flat off Chatsworth Road with stripped wooden floors and original features.

'How can you afford the rent?' I asked. I didn't know anyone else who lived alone.

'It's my dad's flat, so mates' rates.'

'Oh,' I said, mentally adjusting my image of her. 'Are your parents divorced, then?'

'No. My mum died when I was younger.' She came over to take my coat from me. 'Want a drink?'

'I'm sorry,' I said.

'About what?'

'About your mum.'

'Oh. Yeah. It's a bit of a downer. I don't really like talking about it.' She took my hand and pulled me away from the door, towards the bed.

I looked around the flat. There didn't seem to be a dungeon; to be fair, it would be hard to fit one in a studio flat. The bed took up most of the room; it was made of dark wood, like the rest of the furniture, and didn't look like the sort of thing she'd have chosen herself – had she inherited it? There was no clutter, nothing on any of the surfaces – everything seemed to have a place. My mother would have approved of her alphabetized spice rack. It was all a bit grown-up for an artist living in Hackney, and a bit anonymous – there was nothing that gave away anything about Sam. Except, of course, the paintings.

They were of naked women, and they were everywhere, some in frames, some not, luminous in pink and green and yellow and orange, so many of them that you could barely see the walls. Women kneeling, women standing, women kissing, women with their legs spread apart. The paintings were very naturalistic, apart from the garish colours, and very detailed – you could see every dot on every areola, every curling pubic hair. Each of the women stared out of the painting directly out at me, as though daring me to keep looking. I felt like a voyeur.

Weirdly, I recognized one of the women, though I wasn't sure where I'd seen her before. 'Is she famous?' I said, pointing at a nude of a woman with afro hair, painted in shades of brightest purple and orange and red.

'No,' Sam said, taking my coat from me. 'That's Addia. She works at Sh!.'

That's why I recognized her. She was the leather harness-loving sales assistant from the sex shop. 'It's almost like a photograph,' I said. Now I knew Addia had a tattoo of a snake on her torso.

'She thinks it's unflattering,' Sam said.

'It's not,' I said. It was sexy, actually. 'Do you paint all your friends?' I asked, but she was kissing me on the neck now and I wanted her so much I thought I might scream.

She undressed me carefully, with authority, but when I tried to undress her she stopped me, and pushed me gently onto the bed. Still standing, she pulled off her jeans and boxers – she wore boxers – but she kept her T-shirt on.

I had wondered what she'd look like naked; whether she'd have let her body hair grow, how thin she'd be compared to me, how big her breasts would be. I could see now that she didn't shave – not her legs, anyway, or her armpits. I found the soft, curling hairs oddly erotic. I couldn't see her stomach or her breasts yet, though. I tried to touch them, and again she pushed my hands away. It was strange, having her half-dressed when I was naked, and all the women on the walls were naked too.

She knelt on the bed and leaned across to open her wooden sex cupboard – because yes, she did have a sizeable sex cupboard, filled with shelves of mysterious latex objects. The cupboard was only open for a second, but I caught a glimpse of a box that was worryingly labelled *enema kit*. The only thing she took out of the cupboard, though, was a bottle of lube. And she used that lube to do the most wonderful things.

I came five whole times. I'd never come five times before. Not even on a really boring evening in with my Rampant Rabbit.

As I was about to come for the fifth time, I became horribly aware of a very familiar sensation.

'I'm going to piss on you.'

'Do it.'

'I don't want to!'

'It doesn't matter. Relax.'

And then it was too late, and I was a veritable water fountain, spurting all over her T-shirt, all over her face.

'I'm so sorry,' I said, but she wouldn't stop fucking me.

'You're not pissing on me,' she said. 'You're ejaculating.'

And the more she pushed on a certain spot, the more I came, or rather it came — literally gushing out of me, as if I had endless resources of this stuff inside me. I suppose I did. Twenty-six years' worth of it.

As we lay there afterwards, I realized how wet the bed sheets were, and how bad they smelled.

'I am really, really sorry,' I said.

'Are you kidding me? This is what it's all about. This is the real deal right here. This means you had a good time. Don't apologize.'

'But it's gross—'

'I said don't apologize.'

I asked Sam if I could fuck her, too.

She paused, as though weighing up whether to let me, which made me say, 'Please?'

'You're begging me now?' She laughed. 'You're begging to fuck me?'

'Shut up,' I said, laughing too. 'Don't flatter yourself.'

'Too late,' she said. 'I'm already flattered. Let me show you what I like to do.' She leaned over to the sex cupboard again and pulled out a bottle of lube and a box of black latex gloves.

'Here.' She tossed one to me. 'Much sexier than the white ones. Those are a bit too medical.'

I pulled it onto my right hand. 'I look like a murderer,' I said, looking down at my hands. 'I look like I'm about to strangle you.'

'We can play that if it gets you off,' Sam said. 'I like a little bit of asphyxiation now and then. In controlled circumstances, obviously.'

What Sam liked to do, it became clear, was fisting. 'Not up the bum,' she said. 'I want you to slide your whole gorgeous hand into my pussy, then make it into a fist and move it around until I come all over you.'

'I think my knuckles might be a bit chunky for that,' I said, examining them.

'I've had chunkier,' Sam said. She lay back and opened her legs. Her pubic hair was trimmed short. Now, I was worried I should have cut mine shorter for sex purposes. 'Warm me up first, with a few fingers, and keep going till they're all in, and the thumb too.'

'And then I just push it in,' I said.

'By that point I'll just swallow you up.'

'But— what if I get stuck inside you?'

'Happens sometimes,' she said. 'But you just relax and it slides out again.'

'Because I don't fancy turning up at casualty attached to your vagina.'

'It would be more humiliating for me than for you,' she said.

'I'd look like a ventriloquist with a massive dummy.'

'And I'd look like a butch who lets femmes fuck me. Not cool,' she said.

I laughed, and then I looked at her face and realized she wasn't joking. 'Seriously,' she said. 'When you meet my friends, you can't tell them about this. It'll ruin my street cred.'

'Your dad bought you a flat. You don't have street cred.'

'He didn't buy it for me. He lets me live in it,' she said, not smiling. She obviously wasn't that into being teased. 'Anyway, shut up and fuck me before I change my mind.'

I was kneeling at the end of the bed at this point with my hand in the air, not really sure what to do with myself.

'Come up here,' she said, beckoning me towards her.

So I crawled up to her end of the bed and started to kiss her.

At this point I should probably tell you that I've never been a huge fan of being on top. I'd always felt pretty uncomfortable when my ex-boyfriend asked me to 'ride him'; I'm very aware that I don't look attractive from below, all double chins and spots on my jawline. I don't want you to think I'm a lazy lover, but I generally feel most comfortable when I'm lying down, preferably on a firm mattress with a couple of goose-down pillows under my head. Sam was letting me fuck her, though, and it was only polite to give it my best shot.

After a few minutes of really excellent kissing, when I found my mind wandering slightly, wondering if we'd go for breakfast the next morning and whether we could try a new café in Homerton I'd read about, I clambered onto her, one leg between hers, and tried to grind myself into her the way she'd ground herself into me.

'Very good,' said Sam. 'Keep going.'

I could feel her pubic hair on my leg rather than my cunt, though, so I adjusted my position until I heard her groan with pleasure.

I wasn't quite sure how long to keep the grinding up for, so after a minute or two I started trailing kisses down her body. But she called me back.

'Not long enough,' she said. 'Always spend longer than you think you need to warming a woman up. It'll pay dividends in the end.'

So I carried on, and after a while I forgot to be self-conscious any more and my arms began to ache but that didn't matter, because Sam was bucking against me and it was so fucking hot, and she was breathing harder, and then she said, 'Get the lube on your glove. Now.' There was a bit of an awkward pause while I squirted the lube onto my hand. 'Warm up your hands before you touch me,' Sam said, pushing herself into me again, doing a lot of the work from below, it has to be said. And then, 'Now. Fuck me.'

So I slipped a finger inside her and I will never forget how it felt to touch the inside of another woman for the first time. I might have been wearing a glove, but she was so wet and smooth that my hand felt like it was floating and I felt my cunt pulsing in response and I let out a sigh of pleasure and Sam said to me, 'You filthy fucking dyke,' and then she grabbed my wrist and guided my hand in and out, faster and faster. 'More fingers,' she said, and I obliged, and I felt as though I were fucking myself I was so turned on by it. I had three fingers inside her and then four, and then my thumb too, and then Sam said, 'All of you,' and I pushed and then I was inside her up to the wrist, and I looked down and wondered why I'd never learned about this in sex education.

Sam let go of my arm and kept her eyes locked on mine as she started rubbing her clit. I felt incompetent suddenly that I couldn't do all of it myself, but that feeling didn't last because she was so unselfconscious about touching herself that it didn't seem to matter.

'That's it,' she said. 'Open and close your hand. Slowly.'

So I did, and every movement was magnified in her face.

'Now fuck me,' she said, so I pushed my hand forward and pulled it back, and she kept her eyes on mine and said, 'Harder,' so I fucked her harder until I felt like I was punching her and her cunt opened up and soon my hand was coming in and out and I looked down at my hand not quite believing what I was seeing and so turned on and a bit disturbed and then she grabbed my wrist again and pushed me into her harder and started crying out and shouting and then she was coming, so loudly I was jerked out of the moment for a second to wonder whether her neighbours were in and then she was shuddering still, and my hand was still inside her, and she pulled me to her and she was still shaking and moaning, but it wasn't moaning now, it was sobbing.

She was sobbing, like she'd held it in for years and was letting all of her tears out at once, and I was stroking her hair and murmuring 'Shhh' and wondering if this would happen every time I fucked her.

'That was just so good,' she said. 'So good. And you're so gorgeous. And I'm so happy.'

Sam went to the bathroom to wash her face and I lay in her bed, looking up at the ceiling, thinking, I'm a woman who makes experienced lesbians cry because I'm so good at sex. I felt pretty happy with myself, I have to say.

Sam came back to bed carrying two glasses of wine, a bar of dark chocolate and a packet of cigarettes. 'I always crave fags, wine and chocolate after really good sex,' she said. 'And that might have been the best sex I've ever had.'

'You didn't squirt,' I said.

'I never do,' she said. 'Everyone's different. Not many people squirt as much as you.'

'Oh.'

'Don't be embarrassed! It's a gift! It's a wonderful, wonderful gift. You should be proud of it.'

She had a way of making me feel much, much younger than her.

We sat there in satisfied silence for a while, sipping the wine and eating the chocolate. Sam was right: the combination of wine and chocolate really did extend the post-sex high. Sam lit a cigarette. 'You don't mind, do you?' she asked.

'It's your flat,' I said. I was deliciously light-headed and warm and the only thing I was worried about was getting chocolate or red wine on Sam's perfectly white sheets.

Sam began to stroke my hair. 'Don't think I'm always going to let you touch me,' she said. 'Sometimes you're just going to have to lie back and take what you're given.' The way she said it turned me on, and I felt uncomfortable for feeling turned on. If a man had said that to me, I'd probably have run screaming to the nearest

Fawcett Society meeting. But she wasn't a man. And anyway, I enjoyed taking what I was given, when she was giving it.

We stayed up until the early hours, talking. She told me she'd fucked 121 cis women, twelve trans men and three cis men. The whole day was very educational.

'Are the women on the walls people you've fucked, then?'

'Most of them,' she said.

'So are you going to paint me?'

'If you play your cards right,' she said, pulling me towards her and kissing me again.

I woke long before Sam did the next morning, so I walked over to her bookshelves – also alphabetized, by author – and pulled out an old paperback of *The Portrait of a Lady*. I started to read, but Henry James's sentences were too long for my sex-addled, sleep-deprived brain. I flicked to the back to see how it would end and a photo fell out: creased, with a ring on it from a long-cold cup of tea. Sam with her arm around a beautiful, dark-haired woman in her thirties with red lips and impressive cleavage. I turned the photo over. There was a message on the back, dated four years previously, written with what looked like sepia ink:

To my darling Sam. Love Virginie xxx

My heart clenched with retrospective jealousy.

Stupid name, I thought to myself. Pretentious, too, with that stupid sepia fountain pen.

I looked around to see if I could see Virginie on the walls, but I couldn't.

I told myself to snap out of it. The book was dusty – it obviously hadn't been touched recently. There was no evidence to suggest Sam even remembered the photo was in there. Or even that Sam and Virginie were anything more than friends. And anyway, I wasn't Sam's girlfriend. I'd had sex with her once. I had no right to feel jealous.

I felt jealous anyway, though.

14. TEFLON-COATED BY HAPPINESS

The sex was so good, I wanted to tell everyone about it. I told Alice and Dave (who was riveted) and I described the squirting to Cat in a text message. She replied saying *Too much information!!* Which was a bit rich, seeing as I know that the year-five teacher she'd been shagging had a wonky penis.

My swing dance friends were the most interested of all. I told them all about it after our next class over pints and packets of crisps, the bags pulled apart for easy access.

'I knew you'd have fun,' Rebecca said. 'Sam's a legend on the scene.'

'Hey!' said Bo, hitting her arm.

Rebecca leaned forward. 'Did she do that thing with her tongue—'

Bo hit her arm again.

'Probably,' I said, nodding. 'Everything she did with her tongue was amazing. And fisting!' I looked around the table. 'Why didn't I know about fisting?'

Ella looked wistful. 'I can barely remember what it's like,' she said. 'My ex wasn't into penetrative sex.'

'No!' said Zhu, horrified.

'She didn't like it – either way?' I asked.

'No,' Ella said. 'She'd do it to me. But she wouldn't do it hard enough.'

'Wow,' said Bo.

'And how did you feel about that,' asked Rebecca, 'as a gender non-conforming woman? Did you feel emasculated – I know that's not the right word – by the fact that she could penetrate you, but you couldn't penetrate her?'

'No,' said Ella, shifting on the sofa. 'Not emasculated. Just a bit sexually frustrated.'

'You need to get back on the horse,' said Zhu, shaking her head.

'I think I've forgotten how to ride,' said Ella.

'You haven't,' I said. 'I thought I might have done, but it comes back to you.'

The others nodded.

I was so wise and sexually experienced all of a sudden. I had an identity again, one that wasn't 'slightly shit civil servant who drinks wine from cardboard boxes while watching sitcoms'. I was a lesbian. A successful one, it felt like.

Zhu leaned back in her chair and smiled at Ella. 'If you need someone to practise with, you know where I am,' she said.

I laughed, and then I realized that Zhu was completely serious. Ella was folding an empty crisp packet into a tiny square piece. Bo was looking from Zhu to Ella and back again, waiting for a reaction.

'I can attest to the fact that Zhu is a very generous lover,' said Rebecca.

'Rebecca!' said Bo.

'What?' said Rebecca.

It's incredible what a difference good sex can make. Absolutely nothing else had changed, but I felt as though I'd been upgraded to the business class version of my life. I was less anxious, more sure of myself, less bothered by the terrible things I heard on the news every morning, less bitter around couples.

I even felt better about my father, who clearly still had a few issues about my lesbian revelation. He came down to London a couple of days after the incredible sex, and we went for a lunchtime walk along the river. He gave me an awkward hug when we met, and handed over the Stella Gibbons book without looking at me, which I took to mean, 'I'm sorry and I love you.' It was an old hardback of *Nightingale Wood*.

'Thanks,' I said, turning the brittle pages. 'I haven't read this one.'

We walked on for a few moments in silence, watching the boats full of tourists pass on the Thames.

'You seem very cheerful,' he said at last.

'I am. I've met someone.'

He turned towards me. 'A – one of – a lesbian?'

'A lesbian.'

'Well. Great. That's great.' He looked straight ahead again.

'Yes. She's not my girlfriend or anything.'

'Good.'

'What? Why?'

Dad went slightly red. 'Nothing. That's very good news, Julia.'

'No,' I said, stopping in the middle of the path, so a jogger had to swerve past me. 'Why is that good?'

'Well,' he said, walking ahead, so that I had to catch up with him, 'I mean it's good that you're not labelling it. You're too young to put yourself in a box.'

I waited for sadness to hit me, or anger, or something. But I felt nothing. I didn't care what my dad thought about Sam and me, I realized. I had always valued his opinion – too highly, probably – but this time it was clear to me that he was wrong. He couldn't hurt me. I was too happy for anything to hurt me.

In fact, I was so happy that I was probably starting to piss off my friends. I caught Alice rolling her eyes at Dave one Thursday night while I was describing Sam's artistic process.

'She does her portraits really quickly, like Hockney does, in charcoal, and then she uses acrylic.'

'Great.'

'She really *is* great. She's been invited to do a show in Florence next year! They're giving her a studio and an apartment for a month!'

'Sounds amazing.' (Eye roll.)

But I didn't care – I was Teflon-coated, practically, by my newfound happiness.

And anyway, when Alice and Dave met Sam, they were as charmed by her as I was. The four of us went for dinner to a BYO vegetarian restaurant in Vauxhall after we'd been seeing each other for a couple of weeks. Sam turned up late, but with two bottles of wine to make up for it.

'Which one of you is Alice?' she asked, looking from Dave to Alice and back again. Everyone laughed.

I sort of knew Dave would get on with Sam – they had mutual friends, had both been to art school, moved in similar creative circles – but I was surprised by how taken Alice seemed to be with her. She crossed her legs a lot and touched Sam's shoulder and laughed too loudly at her jokes. We all drank too much and soon Alice was quizzing Sam about her coming-out story.

'I've been out forever,' Sam said, refilling everyone's glasses. 'Everyone at school knew. Me and my best friend used to fuck in our dormitory when everyone else was asleep. I had to go back in the closet when I went home for the holidays, though.'

'You went to boarding school?' I asked.

'*That's* what you're picking up on from that story?' Dave asked, leaning forward, ready to ask more.

I spilled a glass of wine all over the table and my legs and Sam jumped up to grab some napkins and the conversation moved on. 'Clumsy,' she said, as she mopped my lap, and I felt as though I had let her down – something about the way she looked at me made me feel guilty, and young, and silly, and a bit incompetent. But then she kissed me, and everything was wonderful again.

*   *   *

'I love her,' Alice told me the next evening over a dinner of over-cooked noodles.

'Do you really?' I asked.

Alice nodded. 'She's so charming.'

'I know.'

'And she's so hot. *So* hot.'

'Don't let Dave hear you say that.'

'He told me off last night for flirting with her.'

'Ha!'

'I know! But she just sort of exudes sex, doesn't she?'

'She does.'

'I wish Dave exuded sex.'

'He probably did when you first met him.'

'Not like Sam.' She twisted more noodles onto her fork. 'What if I never have exciting sex again?'

'You and Dave have plenty of exciting sex.'

'I know . . . but you shine whenever you talk about Sam.'

'But that's just newness. That goes.'

'I suppose so . . .'

I was lying a bit, though. Because I didn't think it would go. I was so happy. I had basically turned into a lesbian Icarus. I should have known it couldn't last.

15. EMERGENCY DOUGHNUTS

The not-lasting started one Tuesday morning at work. Owen was telling me and Uzo about the workout he'd started doing at the gym – an unusually boring conversation, even by correspondence team standards – when Tom marched up to us, self-importantly. He'd been doing a lot more self-important marching since Smriti had arrived.

The three of us looked up at him. Uzo put her phone away. 'Hello,' I said, more of a question than a greeting.

'Hello,' Tom said. 'I was wondering whether you guys wanted to go for a team lunch today? For a good old catch-up?'

Owen, Uzo and I looked at each other. Tom had never suggested a team lunch before. He didn't usually go in for 'good old catch-ups' either.

I made an unconvincing 'Sounds great!' sort of noise.

We went to the Italian restaurant round the corner from the office and ordered the two-courses-for-ten-pounds deal.

'Change is in the air,' Tom muttered darkly, shaking Parmesan onto his lasagne.

'I thought that was the smell of cheap Italian food!' said Uzo, laughing. I like it when Uzo laughs; it makes her statement necklaces rattle.

Tom ignored her. 'There's talk of merging our team with the broader comms team.'

Owen and I looked at each other. 'Merging' was one of the bad words.

'Are they going to make people redundant?' I asked.

Tom furrowed his brow. 'Possibly.'

'They can't get rid of me,' said Uzo, leaning back in her chair. 'I've been here too long. It would be too expensive.'

'They can easily get rid of me,' I said. I was only a contractor. They wouldn't need to pay me off at all.

'They apparently need more people on the Freedom of Information requests team,' said Tom. 'So some of you might be transferred.'

There were gasps and cries of 'No!' and general noises of disgust. No one wants to work on the Freedom of Information requests team.

'I just wanted to give you a heads up,' said Tom. A string of cheese stretched from his mouth to his plate in a slightly disgusting way. 'If I were you, I'd be looking into my options.'

I was reminded of the conversation I'd had with the ballet mistress at the English National Ballet. 'You're young! You did well in your A-levels! You could go to university! You have so many options!' But none of them were options that I wanted to pursue.

Later that day Owen and I left the office for an emergency doughnut to discuss Tom's revelations. Owen went for Raspberry Filled. I ordered Chocolate Glazed (desperate times).

'I know we don't like working here,' Owen said, 'but it's better than not working anywhere, isn't it?'

'Exactly,' I said.

'And compared to loads of people, we have it pretty easy. Laura always has to stay at work till, like, eight. She's a lawyer,' he said. The corners of his mouth turned up smugly. And then he bit into his doughnut and squirted jam onto his shirt, which was satisfying.

I handed him a napkin so he could clean himself up.

'We could apply for the Fast Stream,' I said.

'The next application round isn't till October,' said Owen. 'But there is an SEO recruitment round opening soon . . .' Senior Executive Officers got to do much more interesting work than we did. They had job titles like Senior Policy Adviser and Senior Communications Officer. I liked the idea of being senior.

We looked over towards the door, where two SEOs were standing, chatting animatedly about patient satisfaction statistics – quite a feat, being able to talk animatedly about statistics. They looked important. They had bought their doughnuts to go.

16. NO ONE STARTS WITH JUST ONE JUGGLING BALL

When I was with Sam I didn't have to think about my future, or my past, or the fact that I hadn't done the washing-up, or anything other than whether we had enough lube to get us through the weekend. A month in, we were seeing each other almost every day, and the sex was getting better and more inventive. We'd have sex every time we saw each other, unless one of us was on our period – she was into period sex, she said, but I wasn't ready to bleed all over her nice white sheets yet. I wanted to maintain an element of mystique. I'd never met anyone as uninhibited as Sam. She'd say to me, 'Your cunt is fucking gorgeous,' and then tell me why in graphic, anatomical detail.

'I've never seen such a beautiful pussy,' she said over coffee in Soho one day.

'Thank you. Yours is very nice too,' I said.

'Whenever I think about it I have to wank.'

'Right,' I said. 'That makes me feel . . . shivery.'

What was I meant to say? Were we supposed to be competing to say more and more obscene things? Quite possibly. I wasn't used to talking like this, like the conversation was a big game of obscenity tennis.

She told me I was the best sex she'd ever had. Actually, she said I was 'the best fuck' she'd ever had. Apparently no one had made her come just from going down on her before. And let's remember that she'd had sex with 121 other women. That was probably the pinnacle of my life's achievements.

We weren't just having amazing sex – we walked around Columbia Road flower market together, dodging the tourists and hipsters and amateur street-art photographers; we went out for dinner at her local, laughing at each other's jokes over craft beers and bangers and mash; we strolled up Marchmont Street and browsed the latest LGBT literature in Gay's the Word. We were everything a London lesbian couple should be, except we weren't officially a couple.

She'd never been to my flat, which bothered me. I did love going to hers – it was so clean and quiet, and she didn't have a flatmate or a resident mouse – but I felt it was important for her to see me in my natural habitat. I'd been changing my sheets regularly just in case she decided to come home with me one night, and I'd piled up my most intellectual novels beside my bed, but to no avail. We usually went out in East London, so her flat was more convenient.

One Sunday, I was home painting my nails when the doorbell went.

'Not for me!' Alice shouted from her bedroom.

'Not for me either!' I shouted back.

'I haven't got my trousers on.'

'I'm not wearing a bra.'

I could hear Alice muttering to herself, putting on her dressing gown. She opened the front door and said, 'Oh!'

'Hello,' said Sam's voice.

I opened my bedroom door. There she was, standing on the doorstep in the rain, holding a bunch of peonies.

Alice went back to her room, nudging me unsubtly as she passed, leaving Sam and me alone. Sam was still leaning in the doorway, the top half of her body in our flat, her feet still on the doorstep, as though she might not be staying.

'Are you coming in?' I asked.

'Yes, please,' she said, stepping into the hall. 'I was sitting at home, thinking about your gorgeous tongue going down on me, and I thought I'd come round.'

'Thin walls!' called Alice.

I pushed Sam down the corridor to my room. I could feel her looking around our flat, taking in the damp patch on the ceiling and the dust at the edges of the carpet. I thanked the universe that I had Hoovered my room that day.

She sat on my bed and looked through the pile of books, just as I'd intended.

'Ali Smith,' she said. 'Nice.'

'Yeah,' I said. 'I've read all her stuff.'

'What did you think of *Winter*?'

'Except that one.'

I bunked off swing dance and we had sex and pizza and wine. It was wonderful.

'I haven't been on this many dates with the same person for years,' I told her.

'I don't usually bother with dates,' she said. 'Unless I'm really serious about someone.' She took my hand. 'I'm having the most perfect evening.'

'Sorry about the flat.'

'What about the flat? It's lovely.'

I made a face. 'It's not lovely. You don't have to pretend it's lovely.'

'It's yours, and that's what matters,' she said, looking me in the eye. 'I think everything about you is lovely.'

Every One Direction song and every Meg Ryan film flashed through my mind. I'd never realized how accurate they were until now. I wanted to say something to her, something like 'You complete me,' but I managed to keep my mouth shut and smile at her, a smile that must have told her how I felt.

We had sex again. She wore the strap-on and I got on top, reaching back to make her come with my hand at the same time.

Afterwards, we lay side by side on our backs on top of the duvet, little fingers curled together.

'You are a total natural at lesbian sex,' she said.

'Thank you.' I smiled down at our bodies, my pasty legs against her golden ones, and I realized I felt completely happy with my body and what it could do, for the first time in years.

And that's when she said, 'I can't believe you've only been with two women. Imagine what you'll be like when you've fucked more people.'

It took a while for that to sink in.

'You've got so much to look forward to,' she continued. 'There are so many different kinds of women. Butches, femmes, pillow queens, bull dykes, whatever. Older women, younger women. If I could, I think I'd shag every woman on Earth.'

I couldn't compute what she was telling me. 'I thought you liked having girlfriends,' I said.

She turned to look at me. 'I do. I love sharing my life with someone.'

'Right . . .'

'But I like sharing my body, and my love, with lots of people at the same time.'

I nodded slowly, looking up at the ceiling.

'I wouldn't want to limit myself to one woman. It would be like only eating cheese sandwiches for the rest of your life. Sometimes you just want pastrami, don't you? Which is why I'm non-monogamous.' I felt her shrug, as though her pastrami analogy explained everything.

I pushed myself up onto my elbows. 'So— who else are you sharing your body and love with at the moment, apart from me?'

'No one!' she said, sitting up, suddenly realizing I might not be taking this 100 per cent brilliantly. 'No one since I met you! Of course not! I'd have told you!'

'Oh,' I said, my voice steady. 'OK.'

'But I will at some point. And you will too, if you want to.'

'OK,' I said again, trying to adjust my vision of our future.

'And of course there's Virginie,' she said.

I tried to smile, but the corners of my mouth were turning down treacherously. I knew that name. I'd seen it on the photograph I'd found in Sam's copy of *The Portrait of a Lady*. 'You've never mentioned Virginie before,' I said.

Sam frowned. 'I'm sure I have.'

'You definitely haven't,' I said.

'I'm pretty sure I've told you about her.'

'You really haven't.'

Sam shrugged. 'Either way. She's my lover.'

It's amazing, the power words can have. They're just vibrations, really, over in a second, but I'll never forget the expression on Sam's face, or her intonation, when she told me she had a lover, as if it wasn't important.

'You didn't tell me,' I said. I thought I might cry. I didn't want to cry.

Sam took my hands. 'You don't need to worry about her,' she said. 'I don't see her very often.'

'But when you do see her . . .'

'When I do see her, we have sex,' said Sam, as though she was admitting that she was a vegetarian, or enjoyed a spot of badminton on a Saturday.

I moved the pillow up to cushion my back and sat up. 'So you haven't seen her since . . .' I wanted to say, 'since we've been together.' But we weren't together, officially. So I didn't have the right to be angry, did I?

'No. Haven't wanted to.'

'But you've spoken to her.'

'Maybe once. We mostly text each other. She knows I've got my hands full with you—'

130

'Well, if that's how you see it,' I said, pushing myself to the edge of the bed. I stood up and walked around the room, pointlessly picking things up and putting them down.

'No, babes,' she said. 'Come back here.' She was smiling, but there was something steely in her voice, and I walked automatically back to the bed. She took my hand. 'Virginie has a girlfriend, called Charlotte. They've been together for years. She and I just see each other every three or four months.'

'And Charlotte's OK with this?' I asked.

'Of course,' Sam said, stroking my hand. 'She's non-monogamous too.'

'So it's a relationship. You're in a relationship with her.'

'It's not like that,' she said, sighing, as though trying to explain long multiplication to a particularly slow child. 'We're more like really close friends. You'd love her – she's really funny. She's like a French Tina Fey, or something.'

'I like Tina Fey,' I said.

'Exactly.' She looked into my eyes. 'I've told her all about you,' she said. 'I've told her how amazing you are. She's really happy for us.' And I felt flattered, flattered that Sam was telling people about me, even if they were people she was still planning to have sex with on a semi-regular basis.

I couldn't behave normally with Sam after that. I pretended to be tired, and I locked myself in the bathroom for a long, hot bath.

She knocked on the door after I'd been in there about twenty minutes.

'Julia? Are you OK?'

'Completely fine!'

But I wasn't. Of course I wasn't. I was crying silently, my tears hotter than the bath water. The flattered feeling had faded. I'd thought I'd found someone. I'd been so lonely and then I wasn't lonely but it looked like I was about to be lonely again.

'Can I come in and talk to you?'

'I'm fine!'

'Please. Open the door.'

I leaned over to slide the bolt back.

Sam came in and crouched beside me. 'I should have told you earlier,' she said.

'No, I'm the idiot. You told me you'd shagged loads of women. I should have realized.' I hugged my knees. Something had shifted. I felt too naked now, self-conscious.

'I should have made it clear. I've just been having such a wonderful time with you. I didn't want to spoil it.'

I nodded.

She touched my wet arm. I moved away.

'You really don't need to worry,' she said. 'Having sex with other women doesn't make me want my partner less. It makes me want them more.'

'I don't see how that works.'

'I've told you. Variety. Freedom. And I'm offering you freedom too. Do you see that?'

I didn't say anything.

'We'll have ground rules. I'll tell you when I'm planning to see someone else. And you'll tell me who you're planning to see. And we'll have a veto.'

'What if I want to veto Virginie?'

'That's a bit different. I was seeing Virginie before I met you.' She reached out for my hand. I let her take it. 'I hope this doesn't mean we can't keep seeing each other,' she said. 'You mean such a lot to me already . . .'

Not enough that you want to stop shagging other women, I thought. But I said, 'I'll have to think about it.'

'Of course,' she said. She stood up, wiping her wet hand on her trousers. 'Call me whenever you're ready.'

* * *

As soon as she left, I missed her, with the kind of intensity I used to miss people I had unrequited crushes on. I took a bottle of wine into my room and put on an old Dashboard Confessional album I'd loved when I was at school. I turned on my laptop and looked through Sam's Instagram feed.

I scrolled back through every photo of Sam, at every party, her arm around woman after woman. There she was, graduating from her MFA in New York. She'd gone to Tisch, apparently. She'd won a prize in her final year and she'd worn a very nice black suit to the ceremony. There she was with her arm around another woman's waist – a girl, really, with pastel hair and a gap in her teeth. Had they been dating? Had she been dating someone else and fucking this girl on the side? I tried to imagine her fucking the gap-toothed girl. The thought was painful, but it turned me on a bit, to be honest, and my heart started racing in that addictive, thrilling way it had throughout my teens.

I found photos of Sam in Paris, around Christmastime, nose red with the cold, huddled up next to a woman with curly hair bunched under a woolly hat. The woman from the photograph. Their cheeks were touching. I hovered my mouse over the picture. Virginie Bernard.

I'd found her.

I tried to see Virginie's profile, but it was set to private, so I went back to Sam's profile and clicked on the next photograph. There were Sam and Virginie again, kissing, their eyes closed, with the Eiffel Tower in the background, lit up as if in celebration of their passion. I couldn't stop looking at the photo. I wanted to remember every detail of it, to take the mystery out of it, to make it meaningless, the way saying a word over and over again makes it meaningless.

Alice knocked on my door at about 10.30 to ask me to turn the Dashboard Confessional down a bit. I told her about Sam and the non-monogamy.

'Maybe that's just what lesbians do,' she said, sitting on my bed. She picked up the wine bottle from the floor and took a swig.

'Alice,' I told her, 'That's homophobic.'

'It's not—'

'And anyway, the lesbian cliché is that we move in together after one date and start having children after a week, or whatever.'

'And then stop having sex altogether.'

'Why can't I have a normal girlfriend whose idea of a good night is a little light fingering in front of *Strictly*?'

'I don't know,' Alice said. 'That's all any of us wants, really, isn't it?'

The wine and the whiny guitar music were making us both maudlin.

'I don't want to turn into my parents,' Alice said.

'I deserve a monogamous relationship,' I said.

'You can have too much monogamy,' Alice said. 'Dave keeps talking about getting married.'

'So you don't think I should stop seeing her?' I asked.

Alice looked at me. 'Do you want to stop seeing her?'

'No . . .'

'But how will you feel when she's like, "Have a great time with Alice, babes, I'm off for a quick shag?"'

I considered the question. I pictured myself sitting alone on the sofa, watching *RuPaul's Drag Race* and weeping while she was out fucking anonymous women. Or worse – enjoying a mini-break full of sexy French sex. 'You're right,' I said. 'I can't do it.'

'But it's not one-way, is it? You could shag other people too.'

That did seem like an attractively bohemian idea. 'I *have* only just started sleeping with women,' I said. 'Maybe I shouldn't settle down just yet.'

'I don't know, though,' said Alice. 'It's probably easier in theory than in practice.'

'I know . . . and isn't this all a bit like advanced lesbianism?

Shouldn't I start with one woman at a time and work my way up, like you would with juggling balls?'

'No one starts with just one juggling ball,' Alice pointed out.

I'd never questioned monogamy before. It was a societal norm, after all, like heterosexuality – but since I'd rejected that, maybe I should reject monogamy, too. Did I really only want to have sex with one person for the rest of my life? I've always liked to try new things.

I lasted three days without texting Sam, but that Thursday morning I woke up after a particularly vivid sex dream, frustrated and lonely. I sent Sam a message asking if she'd like to come round that night. She turned up with a bottle of champagne and a bag full of sushi. I didn't regret my decision for a single moment.

I was a bit late to work the next morning, so I was stuck with the desk next to Stan. I ignored his heavy breathing and went through my to-do list. Uzo walked over as I was highlighting the urgent tasks – highlighting things is one of my favourite procrastination techniques, as it makes me feel both organized and artistic – and dropped a letter on my desk.

'This one's for you,' she said.

'It's from Eric!' I said, settling back in my chair to read it.

How marvellous that you've taken up swing dancing! Eve and I loved to swing. I still dance whenever I can; there's a tea dance at the home once a week and me and my friend Irene show everyone what we're made of. Haven't been able to dance so much recently because my legs have been very swollen. Water keeps leaking out of them. Something to do with my heart. I hope you're not eating lunch as you read this!

Anyway, don't tell Irene, but dancing with her isn't a patch on dancing with Eve. We were so comfortable together, you see. It's smashing when you get to that stage, when you know each other inside out.

I have a music recommendation for you. See if you can get hold of

*anything by one of the old dance bands — Bert Ambrose & His Orchestra
or Billy Cotton's band. They were the bee's knees.*

I put the letter down on my desk. Eric's letters were always
uplifting, like good romantic comedies, despite the anecdotes about
the war and the lonely people at his care home and his leaky legs.
But like good romantic comedies, they sometimes left me feeling a
little bit deflated, as though I'd lost a love that hadn't been mine
in the first place. Obviously I knew that was ridiculous. Yes, it was
romantic that Eric had never wanted to dance with anyone but Eve,
till death did them part — but they were from a different time, a
time of suet puddings and women giving up work when they got
married and sixty million people dying in the Second World War.
Things were different now. We had freedom, and equal-ish rights,
and drones killed people so that we could pretend it wasn't happening.
And I *did* like switching dance partners in swing class — it was lots
of fun, even if I sometimes ended up covered in other people's
sweat. Maybe that's what non-monogamy would be like, too.

I turned back to my computer, but Owen was beckoning me from
across the room.
'What?' I mouthed.
He looked over at Smriti, who was standing with the press officers,
laughing (but in a professional way). 'Come to the kitchen,' he
whispered.
I met him by the mug cupboard.
He looked around like an unsubtle spy and said, 'Tom's applying
for a job at the Home Office.'
'Maybe one of us will get promoted, then.'
We rocked with silent laughter at the idea.
'He gave me a heads up — the SEO job ads are going up soon.'
'OK,' I said. I wasn't sure I wanted to apply for an SEO job — I
probably wouldn't get it, and I wasn't sure I could handle the rejection.

But if I ended up unemployed, I'd probably have to move back in with my parents, and sleep in my single bed, and take tourists on Harry Potter tours of Oxford.

'Let's help each other with our application forms,' said Owen.

'OK,' I said.

And then Smriti came into the kitchen, so we pretended to be talking about tea bags.

In the pub after swing dance that week, I ordered two bowls of chips for everyone to share and told the others about my job situation.

'We're looking for someone to take the Wednesday night beginners' class, if you're interested in a teaching gig,' said Zhu.

'I'm not good enough yet,' I said.

'You are!' said Rebecca.

'There's an audition for the Friends of Dorothy coming up, too,' said Zhu. 'Just saying.'

'That's not a job,' I said.

'We get paid gigs sometimes,' said Zhu.

'I won't get in.'

'You will. The audition's next Sunday.'

'Go on,' Ella said. 'I'd try out, if I didn't look like a giraffe when I did the Charleston.'

But I shook my head. Being rejected by the Civil Service was one thing. Failing as a dancer again was quite another.

17. I CAN REALLY SEE THAT YOU ARE A MAMMAL

From the moment Nicky opened the door, I knew the session would be a challenging one. She barely greeted me before walking back down the hall to her living room. 'Full disclosure,' she said. 'I'm premenstrual at the moment. So.'

I told her about me and Sam, and that we were going to give it a go. I wouldn't say she was happy for me.

'You can't be in an open relationship,' she said.

'You're not supposed to tell me what I can and can't do.'

'I can when it's clearly a terrible idea,' Nicky said. 'You are still working out who you are. You shouldn't be in an open relationship.'

'They work for some people.'

'They work for older people. People who have been with their partners for years.'

'Isn't that a bit narrow-minded?'

'We'll see who's right. Let's see, in a year's time, if it's worked out.'

'Fine.'

'Fine.'

Nicky wound her left leg around her right and bent forward. 'Jesus,' she said, one hand on her abdomen. 'Just a warning. PMS gets worse with age. The older you get without having children, the more your womb takes it out on you.' She looked down at her stomach, and said, 'Too bad, womb. My career comes first.' She looked up at me. 'You want kids?'

'I think so.'

'Think you can have kids in an open relationship?'

'I'm really not at that stage yet.'

'Just something to think about for next week.'

The morning after my session with Nicky I woke up, my heart racing. What she'd said had lodged inside me, tilting my opinion of Sam off balance. But I wasn't going to let her tell me what kind of relationship I could and couldn't have. I was in my twenties. I could have sex with whomever I wanted. I could be young and reckless.

I logged on to Facebook and looked at the events I'm invited to but never respond to. A pub quiz, a couple of house parties, a few club nights in East London. And a rave. Ella had invited me to a gay rave. I'd never been to a rave before.

I texted Ella to check she was actually going.

Definitely, she replied. *Zhu's coming too. Wanna come?*

I knocked on Alice's door. 'Alice?'

'I'm asleep.'

'Do you want tea?'

'I want to go back to sleep.'

'Shall we go to a rave tonight?'

I heard a rustling and then a thud, and then Alice opened the door, wearing her duvet like a cape. 'What?'

I made her some tea.

'We don't know how to rave,' Alice pointed out, once we were sitting in the living room, mugs in hand.

'Yes, we do,' I said. 'You just have to wave your arms around a lot and tell everyone you love them.'

'We don't do drugs, though.'

'*You* don't do drugs,' I said. I don't have anything against them,

139

but Alice swore she'd never take them again after we took MDMA in our third year and she spent the night rolling around in a lavender bush that she thought was a nature goddess and woke up the next day to find a voicemail summoning her to the Dean's office; the lavender bush belonged to him, it turned out, and his security camera had caught Alice flattening it with her writhing body.

Alice shook her head and pulled one of the sofa cushions onto her lap. 'I'm hungover. And Dave and I are meant to have a night in tonight.'

'Bring Dave.'

'He won't want to come.'

'Of course he will!'

Alice looked at me and sighed.

'Anyway,' I said, before she could say anything, 'I thought you weren't ready to settle down and you wanted to go out and do young things? Raving is a young thing!'

She sighed again. 'Where is it?'

I smiled. 'Hillingdon.'

'That's hours away!'

'Fine then. I'll just have fun with Ella without you.'

A low blow.

'You think Ella's more fun than me,' Alice said.

'I don't. But I will if you don't come and rave with us.'

She didn't say anything. I was winning.

'I'll pay for us to get an Uber home?'

'I'll come if Dave comes,' Alice said, and I knew it was a done deal. Raves were much more Dave's scene than ours, after all, judging by the number of invitations he received to parties frequented by artists who thought scrawling the words 'blow job' on a canvas qualified you for the Turner Prize.

The rave was in an abandoned carpet showroom. Alice and I both felt quite excited as we climbed in through the broken window, handing our fivers to a 16-year-old boy in a Looney Tunes baseball cap. Here was a London subculture we'd never explored before! We were young and trendy! We'd both been a bit worried about what to wear, but we needn't have been. The rave was an amazing cross-section of society: leathery tattooed men were dancing with blonde teenagers wearing chicken-wire fairy wings and hard-looking men in Reeboks chatted to goths and hippies, everyone united by drugs and beer and electronic music. There were makeshift bars in each of the rooms, selling coke, K, MDMA and laughing gas. It was a bring-your-own-booze situation and we'd come prepared with two six-packs of Red Stripe. We met Ella and Zhu in a corner near the speakers. We began to work our way through the beers, dancing and talking, about Sam, of course.

'I have to say, I think you deserve someone who's really committed to you.' Ella's face flashed white, red, and white again in the warehouse party lights.

'She is committed to me,' I said, waving my arms around, pretty expertly, I thought. 'You can be committed to someone and attracted to other people.'

'Exactly,' Zhu said, taking a swig of beer. 'I'm poly. Wouldn't give it up for anything.'

'Thank you,' I said. Finally, someone I liked, someone who knew what they were talking about, endorsing Sam's way of life.

'Don't you get jealous?' Alice asked Zhu.

'Sometimes,' she said. 'But you only feel jealous when you're scared of losing something. And if you're secure in your relationship, what's wrong with having fun on the side?'

'I don't think a lover in Lyon counts as "fun on the side",' said Ella.

Zhu turned to me and said, 'Ignore Ella. She's terminally monogamous.'

'I wouldn't stand for it,' said Dave. 'It's not like Sam's special, is it? Everyone would shag around if they could, but that's not what you do when you've committed to someone. It's not right.'

'Sam has a very high libido,' I explained. 'Sex is kind of her hobby.'

Dave laughed. Some of his beer dribbled down his chin as he did so; I could see Alice's face register disgust, and I felt a bit sorry for Dave. 'Right,' he said. 'And what if my hobby was rubbing my knob on ladies' coats on the Tube? Would that be OK, then?'

'Dave!' said Alice.

'Ooh,' said Dave, eyes closed, getting into the idea. 'It's all furry.'

'You're disgusting,' I said.

'What?' Dave said. 'You narrow-minded now or something?'

But then he looked at me and saw that I might be about to cry. His face fell, and he said, 'Sorry, Jules.'

I didn't want to cry, and I definitely didn't want anyone to see me cry, so I said, 'I'll be back in a minute,' and stumbled away, taking a long swig of my Red Stripe, forcing myself to nod to the music as the beat travelled up through my legs.

'I just don't want you to get hurt,' Dave called after me. 'You shouldn't let her take you for a ride.'

But I'd bought a ticket for the ride.

'Hey.' Ella was stumbling away from the group towards me. 'Are you OK?'

'I'm fine. I just want to be on my own for a bit.'

Ella stopped. 'You sure?'

I nodded, and she walked back towards the others, looking over her shoulder at me until I turned away from her.

Ella and Dave didn't understand. Sam wasn't taking advantage of me; like she'd said, she was offering me freedom. I would take advantage of that freedom, right here, right now.

I looked around at the waving, sweaty bodies, searching for a likely sex candidate. I wandered around the warehouse, dodging teenagers climbing into speakers. A group of women were leaning against what had been the till point of the carpet showroom. They look like lesbians, I thought – a couple of them had short hair, and one of them was wearing a tie. Perhaps they would like to have sex with me. I walked over and smiled at them, sexually.

'Hello,' I said, still smiling.

The women turned and looked at me. They didn't say anything.

'Can I talk to you?' I said.

The women looked at me some more. They weren't smiling. Nor was I, by this point.

'I'm not hitting on anyone,' I said. 'I just want to make friends.'

'We aren't really looking to meet new people?' said a woman with short dark hair and a high-pitched American accent. 'We're just hanging out together?'

'That's cool!' I said. 'That's totally cool!' I walked away around them, backwards, waving like a loon, and tried to get lost in the crowds.

I really wished I'd taken some drugs.

I walked back towards the others, but Ella and Zhu had wandered off somewhere and Alice had her arms around Dave's neck now. He said something to her and they both laughed, and then they kissed, a long, slow kiss that made me feel like a voyeur for watching them. I should have been happy for them, but I felt self-indulgently miserable instead, so I did the mature thing and hid. I sat down on the floor at the side of the warehouse, my back to the sweaty wall.

A couple of feet in front of me, on the floor, a man was writhing and twisting, muttering to himself, clearly in a K hole. Things could be worse, I supposed. I could be him. But then he probably wouldn't remember anything about tonight when he woke up, whereas I was horribly conscious of everything that was going on.

I saw an abandoned, unopened can of beer, just out of reach, glowing appealingly in the strobe lights. I reached over to grab it. My hand slipped as I tried to open it – what was it, my sixth? My seventh? Whatever. I forced myself to drink it down, ignoring how thick it felt in my throat.

My phone buzzed with a text from Alice. *Where are you? Zhu and Ella were trying to find you to say goodbye.*

Don't worry about me, I texted back.

I can see you, she replied, a minute later. *Wait right there.* It wasn't as though I had anywhere to go.

Alice sat down next to me and put her arm around me. I slumped onto her shoulder.

'No one loves me,' I slurred. 'Everyone has someone to love them except for me. Why am I so unlovable? Why can't I be enough for someone?'

'You are enough, darling,' said Alice, stroking my hair. 'You just haven't met someone who really appreciates you yet.'

'Why doesn't Sam love me?' I said. 'I love her.'

'Maybe she does,' she said. 'In her way.'

It was about 1 a.m. by this point, and Alice was yawning and looking at her watch.

'Just go home,' I said.

'Not without you.'

'I'm not coming,' I said, sulky from the beer. 'I'm going to find someone to have sex with.'

'Please, Julia,' she said. 'I'm getting us an Uber.'

'No,' I said, crossing my arms and slumping further down the wall.

The car arrived. I refused to move. Alice tried to drag me out of the warehouse. I made myself heavy and refused to cooperate. The car left without us in it.

'Fine,' Alice said. 'I'm going. But if you get murdered, don't blame me.'

She let me go and I fell back to the ground. She started to walk away, but then she turned around and marched back towards me. And then she stopped. She had seen someone standing behind me.

'Hello,' she said.

I turned my head, which made everything blur. It was Jane, who had taken my lesbian virginity. She had her arm around a woman with a shaved head and a nose ring.

'Fancy seeing you here,' she said.

'Jane, right?' said Alice, clutching her arm. I'd never seen her so pleased to see someone. 'Will you look after her? I'm going home and she won't come with me.'

'No problem,' said Jane. She sat down and put her arm around me. 'I'll make sure she gets back OK.'

Alice ran off to join Dave, making 'text me' actions at me. She stumbled as they left the warehouse to catch their cab but Dave caught her sleeve and stopped her falling. Rescued by her man, I thought as I closed my eyes. Pathetic.

The world was spinning.

'You're wasted,' said Jane.

I grunted.

'You need something to even you out,' said Jane's friend. 'I'm getting some MDMA. Want some?'

I grunted again. She took that as a yes, and went off to the drug bar.

I opened my eyes and focused on an empty packet of cigarettes on the floor, an anchor to stop the room spinning.

'Is she your girlfriend?' I asked Jane.

'I don't do girlfriends. I told you that,' she said. 'Her name's Tia. We're fucking.'

'She's hot,' I said.

'If you're lucky, I'll share her with you,' said Jane.

I laughed, but she didn't seem to be joking.

Tia came back and waved a tiny plastic bag at us. 'They're out of mandy. I got some E. And some K, in case we need it later. Ready?' she said.

I nodded.

I washed down the little tablet with my beer and slumped back against the wall, waiting for it to kick in.

It didn't take long. The room started pulsing. The lights were the most beautiful things I'd ever seen. I'd never really appreciated electric light before. What a miracle. And the fact that we could colour it red, or green, or yellow. We were gods, really, weren't we?

'Are you rushing?' asked Jane.

I nodded.

'I think there's some acid in this, or some shit,' said Tia.

I nodded again.

Tia and Jane started kissing. I didn't want to be left out, so I crawled over to them on my hands and knees and started stroking their backs.

'We should be somewhere smaller,' said Tia, 'where we can all get really close to each other.'

'Yes!' said Jane. 'You are so intelligent and observant.'

We held hands in a chain and made our way to the toilets. I opened a cubicle door with one hand – it seemed very important that I didn't let go of anyone.

The toilet was blocked. I knocked down the seat and sat down. The back of the cistern was cloudy with recently snorted coke. Tia and Jane knelt on the floor and started stroking my face.

'You have such beautiful skin,' said Tia.

'*You* have such beautiful skin,' I said. 'It's so smooth. I can really see that you are a mammal.'

'That's so true. We are all beautiful mammals.'

'Oh my God,' said Jane, gazing at her palm. 'Look at your hand.'

I looked at my hand, at every line and vein and scratchy cuticle. I looked at every ridge on every nail. I felt tearful, suddenly, connected to my mother and my grandmother and everyone who had gone before me and would come after me. I finally understood what it meant to be human.

146

'We are all so beautiful,' I said.

Tia nodded and kissed me on the lips.

'We need music,' said Jane, and she pulled out her iPhone and scrolled through Spotify. 'Tracy Chapman,' she said, and the opening chords of 'Fast Car' began playing from her phone's tinny speakers. I began to cry.

'Your tears are so beautiful,' said Tia. 'They're like little drops of glass. I'm sorry you're sad.'

'I'm not sad any more,' I said. 'I have you.'

'Yeah, you do have me,' said Tia. 'And I know we're just on drugs and that, but I really feel like I know you. Know what I mean?'

I nodded.

'You're both so great,' said Jane, stroking our cheeks. 'I'm so glad you've met. The three of us together makes so much sense.'

'We should hang out!' I said. 'What are you guys doing tomorrow? Shall we meet for brunch?'

'Yes!' they both said.

I felt too far away from the others so I came down off the toilet seat and squeezed between them, so we were all sitting against the wall, knees hunched, arms around each other.

I didn't feel drunk, or sick, or alone, or jealous. I felt incredibly lucky and grateful to be who I was, and where I was, and to have found such wonderful friends, and such a perfect place to sit, that fitted the three of us exactly.

That feeling lasted for about three Tracy Chapman songs. Just as 'For My Lover' ended, a slow dread began to creep upwards through me.

Jane and Tia didn't like me really. They were putting up with me.

'I should leave you guys alone,' I said, getting to my feet.

'No,' said Jane, tugging me down. 'We want you with us.' She pulled me to her side and stroked my head. 'You're grinding,' she said, rubbing my jaw.

I was, I noticed. My teeth were clenched together. I couldn't seem to relax.

Tia held out a piece of gum. I put it in my mouth. It was like a pillow of ice. I had never appreciated gum before.

I felt tears forming in my eyes again. The world was such a wonderful place, full of such wonderful things, and yet we were all going to die.

'You're coming down,' said Jane, rubbing my hand.

'No, don't come down,' said Tia.

'I feel anxious,' I said.

'No,' said Tia, eyes wide. She knelt in front of me and pushed on my chest. 'Does that help?'

I nodded. It did.

'You need some K,' said Jane. She pulled out a wrap and cut lines on the cistern with her Boots Advantage Card.

'Wow. That's so ironic,' I said.

'Why?' said Jane, smoothing out the lines.

'Because Boots is all about health. And drugs aren't healthy.'

'Boots is a drugstore. These are drugs,' said Jane.

'Oh my God!' I said, everything clear, suddenly. 'You're right!' I saw the lines differently then, as medicine that would make everything better.

Tia opened her wallet and handed me a fifty-pound note. I held it up to the light, marvelling at the magic of the holograph. The note glowed red, like a sunset. I'd never held a fifty-pound note before.

'Hurry up,' said Jane.

I rolled up the note carefully. I hadn't snorted anything since uni and I was worried I'd embarrass myself and do it wrong, somehow, and show myself up as an amateur. The K stung as it hit the back of my throat. My eyes began to water.

The others took turns snorting their lines. We rubbed the rest on our gums.

I don't remember a great deal about what happened next.

At one point I thought the three of us were a triptych in a stained-glass window.

At another point, we definitely kissed – a strange, asexual three-way. As we kissed the background behind us shifted, like a stage set. We were in the toilet. We were on a desert island. We were in a cemetery.

Tia's nose started to bleed.

I could see the crust on her nostrils all of a sudden.

The acne on her forehead.

Jane's teeth were stained yellow.

I had to get out of there.

I stood up very slowly.

'Where are you going?' said Jane, except I don't think she said it that fluently – it was more like 'Wherergo?'

'Home,' I said. I walked out of the cubicle, steadying myself against the walls. The others didn't try to stop me. They were glassy eyed now, lying there, twitching. They were together. They'd be fine.

I edged my way out of the room, while the floor of the warehouse undulated beneath me like the ocean. Somehow I got into a taxi. And then I vomited all over it.

'You pay me for that,' said the taxi driver, furious. 'You pay me.'

He stopped at a cashpoint. I got out, only to find that my wallet had been stolen.

I stumbled back to the taxi and leaned down to the window. 'Wallet gone,' I said.

The taxi driver swore at me and drove away.

It was dawn. The sun was coming up over the motorway, throwing the cars and the gasworks and the trees into silhouette. I took off my shoes to ground myself and walked to the Tube. I don't know how many times I fell over. I don't know how many times I stopped to vomit by the side of the road. I still had my Oyster card, and somehow I made it onto the Piccadilly line. I retched all the way to Manor House. By the time I got home, the sun was up. According to a note on my door, Alice and Dave had gone out for breakfast. I ran a bath. I lay in it, staring at the ceiling till the water was cold.

18. AN UNUSUAL LESBIAN SAINT

I slept till midday, and then I started to vomit again. Relentlessly. There was nothing inside me to vomit up any more, but I vomited anyway, as though my body wanted rid of the memory of whatever I'd put in it. I leaned over the kitchen sink, shaking, unable to hold myself up properly.

My stomach relaxed a little. I made it to bed and slept on and off, waking up sweaty and sick with shame.

A band of the most extraordinary pain formed around my head. I crawled to the bathroom to splash water on my face and lay on the cool floor tiles, my arm covering my eyes.

'Alice,' I bleated. 'Alice? Mum?'

I have given myself a brain haemorrhage, I thought. This is how I die: alone, in my bathroom, because of drugs. I'm not famous, so it's not even glamorous.

I reached for my phone. I called Alice. She didn't answer.

What if I fell back asleep and never woke up? I couldn't risk it. I dialled 999.

The ambulance took about an hour to arrive, by which time I was blind with pain, moaning in agony. They wheeled me out to the ambulance with a cardboard bowl on my knee in case I vomited.

'I'm dying,' I said.

'You're not dying,' the paramedic said. 'You're just stupid.'

They drove me to a hospital. I lay there on a metal bed in the strip-lit room, clutching my cardboard bowl like a teddy bear.

I took my phone out again and texted Alice. *In hospital. Not sure which. Poisoned self.*

Shit! Alice replied. *Dave has taken me on a surprise trip to Brighton! Do you want me to come home?*

No, I texted back, and then my phone died.

A few hours later, a doctor came into my room, grim faced, to give me a lecture. 'You know how much it costs the NHS when people like you drink too much and have a good time and then end up in here?'

I nodded. I was disgusted with myself. 'You're sure I don't have a brain haemorrhage?' I asked.

'You have a bad headache,' he said.

They took me to a bed on the main ward and hooked me up to a saline drip. The band of pain started to release.

I fell asleep.

'Julia?'

I knew that voice. But it wasn't Alice, and she was the only person who knew I was in hospital. I opened my eyes.

Sam was standing there, holding a bunch of grapes. 'I went round to visit you this morning, and you weren't at home, and you weren't answering your phone, so I called Alice—'

'How did you find me? How did you know where I was?'

'This is the closest hospital to your house.' She pulled up a chair next to my bed and sat down. She took my hand and kissed it. 'How are you, my poor baby?' She smelled so familiar and clean.

I began to cry. 'Thank you for coming,' I said.

'You don't need to thank me.'

'I thought I was going to die.'

'I've been there, babes. What did you take? Coke?'

'K.'

She winced. 'That's rough.'

I nodded. 'Will you stay with me?'

'Of course,' she said. 'I'm not going anywhere.'

I closed my eyes and slept. And when I opened them, she was still there, stroking my forehead.

Next time I woke up, it was getting dark outside. A doctor was standing next to my bed.

'I want to talk to you about drug and alcohol counselling,' he said.

'I really don't need that,' I said, pushing myself up, trying to make myself look respectable.

'You ended up in hospital on a drip after a night out.'

'It was completely out of character,' I said.

'I promise it was,' said Sam, standing up. 'She's not going to do it again. Are you?' She looked at me.

I shook my head.

'I'll make sure she doesn't,' Sam said, her hand on my shoulder. 'I'll look after her.'

'Who are you?' said the doctor.

'I'm her girlfriend.' She smiled down at me, her hair glowing in the strip lighting like an unusual lesbian saint.

I'm sure other people have more romantic 'becoming official' stories, but ours felt pretty bloody romantic to me. Sam was willing to take me covered in vomit, in hospital because I had a bloody headache and had taken a few too many drugs. This was me at my absolute worst, and she wanted me.

They let me go at about 11 p.m. Sam took me to her flat and tucked me up in her delicious white sheets. She brought me fish and chips in bed, and when she left me to clear our plates away I cried with gratitude. She was everything I had always wanted in a partner. Apart from the fact that she wanted to have sex with other people.

I slept most of Sunday and called in sick on Monday. I was still in bed when Sam came home. She'd been at her studio and smelled of turpentine. I wondered whom she'd been painting.

'How are you, babes?' she asked.

'Better.'

'Better enough to eat? Jasper and Polly were going to come over. But I can meet them somewhere if you can't face getting up.'

'Oh, no,' I said, sitting up. 'I'll get up. I'll get out of the way.'

'I don't want you out of the way,' she said, sitting on the end of the bed. 'I want you to meet my friends.'

'Well, thank you. I want to meet them,' I said, trying not to show how pleased I was. 'As long as I can borrow some clothes.'

Sam was much taller than me, and skinnier. The best I could do was a pair of baggy jeans that weren't that baggy on me, and an old Bangles T-shirt. 'There might be some make-up in one of the bathroom cupboards if you need any.'

Luckily I still felt rough enough that I didn't care what I looked like, because under other circumstances I'd have felt sick with nerves over meeting her friends.

'So who are Jasper and Polly?' I asked, dabbing on a bit of too-dark concealer, probably left behind by one of Sam's past conquests.

'My oldest friends. Jasper I know from going out when I was a teenager. Polly's a friend from art school. They're a couple now. Met at my birthday about eight years ago and never looked back.'

The doorbell rang and Sam went to let her friends in.

I could hear a deep, quiet voice saying hello and another voice booming, 'Come here! Let me squeeze that gorgeous arse of yours!

You are looking *fine* today! Now, where's this woman who has kept you away from us for so long?'

I flushed the toilet.

'There's our answer!' said the booming voice.

'Hello!' I said, opening the bathroom door. Sam and her friends were squeezed onto a couple of sofas. Polly stood up to shake my hand. She wore red lipstick and had a kind smile. I thought I might like her.

Jasper seemed the most excited to meet me. She was wearing red trousers and DMs and managed to look like a toddler and a middle-aged man at the same time, with white-blond curls and ruddy cheeks. She looked me up and down, lingering on my legs and breasts. 'I can see why you've been busy, Sam,' she said in the booming voice. 'She is one hot mamma.'

I smiled, pleased to be referred to as a hot mamma – though a bit disturbed too, what with Jasper looking an awful lot like a 3-year-old – and then I frowned, because I don't approve of objectification.

'Don't take any notice of Jasper,' said Polly. 'She's overexcited. Sam doesn't often introduce us to her dates.'

Jasper sat back down on the sofa with an 'Oof!' that told me she was in her late thirties at least. 'Come and sit next to me and tell me all about yourself,' she said, patting the seat beside her, so I did. 'Sam's hot, isn't she?'

'She is.' I smiled over at Sam, who was making salad dressing and pretending not to listen to our conversation.

'I only had sex with her once, when she was a teenager and I was in my twenties—'

'That's a bit cradle snatchy, isn't it?' I said.

'What? No! She snatched me! She was very precocious for a 16-year-old. I didn't have much of a say in the matter.'

I was unusually quiet during dinner, shovelling food quickly and taking second helpings to give myself something to do other than talk. I could feel Sam looking at me, checking I was OK. I wasn't massively OK – the conversation seemed to mostly centre around times everyone had fucked each other in various combinations that always involved Sam.

'Do you remember that sex party we went to in Clapham?'

'God, it was so awful. Everyone in their suits, not knowing how to use a strap-on.'

'Sam got off with the only hot women there, as usual.'

I laughed along with my mouth full of bread.

'I can't wait to take you to your first sex party,' Sam said, squeezing my hand.

I nodded.

'Have you never been to one before?' asked Jasper.

'No,' I said.

'You'll be fine,' said Polly, smiling at me. 'I was terrified at my first one, but once you get used to having sex in front of other people it's actually really fun.'

'Are you going to let us play with her?' Jasper asked Sam. She gasped and turned back to me. 'How do you feel about feet? I'd like to do some feet stuff with you.'

'We'll see,' I said, trying to look enigmatic.

'Don't go near Jasper's feet,' said Polly. 'She doesn't know what a pumice stone is.'

'Oi!' said Jasper. 'I'd get a pedicure for Julia.' She raised her eyebrows at me.

Sam took my hand. 'It'll just be the two of us the first time.'

'You *are* a changed woman,' said Jasper. 'Julia's got you under the thumb already!'

Even after everyone left, I was quiet. Sam asked me what was wrong, and I told her I hadn't liked the way Jasper had spoken about me at dinner.

'It's just banter,' she said.

'It's not very feminist.'

'We're all feminists. We're lesbians, for fuck's sake.'

'Jasper's a bit of a chauvinist.'

'That's just Jasper. None of us take her seriously.'

I sat down on the sofa. Sam came to sit next to me. 'Are all your friends non-monogamous?' I asked.

'Pretty much.' She put her arm around me. 'This lifestyle takes some getting used to, but I swear you'll be so much happier when you let go of all that heteronormative bullshit. Do you really think you'll never meet anyone you want to have sex with apart from me, ever again?'

'No . . .'

'Right. Exactly. But the most important thing is us. Isn't it incredible that we found each other? I feel like we have this connection – don't we?' There was worry in her eyes now, which I found reassuring.

'Yes.'

'I don't feel like that very often.'

'I don't either.' I turned and kissed her. I couldn't get over how wonderful it felt to kiss her.

She took my hands. 'There's something I've been wanting to say to you for a while now. I've been telling myself it's too soon. Is it too soon?' She looked at me meaningfully.

I looked back, trying to pretend I didn't know what she was talking about, willing her to back out.

'Shall I say it?' she said.

I didn't say anything.

'I won't say it if you don't want me to.'

'You can say it.'

'You're not ready.'

I smiled.

'That's OK,' she said. 'I'll say it in another way.' She kissed me, and the kiss turned into the most amazing sex, right there on the sofa – really intense sex, the kind where you stare into each other's eyes while you're fingering and then fist each other without gloves and lie there, hugging, for about half an hour afterwards.

I decided to call in sick on Tuesday, too. I still didn't feel stable enough to face the world, stomach-wise. I woke up to find Sam's side of the bed empty, the radio on, the shower hissing.

I walked into the bathroom. Sam was a hazy golden shape behind the shower curtain, humming tunelessly to herself.

'Morning,' I said.

'Go back to bed, babes,' she said. 'Sorry. Didn't mean to wake you.'

'You didn't.'

'Want to stay here today? I like the idea of coming home to you.'

'Or I could come to the studio?'

'Actually, I prefer to work alone,' she said. 'I'd feel self-conscious if you watched me paint. Is that OK?'

'Of course.'

She turned off the shower and pulled back the curtain to give me a hot, damp kiss. She shook her hair, flicking water around the bathroom. 'Make yourself breakfast,' she said. 'Watch TV or whatever. I'll be back about seven.'

The flat hummed with silence after she left.

So many blank cupboard doors and drawers. So many notebooks on the crammed bookshelves. But I shouldn't look at them. I shouldn't open them. No good would come of it.

I climbed back into bed and picked up Sam's laptop from the floor. Five Google Chrome tabs were open: a blog, *Women Painting Women*, about female figurative painters; her Gmail home page, which I shut straight away; and my Twitter page, my Facebook page and my Instagram. I felt a strange little thrill: I put everything about my life up there for people to see – stupid selfies and symmetrical photos of Moroccan floor tiles and inane comments about Saturday-night television – but I'd never considered that someone might actively choose to look at any of it. Sam had been looking through my Facebook photos, back to when I'd started university: me and Alice drinking pints at the Dirty Duck, me with my ex-boyfriend Leon, me in a bikini in Croatia . . . She really did love me. Here was the proof.

19. ALL YOUR EGGS IN ONE BASKET

I was hoping that Sam and I would go on a romantic mini-break over Easter, possibly to Whitstable or Margate – I don't think a relationship is official until you've stayed in an Airbnb together and picked dubious hairs out of a stranger's double bed – but it turned out Sam already had plans.

'I'm going home to see my dad,' she told me a couple of weekends before, as we strolled through London Fields hand in hand, sidestepping cyclists and dogs.

'Oh!' I said, trying and probably failing to keep the disappointment out of my voice. 'Where does he live, then?'

Sam rarely talked about her father. I knew all about Polly's mum and Jasper's brother who lived in St Ives and the MFA crew that Sam visited in New York whenever she got the chance, but nothing about her family, other than that her mother was dead and that her father was rich. 'Dubai,' she said.

'Very nice!' I said.

'Apart from the fact that homosexuality is illegal.'

'Do you have any friends out there?' I asked.

'No,' Sam said. 'He moved there after my mum died, and I was away at school.' And then, 'Fuck.' She had stepped in a puddle. There was a tiny smudge of mud on her right trainer. She knelt down to wipe it clean with a leaf.

'I'll miss you,' I said.

She stood up and put her hands on my shoulders. 'I'll miss you too,' she said, and she pulled me towards her and kissed me.

A teenage boy wolf whistled at us. Sam put her finger up at him and kept kissing me. That felt great, kissing someone and making a political statement at the same time.

I didn't fancy rattling about in the flat alone, eating Easter eggs and worrying about my future while Alice and Dave had loud four-day-weekend sex, so I decided to go home to see my parents.

'Lovely!' Mum had said when I'd called to check it was OK with her. 'And good news: next door's builders are all away for Easter. I suppose it's more of a big deal in Eastern Europe. Thank God! Literally!'

Mum opened the front door before I rang the bell.

'Look,' she said, hands on hips, nodding towards next door. 'They could have cleared the rubble away before they buggered off for a week!'

'Nice to see you too, Mum,' I said, giving her a kiss on the cheek.

Dad was in the kitchen, watching something on his laptop. Whatever it was, he didn't seem to be enjoying it. I walked up behind him. He looked round and smiled at me briefly before going back to frowning.

'Bloody Geoff,' he said, nodding at the screen. Dad was, unbelievably, watching YouTube. 'He's started putting his lectures on the Internet. He has thousands of followers.'

'His face looks even more weirdly smooth on camera, though,' I said, patting Dad's shoulder.

'And the worst thing is he talks such crap,' said Dad. 'It's like he's never read *Silas Marner*.'

'I keep telling your father, YouTube is the future,' said Mum, arranging sprigs of rosemary around the lamb. 'You could get Harry next door to help you, Martin, seeing as you're so chummy with his mother.' She looked at me. 'Harry does make-up tutorials,' she said. 'I watched one the other day, and it explained how to apply base and how to contour. I would need different products, of course, because I don't have stubble.'

Dad looked at me, a pained look. 'Are you listening to this nonsense?' he said.

'I think you'd be very popular on YouTube,' I said. 'You could call yourself The Grumpy Professor.'

'Oh!' said Mum, looking up from the lamb. 'That's good!'

'I'm not grumpy,' Dad said grumpily. He clicked another video. 'Now this chap,' he said, 'this chap knows how to make a YouTube video.'

I looked over his shoulder. A bearded man was standing at the top of a mountain, shouting about how warm he was in his new anorak.

'He reviews mountaineering gear,' Dad said.

'You've never been mountaineering,' I said. 'Has he?' I asked Mum.

'Of course he hasn't,' she said.

'But if I wanted to, I'd know exactly what gear to get,' Dad said.

My exciting new sexuality didn't come up once during lunch, but as I was about to go to bed, Dad said to me, 'Did you enjoy *Nightingale Wood*?' And I said, 'Yes, thanks,' and he nodded stiffly.

I had left my phone in my room and when I went back to find it I had a missed call from Sam. I called her back straight away. The phone rang with a distant, international monotone, which made me feel even further away from her.

'You didn't answer your phone,' she said when she picked up, her voice sulky.

'Sorry,' I said. 'I was with my parents.'

She sighed. 'No,' she said, '*I'm* sorry, babes. I hate being here with my dad. He doesn't know who I am most of the time, and then he has lucid moments and that's even worse because he's so fucking miscrable.'

'Oh,' I said. 'Why doesn't he—'

'Early onset dementia.'

'Oh,' I said again, stupidly. 'I'm so sorry. I didn't know.'

'Of course you didn't. I only just told you. Anyway, it's the depression that's the worst. He's been depressed since my mum died. That's what monogamy does to you – you tie your happiness up with one person and they leave you or die, and then you're fucked forever.'

'That's a cheerful way of looking at it.'

'It's true, though, isn't it?' she said. 'Every relationship has to end, doesn't it? So if you put all your eggs in one basket, you're leaving yourself extremely vulnerable.'

As I lay in bed that night, I thought about what she'd said. We had only just become official, and already I felt her absence like a physical pain, an uneasy, unhealthy kind of missing. I wondered how much more I'd miss her when she was away with Virginie, having tantric sex in a gîte. Maybe I need a Virginie of my own, I thought. An Irish one, perhaps. A Siobhan. We'd have great sexy craic and then drink post-coital whisky together and eat those nice Lily O'Brien's chocolates people always bring back from Dublin. But everything in me rebelled against the idea of being with someone else. I wanted Sam, Sam, Sam. I would do whatever I had to do to keep her.

'You're adorable,' Nicky said in our next session.

'I'm not.'

'You are. You're so sweet.'

'Shut up. I'm not sweet.'

'You think she's your girlfriend.'

'She is. And I met her friends.'

'Her friends who she sleeps with?' Nicky said in a gentle, sympathetic voice that made me want to maim her.

'She's not sleeping with anyone but me at the moment. Plus she called from Dubai over Easter, because she missed me. And she's been looking back through all my Facebook photos. I saw, when I was at her flat.'

'And that's relevant why?'

'Because you only do that if you're genuinely interested in someone.'

'So you think Internet stalking is a sign of commitment.'

'It's definitely a sign of interest.'

'And you're already looking at her Internet history.'

'Not on purpose.'

She shrugged, tapped her pen on her notebook a few times, and asked, 'Have you tried BDSM yet?'

'No. But we will soon. Next week, actually, I think.'

'Right.'

She stared at me. I stared back. A fly buzzed between us, distractingly. I refused to blink. Nicky swatted it, which I took as a victory.

20. MR LOVER LOVER

Sam called me as I was walking to work from Victoria station one Friday in early May, umbrella up against the rain, part of a stream of blue mackintoshes and white shirts heading towards the Department of Health and Social Care.

'Hey, babes,' she said. 'I know we were going for dinner tonight, but Jasper has asked if we want to go to Fuck Everything. Fancy it?'

I didn't say anything.

'You'll love it,' she said. 'It's a really friendly night. And you don't *literally* have to fuck everything. We'll just have sex with each other.'

'In public?' I asked under my breath, as the Minister of State for Health brushed past me.

'Sorry?' Sam said.

'Do we have to do it in public?' I was walking into the office now, past the reporters and television crew smiling despite the rain under transparent umbrellas.

'We don't have to. We can just watch, if we want. Go on, babes.'

I said yes.

'I'm going to a sex club tonight,' I said, as Owen and I waited for our computers to boot up.

He looked up at me, impressed. 'No way.'

'Way.'

'Can I come?'

'No!'

'Is it a gay sex club?'

'I think it's anything goes, actually.' I opened my notebook and flicked casually to my to-do list, feeling pleased with my exotic sex life.

Owen stood up and came to stand by my desk. 'Please let me come?' he said. He straightened his tie, as though that would make a difference.

'Definitely not,' I said. 'I don't think that would be very good for our friendship.'

'I think it would be excellent for our friendship,' Owen said. 'It would be a bonding experience. Tea?'

'Yes, please,' I said, and I handed him the 'Keep Calm and Carry On' mug from my desk.

Owen plodded to the kitchen, and I logged into my computer. I already had an email from Sam: *Can't wait for tonight! Xxxx*

Owen placed my mug, with uncharacteristic carefulness, on my coaster.

'Thank you,' I said.

He was still standing next to my desk.

I looked at him. 'Hello,' I said. 'You're still here.'

'Now can I come?' he said. 'I could bring Laura. One of her ex-boyfriends used to tie her up, apparently. She might be into it.'

'Absolutely not.'

As the hours passed I found it harder and harder to concentrate; I kept starting an email and getting distracted when a new one arrived in my inbox and forgetting what I was doing, or clicking on a marketing email and following all the links until Owen caught me looking at a selection of overpriced French socks with fruit on them and said 'Very sexy!' before I could minimize my screen.

I felt so jittery that I ran all the way home from Manor House station to try and get rid of the excess energy. I needed to calm down. I banged open the flat door and turned on the kitchen light, reaching for a bottle of cheap whisky Alice and I bought for a Burns supper once and keep at the back of the cupboard for drinking emergencies. I took a swig straight from the bottle. The dirty-tasting liquid burned away the anxiety and I felt instantly calmer. Maybe a night out at a sex club was what I needed. I was pretty sure it would take my mind off the prospect of working for the Freedom of Information requests team.

I had a very thorough shower and put on my most flattering underwear and a wrap dress, for easy access. I wasn't planning on having sex, necessarily, but I didn't want to wear jeans and rule myself out of the party entirely. This was all an adventure! A brilliant adventure! Most people never experienced things like this in their entire lives. But as I put on my eyeliner, my hand was shaking.

The club was under a pub down a side street in Kings Cross, defiantly dirty and seedy in amongst the chain cocktail bars and wide pavements and newly planted trees, like a pensioner who refused to sell up in the face of gentrification. I studied the other people waiting to go in; there were two bears in overly tight leather waistcoats, but other than that, everyone just looked like they were queuing up at Tesco for a couple of pints of milk. And then I saw Sam, leaning against the wall near the doorman in leather trousers and a black T-shirt, staring straight at me, unsmiling, waiting for me to notice her.

I waved, feeling stupid, and she walked up to me, hands in pockets, still not smiling, and kissed me on the neck. 'Can't wait to get you inside,' she muttered into my ear, and I shivered. Half of me was terrified, wondering why I'd let myself be talked into this. But the other half couldn't wait for her to get me inside, either.

The club was dark and dank and pretty empty. Clusters of people were standing at the edges, like awkward teenagers waiting for someone to ask them to dance. Just off the main room were three smaller, darker rooms – caves, almost. Occasionally couples would emerge from them, straightening their clothes, smoothing their hair. 'Those are the playrooms,' Sam said. 'Want to go and have a look?'

I nodded, smiling a little too widely.

We walked towards the nearest of the three anterooms. Before we'd even got there, we could hear a woman crying out. 'Someone's having fun,' said Sam.

Jasper was having fun, it turned out, spanking a woman who was lying face down on what looked like a black hospital bed, bum bared, buttocks red. She turned her head as we walked in. It was Polly. She didn't seem embarrassed, but I definitely was.

'Let's leave them to it,' I said.

'It's all right,' Sam said, settling back against the wall, her arms crossed. 'We can watch for a bit.' She put an arm around me and then turned towards the others, smiling passively the way you do when you see a particularly good juggler or street dancer near Oxford Circus Tube on your way to buy tights in Topshop.

I tried to relax; Polly and Jasper didn't seem fazed by our presence. If anything, they were playing up to us. But I flinched every time Polly cried out. The whole thing felt wrong. It was a bit like squeezing your blackheads, or masturbating, or watching reality television – an absorbing solo activity for a Sunday night. Not something you want to do in front of other people. Definitely not something you wanted to watch someone else doing.

Sam looked across at me. 'What's wrong?'

'Nothing!' I said, turning back to watch Polly and Jasper.

Sam was still looking at me. 'Want to play?'

I didn't particularly want to play, not if it involved spanking or being stared at while I tried to orgasm. But I didn't want to stand there watching other people play, either.

'Come on,' Sam said, teasing. 'You're not *scared*, are you?'

'No . . .'

'So let's do it.' She turned to me and kissed me before I could protest. I closed my eyes and pretended I was in Sam's flat, and I was actually getting quite into it until I heard another thwack and another cry and my eyes jolted open. Sam's hands moved from my waist to open the tie of my wraparound dress, but I put a stop to that pretty sharpish. 'Let's go to another room,' I said, as huskily as I could. 'On our own.'

She took my hand and led me from the room, winking at Jasper, and walked me through the main dance floor, which was starting to fill up, to another damp cave. I was very pleased to find it empty. There were a variety of ropes hanging from the ceiling. Luckily, Sam didn't seem particularly interested in those. She didn't seem interested in warming me up either – maybe she assumed I'd be warmed up after watching the spanking. She clearly was – she just pushed me up against the wall and pulled my dress aside to fuck me.

I closed my eyes and tried to forget about the weird ropes and the smell of latex and the muffled cries of 'Yes! Harder!' Fucking in a public place had always been a fantasy of mine, but I'd never pulled it off successfully. I'd once had sex in the back garden of my house at uni, but the risk of being caught and the cold November air had given the bloke a bit of performance anxiety and it was all a bit floppy and disappointing. There was nothing to get floppy this time – but I'd spent years locking changing room doors and generally not taking my clothes off in front of other people, so taking my underwear off and allowing someone to fuck me in front of complete strangers was going to be a bit of an adjustment. Come on, I told myself. Don't be so English. Try to get into it. The techno music pulsed through me. I focused on Sam's hot tongue on my clit, and the cool breeze on my nipples, and the thud thud thud of the beat, and it worked, and I started to come – except as everything was building nicely to a climax, the music changed.

'Mr Lover Lover. Ooh,' crooned Shaggy.

I tried to stay in the moment but my mind was back at a primary school disco.

'Mr Boombastic, telly-fantastic,' continued Shaggy, as Sam soldiered valiantly onwards.

I opened my eyes and took in the damp walls and the curls on Sam's head, bobbing up and down, and the people on the dance floor, dancing ironically.

'I don't think this is going to work,' I said, and just then a woman walked into the room, ignoring Sam completely, and said, 'Sorry, but we're shutting the playrooms now? Can you finish up? Thanks!' She turned around and marched back out as though she did this sort of thing every day, which I suppose she did. That brought me back to myself, and I was suddenly aware that I was half naked.

I grabbed Sam's hair to stop her, but that only seemed to turn her on, and then Jasper stuck her head around the door and watched us for a minute, murmuring, 'Hot,' and then, 'We'll wait for you outside.'

'Let's go,' I said.

Sam looked up at me. 'We're not leaving till you've come,' she said.

I suppose if I'd insisted she would have stopped. But I can't be sure, because I didn't. It seemed easier not to argue.

I clamped my eyes shut again and for the first and hopefully last time in my life, I came, in public, to a Nineties reggae song.

21. THE WEAPON OF MASS DESTRUCTION

The sex club was sexier and more fun in retrospect. I told Ella all about it the next day in swing class and it made a funny story, the Shaggy song, and the woman walking in on us, and me watching Sam's friends spank each other. It felt a bit jarring, talking about playrooms, ropes, etc. at 2 p.m. on a Sunday, as we learned to jive to Cole Porter. A bit like ordering a salad at McDonald's.

'You do realize you don't have to have sex in public, just because you're a lesbian?' Ella said, as we did a turn out. She was wearing a sequinned waistcoat today. It caught the light as we danced.

'Yes,' I said.

'And that most lesbians wouldn't even know what to do with an enema kit.' She spun around on the spot, glittering.

'I'm quite happy not knowing, myself,' I said.

'I just think you've gone in at the lesbian deep end,' said Ella. 'You should try some lesbian bed death to balance it out.'

'That doesn't sound like so much fun, though,' I said.

'It's not,' said Ella, nodding. 'Good point.'

I felt almost cheerful as I walked to work that Monday. I'd started to dread going to work after Tom had told us to 'look into our options', my heart rate speeding up the nearer I got to Victoria Street, but the sex club had helped put things in perspective. What

I did for a living wasn't important – it was how I passed the time until I could go out and dance, and fuck, possibly in public. I did far more exciting things every night than most people I knew. I was part of an underground scene. I'd always wanted to be part of an underground scene.

Owen brought me a cup of tea as soon as I sat down that morning. 'How was it?'

'How was what?'

'The sex club!' He was practically rubbing his hands on his thighs. 'A bit dingy.'

'Did you do it?'

'That's none of your business.'

'You did, didn't you? Just with Sam or with strangers, too?'

'Owen! I don't ask you about *your* sex life.'

'I promise you, if there was anything interesting to tell you, you'd be the first to hear about it.'

'I thought you were banging Laura.'

He flicked a paperclip off my desk. 'She hasn't texted me since last Friday.'

'Oh. I'm sorry.'

'Yeah. I feel like shit.'

'Anything I can do?'

'You can tell me about the sex club.'

'No.'

But he looked so crestfallen, I said, 'The walls were damp. And it was all a lot less exciting than you're probably imagining.'

He cheered up a bit at that. 'You're a much more interesting lesbian than Carys is.'

'Who?'

'My sister. She mostly just Instagrams her breakfast. I think you'd like her, though.'

'Why, because we're both gay?'

'No,' Owen said, put out. 'Because you're both very nice people.'

'Oh,' I said. 'Thank you.'

He gave me a sad sort of smile.

'Have you tried texting her?'

'Who?'

'Laura.'

'Oh. Yes. Quite a lot.'

'But she never replies?'

'She did once, yesterday, to say she needed space.'

'And you kept texting her?'

'Not any more. Carys made me delete her number. I wrote it down on a bit of paper and put it in my sock drawer, though, just in case.'

'Good for Carys,' I said.

Alice was pretty envious of my sex club experience, too. She and Dave weren't having sex nearly as often as they had been, it turned out.

'It's my fault,' she said. 'I had a urinary tract infection about a month ago and that threw things off a bit.'

'They're the worst,' I said.

'I know,' she said. 'He was a love, he kept buying me cranberry juice, but I couldn't bear to look at his penis for a while after that. All that friction.'

'Ugh. Don't.'

'But I need to make more of an effort.' She looked up at me. 'He said something about getting married the other day. Again.' She watched me for my reaction. 'I said I wasn't sure,' she said, almost apologetically. 'And I asked him whether *he* wanted to get married, and he said he definitely did and he wasn't sure he could be with someone who didn't.'

'So what did you say?'

'I didn't say anything. But it would be silly to give up a good relationship because of a piece of paper I don't even believe in, wouldn't it?'

'I suppose so,' I said. 'Dave is great.'

I held out my glass to cheers her, and when she knocked her glass against mine, a little wine spilled onto her jeans. She licked a finger and mopped it up.

'The thing is, I never saw myself with someone as masculine as Dave. I always thought I'd end up with a camp man who liked opera, or used a lot of hand cream and wore pink ties.'

'A Tory.'

'No! A Green voter, probably, the sort of person who goes on protests about the Arctic. Dave's just such a *man*.'

I nodded. 'He even has a beard.'

'And when we're walking down the road, he walks on the outside, because that's what he thinks men should do, and he holds the door open for me in restaurants.'

'Sam does that too,' I told her.

'Do you hate it?' she asked, draining her glass and holding up the empty bottle optimistically as though it might have automatically refilled itself.

'Actually I sort of like it,' I told her. 'She wears men's underwear.'

'No!' Alice said. 'Does she wear a bra?'

'Yes.'

'Hairy legs?'

'Yes. And pits. But almost hairless downstairs.'

'But she behaves like a gentleman,' Alice said, crossing her legs. 'All the trappings of masculinity, but without the weapon of mass destruction. I wish I were a lesbian, sometimes. Apart from having to lick the snail.'

'The snail is integral,' I said.

'You never have to worry about compromising your principles. Even if you married her and took her name, you still wouldn't be giving in to the patriarchy.' She leaned back against the kitchen door and looked at me. 'Tell me the truth. Would you think less of me if I got married?'

I wasn't sure what to say. To play for time, I walked to the fridge, to find something to eat. There was nothing except an ageing piece of cheddar, brittle at the edges. That would do. I sliced off the dry patches and cut it into chunks.

'That's gross,' Alice said as I put a lump of cheese in my mouth. It tasted all right, actually — a little more on the mature side, that was all.

'You ate all the cereal,' I pointed out.

'You haven't answered my question,' she said.

I crossed my arms. 'Of course I wouldn't think less of you.'

'Good,' said Alice. 'Because I'd be happy for you, if *you* got married. I've already thought about what I'd say in the speech.'

'You're making a speech at my wedding now? My wedding to Sam?'

'Of course,' Alice said, put out, apparently, that I hadn't included her in my non-existent wedding.

'I don't think that's on the cards any time soon,' I told her. 'We're a bit too busy having sex in weird padded rooms in front of her friends.'

'You're so lucky,' Alice said, picking up a piece of cheddar between her thumb and forefinger and examining it before putting it in her mouth.

'We're going to an SM club next weekend,' I told her.

Alice grabbed my arm. 'Oh my God! Really? Could me and Dave come?'

I looked at her.

'That would be crossing a line, wouldn't it?' she said.

'A lot of lines,' I said.

'Let's try a new thing this week,' Nicky said as soon as I was settled in the terrible armchair. 'I've been learning about a new kind of therapy called ACT. It's a cross between mindfulness and CBT.'

'I didn't have you down as a mindfulness sort of person,' I said.

'I like to think I'm constantly surprising.'

'You are,' I assured her.

Nicky crossed her legs. 'There's good evidence that ACT is very helpful for anxiety, so I thought we should give it a go.'

'OK,' I said.

'OK,' she said.

I looked at her. She looked back.

'So how do we do it?' I asked.

'Close your eyes,' she said, in a new, strange voice that she obviously thought was 'relaxing'.

I closed my eyes.

'Now. We're going to do a simple grounding exercise to connect to the present moment.'

I couldn't stop myself smiling.

'What?' she said. 'Why are you laughing at me?'

'I'm not!' I said, trying and failing to get rid of the smile.

'You are.'

'It's just the voice,' I said, opening my eyes. 'Do it in your ordinary voice.'

'Close your eyes,' she said again, sternly, in her ordinary voice. I did as I was told. 'Just check in with yourself. How are you feeling, at the level of the body? At the level of the thoughts and emotions?'

'I have a slight feeling of dread,' I said.

'That was a rhetorical question.'

'Sorry,' I said.

'Right. Take a deep breath in. Now empty your lungs completely. Let them fill up again of their own accord.'

I took a deep breath through my nose. Nicky's living room smelled musty, like damp towels that hadn't dried properly. I could smell something meaty, too. Maybe she'd had bacon for breakfast.

'If any thoughts come into your mind, just notice them and let them float gently away, like clouds, or balloons.'

I let the thought of bacon drift away. And then, unbidden, Smriti and Tom's faces came into my mind. I imagined them floating into the air, balloon shaped. And then I thought about Sam. Sam's face. Sam's smell. Sex with Sam.

'If any thoughts hook you in, just let them drift on by, like leaves on a stream,' said Nicky.

Sam wouldn't drift. But I didn't mind being hooked in by thoughts of Sam.

22. GIMP MASKS AND
WAGON WHEELS

I didn't see Sam much in the week leading up to the SM club. She had loads of work to do in preparation for her show, she said, and she cancelled our dinner plans on Thursday night because an artist friend of a friend was visiting from the States.

'Can I come?' I asked.

'It'll be boring, babes,' she said. 'We'll just be talking about art.'

'OK,' I said, but I couldn't help feeling a bit rejected.

I woke up with a racing heart the next day, and felt sweaty-palmed all day at work. What was I letting myself in for? What if I hated SM? What if it . . . hurt? But I had another letter from Eric, describing the first time he went on a bombing raid, which put things in perspective:

The flak they shot at us looked so beautiful from 12,000 feet, like fireworks, red and green and blue and every beautiful colour you can imagine. It felt like a miracle that we got back alive, but I tell you what, there's no high like it.

That was real danger. SM seemed dangerous but it wasn't. That was the point.

I went to Sam's after work, and we ate takeaway sushi and drank beer and discussed what we were going to wear to the SM club the following night.

'Less is more,' Sam told me, with a mouth full of California roll. 'Do you own a corset?'

'No,' I said.

'A thong?' Sam said, dipping a nigiri in my soy sauce.

'Yes,' I said, feeling a little less sure about the whole thing.

'So wear the thong and just tape over your nipples with gaffer tape. I have some leopard-print gaffer tape around here somewhere.' She wandered over to the kitchen and rifled through a few drawers until she found it. 'Boom,' she said, and tossed it to me.

The roll was almost full, but the edge was ragged, curled up at the corners.

'Friend brought it back from America for me,' Sam said.

I knew 'friend' meant 'person I used to fuck'. I let the ripple of jealousy pass through me.

Sam went to the studio again the next morning. I slept late, turned the radio on for company and experimented with the gaffer tape. I managed to make myself quite a supportive bra, though it didn't look particularly sexy – a bit like a sports bra – and it left unsightly marks on my breasts when I pulled it off. I had a long, hot shower, in an attempt to remove the marks. By the time I got out, I had three missed calls from Sam.

'Where have you been?' she asked, when I called her back.

'I was in the shower.'

A silence. 'You're still at my flat?'

'Yes,' I said, not sure that was the right answer, suddenly.

'Are you on your own?'

'Of course I'm on my own!' I said. 'Who else would I be with?'

I heard her breathe out. 'I was worried when I couldn't get hold of you. I thought something might have happened to you.'

'What would have happened?'

'I don't know. I'm being silly. Answer the phone when I call you, babes, OK?'

'OK,' I said. I felt like I'd been told off. 'Sorry,' I added.

'That's all right, babes,' she said. And I resented her saying it, for implying I'd been right to apologize.

She said she wasn't going to be back till seven, so I took a bus home, playing with the gaffer tape as I watched people on the streets of Hackney on the way to their nights out, sticking and unsticking my finger in time to my heartbeat.

I had arranged to meet Sam in the queue to the SM club. I don't know what I expected her to be wearing – nipple clamps or something, I suppose – but when I spotted her, face lit by her phone screen, she was dressed in a Navy uniform, complete with jacket and boots. She hadn't told me that would be an option; I felt a little foolish now, in my thong and gaffer tape, though I was wearing my wrap dress and a coat, too, for the benefit of everyone on the Piccadilly line.

I couldn't see any other women in the queue, only men with artistic facial hair and long coats. We walked to a harshly lit locker room and got rid of our coats. I felt a whole lot less self-conscious when I saw how little everyone else was wearing beneath theirs. Sam kissed me, took me by the hand and led me down a corridor.

Everywhere I looked there were naked male bums attached to buff male bodies. It felt impolite to stare, so I tried to avert my gaze, but there was nowhere to avert it to, because everyone was pretty much naked. The social rules I'd obeyed all my life obviously didn't apply here, not when the outfit of choice for most of the men was a cock ring and nothing else. So I tried to calm the anxious, uptight voice in my head that was screeching 'My eyes!' and breathe, and smile. I'd never seen so many beautiful people. I found myself feeling grateful that I wasn't a gay man; they seemed to have put an awful lot more effort into their abs than I was prepared to.

As we walked past the men's toilets, I saw a man lying on the floor, with a plastic funnel attached to the mouth of his gimp mask.

I shuddered, internally, so as not to offend anyone. He looked like something out of a horror film.

'That's Jim,' said Sam.

'What's he doing?' I asked.

And that's when a man walked up to him and peed into the funnel.

'Yeah,' said Sam. 'He's kind of into extreme water sports.'

We came to a pulsing concrete dance floor filled with writhing, naked bodies. From the wild hand movements and beatific smiles, I'd say most people were on drugs.

'Let's get something,' I said to Sam. 'MDMA?' I noticed a shifty-looking man in a corner, too fully clothed, not joining in with the dancing. 'He looks like he might be selling.'

But Sam didn't like mixing drugs and sex. 'It dilutes the experience,' she said. 'I'm a purist when it comes to fucking.' And I took it from her tone that I wasn't allowed anything either.

The next room we went into was clearly a sex room. Gay porn was being projected onto the walls, the groans of the men just audible over the dance music. I stood in a corner and watched groups of men fucking each other, still feeling strange and distant, as though I wasn't really there. Occasionally a man would walk up to the group and start fucking someone, seemingly at random. Then he'd get bored and wander off again. I felt as though I was watching a nature documentary.

In the middle of the room were rows of slings, laid out like gothic hospital beds with neat little shelves full of toilet paper, latex gloves, lube and condoms. There were men lying in the slings, apparently waiting to be fucked by anyone at all who wandered past. Perhaps the element of surprise was sexy. I wondered what they'd think if I walked up and pulled on a glove.

'Do you fancy it?' Sam said, indicating a sling.

'I don't think they're interested in me,' I said.

'No. I mean, why don't you lie in one?'

I took a step away from the slings. 'No thanks,' I said. 'They don't look very hygienic.'

'Go on,' she said. 'It'll be fun.' She picked up the bottle of antiseptic spray the club had thoughtfully provided, and wiped the sling down. She patted the leather pillow. 'Hop up,' she said.

So I did. Climbing onto it was challenging – a bit like mounting a horse – but I managed it eventually. Sam helped me put my feet in the stirrups. I felt as though I was about to have a cervical smear.

Sam pulled on a glove. 'Wait,' I said. She didn't hear me, so I closed my eyes and pictured myself at home in my nice, clean bed, with my door firmly locked, but the sling was squeaking so loudly it was really putting me off my rhythm.

Just then, I felt someone groping, inexpertly, at my right breast. From the position Sam was in, I knew it couldn't be her. I opened my eyes to see one of the buff gay men touching me curiously, as though my breasts were exhibits in the interactive section of the Science Museum. He didn't seem that impressed.

I felt, distant, bemused. I wondered if I should feel something else – violated, maybe, or angry. I hadn't consented to him touching me. Had I? By being in this place, was I consenting to whatever happened? There didn't seem to be a lot of consent-seeking going on among the men. I shook my head at the man. He shrugged, and wandered off, leaving me wondering if it had really happened. I felt that strange, distracted, floating feeling again.

All the time, Sam was still fucking me. I wasn't really in the mood any more.

'Let's dance,' I said.

'I haven't finished,' Sam said.

I tried to sit up, but Sam pulled me back down and carried on. I could have pushed her away if I'd really wanted to. But there was something so sexy about her wanting to fuck me so badly that I felt myself getting turned on, and being in the sling made the sex more intense, and Sam said, 'My God, you're so open,' and before I knew it she was fisting me.

'That's fucking hot,' said another buff man, sauntering past.

I closed my eyes again, unsettled and aroused in equal measure, and had one of the most bizarre orgasms of my life.

Sam seemed satisfied after that. She said she felt too hot to dance in her Navy get-up, so she'd stand at the side and watch. I was grateful, actually. I was pleased to have some time on my own.

I felt self-conscious on the dance floor, just me in my gaffer tape and hundreds of naked men, but dancing has always relaxed me. I lifted up my hands and closed my eyes, and soon I felt elated, a strange artificial-feeling joy, as if I had taken MDMA after all. I caught the eye of a man wearing nothing but a cock ring. He smiled at me. 'I love your outfit! You look fabulous!' he said.

'So do you!' I said. And then I blushed, as I was essentially complimenting him on his penis. He asked me if I wanted to go outside for a cup of tea, and I realized there was nothing I'd like more.

His name was Gareth. He led me to a food truck selling tea and Wagon Wheels. We sat at picnic tables, which left grooves on our naked thighs, and chatted away to the other naked men.

'Lovely weather for it tonight,' said a man in a gimp mask. He'd unzipped the mouth and was nibbling on a KitKat. 'Feels like Barcelona in the middle of summer.'

'I've never been there,' I said.

'Oh, you must go,' said Gimp Mask Man. 'The Gaudí architecture is stunning.'

Talk soon turned to careers, and I told the others that I worked in the Civil Service. 'My husband does, too!' said Gimp Mask Man. 'Something to do with roads. Sounds very boring to me.'

'What do you do?' I asked Gareth.

'I hate it when people ask me that,' he said. 'It's so embarrassing.'

183

'Go on,' I said. 'Tell me.'

'I'm an accountant,' he said.

'That's not boring,' said Gimp Mask Man. 'That's sexy. So authoritative.'

'Do you really think so?' said Gareth.

Everyone nodded, impressed.

'Julia?' I turned. Sam was standing in the doorway. 'I've been looking for you everywhere.'

'Sorry,' I said, standing up. I had done something wrong again. 'I was worried.'

'Sorry,' I said again. I smiled an apology to my new friends.

Gareth raised his eyebrows. 'I guess we know who wears the trousers in your relationship,' he said.

'Gareth,' said Gimp Mask Man. 'That's homophobic.'

'I'm only joking,' said Gareth, but it stung. I didn't like what he'd implied. I wanted to be in a relationship where we both wore the trousers. Matching ones, preferably, with elasticated waists.

Sam apologized for calling me away from my cup of tea, which made me feel much better about Gareth's trouser comment and everything else. She had just been worried that I'd been abducted by a fetish-loving bisexual with a penchant for gaffer tape.

'I get a bit overprotective sometimes,' she said, as we walked back inside. 'I couldn't bear it if something happened to you.'

'Nothing's going to happen to me,' I said, and she hugged me tight. I was flattered by her fierceness.

I'd had enough of the club, though. The sky was beginning to get light, and my eyes were stinging with exhaustion. Sam and I collected our things from the locker room and walked hand in hand out into the dawn.

'So, what did you think?' asked Sam, on the night bus back to hers. I looked out of the window on the upper deck, my head on her shoulder. We were crossing Waterloo Bridge and the lights of London were reflected in the Thames.

I thought about it: the problematic orgasm, the unsolicited groping, the gimp masks, how uncomfortable and turned on I'd felt at the same time. And then I thought about the attractive gay men, and the strange rush of elation I'd experienced, and the lovely chat I'd had with Gareth over a Wagon Wheel. 'I liked it,' I said.

'Good,' she said, squeezing my hand. 'I was worried you wouldn't get it. Makes you feel alive, doesn't it?'

I thought about it. 'Yes,' I said.

'That's what I love about SM. It forces you to live in the moment.' She pulled me closer. 'Talking of which,' she said, 'I love you.' She smiled at me expectantly. 'I haven't said that to anyone for a while.'

'I love you too,' I said, and saying it seemed to confirm it. The feeling filled me up all of a sudden, like liquid, and it seemed as if some might spill out through my eyes, which would have been embarrassing, because who cries when someone tells you they love you?

'Babes,' Sam said, kissing my face. 'Don't cry. You don't need to worry. You're safe with me. I'm not going anywhere.'

Whenever I wake up with a hangover of shame – when I've cried about something that seemed important at midnight but trivial at 10 a.m., or come on to someone who turns out to be deeply unattracted to me, or had sex in public at an SM club – I go to the most comforting place I can think of, which is the Oxford Street branch of Marks & Spencer. The smell of the cotton pyjamas and chicken-and-stuffing sandwiches reminds me of my granddad, and it's a good opportunity to stock up on black high-leg underpants. The morning after the SM club, I had one of the biggest hangovers of shame I'd ever experienced. The disjointed, floating feeling had drained away while I was asleep, leaving a grainy, dirty guilt behind, like the detritus at the bottom of a sink.

Alice came with me that Sunday morning. We walked around the hosiery department, Alice whispering 'Gimp masks?' and 'Cock rings!' while I said 'Shh!' and tried to look interested in support tights.

'Having sex in a sling . . . that's another thing I'll never do now I'm settled with Dave,' Alice said. She held up the sample tights to her arm and asked, 'Do you think I should get sixty denier, or eighty?'

'Sixty,' I said. 'Is Dave the only thing stopping you going to a gay sex club?'

'You know what I mean,' she said, looking at me with what could have been envy, but I wasn't sure, as it had been so long since someone had looked at me enviously. 'You're really living.'

M&S was working its magic, and as I thought about the previous night, about the extreme water sports and the public fisting and the ripped bodies in leather harnesses, I felt a bit more positive about the whole thing. I'd had fun, and some of it had been pretty hot. Something to tell the grandchildren, if I ever had any. When they were over eighteen.

The best thing had been Sam's declaration on the night bus, and the teary kiss we'd shared, and the intense sex we'd had that night, whispering, 'I love you,' to each other instead of breathing, practically. That was love, and Alice had that already.

'Settling down is really living,' I said to Alice. 'That's what people are supposed to do in their twenties.'

'It's not. Having sex in public is what you're supposed to do in your twenties. Settling down is for your thirties. If you have to do it at all.' She'd walked over to the sock section and was fingering an ankle-length three pack.

'Well, then, you're breaking the mould.'

'I can't do it, Julia.'

She looked at me. She was about to cry.

I could see a shop assistant walking towards us, probably to ask if we needed any help; there's only so long you can look at black cotton socks without attracting attention. I took Alice's arm and led her to the lingerie section.

Tears were slipping silently down her face now. She pushed them away with the back of her hand. 'I'm so spoilt,' she said. 'I love Dave. I just don't want to be a wife.'

I frowned. 'But you're not a wife,' I said. 'He hasn't even asked you to be his wife. He just said he wanted to get married at some point in the future.'

She didn't say anything.

I felt an odd prickle — of jealousy, maybe, or envy, or fear. 'What,' I said, 'you didn't get married in secret, did you?'

She shook her head, but not particularly convincingly.

'But he has asked you to marry him.'

She nodded.

'And you said yes.'

She nodded again. She didn't look the way you might expect a newly engaged person to look: smug and shiny and waving her left hand around so that you'd notice her ring. She looked guilty and miserable.

I said 'Congratulations?' with a question mark at the end.

'You aren't happy about it,' she said.

'*You* don't seem happy about it!' I said. 'I don't know what you want me to say!'

The shop assistant looked over. I picked up a bra to justify our lingering.

'Now it looks like you're shouting at me because I don't like pink bras,' said Alice.

'I'm not shouting at you,' I said, which I realized wasn't actually true when the shop assistant looked over at me again.

'What should I do?' Alice asked, looking so unhappy that I reached out and hugged her. We didn't hug each other that often now that we lived together. As I hugged her I smelled her hair and it took me back to university, and I felt a sudden nostalgia for the girls we had been, no commitments to anyone or anything, everything ahead of us, free to make philosophies about marriage and gender politics and career choices without having to put them into practice.

'What do you think, really?' Alice said, into my neck.

'It doesn't matter what I think,' I said, which told her exactly what I thought, obviously.

I felt Alice begin to shake. I tried to pull away to look at her but she hugged me closer and then heaved out a sob.

I grabbed her hand and pulled her down, out of the sight of the Marks & Spencer staff, so that we were sitting on the carpet, our heads amongst the thongs.

'What was I supposed to say?' asked Alice. 'He went down on one knee in front of *EastEnders*.'

'That's romantic,' I said.

'He didn't think I'd want a fuss.'

'But why did he propose in the first place?'

Alice shrugged. 'His parents got married after six weeks and they're still together. And someone he's friends with on Facebook got diagnosed with testicular cancer, so I think he's decided life is short.'

'Too short to marry someone you're not sure about,' I said.

'But I *am* sure about him. I'm just not sure I want to be a wife.'

'So tell him that. Just tell him that. If he loves you, he'll understand. And you're still sharing a flat with me. You should live on your own, first, just the two of you, see how that works.'

She looked up at me. 'He'll understand, won't he?'

'Yes,' I said, as if I knew anything about it.

'I'll just tell him I made a mistake.'

'That's what you'll do.'

'OK.'

She put her head on my shoulder and we sat there for a while. 'But maybe I *do* want to marry him.'

I looked at her.

'I don't know what I want! I don't want to lose him!'

'Excuse me?' said a voice from somewhere above us. We looked up. The shop assistant had found us. 'Can I help you?' she said.

I stood up with as much dignity as I could muster under the circumstances, which was not a lot, and held the bra up.

'I'm just looking for a bra for my girlfriend's birthday,' I said.

'What?' she said, frowning, and then, 'Oh, right. Right.' She seemed a bit flustered. 'Right. Happy birthday,' she said to Alice, who was still sitting on the floor. 'I'll let you ladies get on with it, then.'

As she backed away, I sat back down next to Alice.

She smiled at me. 'She thought I was a lesbian.'

'That's right,' I said.

'So I don't look boring and conservative at all.'

'No.'

'I'm thinking about getting a tattoo!'

'There you go,' I said.

'And even if I did get married, I still wouldn't be boring or conservative.'

'No,' I said. 'Caitlin Moran is married.'

'You're right!' she said. 'And Chimamanda Ngozi Adichie!'

'And Amy Poehler!'

'She's divorced.'

'Which would be an option for you if it doesn't work out.'

'You're right!' Alice said. We left the shop and walked arm in arm out onto the pavement, and we pushed through the crowds of pedestrians, naming cool married people until it was time to go our separate ways.

23. NOT THAT KIND OF MARRIED PERSON

Alice and Dave went away to the country for a long weekend in June, which was nice, as it meant Sam and I had the flat to ourselves. We had sex on the kitchen worktop, which made me a little anxious for food hygiene reasons, and on the sofa (wipe-clean, as I've mentioned). We did it in the shower, too, though I kept choking on the water when I was going down on her, which wasn't very sexy.

When Alice and Dave came back, she was wearing a lovely antique emerald ring, and their engagement was official. I hugged Alice, and Sam and Dave slapped each other on the back, and we toasted their future with warm Freixenet from the off-licence. Alice looked really happy. She even asked me to be her bridesmaid.

'You won't have to wear a terrible dress,' she promised. 'And I don't want a hen party.'

'I'm fine with organizing a hen party.'

'I just want you to help me choose a dress and stop me freaking out.'

'I'd be honoured,' I said, and I meant it. But then I thought of something. 'Do you want me to move out?' I asked in a quiet voice, so Dave wouldn't hear.

Alice grabbed my sleeve and pulled me towards the window. 'No! Why would I want you to move out?'

'Married people don't usually live with flatmates,' I said, although the idea of leaving gave me a horrible lurching feeling, like vertigo, or riding on a night bus after too many vodkas.

Alice looked horrified. 'Please don't move out. I don't want to be that kind of married person.'

'What,' I said, 'a married person that can walk around naked whenever they want?'

'No!' she hissed. 'A grown-up married person! And just because we're married, it doesn't mean we'll suddenly be able to afford the rent on our own. We'll be skint. We'll have spent all our money on chair covers and two weeks in Mauritius.'

'You could move somewhere cheaper. You could move to Zone Four.'

'Oh God.'

'Don't you think Dave will want it to be just the two of you?'

We looked across at Dave. He was doing a bicep curl to show Sam how much his muscles had developed since he'd started doing yoga videos.

'I don't know,' Alice said in a small voice.

'You might actually like it,' I told her, and I gave her a hug. I didn't want to have to find a new place to live. In my experience, looking for a flatshare in London is like going to a series of interviews for jobs you don't really want, and being accepted or rejected (but mostly rejected, let's face it) on the basis of your taste in Netflix box sets.

I was happy for Alice and Dave, though; I was so in love with Sam that my anti-marriage principles were flying out of the window. I found myself having daydreams about a wedding in a registry office somewhere, Sam in a suit, me in an ironic white dress, making a political statement of the whole thing but still meaning every word of our vows. Virginie could be Sam's bridesmaid, I decided. In my daydreams, Sam had ended things with Virginie because of her overwhelming love for me. Virginie had taken it brilliantly and bought us the Le Creuset casserole dish from our wedding list.

My wedding fantasies intensified a few nights later. I was lying next to Sam, about to fall asleep, when she said, 'If Alice and Dave want to live on their own, you could move in with me.'

Those were the most romantic words I had ever heard. They implied love and commitment and visits to IKEA. They were the opposite of, 'I have a French lover who enjoys being spanked with a hairbrush.' I looked at Sam. 'Really?'

'Really. Like I said, I love you.'

'I love you' was still new and powerful. I leaned across to kiss her, feeling slightly drunk with happiness. 'I love you, too,' I said.

Absolutely no one else thought that me moving in with Sam was a good idea. Ella told me that three months was way too soon, even for lesbians, and said she'd ask around to see if any of her friends needed a flatmate. Zhu agreed. 'You don't know if you're going to like being poly yet. You should have your own space.' And Cat, who was in Birmingham, deep in rehearsals for her next show, a Theatre in Education production about the solar system in which she was playing both the planet Mercury and the spaceship *Vostok 1*, begged me not to 'do something so fucking stupid'. She would be back in London after the summer. If I could just hang on until then, I could move in with her.

I was disappointed; I wanted my friends to feel as recklessly enthusiastic about Sam as I was. But I'd told them too much about her.

So when Sam called me a couple of days later during my lunch break and asked what I was thinking about moving in, I told her I didn't think it was a good idea. I felt I was making an extremely mature, sensible decision.

'That's cool,' she said. 'I totally get it.'

'We haven't met each other's families,' I pointed out.

'We should change that, anyway,' she said. 'Parents love me. We could go up to Oxford this weekend if you like.'

'Can I meet your dad too?'

Sam didn't reply straight away. 'It's not like we can just go to Dubai for tea,' she said. And then: 'Let's start with your parents. You actually like spending time with your parents.'

Which was putting it a bit strongly, but I took her point.

24. I HOPE YOU'VE BROUGHT YOUR PYJAMAS

A couple of weeks later, Sam and I were standing on my parents' doorstep, hand in hand. She was wearing a suit – all black, as usual – and I was wearing a dress that I'd actually ironed. I'd never felt more heteronormative, apart from the fact that we both had vaginas.

Mum was very welcoming. 'Sam!' she said as she opened the door. 'Lovely jacket. I was wondering if I could get away with masculine tailoring, what do you think?'

'Definitely,' Sam said.

'I hope you've brought your pyjamas,' Mum said, as she led us through the hall.

'I haven't, actually, Mrs Blunt,' Sam said. 'But I hope you'll let me stay anyway.'

'Yes! Ahahahaha! Ahahaha!' said Mum, nudging Sam to show how OK she was with the whole thing. 'And call me Jenny, please.'

'I will.'

Mum giggled and looked away. I hate the word giggle, but unfortunately that's what she was doing. I felt queasy. My mother was flirting with my girlfriend.

Dad was in the kitchen, chopping vegetables. He didn't look up when we came in.

'Martin? Julia and Sam are here.'

'Hello,' said Dad, still not looking up.

'I've brought some wine,' said Sam, waving the bottle.

'Lovely,' Mum said, taking it from her. 'Claret. Martin loves claret, don't you, Martin?'

Dad grunted and kept chopping.

Sam and I looked at each other.

'Why don't you take Sam to your room?' said Mum. 'I'll give you a shout when dinner's ready.'

We stepped over the optimistic airbed my parents had made up on the floor and lay down, side by side, on my childhood single bed.

'I don't know why my dad's being so weird,' I said as we stared up at the glow-in-the-dark stars I'd stuck on the ceiling as a teenager.

'Don't worry about it,' Sam said.

'He's not normally like this. He's being so rude—'

'He's getting used to the idea of you being with a woman. Give him a bit of time.'

'This is the twenty-first century.'

'But things were different when he grew up.' Sam stroked my hair. 'My mum went nuts when I told her I was gay.'

'How old were you?' I asked, trying to sound casual. Sometimes Sam shut me down when I asked her too many questions about herself. I'd asked her about her coming-out story before, but she'd been oddly vague about it.

'Thirteen,' Sam said, flicking a speck of lint from her trousers.

'Did she come round?'

She shook her head. 'She was diagnosed just after I came out to her. We never talked about it properly, or made up.'

'I'm so sorry. That's really shit.'

'It is.'

'When did she die?' I asked, trying to look appropriately serious, trying not to show how pleased I was that she was opening up at last.

'About a year after that.'

'God, I'm so sorry.'

'You said that already.'

'I don't know what else to say.'

'There's nothing to say. It's just shit. That's why I don't talk about it.' She shifted closer to me. 'Anyway. Things are different these days. Your dad will get over it.'

'You're right.'

'I'm always right.' And she started to kiss me.

'Stop it,' I said. I could hear my parents in the kitchen, voices raised.

'Why?' Sam said. 'Have you ever had sex in this bed?'

I shook my head.

'Time to christen it, then. Better late than never.' She pulled my dress over my head and pushed her hand into my pants and fucked me as I bit my hand to stop myself crying out as I came, which I did just before Mum called 'Dinner!' conveniently.

Dad warmed up a bit during the meal itself; he couldn't keep ignoring Sam, because he's not a rude man really, and Sam was asking very thoughtful questions about his academic work. I was really touched by how lovely Mum was with Sam – touched and ever so slightly disturbed, as she brushed Sam's hand every time she asked her a question and laughed so hard at her jokes that I could see the fillings in her back teeth.

After we'd finished our main course, Mum cleared the table, and there was a bit of a lull in the conversation – a pretty uncomfortable lull. I decided to fill it by announcing to the room that Alice was getting married, which I soon realized was a mistake.

'Good for her,' Dad said. 'To that northern chap?'

'Yes,' I said. 'Dave.'

'Ah well,' he said.

'Martin,' warned Mum from the other end of the kitchen.

'What?' Dad said, wiping his mouth with his napkin.

'Don't,' said Mum.

'I didn't say anything,' said Dad.

'But you were thinking something,' I said.

'What? I just said, "Ah, well." A perfectly normal thing to say, under the circumstances.'

'What circumstances?' I asked, ignoring Sam, who was shaking her head.

'Well. I don't suppose you'll be getting married now.'

'Now what?'

'You know what.'

'Now that I'm going out with a woman?'

'Yes.'

'Maybe I won't.'

'You know perfectly well that lesbians can get married, Martin,' said Mum.

'Not in a church,' said Dad.

'Dad. You never go to church.'

'Your mother and I got married in a church, thank you very much.'

'And you'll be buried in a church. Soon, if you don't stop this,' said Mum.

Saying goodnight after we'd had our coffee was a bit awkward, too. Dad seemed very aware that we were going into the same bedroom. I fucked Sam that night – it seemed a waste not to, seeing as my parents clearly assumed we'd be shagging anyway. Afterwards we slept top-to-toe in the single bed like children at a sleepover.

I woke up the next morning to find Sam already awake, standing at the window. I'd slept for ages, judging by the angle of the sun, which was lighting up Sam's hair and her cheekbones and the curve of her thigh. How was it possible that someone so absurdly attractive fancied me? I felt stupidly lucky.

I shifted in bed and Sam turned to look at me. 'You're beautiful,' she said, which made me *feel* beautiful.

'What time is it?' I asked. I could hear my parents in the kitchen, clattering cutlery and arguing in their morning argument voices (quieter than their evening argument voices). 'What do you want to do today?' It was a bright blue day, a perfect day for punting. I had a vision of rowing Sam down the Cherwell, showing off my superior steering skills, while she lay back, sipping Pimm's in a straw boater, admiring me.

'Nearly eleven. I'd like to see what's on at Modern Art Oxford. We could stay for dinner if you want.'

'I have to get back by about five,' I told her. 'It's the swing dancing social tonight.'

Sam turned to look out of the window. I couldn't see her face, but she had extremely expressive shoulders, and her shoulders were not happy with me.

'Come, if you like,' I said.

'Obviously I don't want to come,' she said. 'I don't like swing dance.'

'OK,' I said.

She turned to look at me. 'You always choose your dance friends over me.'

That was so blatantly untrue that I laughed.

'Don't make fun of me,' she said.

'I'm not,' I said, walking over to her. I wasn't going to let her guilt-trip me out of going. 'Come on. I can take you to my favourite brunch place in the Covered Market. Shall we do that?'

She didn't say anything, but she let me hug her.

And then she looked up at me and said, 'Sorry, babes.'

'That's OK,' I said.

'I just miss you when you go out without me.'

'Come back soon, darlings,' Mum said as we left the house. She walked out onto the front step in her slippers to give Sam a too-tight hug.

'We will,' said Sam, once she had been released. 'So lovely to meet you. Come and see us in London! I promise to show you a good time . . .'

'I'd love that!' giggled my mother.

I was glad I hadn't eaten breakfast yet.

'Aren't you going to come and say goodbye, Martin?' Mum called.

Dad padded out into the hallway. 'Lovely to meet you,' he said, holding out his hand, but Sam pulled him into a hug.

He stood there for a few moments before bending his right arm at the elbow, like someone doing an impression of a robot, and patting her three times on the back.

'God, Martin, relax!' Mum said, rolling her eyes at Sam, hand on hip. She reminded me of myself, trying to be cool. I resolved never to try and be cool again.

Sam didn't hold my hand as we walked into town. I pointed out places from my childhood as we passed them – my primary school, the community centre where I had done my first ballet lessons. I took her to Christchurch Meadows and pointed out the cows that students had once painted blue and the sprawling plane tree that had inspired Lewis Carroll to write 'Jabberwocky'. She nodded and smiled, but smiling looked like an effort.

'It's funny that people still read *Alice in Wonderland*, even though Lewis Carroll probably wrote it for an actual child that he was in love with, but it's not OK to watch Woody Allen films.'

She nodded again.

I was beginning to feel desperate. I wasn't sure where the weekend had gone wrong. My punting fantasies were fading rapidly. There's no point rowing someone down a river if they're not going to appreciate it. It's a waste of upper body strength. 'Please talk to me,' I said.

'I'm just hungry,' she said.

So I took her to the Covered Market, up a rickety staircase

to a little café that was plastered with posters of Jim Morrison and served lentils and chickpeas and generally wished it was in the Seventies. We ate a heavy vegetarian breakfast in a heavy silence.

And maybe she had just been hungry, because as Sam ate her last mouthful of eggs, she looked up and smiled at me.

'You're back,' I said.

'Sorry,' she said.

'That's OK,' I said. 'Better?'

She nodded. 'Art gallery now?'

'Sure,' I said.

On the way out of the market, we passed the unapologetic butcher where pheasants and rabbits and deer hang upside down by the legs, dripping blood on the stone floor, staring at you reproachfully for not being vegan.

'Fancy some venison for dinner?' Sam said, pointing.

'No thanks,' I said.

'Polly told me about a lovely restaurant on the river—'

'The Cherwell Boathouse?'

'That's the one,' she said.

She took me by the shoulders and turned me towards her. I looked into her eyes and laughed, they were so beautiful.

'You don't really have to go to the dance thing tonight, do you? Let me buy you dinner. To celebrate me meeting your parents. What do you say, babes?'

I sighed. I wanted to stay with her. I wanted to stare at her amazing face in flickering candlelight and toast our relationship with cava. 'I told everyone I'd be there,' I said.

'You can just say you changed your mind.' She kissed me. 'I hear they do an amazing chocolate tart,' she said.

She had chosen her words wisely.

'OK,' I said. 'I'll stay.'

And Sam pumped the air with her fist and kissed me properly, right there on the High Street, watched by old men drinking lunchtime pints in the Mitre and blonde students about to spend their student loans in Reiss.

I called home on the way back from Sam's the next day to say thank you for dinner. Dad picked up the phone.

'What did you think?' I asked.

'Of what?'

'You know of what.'

'She seemed perfectly nice.'

I laughed.

'Why are you laughing? What am I supposed to say?'

'You're supposed to say she seems lovely and that you're happy for me.'

'Well—'

'Well what?'

'Never mind.'

'What were you going to say?'

'Well. If you're going to go out with a woman, fine. I like women myself. Totally understand the attraction. But why don't you go out with one who actually *looks* like a woman?'

I could hear my mum in the background saying, 'Martin!'

'She does look like a woman,' I said. 'She looks like a butch woman.'

'She looks like a man. She has short hair—'

'So does Mum!'

'But your mother doesn't wear men's suits, does she?'

'I hope none of your students know about your reactionary views,' I said. 'Haven't you heard of no-platforming?'

'They can't no-platform me,' said Dad. 'I basically *am* the platform!'

My mother took the phone from him at that point. 'Please don't pay him any attention,' she said. 'I don't know what's got into him. He's like William Wordsworth. Liked to think of himself as a radical in his youth, but he's got horribly conservative in his old age.'

'I am not like William Wordsworth!' shouted Dad. 'I am not conservative!'

'Tell him he is,' I said.

'You are,' Mum said to him.

I could hear Dad ranting on about always voting Labour and young people moving the goalposts and how much he'd always loved Noël Coward, who was 'very queer indeed', but Mum was ignoring him. 'Sam's lovely,' she said. 'I've always found masculine women rather attractive myself.'

'Thanks, Mum,' I said, willing her to stop speaking.

'Something nice about people on the boundaries of gender, I've always thought.'

Dad was still muttering in the background, something about how it wasn't 1979 any more.

'And she has beautiful hair. I'm rather envious of it, in fact. Tell her she's welcome any time. I'm very pleased you've found each other.'

25. ALL OF THE BAD WORDS

Owen and I were standing by the biscuit cupboard that Monday when Smriti walked up to us, trailed by Tom, who looked even more miserable than usual. 'Can we have a quick chat?' she said, motioning to Uzo who was walking slowly back from the kitchen with a peppermint tea. 'In the meeting room?'

Owen looked as apprehensive as I felt. I'd had several 'quick chats' in meeting rooms over the years and nearly all of them had ended in tears (mine). I'd had one with the ballet mistress at the English National Ballet after breaking my ankle and with the physiotherapist who told me I'd never dance *en pointe* again.

We took our seats in the meeting room. Owen tapped his pen against the table until Uzo said to him, 'Stop it, eh?'

Smriti steepled her fingers and smiled at us all. 'I just wanted to let you know that we're undertaking a strategic review of the unit.'

I looked across at Tom who was slumped in his chair, muttering darkly. I looked at Owen too. He was staring straight down at the table. My heart started hammering. I did care about losing my job, it turned out.

Smriti carried on talking, using all of the bad words – 'merging' and 'restructuring' and 'rationalizing' and 'fit for purpose'. 'I want you to know that each and every one of you adds value to the team,' she said. 'But there is a possibility that some of you will be redeployed, and there may be some redundancies.'

The word 'redeployed' made me think of Eric. I told myself to look on the bright side. There were worse things in the world than being made redundant.

'It's going to be OK,' Owen whispered, when we got back to our desks.

'How is it going to be OK? She said they were going to keep one Correspondence Officer in the merged team. One! And there are three of us! Uzo's definitely getting it.'

Owen crouched by my desk. 'They've posted the SEO jobs. Two Senior Account Manager roles in Internal Comms.'

I turned back to my computer and loaded the Civil Service jobs website. The Senior Account Manager jobs were right at the top of the page. 'We need excellent verbal and written communication skills, and the ability to think creatively.' I looked at Owen. 'We might actually be qualified.'

'Want to go to the pub tonight and work on the application form together?'

My fear of unemployment had taken over my fear of rejection, so I said, 'OK.'

Uzo wandered over, mug in hand, on the way to the kitchen, and saw what was on my screen. 'You applying for the Senior Account Manager jobs?'

'We both are,' said Owen.

'Shh,' I said.

Uzo made a tutting noise. 'You two are crazy,' she said. 'Why would you want to be in charge of things? Do you know how hard you have to work when you're in charge?'

Owen and I spent two hours going through the application form, ignoring the shouts of the middle-aged men watching football on the other side of the pub. We had to give 250-word examples of times we had embodied Civil Service Behaviours and Strengths.

'I don't think I'm analytical,' I said, looking at the list of strengths. 'But I'm quite inclusive. Don't you think?'

Owen nodded. 'You never leave anyone out of a tea round.'

I like to think I'm quite good at writing, but there's nothing more frustrating than trying to describe a time you Delivered at Pace in a limited word count, particularly when you've never delivered anything at pace in your life, except the lattes you made during your summer job at Starbucks. By 8.30 p.m. I'd only answered one question out of twenty. And then Alice texted, saying she'd made Bolognese and did I want some, so I decided to go home. The deadline wasn't for a couple of weeks, anyway.

As Owen hugged me goodbye, I asked him, 'Do you want to come? Alice says there's enough food,' to prove how inclusive I was.

He shook his head. 'I'm going to keep going,' he said, 'because I have determination and persistence.'

I had just finished washing up the Bolognese pan when Cat called.

'How's the solar system show going?' I asked her.

'Shit,' she said. 'A kid threw up on my shoes when I was singing my planet Mercury song today.'

'Poor you,' I said cheerfully.

I told her about the redundancies at work.

'Just quit!' she said. 'You can be in *Menstruation: the Musical!* Did I tell you we got funding?'

'No!'

'I know! Actual Arts Council money! We're being paid, baby! We're going to Edinburgh!'

'Wow!' I said. I hugged a cushion for comfort.

'It's going to be funny but really political. Lacey wrote this proposal, all about how the show's going to increase awareness of period poverty. Did you know that asylum seekers only get about £38 a week to live on? And they're not allowed to work? So most of them can't afford sanitary products?'

'I didn't. The show sounds amazing.'

'We're still looking for someone to play the tampon. It's quite a big part.'

'I'm not sure I've got the gravitas to pull off a role like that,' I said.

Cat sighed. 'Just admit that you're scared.'

'OK,' I said. 'I'm scared.' And as soon as I said it I started to cry. 'I can't not have a salary,' I said.

'If you lose your job you won't have a salary anyway,' Cat pointed out.

'I'm not going to do it. I'm sorry,' I said.

'Yeah, well. I'm sorry too,' said Cat.

'Will you sing me the planet Mercury song to cheer me up?'

'Fuck off.'

Saying no to the musical made me feel even more determined to get the SEO job, so the following evening I came straight home from work and sat down at my laptop. I did my best to pretend I had 'pride and enthusiasm in public service' and that I 'allowed colleagues the time and authority to meet objectives', and by the time Alice banged through the door at midnight, drunk after a book launch, I'd finished the whole application.

'Want me to proofread it?' Alice asked, swigging orange juice from the bottle.

'Oh, yes please,' I said, standing back to let her see.

She bent over my computer. She smelled of stale wine. 'There's quite a lot of jargon in this,' she said.

'I know,' I said. 'It's the Civil Service. You have to use jargon.'

'But it doesn't make sense.'

'I don't think it matters.'

Alice gave an exaggerated, drunken shrug. 'I'm going to eat some cheese. Want some?'

'No thanks,' I said. I sat down in front of my laptop again and pressed submit. It was time to start believing in myself.

26. SAM LOVES JULIA

That June, London was hotter than I ever remember it being – too hot, really, considering the number of extremely sweaty men on the Underground. But the city was beautiful – the buildings looked as though they were posing for photographs, turning their best sides towards the light, and as I looked out at the Houses of Parliament and Westminster Abbey from my office window each morning I felt lucky to be where I was, in London and in love.

That July I went to my first Pride as an out lesbian, the first where I could walk down the road in rainbow face paint, holding hands with a gorgeous woman, willing people to take photographs of us kissing. Pride is exactly what I felt. I was bursting with the newness of being queer, and it was wonderful.

The Stepping Out crew were marching in the parade, dressed in sequins, behind a group of lesbian volleyball players, but Sam and I rode on the Stonewall float, just the two of us; a friend of a friend of hers worked for them. We sailed down Regent Street, waving like queens, watching Barclays employees hand out leaflets about savings accounts and socialists shouting about the commercialization of Pride. There were queer Muslims and drag queens on stilts and a bus full of LGBT pensioners and men in leather, and all of them were smiling, and I felt so grateful to be one of them that I almost cried. I put my arms around Sam's waist and kissed

208

her cheek. Lady Gaga was pumping from the float's sound system. Balloons swayed and twisted in the breeze. On the pavement below, a man in a sequinned jacket played with a yoyo. A group of football fans leaned out of a pub window to cheer for us. I felt gloriously alive.

Whenever I stayed at Sam's she would make me breakfast and we'd open the windows wide, breathing the fresh air and marvelling at the birdsong, wondering what the birds were saying to each other. One morning, as I was washing up our bowls, Sam wrote *SAM LOVES JULIA* on the steamed-up kitchen window and I finally understood what swooning felt like. After work every day, we hurled ourselves at the nearest green space to drink corner-shop wine or went to pretentious street food pop-ups to Snapchat our rice noodles. We went to the open-air theatre once to watch *A Midsummer Night's Dream*, and laughed at all the Shakespearean jokes. I even got a few of them.

I wanted to tell everyone about my relationship and the incredible sex I was having. I found myself coming out to baristas at Starbucks and smiling at lesbians in the street in the hope they'd recognize me as one of their own, and I even described fisting to Owen over lunch one day. He was very grateful for the information.

'Carys never tells me anything,' he said.

'That's probably appropriate,' I pointed out. 'She's your sister.'

'I guess,' he said. 'So – gloves?'

'And lube. And take it slowly.'

'Right,' he said. And then: 'How can I tell if a woman's up for it, though?'

'You could ask her,' I said.

'OK,' he said. 'I mean – in theory. Next time someone agrees to have sex with me.'

That afternoon we got back to our desks to find that we had both been invited to interview for the Senior Account Manager jobs. We ran into a meeting room and jumped up and down, and that night we celebrated with a picnic in Green Park. Maybe we had futures after all.

Sam decided to combine the private view for her show with her thirtieth birthday and throw a massive party. 'The woman who owns the gallery owes me one, to be fair. I made her come, like, nine times last time I saw her,' she told me one hot night as we drank beers in London Fields, the smoke of other people's barbecues stinging our eyes.

I had a vision of the gallery owner lying back on a pile of David Hockney canvases while Sam licked champagne off her nipples. Clearly the sensible part of me knew that Hockneys are kept in carefully controlled atmospheric conditions and the best you get at most private views is a warm can of Stella, but I've always had a strong imagination.

'Don't you miss it?' I asked.

'Miss what?'

'Miss having sex with other people.'

'Not at the moment,' she said, reaching for my hand. 'You and I have only just got started. And anyway, I know we'll enjoy other people eventually.'

I put my beer down and kissed her, hard. She seemed surprised, but she kissed me back, and we ended up having fully clothed sex right there on the grass, Sam looking at the people around us, daring someone to notice. I tried to unbutton Sam's jeans so I could fuck her too, but she stopped me, gripping my hand a little too tightly. 'No,' she said. 'You only get to touch me in private.'

27. THIS IS WHERE
THE MAGIC HAPPENS

Sam was spending almost all of her time in the studio now, adding finishing touches to some of her more recent portraits. I didn't like to think about how recent they were, or what had happened just before she'd painted them, or why she hadn't painted me yet. It's not that I thought I deserved to be immortalized in art – I'm not a Tudor aristocrat or a nineteenth-century horse – but I wanted her to *want* to paint me.

I went to her studio for the first time one hot Saturday. The entrance was behind an unmarked door off Kingsland High Street, down an alley speckled with pigeon shit. Sam led me up the concrete stairs to the large damp room she shared with Polly.

'This is where the magic happens!' Sam said, arms spread wide, turning around in the space, gazing up at the ceiling as if it was the Sistine Chapel rather than a corner of a warehouse with foam ceiling tiles and graffiti on the front door reading *WEEP* and *Where's the East End gone?* and *Hackney has cancer.*

'I think this is the most hipster place I have ever been,' I said, waving to Polly, who was sitting at a slanting desk under one of the windows. 'You could rent it out for weddings. You'd just need one of those giant *LOVE* signs, made out of light bulbs.'

Polly gave me one of her half-smiles. 'That's not a bad idea. It's not like I'm making any money from my paintings. Maybe I should become an events planner.'

Sam laughed and put her hand on Polly's shoulder. 'Babes. You couldn't organize a piss-up in a brewery. No offence.'

I could see Sam's point – even if Polly hadn't been there, it would have been clear which side of the studio was hers and which side was Sam's. Polly's side was messy and personal and chaotic, like a teenage girl's bedroom, with piles of magazines beneath the desk, tubes of half-used paint lying all over the place, photographs torn from magazines pinned to a board, along with photos of Jasper, and her, and Sam. Sam's side was orderly, private, controlled. Her paints were arranged in plastic IKEA boxes. Her canvases were lined up beneath the window in size order. It looked less like an artist's studio and more like the sort of place a psychopath might dismember you, tidily.

'Cup of tea?' Polly asked, pushing her chair back from her desk.

I started to nod, but Sam said, 'No, thanks. We're going out for tacos in a minute, aren't we?' She took my hand and led me to her side of the studio. 'I just wanted to show Julia my paintings.'

She turned the canvases around and spread them out so that they were lined up like suspects for a very sexy crime. I didn't recognize any of the women, and I was glad at first. But then I wondered who they were, and when she had painted them. Had they come here and sat for her while I was at work?

'I think there's a piece missing,' Sam said, hands on hips. 'It's just a collection of portraits at the moment.'

'So?' I asked, turning to look at her.

'So, there's not enough edge. I've had an idea. I think you'll like it.'

I turned back to the paintings. One of the women had an awful lot of pubic hair. Sam had painted each hair painstakingly in different shades of black and brown and red and gold.

'What's your idea?' I asked.

She raised her eyebrows, jogged over to a shelf and picked up another canvas to show me. It was a painting of her right fist, fluorescent pink and orange and yellow, so detailed that I recognized it instantly; there was the freckle on the knuckle on her ring finger, the sickle-shaped scar near her thumb.

Sam was looking at me, waiting for a reaction. I felt Polly looking at me, too. 'What do you think?' asked Sam.

'It's wonderful,' I said, which it was, in a way.

'Do you get it?' she asked.

I nodded, but I didn't get it at all. And I didn't really like it.

The night before the private view, Sam and I went down to the gallery for the hanging. It was one of those large, cold East London spaces that used to be a tram shed and features a lot of concrete and corrugated iron. Sam liked the roughness of the space – it would contrast nicely with the refined, curving lines of her paintings. The show was called *Women, Naked*, and she had decided to hang the bare canvases on the rough walls, so that the paintings would be as naked as their subjects. That's what she said, anyway. I think she might just have been trying to save money on frames.

Sam put me in charge of stickering the paintings that weren't for sale. She was pretty stressed, I could tell; her movements were quicker than usual, and she was quicker to anger, too. At one point she checked her phone and swore. 'Fucking cunts from *Creative Review* aren't coming after all.'

'Bastards,' I said, though I hadn't known they were coming in the first place; I wasn't really sure what *Creative Review* was.

'Someone from Concrete Street Gallery is coming, though.'

'Is that a good one?'

'They represent Anna Wypych,' said Sam, as though that would answer the question.

'Would you want them to represent you, then?'

'I don't know. Maybe.' She put her phone away and stood back, hands on hips, to look at the paintings on the walls. She straightened one of them – a woman with her hands over her breasts, her face and pubic hair in focus, the rest of her hazy. 'It's not like I'm struggling without representation over here. And people in London are such wankers about figurative paintings of women. Did you hear what happened to Loretta?'

I didn't know who Loretta was. 'No,' I said.

'She exhibited this great painting, of her friend, a burlesque dancer, and her bush was showing. And loads of idiots complained to the gallery because they were offended by seeing a woman's pubic hair in a sexual context, and the twats that ran the gallery took it down.'

'That's so – reactionary.' I was pleased with myself for coming up with the word reactionary on the spot.

'I know. But that's what it's like. People can't handle women presented as sexual objects. Even when the person painting them is a woman.'

'I bet it was a man who decided to take that painting down,' I said.

'Probably,' Sam said. She looked over and gave me a quick smile. 'But I bet they'd have no problem with Jane's stupid *Cunt* paintings.'

'Is she coming tomorrow?'

'Nah. We don't really get on,' she said. She pointed at a painting just above my head. 'Jasper's buying the one of Polly.'

I added a red dot below the painting. Polly's nipples were very red in the painting. They looked a bit sore, actually.

'The fist isn't for sale. That's staying in my flat. Or you can have it for yours, if you like.'

'Thank you,' I said, stickering it, though I wasn't sure I wanted it in my flat – I didn't really want to think about fisting when I was eating my Alpen, and the colours would clash with Dave's Ercol coffee table.

'Are any of your friends coming?'

'Ella is,' I said. 'And Alice and Dave.'

'Don't hang out with them the whole night though, yeah, babes?' Sam said, kissing me. 'I'll need to you mingle with the collectors. You'll be, like, my first lady.'

'I don't want to be first lady,' I said. 'I want to be vice president.'

'All right, babes,' she said, 'whatever you want,' but she was doing something important-looking with a tape measure and I got the impression she was humouring me.

28. A VERY ATTRACTIVE CAR CRASH

'You didn't have to get me anything!'

We were at Sam's, getting ready for her private view, and I'd just given her a birthday present. Choosing it had been impossible – I'd spent hours in Selfridges, picking up things like gold nail clippers and velvet bow ties before remembering she wasn't a fifty-year-old Russian businessman and putting them down again. Her friends hadn't been much help. 'She's impossible to buy for,' Polly had said. 'Just give her a good seeing to. She'll like that.'

Sam felt the parcel I'd handed her, trying to guess what was inside.

'It's really not very exciting,' I told her.

She started by unwrapping it slowly, but she soon grew impatient and ripped the wrapping off. She examined each present in turn, making small noises that were meant to sound like approval but which were definitely disappointment.

'Novels!' she said. 'And prosecco! We'll have that later. And a T-shirt!'

The T-shirt was black, and had cost £80 for no apparent reason.

'You always wear black T-shirts,' I said, by way of explanation.

'I know!'

'You don't like it.'

'I do. I do! It's just – nothing, it's great.'

'What?' I said.

'Well,' she said, crumpling the T-shirt on her knee. 'It's all just a bit impersonal.'

'Oh,' I said, trying to sound less crushed than I felt.

She gave me a sad half-smile. 'It's fine,' she said. 'It's just you're my girlfriend, so I thought—'

'What?' I said.

'Nothing.' She looked down at the T-shirt. 'I just thought you might make more of an effort.'

I sat there, looking down at my hands in my lap. I had made an effort – I'd spent all of my lunch money for the month on her presents. I was going to be eating Weetabix at my desk till August. 'Sorry,' I said, but saying it felt wrong, like saying 'Excuse me' as a reflex when someone bashes into you on the Tube.

'That's OK,' she said.

I boiled quietly, like an angry kettle.

She opened the card I'd made for her. I'd borrowed some coloured pencils from Dave to draw a rainbow on the front. Inside I'd written, 'This voucher entitles the bearer to a session of extremely good sex.'

'Now that's more like it,' she said, and she kissed me. She turned to look at the front of the card again. 'This is very sweet. It looks like a child drew it.'

'Shut up,' I said, but she rubbed my head like a parent would, and I felt a bit better.

That night, the air was heavy with heat. We walked through Clapton, hand in sweaty hand, until we reached the gallery. The brick walls were covered with jasmine.

'Smells a bit like vagina, doesn't it?' Sam said.

'That's not the first thing that came to mind,' I said.

'You haven't fucked enough women yet,' she said, and she pushed the heavy door open.

*   *   *

217

A few people were already there, milling around, not really looking at the paintings, drinking cheap rosé from plastic cups. Friends of Sam's I'd never heard of crowded round her to congratulate her and wish her happy birthday, mostly lesbians and other artists. I was expecting everyone to be stylish, in shapeless clothes and thick-framed glasses, but most people were dressed in paint-splattered DMs and old Barbour jackets and faded dungarees. Artists obviously washed less often than I thought they did, probably because they were too busy being inspired and creating things. Maybe if I washed my hair once a week I'd get a sudden urge to write a villanelle or take up crocheting? Might be worth a try. There were a couple of older people there who I thought might be collectors; they were studying the art and the price list more carefully. They didn't look as rich or eccentric as I'd expected collectors to look, either. They looked like paediatricians, mostly.

I stared at the paintings, feeling slightly out of my depth, art and socializing-wise. I looked around for my friends, but they hadn't arrived yet. I noticed Jasper over in the makeshift bar area. Alcohol. That's what I needed.

I walked over to the bar, listening to other people's conversations.

'I fucked a really hot bi guy last night.'

'Did you catch *The Dark Wood* at Transition?'

'Which one's her girlfriend?'

I turned my head. A couple of women were studying the paintings on the wall.

But Sam hadn't painted me. Why hadn't she painted me?

I picked up a bottle of vodka and was about to pour myself a glass when I heard someone say, 'Hey. Bring that up here.'

Polly was standing on the mezzanine above me, beckoning me to join her.

'How do I get up there?'

She pointed at a spiral staircase in the corner of the room — a cast-iron Victorian one, fragile and out of place.

I climbed up, almost dropping the vodka on the heads of the people below at one point as the staircase juddered under my weight. At the top, Polly took the vodka from me and swigged from the bottle. We looked down at everyone in the gallery, laughing and talking and drinking. Polly pointed out various people: a woman who was into scat, another who'd had an affair with a newsreader, a bloke who had a fetish for spanking really old people.

We stopped speaking as we felt someone climbing the staircase to join us, the floor trembling each time they took a step. We turned to see Jasper trying to catch her breath as she heaved herself up the last few steps.

'Thought that might be the end of me!' she said, putting an arm around each of us. 'What are you doing, gorgeous girls? Plotting the femme revolution?'

'Oh, shut up, you old chauvinist,' said Polly, pulling away.

'Julia,' Jasper said, apparently unfazed, 'we're recording video messages for Sam's birthday. I'm going to play them later on the projector. Do you want to make one?' She held up her phone.

'I'm a bit drunk,' I said.

'It'll be easier that way,' Polly pointed out.

I didn't really want to record a message; I've never been much of one for public declarations of affection. But it would have been weird to say no. I followed Jasper to a blank wall – 'Nice neutral background' – and when she pressed record I stammered out something about how happy Sam made me. I think I might have accidentally plagiarized some Lionel Richie lyrics. it was all a bit embarrassing.

'That was very sweet,' said Jasper, playing back the video to check that it had recorded. 'I hope Sam knows what a lucky woman she is!'

Sam was manic that night, practically jogging between different groups of people, throwing back her head with laughter in a way I didn't recognize. She barely seemed to see me; she kept glancing over my head in case there was someone more influential to talk to, and there always was.

'The bloke she's talking to now is from Concrete Street,' Polly told me, when Sam was deep in conversation with a guy with dreadlocks and a mustard suit. And later: 'That guy is a collector from China. Think he's a bit of a creep. But still, he's got money.'

Alice, Dave and Ella turned up at about eight. I saw them standing in a corner, drinking their wine quickly, looking around warily at the other guests. I ran over to them and grabbed their shoulders, like I'd reached dry land. 'Thank God you're here,' I said. 'I keep having to pretend I know things like who Bob and Roberta Smith are.'

'They're one person, Jules,' Dave said, bending down to kiss me on the cheek.

'Fuck.'

'It's very exciting!' Alice said, looking around, smiling. 'Look at all the breasts! And the vaginas!'

'It's like being in a vagina showroom!' said Ella. 'I like that one over there, the one with the heart-shaped pubic hair.'

'I wonder if she got it waxed like that for a special occasion, or if that's her everyday look?' Alice said.

'Maybe she varies the shape, depending on the month. Like, maybe that was for Valentine's Day, and she gets a Christmas tree in December,' said Ella, and she and Alice bent double with laughter. I didn't laugh, out of respect for Sam's art.

Dave gave me a sympathetic smile, which annoyed me. I didn't want sympathy. 'She's very talented,' he said.

'Yes,' I said.

'There isn't a painting of you here, is there?'

'No,' I said, and for once I was grateful for that; I didn't want my friends laughing at my pubic hair.

At nine, Sam ting-tinged her glass and stood on a chair to give a speech. She looked around the gallery, smiling everyone into silence. When the last murmurings had died down, she began to speak.

'Thanks so much for coming,' she said. 'So. My work is all about foregrounding female desire and celebrating women's bodies.'

'Foregrounding. Good word,' Alice whispered, nodding.

'My paintings shouldn't be radical,' Sam continued, 'but in some senses they are, and I want to thank Alyssa and the Tramshed Gallery for inviting me to show here.'

There was a round of applause, and Alyssa, a woman with an aggressively short fringe and fishnet tights, took an ironic bow. Sam made her come nine times last time she saw her, I thought, and took a deep drink of my vodka.

'There are loads of other people to thank – my studio mates, for keeping me company and stopping me going insane; anyone who has ever bought my work or reviewed my work; the Arts Council, for supporting me over the past year . . .' she was looking around for something or someone, and then she saw me and raised her glass. 'And Julia, my beautiful girlfriend,' she said, 'for being so completely delicious and for teaching an old dog new tricks. I love you, babes.'

Heads turned towards me. There were whoops and cheers. I covered my face, embarrassed but pleased at the same time. Had she essentially just told the room I was good in bed?

Sam beckoned me over and hugged me. 'I really do love you,' she said into my hair, and I felt warm and safe and smug.

Most of the art people drifted off before ten, when the wine ran out, around the time some of Sam's proper friends started disappearing to the toilet to take coke. Dave went to the off-licence and came back with another bottle of vodka and some lemonade, and we drank our way through it steadily until we'd reached the 'I love you!' 'No, I love *you!*' stage of drunkenness. A couple of stickers had appeared on the walls next to the paintings. Some of the collectors had shaken Sam's hand. She seemed satisfied.

Around eleven, Sam shouted 'Lock in!' and shut the doors. The second part of the evening began. The Yo Majesty tunes started up on Spotify and people did shots of whatever alcohol was left on the trestle table. There was dancing. Someone ordered takeaway pizza and put a candle in the middle of a quattro formaggi for Sam to blow out.

And then, before the evening got completely out of control, Jasper stood up on Sam's speech-giving chair and shouted, 'Oi, Sam! We have a surprise for you!'

Two women pulled a chair into the middle of the room in front of the projector and Sam sat down. She called out, 'Where's my baby?' and Alice pushed me forward. I knelt on the floor next to Sam and she bent down to give me a kiss. A drunk woman behind us shouted 'Fucking lezzers!' and everyone laughed.

And then there was silence. A square of yellow light appeared high on the white wall of the warehouse, above three paintings of the same woman, standing, kneeling and sitting. The light danced and flickered for a moment before the words *HAPPY BIRTHDAY, YOU PERVY BITCH!* flashed onto the wall, to more cheering and more applause. Sam looked at me and squeezed my hand, excited.

One by one, Sam's friends appeared on the screen, talking about how great she was. And then it was my turn.

There was my massive head on the screen, saying things about how much better my life was with Sam in it and blowing her a kiss. My head was in my hands by the end of it, but I could hear everyone saying, 'Awwww!' and 'How sweet!'

Sam rubbed my back. 'Hey,' she said. I opened my eyes. 'That was gorgeous. I love you, too. So much.' She kissed me, and her friends cheered, and everything was all right.

For about five seconds.

Because that's how long it was before a woman – a beautiful woman – appeared on the screen, pouting and waving her fingers.

She was like a caricature of a sexy person, with oversized lips and huge brown eyes and dark curly hair, styled like a Forties pin-up. '*Bonsoir!*' she said.

Virginie.

Sam was smiling, her hand over her mouth in surprise. She turned to Jasper. 'How did you get her to do this?'

'Sam, my darling girl,' said Virginie, in an almost cartoonish French accent, 'I am so sorry I'm not there with you today. You know how much I miss you, and how much I love you. But don't worry, OK? I'll reward you with the most delicious spanking the next time we're together. OK? *Bisoux!* Charlotte sends her love too!' She blew a kiss to the camera, and a young butch woman's head popped into the frame, waving and saying '*Bon anniversaire!*'

Sam was still smiling and shaking her head. I was smiling too, smiling and smiling, because if I didn't force the corners of my mouth upwards, I knew they'd turn down, and then I'd cry, and I couldn't have that. I didn't want to make a fuss and ruin Sam's birthday. Why *shouldn't* Virginie send her a birthday message? Sam had been nothing but honest about their relationship.

And then, from the back of the room, that voice again. '*Bonne anniversaire!*'

The atmosphere in the room changed. People were looking at each other, looking at me. I registered gasping, and chairs scraping back and people turning to look, and Sam saying, 'No fucking way.'

She was taller than I thought she'd be, and horribly, unfairly charismatic. It was a shock to see her moving, to hear her talking, to be reminded that she was real. Everything about her was exaggerated – her large eyes, her small waist, her big hips, her cleavage. She even walked with a wiggle, like Marilyn Monroe. So twentieth century, I told myself. She's basically designed herself to appeal to the male gaze. I wouldn't want to look like that, even if I could. But who was I kidding? Definitely not myself. I wanted to cry.

And yet I couldn't stop staring as she made her way from the back of the room towards Sam, her arms outstretched, her curls bouncing. I felt like I was watching a very attractive car crash.

They hugged – they didn't kiss, thank God – and they were murmuring things to each other that I couldn't hear, and the other guests started clapping and chattering to each other.

Virginie turned to me and said, 'And you must be Julia! You are even more beautiful than Sam said you were.'

'Thank you,' I said, trying to smile.

Alice put a hand on my shoulder, but I shook her off; if anyone was nice to me I would cry. I shook my head, lips tight, and walked towards the toilets without looking back. I locked myself in and sat on the concrete floor and thought, what the fuck just happened? I began to feel dizzy, as though I was losing my grip on everything, like I might just float away, so I tried to concentrate on how pretentious the copper-pipe taps were.

Someone was knocking on the door. 'Julia?' It was Polly.

'I'm fine!' I said, as brightly as I could. I was going to pull myself together and be the life and fucking soul of the party. I was going to kiss Virginie on both cheeks and share in-jokes about Sam with her, like the way she sings in the shower, and how angry she gets when she accidentally puts on one navy sock and one black sock. And tomorrow I was going to tell Sam that I'd changed my mind and that I couldn't do it, and that if she wanted to be with me she would have to break up with Virginie.

I looked at myself in the mirror. My eyes were a little on the shiny side, maybe, but other than that, you wouldn't know I'd been crying. I took a deep breath and opened the bathroom door.

Polly was waiting for me outside, her arms crossed, next to Alice and Dave and Ella. Alice rushed up and hugged me. She didn't say anything. She probably didn't know what to say.

'What the fuck,' Dave said.

'I had no idea she was coming,' Polly said.

'I know you didn't,' I said. 'It doesn't matter.'

'I'm going to fucking kill Jasper.'

'You should,' said Dave. I could tell from his voice that he was furious, and I was so grateful, because I didn't really feel like I had the right to be angry.

'You're the one she loves,' Polly said. 'She's always calling Jasper up and telling her how you've changed her life.'

'But she's not the one who came over to talk to me,' I said. 'You are.'

We all looked over at Sam, who was doing tequila shots at the bar with Jasper and Virginie, one arm around Virginie's waist.

'I'm sorry,' Polly said.

'You shouldn't be apologizing,' I said. And as I looked at Sam I knew I couldn't do it; I wouldn't be able to get through the evening, pretending to be OK with Virginie, pretending to have a lovely time with them both. 'Tell Sam I'll see her tomorrow,' I said.

'Any time you want a drink,' Polly said.

'Thanks.'

Ella put an arm around my shoulder, and Alice took my hand on the other side, and Dave walked in front of us to open the door for me, and I must have felt very numb and detached from reality because all I remember thinking was, I wonder if this is how celebrities feel when they're being rushed away from the paparazzi?

I heard Sam slurring, 'Where's Julia?' but I kept walking. 'Julia!' Sam called. 'Wait!' But the four of us ran around the corner. Dave ordered us an Uber, and we rumbled back to our flat in silence. Ella came with us, and she put me on the sofa with a blanket around me, and Dave cooked us pasta. We didn't talk much. I didn't feel sad or angry or guilty. I didn't feel much of anything, really.

29. BAISE-MOI!

Ella borrowed a pair of pyjamas and slept in my bed that night. It felt strange having someone else next to me, someone with an unfamiliar smell and an unfamiliar heat, but I was grateful not to be alone. I woke up in the night and started to cry and she fetched me a cup of water and told me funny stories till I fell asleep again.

She wasn't there when I woke up the next morning. I couldn't seem to get out of bed. At about eleven, Alice brought me a cup of tea. She sat on my bed as I drank it.

'Ella's getting pastries,' she said.

I nodded.

'Heard from Sam this morning?'

I shook my head. 'She's probably still asleep. She was wasted.'

'You have to talk to her.'

'I know,' I said, trying to breathe away my anxiety, like self-help books tell you to. 'Why can't she just be normal?'

'Maybe if she was, you wouldn't be so into her,' Alice said, playing with the duvet. 'Dave's completely normal, and completely committed to me, and I find myself thinking all the time about what it would be like to be single. I know that makes me sound ungrateful.' She looked at her hands. 'Sorry,' she said. 'I didn't mean to make it all about me.'

'It's all right,' I said. 'I'm bored of my own drama already.'

She looked up again. 'So, are you going to call her?'

'Of course I'm not,' I said. 'She's the one who needs to apologize.'

But she didn't call. Not till it was nearly dark, anyway. I lay on the sofa all day, imagining Sam and Virginie together in bed. I bet Virginie did things I didn't know were even options, sex-wise. I bet they'd had sex on the Eiffel Tower and used a baguette as a sex toy and smeared foie gras all over each other's bodies, or whatever it is that French people do. It wasn't until I was running myself a bath that the phone rang. I checked my watch: almost 8 p.m.

'Babes,' she said, 'I'm so sorry about last night.'

I didn't say anything. To be honest, I was feeling relief – relief that she'd finally called, that she was apologizing – but I had the high ground, and the view was lovely from up there so I didn't want to give it up just yet.

'I had no idea she was going to show up,' Sam said.

'I know you didn't.'

'And I'm sorry I'm only just calling now. She's just left.'

'Did she sleep in your bed?'

A silence. 'Where else would she have slept?'

I know honesty is a good quality – up there with 'earns money' and 'makes me laugh' on the list of things I've always wanted in a partner – but I was beginning to think there was such a thing as too much honesty. 'Did you have sex with her?' I asked, closing my eyes, wincing, waiting for the blow.

'No.'

I opened my eyes. 'Promise?'

'Babes, I wouldn't have done that to you. I know you're not ready for that yet.'

I felt horribly, pathetically grateful. I almost said thank you, but I stopped myself.

227

'Where did you get to, anyway?' Sam said then. 'It was a fun night, wasn't it? Before that, anyway.'

'Sure.'

'Marlon from Concrete Street asked for my number!'

'Great.'

'You were the biggest hit of the night, by the way. My friends all thought you were a hot slut.'

'Don't call me a slut.'

She paused, clearly taken aback. 'It's a compliment in our community.'

'I don't like it.'

Another pause.

'Please don't be like this, Julia. I didn't invite Virginie. No one meant to hurt you.'

'Well, I am hurt.'

'Please let me see you, babes.' Her voice was rising. She was beginning to worry, and I was glad. 'Please come over. I'll buy us takeaway and look after you. Please?'

What was the point in putting it off? I had to talk to her about this while I was in the driving seat.

On the bus, I rehearsed what I was going to say to Sam, feeling sick with nerves. I was going to give her an ultimatum. She had to choose between me, a beginner lesbian who thought 'That's very nice' counted as talking dirty, and a stunning woman who knew how to say 'Fuck me' in several European languages. But then she opened the door and smiled. I tried to look stern but she kissed me and I forgot what I had been planning to say.

The most important thing was to hold onto her, at any cost.

We went upstairs and had slow, hungover sex. As we lay in bed afterwards, Sam stroking my arm, she said, 'I've been thinking. I really want you to meet Virginie properly. You'll feel so much less threatened if you actually talk to her.'

228

I propped myself up on my elbow. 'I don't think I can.'

Sam looked into my eyes. 'If you really want me to break up with her, I will.'

'Really?' I felt dangerously hopeful.

She nodded. 'But will you come and meet her first? Before we throw in the towel without even trying to make it work? Meet me halfway?'

And my heart, as they say, sank.

'Come with me, next time I go!'

Which was such a hilarious idea that I laughed out loud. Did she actually think I would happily swan into Virginie's house, shake her hand and maybe have a cup of tea with her, and then sit at the kitchen table painting my nails while she fucked my girlfriend? 'Absolutely not,' I said.

'Please? There's a big sex party that Virginie and I go to every year, in this big old chateau outside Lyon. It's happening in a couple of weeks. There are still tickets.'

I didn't say anything.

'We could just watch. You wouldn't have to do anything you weren't comfortable with.'

'I can't just sit there while you fuck her,' I said.

'That's not going to happen. We won't just ditch you and go off to have sex. Charlotte will be there, too—'

'I suppose you expect me to hook up with Charlotte, do you?'

'Of course I don't!' She looked at me. 'If you wanted to, you could play with someone at the party and I could sit it out. To ease you in.'

'I don't think I'm going to want to do that.'

'Or we could have a threesome—'

'But you will have sex with Virginie.'

She took her hand away. 'It's like you're obsessed with the idea of me having sex with her.'

I laughed. 'Oh, I'm the one obsessed with you having sex, am I?'

Sam sighed. 'If you come with me, I'll share a room with you. But if you stay here, I'll probably stay in Virginie's room.'

'Are you blackmailing me?'

'I can't believe the woman I love just accused me of blackmail.'

'I didn't—'

'You did. It's fine. If that's what you think, that's fine,' she said, standing up. 'Maybe it's best if I go on my own.' She walked to the door.

I felt like something was breaking inside me. Who was I before I met her? Sexually inexperienced, lonely, depressed, a breaker of penises.

'I'll come,' I said, because in that moment it seemed the only thing I could say.

She turned around. 'You will?'

That smile.

I nodded. I could do this.

'You won't regret it,' Sam said, kissing me on the cheek. 'I promise you, we'll have a great time.'

30. CONDOMS ON THE PILLOWS

I lied and told my friends I was going to Paris with Sam – I didn't want to tell them we were visiting Virginie. They would think Sam was taking advantage of me, but she wasn't; if anything, I was taking advantage of her. I was getting a free holiday and several three-course meals (plus cheese, if I had anything to do with it). Yes, I might have to sit through a bit of sex. But if I really couldn't handle it, Sam would break up with Virginie. I had nothing to lose. And I didn't want anyone else's voice in my head telling me I was doing the wrong thing.

As the trip drew closer, I could feel myself starting to snap at people. I started ignoring Cat's texts and calls, and I stopped going dancing, and I longed for the nights when Alice and Dave went out till late. I was using all my energy trying to behave like a normal person in the face of impending Virginie-based doom. I didn't have anything left for anyone else.

Owen kept trying to corner me at work, to ask what was wrong. He was preparing for his Senior Account Manager interview, and he kept asking me things like, 'Do you think this tie makes me look like I have a Strategic Approach to Objectives?' I knew I should start preparing for mine, too – it was scheduled for the Tuesday after I got back from Lyon – but I've always liked the adrenaline rush that comes with leaving things to the last minute. Besides, it would be nice to have something to distract me while Sam was busy having Gallic sex.

Work, strangely, was an escape. I focused on the emails I received, from people whose problems were far greater than my own. I focused on replying to Eric, who had written to tell me he'd been referred for an operation on his heart, and complaining about the waiting times.

> *I've been told that I might have to wait eighteen weeks — that's nearly five months! I don't think it's acceptable that someone with more money can pay to have it done right away, and poor old sods like me have to wait five months. I'm trying not to feel down in the dumps about it. My aorta's lasted me ninety-six years, so hopefully it can hang on in there for a few more months. Besides, I'm dreading the op, to tell you the truth. Almost as much as I used to dread the Bomber Command ops. Tell you what, before we went out on a bombing raid, we each used to widdle on the back wheel of the plane for luck. I'd widdle on my hospital bed if I thought that would do me any good.*

I hated the idea of Eric worrying about his operation. Just before my granddad died, he had a knee replacement, and he'd been very nervous about it. I'd visited him on the ward beforehand, and we'd played cards, but he'd gossiped too loudly about the man in the bed next to him and everything had smelled of disinfectant, so I'd only stayed for half an hour. I can still see the way he looked at me when he asked me to stay for another round of Rummy, a bit shy, like he knew I'd say no. And I had. I'd made an excuse and walked away. I was going to do better by Eric.

I wrote him an official reply, reassuring him about the government's commitment to reducing waiting times, but I went out at lunchtime and bought him a Get Well Soon card, too — one with tulips on the front, because he'd told me they were Eve's favourite flowers. I wrote that I hoped he'd be jiving again before too long — and then I added: *I would love to come and see you in Brighton one day soon, if you'd like a visitor?* I put my home address at the top of the card. Eric had become a friend, after all, even though we'd never met. The only one who wouldn't judge my relationship with Sam. Because he didn't know anything about it.

Two weeks later, I was sitting on a Eurostar train, looking out at a blur of red bricks and sky-blue arches as we pulled away from St Pancras station. I had briefly considered pissing on the back wheel of the train for luck, Eric style, but I've never been good at peeing in front of other people. I very much hoped no one would be doing water sports at the French sex party; I bet Virginie looked amazing when she peed, like a sexy public fountain.

Sam had been particularly wonderful to me since I'd agreed to go to Lyon; she'd held me closer and kissed me more deeply and told me again and again how much she loved me. But now we were on the train and I felt anxious again. It was almost comforting, like having an old friend with me for the ride. I took a deep breath in and out. Sam looked over at me and smiled.

'We'll just chill out tonight. Go out for dinner. Save our energy for the party tomorrow.'

'OK.'

'It's going to be OK, babes,' she said.

'I know,' I said quickly. She didn't need to patronize me.

Virginie and Charlotte were waiting for us at Arrivals. I had wondered whether Virginie would be less beautiful than I remembered — wrinklier or a bit powdery close up, maybe — but she wasn't; I actually had to stop myself asking her which moisturizer she used. She was wearing a musky, old-fashioned perfume that made me think of sex. Charlotte was much less intimidating — about my height, with lots of piercings and low-slung jeans. She was quite attractive too, though.

She looked like she might push you up against the wall and give you a good seeing to. Not that I was in the market for that sort of thing.

'My darlings!' cried Virginie, hugging both Sam and me at once – an equal opportunities hug, wedging our heads against her bosom. She was the sort of woman that had a bosom. She released us, gave Sam a quick kiss on the lips, so quick that it took me a while to register it. Then she turned to me. 'You ran away so quickly last time I met you! I am so glad we will have the opportunity to get to know each other properly!'

'Me too!' I said, in my cheeriest, most carefree voice.

I felt Sam's eyes on me, but I wasn't ready to look at her just yet.

'Welcome to Lyon!' Virginie said. 'Our flat isn't far – we'll walk. OK?' She walked away across the station concourse.

Sam touched my shoulder so that I had to look at her, and mouthed, 'You OK?'

I mouthed back, 'Totally fine!'

Sam smiled and kissed me on the cheek. Then she ran to catch up with Virginie. They linked arms and began talking quickly, catching up on news. Like old friends, I told myself. Just like me and Alice. With a tiny bit of fisting thrown in.

'Please, let me take your bag?' Charlotte asked.

'No, thanks,' I said.

'I insist,' she said, reaching down to take it. 'Let me.'

'I can do it,' I said, pulling the bag towards me.

'As you wish,' she said, shrugging, and we walked on in silence down the long, wide streets of Lyon.

We crossed a river to a pale, picturesque part of the town. 'We are very lucky with our apartment,' Charlotte told me. 'Lyon is so cheap compared to Paris . . .'

'You used to live there?'

She nodded. 'But life in Lyon is much easier. I work in music, but I can afford a flat like this?' She did a flicky thing with her hand, which I think meant she had a good deal.

'What does Virginie do?' I asked.

'She's a therapist.'

'Of course she is,' I said.

'Sorry?' asked Virginie, hearing her name.

'Nothing!' called Charlotte, and Virginie turned back around. 'She works a lot with lesbians and gay men. France is still very homophobic.'

'Do you two get hassled?' I asked.

'Sometimes, when we hold hands. But we go to a lot of gay places. And also, people often mistake me for Virginie's son!'

I laughed along, but then, ahead of me, Virginie put her head on Sam's shoulder, and Sam brushed her hand over Virginie's bum. Just for a second, but I saw it. I stopped laughing and I felt my face growing hot. But Charlotte didn't seem bothered at all, so I told myself I shouldn't be either.

Virginie and Charlotte's apartment was off a street known for its gay bars. We walked up a slippery stone staircase to get to it, and Virginie walked ahead of me, hips swaying as she put one foot in front of the other. I watched the others watching her, too.

The apartment was cool and bohemian, with comfortable-looking fabric sofas and an open-plan kitchen. There were three bedrooms off the living area. Virginie pointed to the one in the middle. 'That's Charlotte's room,' she said. 'The one on the right is mine. And you and Sam will be sleeping in the guest room tonight. OK?'

'Thank you,' I said.

Virginie bowed. 'You are welcome. I have a little gift for you later, OK? To welcome you to our way of life. Something that really helped me when I was young, like you.' She said 'young' to rhyme with 'wrong'.

'How are you feeling, babes?' asked Sam, as we unpacked our things.

'Fine,' I said – and I did feel fine, sort of. 'Charlotte's nice.'

'Yeah, she's cool,' Sam said. 'I think she likes you, by the way. I can tell.'

'That's good. I'm still not going to have sex with her.'

The guest room was pretty innocent-looking – floral bedspreads, a Matisse print, a bowl of potpourri, even. Until you looked at the bookshelf, which was full of SM erotica, or opened the bedside cupboard, which was full of dildos and harnesses.

There were condoms on the pillows.

'But we don't have penises,' I said, picking one up.

'You should always use condoms with a dildo if you're using it with more than one sexual partner,' said Sam, and I felt a bit silly.

'They're ribbed,' I said.

'Virginie really cares about her guests' pleasure,' Sam said.

I walked over to the bookshelf and picked up a book called *Gimme Hot Butch Pain*.

Sam came up behind me and kissed my neck. 'I'm glad we're sharing a room tonight.'

'Me too,' I said, putting the book down and grasping her arms as they wrapped around my waist, holding them around me, tight, fierce.

'Going to strap one of those dildos on when we get back here.'

'As long as they've been sterilized.'

'Of course they have,' Sam said, in an offended sort of voice, pulling her arms away from me. 'You didn't have to come, you know. It was nice of Virginie and Charlotte to invite you. You shouldn't laugh at them.'

I didn't want to annoy her. There was a hot French woman two doors away, literally waiting to fuck her. 'I'm sorry,' I said. 'I'm not laughing at them. This is just a bit weird for me.'

'I know,' she said, giving me a sympathetic little smile. She sat on the bed and patted the spot next to her. 'You do know Virginie will probably want me to stay with her one night before we leave, don't you? It's been a long time since we've seen each other. But tonight I'm all yours.'

'Lucky me!' I said, in my too-cheerful voice. It would be fine. I hadn't seen any of the Godfather films or read any Anthony Trollope, or researched the history of Lyon. I had lots of job interview prep to do, too. Lots to keep me occupied. Lots and lots. I'd be totally fine. Totally.

31. *MÉNAGE À TROIS*

That first night, Virginie and Charlotte took us out to a lesbian bar. We sat at a tiny table and ate piles of bread, cheese and cornichons. Virginie and Charlotte were both heavy drinkers, which made everything a lot easier. They ordered a bottle of delicious red wine, and then another, and after the first glass I felt warm, relaxed and impulsive. It was as though the four of us were embarking on a strange adventure together.

'The most wonderful thing about being with Virginie is that I never have to compromise,' Charlotte shouted to me over a RuPaul track. I nodded, but I was a bit distracted by Virginie and Sam, who were whispering into each other's ears on the other side of the table. 'It's like being single but better, you know?' she said, shrugging Frenchly. 'If I see another lady I like, I take her home, and Virginie is fine with it. Can you imagine?'

I could not. 'I'm not sure I would find many women who would want to go home with me,' I told her.

Sam was tucking a strand of hair behind Virginie's ear.

'You?' said Charlotte. 'You could get all of the ladies here if you wanted them.'

'Oh stop,' I said.

Virginie put a hand on Sam's thigh.

'I am serious!' Charlotte said. 'You are feminine, but you have

238

an edge. You would appeal to the butches and some of the femmes as well, I think.'

'Thanks,' I said.

'Who would you go for here?'

I looked around. There was a woman at the bar in a black leather dress with hair that was so blond it was almost white; there was something exciting about her – a dangerous energy. I nodded in her direction. 'She's not my normal type,' I said, proud that I'd made it sound like I was a seasoned fancier of women with an established type to go against.

Charlotte laughed. 'You are joking.'

'No,' I said. 'Why?'

Charlotte laughed harder.

'What?' I said.

'Yeah, what?' Sam asked.

'Out of all the women in this bar, she is Julia's favourite,' said Charlotte, pointing towards the tall blonde woman.

Sam looked over. The woman was downing a shot with the barman. 'Is she——' she started.

Charlotte nodded, unable to breathe by this point, practically.

Sam and Virginie started laughing, too.

'Literally, what's so funny?' I said, but they were laughing too hard to answer.

'She is a celebrity in Lyon,' explained Virginie. 'She's a famous drag queen.'

Ah. Aaaaaaah. I looked at the woman again. She had an Adam's apple.

'Whatever,' I said. 'I still fancy her. I've enjoyed penises in the past. Sporadically.'

Virginie smiled. 'Sporadically?'

'She means penises don't do as much for her as my fingers do,' said Sam.

'Maybe I just haven't found the right penis yet,' I said.

Charlotte leaned across the table to give me a high five.

'That's right, darling,' Virginie said to me, approvingly. 'Keep this one on her toes. OK?'

As soon as we got back to our room, I pushed Sam onto the bed and pulled off her T-shirt. It caught on her ears, which probably hurt, but that was sort of the point.

She tried to kiss my neck, but I told her not to touch me, and to shut up. I actually sounded quite assertive. This is what it felt like to be on top, then.

I opened the bedside cupboard and chose a harness and the biggest dildo I could find.

Sam seemed a little out of her comfort zone. She tried to roll me onto my back but I pushed her hands down. She tried again, really tried, but she couldn't overpower me, the angle she was at, and I held her arms down to the bed until she stopped struggling. I didn't kiss her – I didn't really feel like it. I just fucked her as hard as I could, holding onto the bed frame to force myself deeper into her as she cried out. This was what she must feel like when she was fucking me – powerful. A little bit vindictive. Which worried me. I was fucking her this hard because I was angry. What was driving her when she fucked me?

She came pretty quickly, which was satisfying. I pulled myself out of her and lay on my back, breathing hard, making a mental note to go running more often.

Before I'd caught my breath, Sam pulled off the harness and straddled me. She didn't bother putting a glove on – she just squirted on some lube, slid her hand inside me and began to fist me. I felt like she was trying to correct the balance of things. I closed my eyes, determined not to look at her. I thought about anyone but her – the fit drag queen. Jane. Charlotte, even. Every celebrity I'd ever fantasized about. But then, unbidden, I saw Sam with her hand on Virginie's bum. I thought about Sam fucking Virginie, and Virginie fucking Sam, and I hated it, but it turned me on, and I felt my anger turn to jealousy. I opened my eyes. Sam was sweating and her eyes were focused on me and I came, and the instant I did I started crying and I couldn't stop.

Sam stopped moving inside me, but I had closed up around her wrist. 'Relax, babes,' she said, stroking my clit until she could slide her hand out. 'It's OK,' she said. 'Everything's OK. I'm here.'

Virginie and Charlotte took us to lunch the next day at a dark, cave-like *bouchon*, which suited me, because it was hard for everyone else to read my facial expressions and easy for me to refill my glass without drawing attention to myself. Part of me was looking forward to the party; it was being held in a French chateau. I had been assured there would be free champagne. This wasn't the sort of opportunity that presented itself to civil servants very often, certainly not these days – who knows went on in the Eighties? But the rest of me was apprehensive. I didn't want to watch Virginie and Charlotte having sex, or let them watch me have sex. I wanted to pretend that we were a group of platonic friends, like WI committee members, maybe, or Anglican priests.

As our main courses were being cleared away, conversation turned to the party. 'Some people will be doing scenes tonight,' Virginie said.

'SM scenes?' I asked.

Virginie nodded, smiling. 'They might pretend to be kidnappers, or dogs, maybe, or even housewives!'

'Something for everyone!' I said, in my cheerful Anglican priest voice.

'Exactly!' said Virginie. 'There's gender play—'

'And age play,' said Sam.

'Lovely,' I said. 'At ballet school, I always used to be cast as the old woman, so I'll be good at that.' I refilled my wine glass.

'I pretend sometimes that I am Charlotte's aunt,' said Virginie.

'What's that,' I asked, 'incest play?'

'Some people call it family play,' Sam said. 'But yes.' She smiled at me. I was catching on quickly.

'And there's animal play, which can be—' Virginie searched for the word in English. '—embarrassing.'

Charlotte nodded. 'When I was first out, I had a mistress who wanted me to be her puppy all the time, even in public.'

'Even when you were going to the post office?' I asked her.

Charlotte nodded again. 'But I cheated when she wasn't there.' She laughed and shook her head. 'She would make me do tricks and reward me with food.'

'Did you have a name?' I asked.

'Yeah,' said Sam, 'what was your name?'

'Bisou,' Charlotte muttered.

Virginie laughed and clapped her hands. 'That means kiss,' she said to me. 'Such a silly, girly name!'

Charlotte crossed her arms and spread her legs, as if to counteract the girliness.

I was actually beginning to enjoy myself. We were laughing and joking about sex, and teasing each other, and the world hadn't ended. I looked across at Virginie, who was talking about custom leather whips with the same enthusiasm that my dad talks about obscure passages from William Blake poems. She wasn't the least bit jealous of Sam or suspicious of me, even though she had a right to be – she'd been with Sam longer than I had, after all, and I was the one threatening to make her choose between us. But I'm an only child, and I've never been good at sharing. I used to get into trouble for eating more than my fair share of Smarties at nursery, and whenever I go out to dinner and someone says, 'Shall we just get loads of mains and have a bit of everything?' I feel like I'm going to break out in hives. Virginie was a better person than me, is what I'm saying. Less selfish, more evolved.

Because I wanted to be OK with all of this. I wanted to be able to approach drag queens in bars and persuade them to come home and fuck me, if they happened to be that way inclined. I wanted to be OK with who Sam was. Because now that I'd met Virginie, I felt arrogant for ever believing that Sam might choose me over her. And ending it with Sam didn't feel like an option.

We ate so much that by the time we left, my stomach was bubbling and prickling with indigestion, though that might have been anxiety, too. Sam put her arm around me as we walked back to the flat, and I leaned into her. She was smoking now, a long, elegant cigarette of Virginie's that looked out of place in her hand.

'You're cool with coming to the party, right?' she said, flicking the ash.

'Yes,' I said. The wine was turning the anxiety into adrenaline and I felt brave and reckless, as I so often did when I was with Sam. I crossed my arms tight across my chest. I could feel my heart beating. With excitement and anticipation, I told myself.

We caught a cab to the chateau, which was only about twenty minutes outside Lyon. Sam held my hand the whole way, massaging my palm with her thumb. I was finding it challenging to breathe in my tight black dress; I was perched on the edge of the back seat, back straight, the seams of the dress creaking every time my ribs moved. 'You will not have to wear it for long!' Virginie had told me. 'The guests strip off to their lingerie early in the evening!'

The car smelled of dogs and old fags, which made me feel a bit sick, and I felt sicker still – an excited sort of sick – as we turned into the long driveway towards the chateau. It was all turrets and shutters and narrow windows, like something out of a fairy tale – a Brothers Grimm one, probably. Everything looked grey and ghostly in the moonlight, but I could see lights on in the room downstairs, and silhouettes of people drinking and talking. The cab slowed down on the gravel with a satisfying crackle and we got out and stood on the huge stone doorstep. Sam pulled the old-fashioned doorbell – a rope which rang a bell somewhere deep inside the house. A woman in a red satin dress opened the door. She said something in French, which I assume meant, 'Come in!'

We walked through into the vast, cold living room. Everyone was crowded around a fire at one end of the room, sipping champagne, talking and flirting. A couple were kissing on the sofa. I noticed a woman with a dog collar around her neck, and another woman holding the lead that was attached to it.

Virginie saw me noticing them. 'They are friends of ours,' she said. 'They are in a 24/7 sub-dom relationship. Elodie dominates Sophie all the time, not just during sex.'

'Doesn't seem very practical,' I said. 'What does Sophie do at work?'

'Oh – she doesn't have a job.'

I wished I could get Sophie on her own and ask her about the choices she had made and why she had made them, or even if she had made them, but the lead was a bit off-putting.

Sam came up behind me and put her chin on my shoulder.

'This is where we check each other out,' she said. 'Because it's pretty dark, down in the dungeon.'

I turned to look at her. 'There's an actual dungeon?'

'It's a wine cellar most of the time. But they take out the barrels and put in a few slings and things for the party.'

'I think wine cellars are sexier than dungeons,' I said. 'More aspirational. Not so many rats.'

'It's not really meant to be aspirational,' Sam said. She looked a bit impatient, like she was bored of me making a joke out of everything. 'Anyway,' she said. 'I just want you to know, you can play with someone else tonight if you want to.'

'I don't want to.'

She put her arms around my waist. 'I want you to be the first one to play with someone else. I think it's important.'

I didn't say anything.

'We can start with a threesome,' she said.

'Not with Virginie or Charlotte,' I said.

'No, obviously,' she said. She nodded to a woman across the room with long dark hair and a big laugh and a big body, her curves defined by the firelight. She turned and looked at us, and raised her glass.

'What do you think of her?' Sam asked.

'She's hot,' I said, because she was, objectively. I wouldn't have thought of her in a sexy way if Sam hadn't suggested it. But she had suggested it, and there was something thrilling about the thought of fucking someone so different from Sam.

'Let's just see what happens, shall we?' said Sam, and she turned me around and kissed me again. I could feel the woman watching us.

As the hours passed, the party got louder and looser and drunker. People kept refilling my champagne glass.

'I'd better stop,' I said to Sam at one point. 'I'm going to feel like shit tomorrow.'

'You can't get a hangover if you just drink champagne and nothing else,' she said.

'Bollocks,' I said, but I kept drinking anyway.

Before long, people started taking their clothes off, heading downstairs in various combinations of twos and threes and fours. I saw one group of five women heading off together. Ambitious, I thought. Virginie and Charlotte disappeared with the 24/7 BDSM couple, probably to try out some sort of pet shop-themed sex that I wanted absolutely nothing to do with. I felt much lighter and happier without them there.

Sam and I danced by the fire for a while, kissing, and I felt fizzy with wine and bolder than usual. I put my hand on Sam's arse, experimenting with taking the lead. Sam kissed me harder in response. And then, because I was feeling powerful, I said, 'Let's go downstairs.'

'All right then, babes,' she said. 'If that's what you want.'

Downstairs it was dark and the music was loud and everywhere I looked I saw naked flesh, everything luminous in the gloom. I took Sam by the hand and led her around the main dance floor to the dimmest corner I could find. To our left, a woman was tied to a column, wearing nothing but a thong and heels. She had clothes pegs attached to her nipples, and her partner was lashing her breasts with a whip, apparently trying to remove the pegs. A few feet away, a woman paced the floor with a tray of cutlery, tossing forks and spoons onto the floor while another woman scrabbled around on her hands and knees, trying to pick them up. The scenes all seemed oddly domestic, what with the pegs and cutlery. Was that because we were women? I wondered. Did men toss spanners around and lasso each other with car tyres?

'Yeah,' Sam said, as the scenes played out before us. 'Sometimes SM isn't actually that sexy to watch.'

It didn't look like it would be that sexy to do, either.

And as I was having that thought, the woman with the big smile walked up to us and said something to me in French.

'*Je ne parle pas Français*,' I said, feeling stupid and English and not very sexy.

'English?' she said, still smiling. 'Do you want to play?'

Sam put her arm around me. 'We're only playing together today,' she said, possessively, I thought. I felt a pleasant sense of sexy power.

The woman shrugged. 'Three is good for me. It'll be fun.' And in that moment, I felt that it would be; unlike most of the people in the dungeon, who were yelping or moaning or doing unspeakable things with wooden spoons, she didn't seem to take sex or herself too seriously. I was attracted to her confidence, and to how completely different her body was from mine and from Sam's.

'I'm Julia,' I said to her. For some reason, I felt it was important that we introduced ourselves before the sex got under way.

'Emma,' she said. '*Enchantée.*'

'*Enchantée* as well,' I said, which obviously wasn't the standard response, but I was preoccupied, wondering how the mechanics of this encounter would work.

I didn't really know how to have a threesome. I should have done some research in advance, or at least paid more attention to the logistics on Pornhub. I stood there stupidly for a while, but then Sam took control. She kissed me and unzipped my dress – there was an awkward moment when I tried to step out of it, and got my heel caught in the fabric. Emma started playing with my pony-tail, which reminded me of the way my friends and I had plaited each other's hair during school assemblies. And then Sam stopped kissing me and made an 'after you' gesture to Emma – the sort of gesture men in suits make when you're queuing for the bus. And then Emma kissed me, and I stopped thinking about assemblies.

Kissing someone new is always strange – it can take a while to get the rhythm right, and the other person's mouth can be too wet, or oddly full of teeth. Emma was a good kisser, but it still took me a while to relax into it. Her mouth felt bigger than Sam's. She tasted of peppermint. And then, of course, there was the fact that Sam was watching us. I didn't feel as self-conscious as I thought I might. I felt powerful, like I used to feel when I was onstage. And then Emma pulled away and started kissing Sam instead. I waited for the jealousy to hit me. But it didn't. And that gave me a rush of elation. Maybe I could do this, after all! Maybe I had ascended to a higher, jealousy-free plane!

Emma took her dress off, too, revealing some very impractical underwear – more holes than fabric. She had let her underarm hair grow and I loved how womanly that made her look. I felt small compared to her, and I liked that too. She started kissing me again, and I heard Sam say to her, 'I want you to fuck Julia.' Which pulled me back into myself for a moment. Why was she the one giving the orders? But I didn't want to contradict her in public, and anyway, by this point I wanted Emma to fuck me too, so I didn't object when Emma pushed me up against the brick wall of the dungeon, or when she pushed her fingers inside me. Her breasts were pressed up against me, and I stopped thinking about the politics of what was going on, and I closed my eyes – but then Sam said, 'Look at Emma,' and I did, because I've always been good at following instructions, and I noticed that a crowd had gathered to watch us. Virginie and Charlotte were there, arms round each other's waists. I didn't want to stop the sex, but I didn't want to think about them when I came, so I turned around and leaned on the wall. It was warm and clammy. Emma kept fucking me from behind, and then someone – Sam, I think – started to finger my arse, and as soon as she did, I came, an orgasm that left me weak and shaking and out of breath.

I wondered whether Emma would try to fuck Sam after that, or whether Sam would fuck Emma, but there seemed to be a tacit agreement that everyone had got what they came for.

'I feel bad,' I said, as Sam and I walked upstairs. 'I feel like that was all about me.'

Sam grinned and kissed me. 'Watching you have fun gets me off.'

It was just after 3 a.m. The party was beginning to wind down; people began drifting to the bedrooms upstairs or catching taxis home. There were a few knots of friends still drinking and laughing together in the living room.

Virginie took my hand as we waited for the taxi. 'I am so pleased you enjoyed yourself,' she said. 'Emma is a good fuck, isn't she?'

'Yes,' I said, suddenly assaulted by images of Virginie and Emma together.

'And you, Sam?' said Virginie. 'Did you play with anyone?'

Sam shrugged. 'Not really.'

'You joined in with Emma,' I said.

'Barely,' she said, kissing me on the head.

I put my head on Sam's shoulder as the taxi rumbled home, listening to Virginie and Charlotte tell Sam about the sex they'd had at the party, and the scenes they'd seen, and the toys they wanted to buy — 'I saw a woman with a butt plug with a little fox-fur tail coming out of it. I think we could have a lot of fun with that!' The sex and the champagne and the movement of the car and the murmur of the voices lulled me to sleep, and I dreamed that Virginie and I were having a cup of tea together, sharing a piece of cake, such good friends.

32. POLYAMORY FOR BEGINNERS

I woke around noon the next day, dry-mouthed and heavy-headed. Unhelpful tabloid-style headlines about the night before were sloshing around inside me, along with all the champagne I'd drunk, phrases like *LESBO LOVERS IN SLIGHTLY AWKWARD THREE-WAY ROMP* and *BUSTY BRUNETTE BEDS LESS BUSTY BRUNETTE IN MOULDY WINE CELLAR*. I wasn't feeling a hundred per cent fantastic about what had happened, in other words.

I looked at Sam, lying next to me, curled in on herself with her back to me. She wasn't moving. I was suddenly afraid that she had died during the night. I put my hand in front of her mouth to feel for breath.

'Babes. What the fuck are you doing?'

'Sorry.' I pulled my hand away. 'Go back to sleep.'

'You've woken me up now.' She turned onto her back and covered her eyes with her hand, against the sun.

'Sorry,' I said again.

She shifted onto her elbows and smiled at me.

I smiled back. I felt shy.

'So,' she said, 'you popped your non-monogamy cherry.'

'I suppose I did!' I said, extra cheerfully.

'Did you have fun?'

'Yes,' I said. 'I was glad you were there, though.'

'Hardly. You were like a kid learning to ride a bike. I let go, and you didn't notice, and kept on riding.'

'I don't think it's very sex-positive to compare a woman to a bike,' I said.

'Oh, shut up,' she said, grinning. 'What, are you more sex positive than I am now?'

'Maybe,' I said.

She kissed me. 'You know I'll be sleeping with Virginie tonight? You OK with that?'

She was just being honest, I suppose, but I am actually quite a fan of denial. I would much rather she'd pretended that she and Virginie were going to stay up late watching *Golden Girls* and doing face masks.

I nodded, but it can't have been very convincing, because she said, 'You kind of have to be OK with it.'

'I am!'

'You're not. I can see you're not. That's really not fair, babes.'

'What am I supposed to say?' I asked. '"I'm thrilled you're going to be having sex with another woman tonight. Make sure you knock on my door as soon as it's over and tell me all about it, especially the anal?"'

'We probably won't be—'

'Please don't tell me what you will and won't be doing,' I said, closing my eyes.

Sam stood up, shaking her head. 'You're such a hypocrite! You fucked someone else last night!'

I felt absolutely alive with injustice. 'But you *told* me to fuck someone else! You *wanted* me to be the first to fuck someone else!'

'Right!' she said. 'And you *literally just said* that you enjoyed it! And did I give you a hard time about it?'

'No . . .' I crossed my arms; I felt too naked, now that we were arguing. 'I'm not telling you not to sleep with Virginie. But I can't help feeling weird about it.'

'It's not fair to make me feel guilty,' Sam said. 'I'm not having that.' And she opened the door and slammed off to the bathroom.

I sat there on the bed, tingling with rage. I ran over the facts in my head, to reassure myself that I wasn't going mad: Sam had actually encouraged me to fuck someone else. She had picked Emma out for me. And then she had choreographed the whole encounter, like a kinky Twyla Tharp. It wasn't fair of her to compare that to what was going to happen tonight. Virginie wasn't a stranger and I hadn't been invited to join in. Not that I'd have RSVPd 'Yes' to that particular invitation.

I worried I was going to slide into a panic attack, right there in the bedroom, which would have been embarrassing – not ideal weekend guest behaviour. I walked over to the window and held onto the sill to steady myself. Outside, it was a lovely blue-and-yellow day, the trees and houses in sharp focus, like a vivid memory. I could get through this. I had been through worse. Soon this would all just be a memory too.

Sam came back into the room ten minutes later. I was still standing by the window, not sure what to do with myself. She hugged me from behind. She was damp. She'd had a shower. I let myself lean back into her. I felt better when I was touching her.

'Sorry, babes,' she said, into my hair. 'I guess it was harder than I thought it would be to see you with someone else, last night.'

And the anger was back again. 'But you *told* me to—'

She held me tight, so I couldn't pull away. 'I'm not blaming you, babes. But you have to let me do this tonight. Even things out. Fair's fair. Yeah?'

'Yes,' I said. I didn't want to argue with her, not today, not when she was going to be spending the night with Virginie.

I didn't say much at breakfast. The others chatted about the sex party – about how they shouldn't have drunk so much, and how much fun they'd had with the 24/7 sub-dom couple, who were experts in Japanese rope bondage, and about their friend Sylvie, who'd burned all her arm hair off during fire play. I focused on the coffee and croissants and cheese and ham and jam (raspberry), all of which were extremely restorative and delicious.

'And Julia,' Virginie said, 'you were so hot!'

'Thank you,' I said, looking down. I'd spilled jam on the table.

'That reminds me,' Virginie said, standing up and walking to her overcrowded bookshelves. She pulled out a worn paperback and handed it to me.

Sam leaned over to see what it was and nodded approvingly.

I looked at the cover and almost laughed – it featured hyper-real illustrations of naked, mulleted people holding hands, apparently all orgasming in unison. There was a cat on there, too, for some reason. The title – *Polyamory for Beginners: Infinite Pleasure Minimal Pain* – was in a font that looked worryingly like Comic Sans.

'Someone should reissue it,' Sam said, correctly interpreting my reaction.

'This book changed my life,' Virginie said. 'It freed me from the pressure of being monogamous.'

'Right,' I said. 'Thank you.'

'You will love it,' Charlotte said, smiling at me. 'I used to be a very jealous person, but this book, it totally cured me of all that.'

'It's pretty much the non-monogamy bible,' Sam said.

'Well, I'm looking forward to reading it,' I said. And I was. I wanted to be cured.

That day passed very quickly; days do when you're dreading what's at the end of them. Virginie and Charlotte gave us a proper guided tour of Lyon – a beautiful city, full of apothecaries and sweet shops selling incredibly strong liquorice – but I couldn't relax. Live in the moment, Julia, I told myself. Listen to those melodic French accents.

Smell that buttery French air. But my mind kept flashing forward to the night ahead when the others would once again be experiencing infinite pleasure and I would be trying to cure myself of monogamy by reading an Eighties self-help book.

Dinner that night saved me; the food was so delicious that I was completely absorbed in every mouthful and the three glasses of Sauvignon Blanc I drank silenced the voice in my head that screamed, 'What the fuck are you doing?'

We finished eating at about 10 p.m. and went to a lesbian club. Sam put her arm around me as we walked in. 'OK?' she said.

'OK.'

'You're amazing. You know that?'

'I know,' I said.

'There's no one in this world I love or desire more than you.'

'Right.'

'I mean it,' she said. And I believed her. That's what made the whole thing so complicated. 'I want you to feel free to take someone home tonight, if you want to.'

'That's not going to happen,' I said quickly. The very idea exhausted me; I'd had enough random sex for one weekend.

But after Charlotte had ordered us a round of tequila shots and Sam had started dirty dancing with Virginie, taking someone home started to seem like a pretty good idea. Charlotte wandered off to chat up a boyish-looking woman at the bar, and soon they were kissing, pushing each other up against the wall. I was left alone, bouncing along to the music in a manner that I hoped said 'I'm broad-minded and open to casual sex.' It worked; after a couple of minutes an attractive older butch with kind eyes and a nose piercing tapped me on the shoulder and said something in French.

'My name is Claudette,' she said, after I'd explained about my lack of French.

'Julia,' I said. I looked at her; she reminded me a little bit of my GCSE physics teacher, who probably was a lesbian, I realized now, just like the rumours had suggested. There was something attractive about her, though.

'I can kiss you?' said Claudette.

And I said, 'Yes.'

Claudette tasted of stale beer – a little like Finn, in other words – but I closed my eyes and tried to get into it. She began to run her hands down my back. I opened my eyes and saw Virginie and Sam on the other side of the club, kissing and swaying to the music. I closed my eyes again and put my hands in the French woman's hair, but all I could see was my girlfriend with her hands on another woman's arse and sure, maybe it was hypocritical, but I felt like I'd been slapped.

Claudette pulled away and wiped her mouth with the back of her hand, which I took as an implied criticism of my kissing technique. 'Shall we go back to my flat?' she asked.

I had never felt less turned on in my life.

'Thank you,' I said, 'but no.'

So I only had myself to blame that two hours later I was sitting propped up on floral pillows in Virginie and Charlotte's guest room, listening to aggressively loud metal music and flicking through *Polyamory for Beginners*, trying to distract myself from what was going on in the other rooms. Charlotte had brought her boyish woman back with her – they tried to persuade me to have a threesome with them, but I politely declined. I turned down a nightcap, too. I took a half-finished bottle of wine into my room instead and tried to create a *cosy, serene, self-loving space* for myself, as the book recommended.

The book was actually very absorbing, particularly the diagrams. I looked at a line drawing of four people in a complicated, Twister sort of arrangement. *Four isn't a chore!* read the caption, but I wasn't convinced. Unfortunately, though, not even the book could distract me from the dull thumping noises coming from the other rooms. Every time I heard someone moan, I told myself it was Charlotte, but who was I kidding? I'd had sex with Sam enough times to know what she sounded like in bed. Plus I didn't think a French woman would be able to say, 'Harder!' or 'You like it, do you, you filthy whore?' in such a convincing London accent. *Polyamory for Beginners* offered:

> *When my partner is in the guest room with another lady, I sometimes find myself feeling jealous. I know that in situations like that, the best thing to do is to treat myself! I ask myself, what would I be doing if my partner was just out at work and I had the evening to myself? I run myself a scented bath and lie there listening to classical music; I read a few chapters of a gripping novel; I put a face pack on and watch old movies. Audrey Hepburn films are my favourite! The possibilities are endless. Take this time for yourself. Enjoy it! And then, when your partner comes back into your room, still smelling of her juices, kiss him and say, 'Did you have fun?' He'll be so impressed that you care so much about his pleasure. By then, it'll all be over, and you'll think, it wasn't that bad!*

I tried to read up on the competencies for my job interview, but I couldn't concentrate. I listened to a meditation podcast, but the soothing voice kept telling me to pay attention to the noises around me, which was the last thing I wanted to do. I began to cry hot, silent tears.

Treat yourself as you would if you had a cold, advised *Polyamory for Beginners*, but I didn't have any Vicks VapoRub with me, and I didn't think it would be very helpful if I could find any. Maybe I was taking the book too literally? *Try to put things in perspective*, said the book. *When your partner is with another woman you might feel like you're being tortured. But you're not! Think of what other people around the world are suffering right at this very minute.* Good point, I thought; I plugged myself into my laptop and watched documentary after upsetting documentary, about genocide, murder, racism and homophobia. I cried about the things humans do to other humans, and I cried for myself, too, and I felt better, until my laptop battery ran out and I realized I'd left the charger in the living room.

Things went downhill after that. I paced the room, biting my fingers till they bled. Was Sam curling into her, like she curled into me? Did she kiss her in the night whenever she turned over? Was she whispering 'I love you' in her ear? And was I a hypocrite to mind this so much, considering what had happened the night before? I felt like I was going mad. It was nearly four in the morning, but this was an emergency, so I called Alice. She picked up on the fourth ring.

'Are you OK?' she asked. I could tell from her voice that I'd woken her up.

'No,' I said.

I could hear her sitting up in bed. 'What's happened? Are you still in Paris? Where's Sam?'

'I'm not in Paris,' I said in a small voice. 'I'm in Lyon.'

'But – isn't that where Virginie lives?'

'Yes. They're having sex in her room and I'm on my own, and I can't believe I let this happen—'

'Wait there,' said Alice. 'I'll try and get a Eurostar or something.'

'No, it's fine.'

'You are not staying there. Get out of there. Get a hotel.'

'No,' I said, 'It's not like that. I knew this was going to happen.'

'Julia,' said Alice, 'this is not OK. It is not OK that she has asked this of you.'

'But I had sex with someone else last night—'

'What?'

'Sam was there too—'

'Did you *want* to have sex with someone else last night?'

'Sort of. At the time.'

She didn't say anything. I sat there, listening to the comforting not-quite-silence on the other end of the phone for a while.

'I love her,' I said.

'Julia,' she said. 'I think you're obsessed with her.'

'I'm supposed to be obsessed with her. She's my girlfriend.'

'No,' she said. 'You're not.'

'I need her.'

'We need to get you home.'

'I'm coming home tomorrow,' I said.

'Is there somewhere you can go now?'

'No, it's OK. Really, it's fine. I'm sorry I woke you up.' I hung up the phone and sat there, breathing erratically. Alice called back a few seconds later but I rejected the call. She didn't understand. I barely understood myself. I wasn't well. All I knew was that I had to do something to change the way I felt, and I wanted to hurt myself in some way.

That isn't a feeling I've had often in my life; just once before, actually, shortly after the end of my dance career. I've never been a very practical person, so I wasn't really sure how to go about it. And I can't have wanted to hurt myself that badly, because instead of a kitchen knife or the prescription painkillers my dad used for his sciatica I used a ladybird-shaped drawing pin from my parents' noticeboard. I tried to push it into my wrist, but I didn't try particularly hard; I ended up with the world's tiniest bruise, and even that was gone a day later.

Tonight, that out-of-control, sliding-off-the-world feeling was back. I opened the sex cupboard and found a nipple clamp. I put it on my arm and tightened it till my skin turned red, then white. I felt calm; the pain was focused and clean, white and cold and outside me. And then I realized what I was doing, and I pulled the nipple clamp from my arm and rubbed the place where it had been. 'Get it together, Julia,' I said to myself out loud. I forced myself to breathe in and out until the sex noises stopped at about 5 a.m., and then I finally, finally fell asleep.

I managed about three hours of sleep, punctuated by strange dreams about having sex with the blonde drag queen from the bar, before I was woken by the smell of coffee and the tinkle of sexually fulfilled French laughter. I sat up in bed and tried to work out what I'd say to everyone over breakfast. 'I had a great night, thanks. Learned about conditions in Bergen-Belsen and then self-harmed with a nipple clamp'?

I spent a long time in front of the mirror making sure my make-up was flawless while I listened to the voices in the other room. They were speaking English, so I guessed Sam was out there. I waited until I heard someone shut the bathroom door and turn on the shower, so I wouldn't have to face all of them at once, and then I smiled an unfeasibly wide smile and opened the bedroom door.

It's fair to say I've had pleasanter breakfasts than the one I ate that morning, and I'm including a fruit salad in Marrakech that gave me diarrhoea. I opened the bedroom door to find Virginie, Charlotte and Sam sitting around the kitchen table, drinking coffee and eating croissants in their dressing gowns. Virginie's hair was rumpled. Sam's lips looked red and puffy.

'Sit here!' said Virginie, pulling out the seat next to her. 'How did you sleep?'

'Fine, thank you' I said, sitting down.

'The coffee is fresh,' said Charlotte, pushing the cafetiére towards me.

'Great,' I said, and poured myself a cup, grateful to have something to do with my hands.

'Chloe is in the shower,' said Charlotte.

'She's the woman you brought home?' I asked, glad not to have to look at Sam or Virginie.

'Yes. We had a lot of fun,' she said.

'And you, Julia, what would you like to do this morning? What time is your Eurostar?' asked Virginie.

I let Sam answer. Then everyone discussed the weather and if we had time to go for lunch before we left. I focused all my attention on taking a croissant, buttering it and eating it in small bites; swallowing wasn't easy. No one was acknowledging what had happened the night before. No one had asked me how I was, or how I'd found giving up my girlfriend for the night; I don't know what I'd expected — it wasn't as though I wanted them to act ashamed, or to pity me, but I felt like someone should have acknowledged the sacrifice I'd made.

'I missed you,' Sam said, coming over to kiss me on the head. She smelled of Virginie's perfume.

I got through the rest of the day somehow, and by 'somehow' I mean 'by drinking a lot of red wine'. Luckily Sam was so tired from her night of hot French sex that she was happy to sleep all the way home. But when we got back to her flat and she asked me how I'd enjoyed the weekend, I couldn't stop myself bursting into tears.

'Shh,' she said stroking my head. 'That was all a bit new for you, wasn't it?'

'Please could you have another shower? You still smell of her.'

'OK, babes,' she said. 'It gets easier, you know. It really does.'

'I don't know if I want it to get easier,' I said. 'I think I'm going to go home tonight.'

'Please don't go,' she said, reaching for my hand. 'You still want me, don't you? You have to tell me you still want me.'

'I still want you,' I said. And then I made myself say, 'But I don't think I can share you. It hurts too much.'

'You'll feel different tomorrow,' Sam said, her voice decisive. 'Everything is very raw right now.'

But I felt stronger than usual — something to do with the heady cocktail of anger and humiliation and sleep deprivation. 'I don't think I will,' I said. 'Virginie isn't just some random woman you've had sex with. It's not the same as having a threesome at a sex party. You love her. I didn't sign up for that.'

Sam dropped my hand and made a strange little scoffing noise. 'You're not seriously asking me to choose between you?'

I wanted to say 'No,' and have her hold me again, and maybe have some sex and eat Chinese food and forget about the whole thing until she next went to France, but that was the problem – there would be a next time, and I didn't want there to be. So I said, 'Actually, yes, I am.'

I took the Overground home. My mind felt clean. As I walked up Green Lanes, I could see people playing tag in Finsbury Park. I could smell chargrilled meat. I was hungry.

I didn't see Sam for two weeks after that.

33. SAVING CONTENTMENT FOR MY RETIREMENT

I called in sick the day after we got back from Lyon and lay in bed, crying and threatening never to get up again. Alice came in to see me when she got home from work and insisted that we watch a period drama together, so that I would remember there were good and beautiful things in the world – BBC adaptations of classic novels, for example – and I shouldn't give up on it altogether.

I did get up the next day – I had to, to go to my job interview. To say that I was underprepared is an understatement. I had tried to do some work the night I got back from Lyon, but it's hard to come up with an example of a time you dealt with a mistake at work when you're shovelling peanut butter cups into your face and sobbing. I had hoped that my verbal communication skills would get me through (they 'exceeded expectations', according to my last appraisal), but as soon as the interviewers came out to meet me, I knew the whole thing was hopeless. Even my handshake was weaker than usual.

'How did it go?' Owen asked, when I got back to the office after the interview.

I dropped my bag on the floor and sat down. 'Shit,' I said.

'What did you say for the question about influencing a senior manager?'

'I told them about the time we asked Tom for database training,' I said to him.

Owen nodded.

'What?' I asked.

'Nothing,' he said.

'You think it's a rubbish example.'

'I don't!' he said. 'It's just – you're supposed to say "I" not "we", so it's clear you're not taking credit for something someone else did.'

I closed my eyes. 'I'm not going to get the job.'

'You don't know that.'

'I do,' I said.

'I probably won't get it either,' said Owen. 'We can be unemployed together and do fun unemployed things.'

'What,' I said, 'like not have enough money to eat?'

As the days passed, the memory of the terrible interview faded. Anyway as Ella and Zhu pointed out, it wasn't as though I really wanted the job anyway. It was July and London was in the throes of a heat wave; I felt weirdly high during those two Sam-free weeks as I walked the baking streets, listening to songs about being young and single, smiling stupidly at blue skies and people in shorts. It turns out that when you're not having extremely satisfying sex all the time, or talking about having sex, or getting drunk with the person you have sex with, you have time to take part in the Women's March, watch queer cabaret acts at Bethnal Green Working Men's Club and experiment with recipes for strawberry cake. But then I'd see something that reminded me of Sam – a packet of Marlboros, an advert for the Eurostar, the Tate Modern – and I'd break down again, sobbing on Alice's shoulder that I'd lost the love of my life.

Alice would make soothing noises while I bleated, 'I love her! She makes me feel alive!' But that first Saturday, as we were browsing for feminist literature in Waterstones, she said, 'I just think she's trying to have her *tarte tatin* and eat her Victoria sponge, too. There are people I fancy, but I don't do anything about it, because I'm engaged to Dave, and that's that.'

That perked me up a bit. I looked up from the three-for-two table and asked, 'Who do you fancy?'

'Never you mind.' She held up a copy of *The Blind Assassin*. 'Have you read this one? I haven't read enough Margaret Atwood.'

'No,' I said. 'Tell me who you fancy.'

'Fine,' she said, putting the book down. 'Ahmed at work. And Owen.'

'Owen from my office?' I asked.

'Yes. And John from next door. And the Turkish bloke from the corner shop.'

'Wow,' I said.

'But I'm not going to have sex with any of them, because I've made a vow.'

'Are you and Dave all right?' I asked.

Alice nodded and smiled. 'We're fine!' she said.

'Great.'

'Most of the time,' said Alice.

'OK.'

'Except for the sex drought.'

'That's normal, though,' I said. 'You've been going out for years.'

'But you and Sam have been together for a while now.'

'Only a few months, really. And I'm not sure we're even together any more.'

'OK. But whatever. When you see her, you have sex all the time.'

'Yeah, but Sam's special. She's got an unusually high sex drive for a woman.'

Alice gave me a cold little smile. 'You're right. I should be grateful I don't have to sit there while Dave has sex with a French woman and then disappears for a week.'

*   *   *

But Sam hadn't disappeared altogether; photos kept popping up on Instagram. Sam dry-humping Jasper at a polysexual club night; Sam smoking in London Fields; Sam apparently shopping on Bond Street (quite uncharacteristic – she usually bought her clothes in the Dalston branch of Oxfam). Some of the photos were selfies, but most weren't, and I drove myself ever so slightly mad trying to work out who had taken each photo based on the angle they were taken at. Was she taller than Sam? Was she some sort of high-maintenance West Londoner, hence the Bond Street trip? Or had Sam just purchased a selfie stick? Anything was possible.

I was having fun too, though – pretending to on social media, at least. I arranged to see friends every night after work so that I wouldn't have to be alone with my thoughts. I surprised Owen by suggesting a team drink, and we ended up doing shots with Uzo, who turned out to be very good at karaoke. I actually had a little cry during her rendition of 'Without You'. I did a yoga class with Cat, who was back in London briefly before going up to Edinburgh for *Menstruation: the Musical* which was widely tipped to be the cult hit of the Fringe.

'Sam's a twat,' Cat whispered, trying to wedge her left foot into her groin – quite challenging. 'Come to Edinburgh with me. There'll be loads of queer people for you to choose from.'

'I don't want loads of queer people. I want Sam,' I said.

And then the teacher shot us a look, because if you can talk when you're doing one-legged pigeon pose, you're not doing it properly.

I went back to Stepping Out too; Ella and I discussed the ethics of BDSM as Zhu taught us the shim sham.

'I'm obviously more conservative than I thought I was,' I said, shuffling to the right.

'If being conservative means you don't want to be led around on a lead, I think that's OK,' Ella said, shuffling to the left.

'Obviously I believe everyone has the right to wear leads if they want to. And clothes pegs on their nipples,' I said, doing a step ball change.

'Is that a thing?'

'Apparently,' I said. 'Though maybe it was just that one woman? I haven't been to enough sex parties.'

'Sounds to me like you've been to too many of them.'

Pretty much all of my friends agreed that I should ditch Sam if she refused to break up with Virginie. I felt both strengthened by their opinions and weak for relying so heavily on what they thought. But no one understood what Sam was like when we were alone; the way she looked into my eyes; the way she pretended to be a tiny hippo when she was in the bath, which I realize sounds obnoxious, but was honestly completely adorable; the way she made me come. Let's not pretend the sex wasn't a massive part of it.

The days passed, and she didn't call. I found myself snapping at the people who did call me, because they weren't her – the poor woman from the local pharmacy didn't deserve my wrath – and I couldn't concentrate at work; I'd be writing a letter about working conditions for junior doctors and I'd drift into a daydream about Sam, and my heart would start racing, and the only way I'd be able to calm myself down would be to read old texts or look at photos of us together.

But when my heart was racing, at least I was aware of it beating. I wasn't comfortable, but I didn't want to be. I was saving contentment for my retirement. You're not supposed to be content at 26.

'You sabotaged yourself,' Nicky said, at my next session, when I told her about my job interview.

'I wouldn't say that,' I said.

'Of course you wouldn't,' said Nicky. 'You're terrible at taking constructive criticism. Let's look at the facts: you had weeks to prepare for the interview, and you left it till the night before, and didn't go to bed until one in the morning.'

'My head wasn't in the right place,' I said. And I explained about Lyon and everything that had happened there.

She stared at me open-mouthed while I was telling her the story, and when I'd finished, she said, 'So. First you had a threesome.'

'More like a semi-threesome. Kind of a two-and-a-halfsome.'

'In public.'

'In front of other people.'

'And then the next night she had sex with another woman without you, and you could hear the whole thing through the walls.'

'Yes.'

'While you were watching a documentary about AIDS.'

'HIV.'

'And did she sound like she was having a good time?'

'Yes.'

'And did the noises turn you on?'

'No!'

She raised her eyebrows at me.

'I was trying really hard not to be turned on.'

'You should keep that bit in the story when you tell it. It makes the whole thing much more interesting.'

I thought about that. 'It is a good story, isn't it?' I said.

'Are you kidding? You're going to be dining out on it for years!'

'Trying to self-harm with a nipple clamp is pretty funny,' I said.

She looked at me, suddenly serious. 'That's not funny,' she said.

I started to cry.

'As your therapist, I advise you to send her a text right now and tell her it's over.'

'You're not supposed to tell me what to do.'

'I see it as my duty to intervene when my clients make decisions that could lead to them getting hurt.'

'I won't get back together with her unless she ends it with Virginie.'

'But she's still free to have casual sex with as many anonymous people as she likes.'

'And so am I!'

'I can help you decide what to say.'

'I don't want to send her a text,' I said. But I took out my phone. And there on the screen was the green glow of a new WhatsApp message.

I couldn't stop myself from smiling. 'It's from her,' I said.

'What does it say?'

'We need to talk. I love and miss you and I am prepared to compromise but you'll need to compromise too.'

'How romantic.'

'I'm asking her to break up with someone she's been seeing for years. It's a big deal.'

'This is going to end in tears.'

'It won't!' I'd had enough of people telling me not to be with Sam. Bloody Cat and self-righteous Alice and now Nicky, who wasn't even a proper therapist yet—

'It will, and I'll have to pick up the pieces. I mean, you'll need a lot more therapy, which is good from my point of view, but you're my client and I'm telling you what's best for you.'

'She's what's best for me.'

'If what you want from a relationship is a collection of outrageous stories to tell at dinner parties, sure.'

'She makes me feel alive.'

'You're a masochist. You know there are clubs for that sort of thing?'

'I do. I've been to several of them.'

She blinked at me. 'Tell me everything.'

So I told her, about the slings, and the gimp masks, and the water sports, and the clothes pegs, and the cutlery, and the leads, and the KitKats.

She sat there for a while and then said, 'Well. That all sounds very interesting.' A pause. 'Are your friends jealous?'

'Envious,' I said, before I could stop myself.

'Excuse me?'

'Nothing. It's just – you're jealous of something you have. You're envious of something you don't have.'

She wagged her pen at me. 'You're my most pedantic client. You know that?'

'Sorry,' I said. 'I need to be good at grammar and things, for work.'

She looked at me for a while. 'Here's the way I see it.'

'I don't really want to know the way you see it.'

'Then why are you paying me £25 a session?'

'Because literally every other therapist in London charges four times that much.'

'The way I see it is this: you find it arousing to be dominated during sex.'

'Yes. Fine. Definitely think we should talk about something else now.'

'But Sam is starting to dominate you the rest of the time too.'

'That is completely untrue.' I could feel myself getting flushed and agitated, like my mother does when she hears words like 'steel beam' and 'subsidence'.

'You're an intelligent woman—'

'A compliment!'

'I haven't finished. You're an intelligent woman. You claim you want to be independent. But you're letting your girlfriend control you.'

I stood up. 'You're just prejudiced against people who do BDSM. You're a kink shamer.'

Nicky smiled and crossed her legs. 'You learned that phrase from Sam.'

'You don't know what you're talking about.'

'Are you actually happy with Sam?'

'Yes. I am.'

'And what are you going to do about the fact you're going to be unemployed in a few months?'

'I'm not thinking about that right now.'

'I can see that. You're distracting yourself with lesbian drama. How's the anxiety?'

'Fine,' I said, but my hands were shaking, which slightly gave the game away. I thought I might be about to cry, so I said, 'I think that's enough for this week,' and stood up.

'Julia. Come back,' Nicky said.

I didn't trust myself to speak, so I shook my head and shut the door behind me. As I made my wobbly way out into the street, I took my phone out and texted Sam back.

34. ELIMINATION DAY

Sam suggested meeting at The Glory. You could read that in two ways, I decided. It was intimate and welcoming and dark – the perfect spot to tell me how sorry she was, vow to break up with Virginie and toast the future of our relationship with a bottle of house red. But it would also be a good place to dump me: the sort of place you could have a serious chat, and small enough that I wouldn't want to make a scene, not in front of all the trendy queers.

As I walked in, Sam waved at me and gave me a warm, gorgeous, uncomplicated smile and I just wanted to run away from the non-monogamy and the disapproval of my friends and therapist and the voice in my head that said, 'She'll never change' and stare at her forever.

She held my hand as I sat down and said, 'I've missed you so much, babes. I'd forgotten how beautiful you are.'

I hadn't forgotten how beautiful she was, obviously, because I'd spent so much time watching her Instagram stories, but I had forgotten her charisma, and how completely, hopelessly attracted to her I was.

Sam ordered us a couple of glasses of wine. Large ones. We drank them quickly, asking each other banal questions about work and what we'd been up to over the previous two weeks.

'Concrete Street are going to represent me!' Sam told me.

'That's great!' I said.

'And you? How's work?'

271

'Fine. Still waiting to hear about the Senior Account Manager job, but I know I messed up the interview. Cat's going to be a famous actress, though. Five-star review in the *Scotsman* for *Menstruation: the Musical*.'

'Are you pleased for her? Or are you secretly a bit bitter? I would be.'

'Massively bitter,' I said. It was a relief, being able to admit that. 'She keeps asking when I'm coming up to see the show but I don't think I can bear it. I'd probably cry through the whole thing, which wouldn't be appropriate, seeing as the *Guardian* called it "hilarious and uplifting".'

'They called it "timely", too. I saw the review.'

'God. Don't.'

Sam laughed. And she looked me straight in the eye. And in that moment I didn't care that Cat was probably going to move to Hollywood and appear on the cover of *Vanity Fair* in a ball gown, sitting on Glenn Close's lap, because I had Sam back. Or I would, if this evening went to plan.

We were on our second round before we got down to business.

'I should have known it was too soon for you to come to Lyon,' Sam said, fiddling with her glass.

I nodded.

'That was pretty full on, meeting Virginie for the first time and staying in her house.'

'While you had sex with her.'

'Which you knew was going to happen.'

We looked at each other across our glasses of wine. This was starting to feel less like a conversation and more like a negotiation, and I've never been much of a negotiator. I actually talked myself into a pay cut when I got my job – the recruitment consultant who sent me for the interview said, 'Will you take the job for £28,000?' and I said, 'I'd take it for less, to be honest.' So they offered me £25,000, and I hated myself for months, until I decided to do three grands' less work over the year, turning up late and taking long lunches and looking at Twitter when I should have been answering letters about the IVF postcode lottery.

Sam took my hand. 'I really don't want to lose you.'

'I don't want to lose you either,' I said.

'But I can't change who I am.' She gave me a sad smile.

'I'm not asking you to.'

She laughed. 'Well. You are. A bit.'

Which was true. But she was asking me to change too, obviously. So I pointed that out.

Sam took a sip of wine. 'I made a very difficult decision last week,' she said. She took a deep breath and let it out, looking at me earnestly, letting the tension build, like a reality TV judge preparing to announce a contestant's elimination. 'I told Virginie it was over between us.'

I let out a breath. I felt relieved, sure. But I also felt guilty. Much more guilty than I'd anticipated.

'It wasn't easy,' Sam said, looking at her hands. 'She was very angry with me. Charlotte's very angry, too.'

'Mmm.' Anger. That's the other thing I was feeling.

'You should know that I'm going to be grieving for her and I'll need you to support me.' She started to cry. 'I'm sorry,' she said. 'I'm just going to really miss her.'

It hadn't occurred to me that seeing Sam cry over breaking up with Virginie would be as painful as listening to them fucking.

'*I'm* sorry,' I said, putting my hand on hers.

Sam pulled a tissue from her pocket. 'I have to be free to have casual sex. Otherwise this will all just end in tears.'

'I know,' I said.

'And I want you to have it too! It was fun with Emma in Lyon, wasn't it?'

I thought back to that night. 'Yes,' I said.

'See?' Sam said. 'It doesn't have to be threatening.'

But I was still threatened. 'Why am I not enough for you?' I asked.

Sam's eyes widened. 'That's not it,' she said. 'That's not it at all! The fact that I want to have sex with other people is completely separate from the way I feel about you!'

I nodded. 'It's hard to feel like I'm not being made a fool of. Nicky really doesn't get it—'

Sam pulled away from me. 'You don't tell your therapist about what we do in bed, do you?'

'Well – yes,' I said.

'She knows you're into SM?'

'She knows *you're* into SM,' I said.

'And what does she think about that?'

'She has a lot of opinions about everything,' I said.

'What does she think about SM and non-monogamy?' Sam asked again.

'She thinks SM is fine as long as the power dynamic doesn't spill over into real life.'

I shouldn't have told her that. Obviously, obviously, I shouldn't have told her that.

'You need to stop seeing her.'

'I don't,' I said, pleading, touching Sam's arm. 'She says loads of stupid things. She thinks Alice secretly wants to be a housewife and that's why she's having doubts about marrying Dave.'

'That makes no sense.'

'Exactly. That's what I'm saying. You can't tell me to stop seeing her,' I said.

'No,' Sam said, her voice softer suddenly. 'No, that's not what I'm doing. I'm sorry.' She reached out for my hand again. 'I just think you should find a counsellor who understands alternative life-styles. It sounds like she's a bit judgemental, OK, babes?'

If I stopped seeing Nicky, Sam and I would both have sacrificed something for our relationship. We would be even. So I said, 'OK. I won't see her for a while if that's what you want.'

Sam sighed, her eyes squeezed shut, eyelashes flickering. 'Thank you,' she said, taking my hand. 'Thank you.'

'She's controlling you.'

'She's not. I just don't know how useful these sessions are at the moment.'

'She told you to stop seeing me.' Nicky did her trick of staring at me until I had to look away.

'I'm finding it all a bit confusing. You don't think I should be with Sam. And I want to be with her. So coming to see you isn't making me feel better.'

'Therapy isn't supposed to just make you feel better. It's meant to be hard work.'

'I don't want to work hard,' I said. 'I want to be happy. Sam makes me happy.'

And then I started crying, which undermined my point a little bit, and I tried to make myself stop crying, but that only made me cry harder and longer, my mouth turned down in a sort of pantomime of grief.

Nicky passed me the tissues. I glanced up at her, expecting her to be looking at me triumphantly, but she wasn't. She looked concerned. Which was much worse.

'Stop looking at me like that,' I said.

So she looked at her notebook and said, 'Have you really made up your mind?'

I nodded.

Nicky put down her pen. 'Any time you want to come back,' she said, 'just call me. Call me in the middle of the night if you need to. I'll always pick up. Unless I'm in a compromising position.'

As we said goodbye she hugged me, tight, which probably isn't the sort of thing a therapist is supposed to do. She was wearing the same perfume as my mum. I pulled away and waved a vague goodbye and ran home down Green Lanes, crying harder than ever.

35. VINDICTIVELY CALM

I thought I'd feel more secure in my relationship with Sam now that Virginie was out of the picture. I thought we'd do the sorts of things really committed couples do – go on shiatsu massage courses, host dinner parties, describe each other as 'my other half' – but instead of throwing herself into being with me, Sam pulled away. I'd go for dinner at her flat and she'd open the door in her dressing gown, unsmiling, and put pasta on the hob without attempting to make conversation. I'd try and do enough talking for both of us, but she'd give one-word answers to my questions, and when I asked what was wrong, she'd say, 'What do you think's wrong?'

I'd find myself stroking her back and saying, 'I'm sorry you're having a bad time.' She would huff in response, and say something like, 'Could you not touch me? I'm feeling a bit sensitive right now. I just need some space.'

The trouble is, whenever someone asks me for space I want to spend every waking moment with them. The more monosyllabic and, frankly, unpleasant Sam became, the more I tried to fix her, sending her sweet text messages first thing in the morning, cooking dinners for her, making up little songs about how much I loved her. Some of them even rhymed.

A few weeks after Sam had broken up with Virginie, I persuaded her to meet me for a drink after work. She turned up carrying a large cardboard box. As she sat down, I saw that her eyes were swollen. 'What's wrong?' I asked.

'Nothing,' she said. 'You wouldn't care.'

'Please tell me,' I said.

'Fine,' she said, like she was doing me a favour. 'Virginie sent all my things to the studio.' She put the cardboard box on the table. 'She sent back all the presents I ever gave her.' Sam started pulling things out of the box – a silver necklace, small stuffed animals, endless cards. 'This was the first thing I ever bought for her,' she said, holding up a small vibrator. 'I know I've hurt her, but she's being cruel.'

'You poor thing . . .'

I know I sound weak and pathetic, and I felt weak and pathetic at the time, but I was furious, too. Did she really expect me to comfort her about her break-up with another woman? Yes, was the answer. But I couldn't tell her how angry I was, because she would think I was being unreasonable, and we would fight, and that might be the end of us.

That night I cried on the Tube home. The balding man in the seat opposite said, 'Cheer up, it might never happen,' which made me cry more. A woman in a floral beret offered me a tissue that smelled strangely of cinnamon.

The flat was quiet and empty when I got home. I changed into my pyjamas and lay on my bed, listening to the traffic until I fell asleep.

I woke up at three in the morning, sweating, from a dream about Sam and Virginie and the tiny vibrator. I could barely keep my eyes open at work the next day. I offered to make a tea round, and ended up putting milk in Uzo's peppermint tea, which is the sort of thing that can ruin the office dynamic if you're not careful, particularly in an office where you pay for your own tea bags. As I was waiting for the kettle to boil a second time, I heard a buzz of activity around Owen's desk. Uzo was hugging Owen – an unusual occurrence – and Tom was saying something about a feather in Owen's cap.

I walked over as quickly I could without spilling Uzo's tea.

'What's going on?' I asked.

Owen scuffed the floor with his foot and shrugged. 'Got a second interview,' he said.

'Oh!' I said.

'Check your email!' he said. 'Maybe you've got one too!'

So I did – with Uzo and Tom and Owen all looking over my shoulder at my inbox, which was unfortunate, because there was a five-message exchange with Cat near the top, titled *Is this costume too tight around the vag area?*

And there, in the middle of the unread messages, fat and bold, was an email from Civil Service Jobs. I clicked on it. And then I wished I hadn't.

We regret to inform you that you have not been successful at this time. The standard of applications was very high . . .

There was a sympathetic silence.

'Oh well!' I said, brightly, turning and smiling at the others.

Uzo rubbed my shoulder.

'Don't let the bastards get you down,' said Tom. 'It's all a matter of jumping through hoops. Not everyone can be a bloody performing pony. No offence, Owen.'

'I'm sorry,' Owen said.

'Don't apologize!' I said.

'I probably won't get any further, anyway.'

'You will! I bet you will!' I said, with audible exclamation marks. 'I'm really happy for you!'

'Thanks,' he said, looking down, still shuffling.

'I always knew Owen was smarter than he looked,' Uzo said, hugging him again, mug in hand – a dangerous undertaking.

'Thanks,' said Owen again, escaping unscalded. Part of me – the nasty part of me – was disappointed.

278

Owen didn't seem to want to look at me, which was just as well, because my face was doing an odd, twitchy dance. I was trying to make it smile, but it seemed determined not to. I knew I probably looked extremely upset, which was not an appropriate way to look under the circumstances, so I took my face to the toilets where no one would be able to see it for a while.

I went to Sam's that night and told her what had happened, crying into my fish pie at the kitchen table as she rubbed my hand absent-mindedly.

'I feel like such a failure,' I said.

'Don't be silly,' she said. 'If you had really wanted the job, you'd have done more work for the interview.'

I suppressed another flicker of fury, because I'd probably have performed better if I hadn't been distracted by the memory of French women offering me coffee one minute and fucking my girlfriend the next.

I helped Sam clear the table and then sat down while she stood with her back to me at the sink, scrubbing the dirty plates. The steam from the hot water filmed the kitchen windows and the SAM LOVES JULIA she'd written with her finger months before reappeared, like the ghost of what our relationship had once been, mocking me.

That night I slept pressed up against her, desperate to feel the comforting heat of her body, but she edged away from me, muttering again about needing space. I lay on my back, thinking of all the withering things I could say to her, things like, 'Polly is a more interesting artist than you,' and 'Your Barbour jacket makes you look like a retired policeman,' and 'You look a bit like an owl when you're about to come.' Just thinking them made me feel calm, in a vindictive sort of way. I realized 'vindictively calm' wasn't an ideal way to feel when lying next to your girlfriend. Perhaps some time apart wasn't a terrible idea.

So the next morning, when we were lying in bed, I told her,

'Alice and I are going to go and stay with Cat in Edinburgh for the weekend.'

She smiled — the first real smile she'd given me in ages. 'Good idea,' she said. 'I'll miss you. Don't do anything I wouldn't do.' And she winked at me. I'd definitely made the right decision, if she was winking.

36. VERY SCOTTISH TINNITUS

Alice and I took Friday afternoon off work and arrived at Terminal 5 three hours before our flight. Alice hates to be late for things, and she loves shopping in airports. 'It feels like free money, when you're about to leave the country!'

'Scotland isn't a different country,' I pointed out, but she was already in Boots, looking at the travel-sized shampoos.

My favourite thing to do at airports is to get drunk, so that's what we did next.

'I'm so glad we're getting out of London,' Alice said, when the wine kicked in. 'Dave keeps emailing me about wedding lists. He wants us to register for fish knives. Who in the twenty-first century uses fish knives?'

'Dave doesn't strike me as a fish knife sort of person,' I said, opening the peanuts I'd been intending to eat on the plane.

'I know! He's turned into a weird Victorian gentleman since we got engaged.'

'At least he's not at home crying because he's broken up with his bouncy-haired lover.'

'Let's not talk about our stupid relationships any more,' Alice said. 'If we were a movie, we'd fail the Bechdel test.'

'All right then,' I said.

'All right,' said Alice.

We looked at each other blankly for a few moments.

'How's work?' I asked.

Alice shrugged. 'I'm editing the biography of a man who used to be in *The Archers*. Lots of photos of his grandchildren and jokes about pig farming. How's yours?'

'You know how mine is.' I'd moaned to her about Owen and his second interview the night before.

We looked at each other a bit longer.

'Would you like to talk about politics?' Alice asked.

'No thank you,' I said. 'I've had too much wine for politics.'

'I saw a really good hedgehog video on Instagram earlier,' Alice said, and she got out her phone.

We drank gin and tonics on the plane, and the safety announcement seemed funnier than usual, and we were still a bit tipsy when the plane landed an hour later.

'We need to sober up,' Alice said, as we waited for our bags. 'We're going to see a Pinter play tonight.'

I wasn't in the mood for a Pinter play, but it's hard to be in the mood for anything when you're waiting at baggage reclaim. According to the airport clock, it was almost eight at night. I wondered what Sam would be doing without me. I WhatsApped her to let her know that I'd arrived, and to tell her that I loved her. The blue ticks let me know she had read the message straight away. She didn't text me back.

Because we were in Edinburgh, it was raining. We narrowed our eyes against the wind and dragged our bags towards the New Town, passing jugglers and student sketch groups and tourists queuing at street food vans for haggis toasties. Everywhere we went, we could hear bagpipes playing 'Scotland the Brave' in a variety of keys and time signatures. It was like having very Scottish tinnitus.

Cat was staying in a two-bedroom Georgian flat just off Princes Street with eight other people. She met us at the front door, still in her stage make-up. She hugged me. 'You came!'

We sat in her room and drank beers, shouting our news to each other over the sound of her flatmates singing improvised comedy songs in the living room.

'You have a room to yourself?' Alice asked Cat.

'I kicked Lacey out to make room for you two. She's staying with her boyfriend.'

'The tadpole?' I asked.

'He's a sanitary towel this time!'

'So the show's going well?' Alice asked.

'Look!' Cat said, showing us a photo on her phone: a blackboard with *SOLD OUT* written at the top and *Menstruation: the Musical* in looping pink chalk letters halfway down.

'You've actually sold out?' Alice said.

'Just yesterday's show,' Cat said. 'No need to look so surprised.'

Cat seemed different – louder than usual, her gestures more exaggerated, probably because she'd spent three weeks surrounded by actors and comedians and the odd mime artist. As she talked about the agents that had come to see her show, and the brilliant reviews, I slipped further into a well of self-pity.

'You're very quiet,' she said to me. 'What's wrong?'

'Just work,' I said.

'Not Sam?' said Cat.

'I don't want to talk about Sam,' I said. She still hadn't texted me back.

'I do,' said Cat.

'Cat,' said Alice, a warning.

'She's guilt-tripping you for asking her to be monogamous.'

'We're still not actually monogamous,' I said.

'For fuck's sake,' said Cat.

'Don't you think that monogamy is a patriarchal construct?' I said.

'If it is, it's one of the better ones,' said Alice.

'Why aren't you angry with her?' said Cat.

'I am,' I said, and as I said it, I let myself properly feel it. Fuck her, I thought. Fuck her and her 'I'm going to be grieving for Virginie' and 'I'll need you to support me' and 'I still need to have sex with other people.'

'Fuck her,' said Cat.

'Don't say that,' I said.

I don't remember much about the Pinter play except that it was long and involved a boarding house and a character named McCann. I fell asleep during one of the pauses and the next thing I knew, Cat was shaking me awake and the cast were onstage taking their curtain call.

I do remember how grateful I felt to be sharing my bed that night with my two best friends. 'I love you,' I muttered, as we settled in.

'Shut up and get to sleep,' Cat said, adjusting the silk scarf she'd wrapped around her hair. 'You're helping me flyer tomorrow and it'll be a thousand times worse with a hangover.'

There are many terrible things about flyering during the Edinburgh Fringe – the baking sun, the pouring rain, the awful stand-ups who tell the same jokes over and over again, the fact that everybody hates you. I hated myself quite a lot that day as I stood there on the Royal Mile, thrusting glossy leaflets at passers-by, trying not to throw up on my shoes. The best thing about flyering is that it's all-consuming. I didn't have time to think about whether I'd have a job when I got back, or about Sam, or anything much, except how long it would be before I'd be able to eat something – a kebab, possibly – and start drinking again. Drinking seemed to be the answer to everything in Edinburgh.

I was fantasizing about what kind of kebab I'd have – chicken shish? – when I heard a voice behind me say, 'Isn't that the girl we hung out with at the rave?'

I turned around.

'Is that——' said Alice.

'Yes,' I said. 'Hello, Jane.'

There she was, with her sharp bob haircut and her trendy dungarees and her friend Tia, the one with the shaved head and the gum. Tia smiled and I had a sudden flashback to rubbing her back and telling her that she was a mammal. I wanted, quite badly, to die.

We hugged hello.

'What are you doing here?' I asked.

'Tia's doing a show.'

Tia handed me a flyer.

'You should come,' said Jane. She held my gaze. I held hers. My heart sped up. It was all a bit intense, for noon on a Saturday.

Cat's show was on at 5.15p.m. in a cabaret venue in the Old Town. Alice and I had seats at the front. We ordered a bottle of red wine, which felt appropriate, considering the period theme, and soon the overture was booming out from a sound system. I felt a rush of envy as the cast stepped onto the stage, but I soon forgot to be envious, because the musical was brilliant – funny and political and oddly moving, which was an achievement seeing as Cat spent most of the second half dressed as a Mooncup. She closed the show with an impassioned torch song about period poverty and it didn't feel like a choice when I got to my feet to join in the standing ovation; I felt as though I'd been swept up there by the power of her voice and the surprising beauty of the music, and I clapped until my hands were numb. And I cried a bit. I wished and wished and wished I'd auditioned for the part of the tampon.

Cat was hyperactive after the show, hugging everyone repeatedly, speaking too quickly, laughing extra loudly at jokes. She introduced us to Lacey, who immediately dragged her away to meet someone else, so Alice and I were left on our own. We sat down at a table and poured ourselves some wine from an abandoned bottle.

'My feet hurt,' Alice said, looking down at her heels.

'Of course they do,' I said. 'You're wearing ridiculous shoes.'

'I want to go to bed.'

'Come and see Tia's show with me,' I said. 'It's just around the corner.'

Alice shook her head. 'I've had enough of clapping at things.'

'What's that?' Cat was back, arms around both of us.

'Julia wants to go and see Tia's show.'

'Fuck it,' said Cat. 'If Sam wants you to sleep around, you might as well go for it. Jane's a babe.'

'I'm not going to have sex with her,' I said.

We left Cat with her cast, telling a loud anecdote that involved a lot of arm movements, and walked out into the street. The cool air made me feel more awake, yet more aware of how drunk I was. I checked my phone. Still nothing from Sam.

'Are you coming back to the flat?' Alice asked.

I shook my head. And as she walked up the hill, to bed, I walked down, unsteadily, mouth fuzzy with drink, towards Tia's show, towards Jane.

37. SHUT IT, YA BAWBAG!

Tia's show was in the back room of a pub. There were only ten of us in the audience, but we were all drunk, and laughed easily. My favourite bit was when she talked about how she liked to be touched officially – patted down in the airport, examined by a doctor, etc. Jane caught my eye when Tia talked about her nipples going hard during a breast examination.

The bar had stopped serving by the time the show was over, and Tia and her friends were talking about going to a club. Jane asked me if I wanted to come.

'I don't think I should,' I said.

'We can go back to my flat instead,' Jane said.

I could have said no.

I could have texted Sam, to check she was OK with what I was about to do.

But I knew she wouldn't be.

And I was hurt, and angry, and sick of following rules someone else had come up with.

And I wanted to forget about everything – about my failed job interview, and the fact that I'd missed out on being in the cult hit of the Fringe, and my girlfriend, who missed her lover.

So I said, 'OK.'

When she kissed me, I kissed her back. I did it without really meaning to. It was sort of a Pavlovian response. Which makes me a dog, doesn't it? That seems appropriate.

Just like that we were back at Jane's flat and she was pushing me back onto the bed and undressing me. As she kissed my neck I noticed how different her skin felt to Sam's, and I didn't really like the difference, but I was turned on by it at the same time. She bit me, a playful bite, but probably harder than she'd meant to, and it released something in me – some of the anger and frustration – and I scratched her back in retaliation.

'You like it rough now, then,' said Jane, and she pulled my hair so hard that my eyes watered. I pulled her hair, too, and the whole thing was starting to feel like a school-playground fight, but then Jane kissed me again, and I bit down on her lip, and she pushed her fingers into my mouth, and I bit them too, and she pushed my legs open, and then she was fucking me.

I took hold of her wrist and pushed it further inside me. I wanted her to hurt me, because I was full of fury now, with Sam and with Jane but mostly with myself, and this seemed the best way of getting it out of me. I reached out and touched Jane's breast, because Sam rarely let me touch hers.

And as soon as I did, I came.

And coming was like a victory.

And then it was over, and I was left with a crawling emptiness and dread.

'Fuck,' Jane said. 'You've been doing your homework.'

She wiped her hand on the bed.

Outside the window, a lone bagpiper was playing 'The Bonny Banks o' Loch Lomond'.

Someone on the street shouted, 'Shut it, ya bawbag!'

I closed my eyes. A tear slipped out. 'Fuck,' I said. That had been so easy to do. I had barely noticed the line as I'd crossed it.

At some point I must have fallen asleep. I woke up with Jane still next to me and checked my phone. Two missed calls from Alice, and a text from Sam.

So sorry for the late reply, babes. I got an early night. When are you home? I miss your gorgeous cunt. And your gorgeous face, obvs xxx

I could hardly bear to be in my own body, I felt so ashamed. I'd always thought of myself as a good person, the sort of person who buys sandwiches for homeless people and votes with less privileged people in mind and would never, never cheat on her girlfriend.

Jane opened her eyes and smiled at me. 'Morning.'

She sat up in bed. She was still topless. I looked away.

'Please don't tell Sam what happened,' I said.

She laughed. 'Don't worry, I won't. Sam's scary.'

'She's not.' My anger was long gone. There was no room for it inside me, what with all the shame and self-hatred. I had never loved Sam so purely. I couldn't believe what I'd done. I got out of bed and looked around for my clothes, because being a terrible person is much easier to deal with when you're wearing underpants.

'Well, I'm scared of her,' Jane said. 'She pushed me up against a wall once and accused me of turning her ex against her.'

I paused, about to put my T-shirt on. 'Didn't you?'

'No! She turned Marie against *me*, and all her other friends. She started making comments when Marie went out in certain clothes—'

'She's never done that to me.'

'—and she started telling Marie who she could see and who she couldn't see, and when Marie got sick of Sam controlling her, she was too scared to break up with her on her own, so I went with her.'

I sat down on the end of Jane's bed, slightly sick with dread. 'And how did Sam take it?'

Jane shrugged. 'She was very grown-up and polite about it, actually. But then a couple of weeks later she came up to me as I was walking down that cycle path, you know the one between Hackney Central and London Fields? And she pushed me up against the wall and accused me of breaking up their relationship and fucking Marie behind her back. Which I wasn't, by the way.'

'OK,' I said. 'That's your side of the story.' I pulled my T-shirt on.

'That's the only side of the story.'

'It isn't though. Obviously.' I started to do up my jeans. The button was fiddlier than I remembered it being.

'Whatever.' Jane grabbed a towel from the floor. 'Just be careful.' She walked to the bathroom and turned on the shower.

I closed my eyes. For a moment I could imagine I was back at home, in my bedroom, about to join Alice and Dave in the living room for brunch and Netflix in our pyjamas. I opened my eyes again. I was still in Jane's bed. I was still an awful human being.

I got an Instagram message from Jane as I got on the plane that evening. *Didn't want to text you just in case . . . Last night was hot. Don't worry, I won't tell her. Call if you ever need someone to talk to, and look after yourself.* I turned the phone off without messaging back.

38. SHRIVELLED PEA

The worst thing was how happy Sam was to see me when I got home. The way she smiled when she opened the door, how tightly she hugged me.

'I know I've been awful these last few weeks,' she said. 'I shouldn't have asked you to be there for me through that. I'm through the worst of it now, promise.'

I couldn't say anything, because of the guilt.

'I've been terrible, haven't I?'

'Not terrible . . .'

'Let me make it up to you?'

She started to kiss me, to take off my cardigan. I was sure she'd be able to tell what I'd done, taste it on my lips the way when you can tell when someone has been drinking or eating tuna melts. I had to tell her. Rip it off, I told myself, like a plaster.

So I closed my eyes and said, 'I ran into Jane in Edinburgh.'

She let go of my cardigan. 'What happened?'

But there was something dangerous in the way she asked the question, and all of a sudden I realized that telling her was a terrible idea, so I said, 'I just ran into her in the street, when we were flyering,' and walked over to the sink and examined the taps, as if they were interesting, which they weren't.

'Good,' she said. And then: 'I'd rather you didn't have sex with Jane, if that's OK.'

Did she know? Was she testing me? I stared at a droplet of water on the base of the tap, the way it reflected the whole kitchen distorted, upside down. 'OK,' I said, nodding too much. 'Noted!'

I wasn't the sort of person who usually said things like 'Noted!' But I was doing all sorts of things I didn't usually do at the moment, it seemed.

I felt like a worm. Less than a worm, actually – I felt like one of the shrivelled peas I always find underneath the fridge, no matter how carefully I've Hoovered the kitchen. I couldn't bear what I had done. I needed someone to tell me it was OK, justifiable somehow. After dance that Sunday, some of us went for lunch in Soho – expensive noodles, uncomfortable seats – and afterwards, Ella said she needed to go to Foyles to get a birthday present for her mother.

I thought the cookery section might be a good place for a confession – the comforting smell of books, the promise of many meals to come – so as Ella was contemplating buying a cookery book all about butter, and Zhu was trying to persuade her to buy something about Middle Eastern food instead, and Bo and Rebecca were off to the side, leafing through a book about mindfulness, I told them what I'd done.

'What?' said Ella, clearly appalled.

'I know,' I said.

'You have to tell her.'

'Do I really?' I said. I leaned against the Jamie Oliver shelf. He was staring straight at me from one of his covers, brandishing a roast chicken, as though even he thought I was a coward.

Rebecca walked over and rubbed my back. 'You might think, ethically, that honesty is the best policy. But ask yourself *why* you want to be honest. If you're just doing it to make yourself feel better, and you know it will hurt her, that isn't a particularly noble course of action.'

She had a degree in PPE from Oxford. She had to be right.

'I don't actually think you've done anything particularly terrible,' Zhu said, shrugging. 'You're non-monogamous, aren't you? The only thing you did wrong was not tell her.'

'I really don't want to tell her,' I said. 'She would go – I don't even know what she'd do.'

Bo handed me a book called *How to Break Up with Anyone*. 'I'm just saying.'

'I'm not going to break up with her,' I said.

No one seemed particularly pleased to hear that.

The guilt didn't go away, but I learned to live with it, the way you learn to live with back pain, or the Conservatives winning the general election. As long as I didn't think about it too much, I could fool myself into forgetting about what I'd done. The trouble was, whenever I spoke to Cat or Alice, they brought up the bitey sex I'd had with Jane – Cat didn't see what was so bad about it, but Alice thought it counted as cheating. I knew in my gut that telling Sam was the right thing to do. But although I'd told Jane I wasn't scared of Sam, I was, a bit. I didn't want her to push me up against the wall, unless it was in a sexy way.

Alice told Dave about me and Jane, which made me so angry I didn't speak to her for several days, until she made a banana bread that smelled so good I couldn't help asking for a slice. I learned my lesson after that; I wouldn't talk to my friends about my relationship with Sam any more. Sam didn't want me to, and after what I'd done, respecting her wishes seemed like the least I could do.

Owen bought me a Pret brownie one lunchtime and said I didn't seem myself. He asked if I was upset about him getting a second interview. I said I was, which was true. He seemed very flattered by that.

'No one's ever been envious of me before,' he said.

'I'm sure that's not true. You always queue up and get the latest iPhone before everyone else.'

He nodded thoughtfully. 'But no *cool* person has ever envied me before.'

'You think I'm cool?'

He shrugged. 'Come for a drink with me and Carys next week,' he said. 'She's cool too.'

'Maybe,' I said.

'Oh, come on,' Owen said. 'What's the worst that can happen?' So I agreed.

But I went to Sam's that night, and as we got into bed, my phone lit up with a text from Owen: *Carys is free next Weds if you are?*

'Why is he texting you this late at night?' Sam asked, reading the message over my shoulder.

'We're going for a drink next week with his sister.'

'How come?'

'He thinks we'll get on.'

'Why?'

I should have said, 'Just because.' But instead I said, 'She's queer, and Owen thought we might get on.'

'You don't need more friends,' Sam said.

Sam had always encouraged me to look at other women in the street, to imagine what they'd look like in a strap-on, etc., but things were clearly different now she'd broken up with Virginie.

'I don't want you to go,' she said.

'What?' I said. 'Why?'

'I just don't.' She lay back on the bed and looked up at the ceiling.

I thought of what Jane had told me about Sam and Marie, and I said, 'You can't tell me who I can be friends with.' But it sounded like a question.

'I'm not,' she said, turning to me, softening. 'I'd never do that.'

She kissed me on my forehead. 'It's just – I'm finding it really hard, now that I've broken up with Virginie. I couldn't bear to lose you too.'

'You're not going to lose me,' I said, glad the light was out because I felt as though my face was flashing with guilt.

She took my hand. 'I just think our love is a delicate thing at the moment. We don't want to tip it off balance by bringing new people into the mix, do we? So maybe text Owen back and put the drink off.' She smiled at me. She was waiting for me to text him.

I felt like she had a right to be jealous, considering what I'd done. So I typed out a message, very aware of her eyes on the screen. *Actually I can't do Wednesday . . . maybe another time*, I wrote. And I put my phone on silent before he could reply.

'Thank you,' she said, and she kissed the top of my head.

The next morning, a card flopped through my letterbox, just as I was about to leave for work. I recognized the spidery handwriting, so I sat down to read it.

Dear Julia,

I'm sorry I'm only just replying to your lovely card. I'm afraid I've been in the wars. I haven't been sleeping well; the war has been playing on my mind. I can still see myself in my bomb turret, looking down on the German cities, well alight. The things we did don't sit easy with me. I've been very breathless, too; apparently it's my dicky aortic valve playing up. But the good thing is they're moving my surgery date up. Or is it bad news???

It would be absolutely smashing if you came to visit! If I'm up to it, I'll take you down to the seafront for a bowl of soup. Or rather you'll take me (I'm afraid I'm in a wheelchair at the moment. I hate the thing. It makes me feel old!).

Anyway. Mustn't grumble!!! My daughter's come to look after me for a few days. She's very good. She's here now, telling me to stop writing this letter and get some rest. I have to go for an appointment at the hospital tomorrow, to the Geriatric Unit. Geriatric! I ask you. That's adding insult to injury.

Please write back and tell me how you are doing. I'm always wittering on about myself. I'm sure you have a much more exciting life than I do. How's the swing dancing going?

Look after yourself and I look forward very much to seeing you soon.

P.S. — Here's another tune for you: 'Ain't Misbehavin''. It's nice and slow, which suits me these days!

Your friend,

Eric

I folded up the letter and sat down on the sofa. And then, I started to cry. The tears had been pretty close to the surface, it has to be said, but they caught me by surprise. Caring about people over the age of seventy-five only ever led to heartbreak. Mind you, caring about a thirty-year-old wasn't going brilliantly either. I'd send Eric some flowers, I decided.

When I got to work, I searched the Interflora website, but everything looked a bit funereal. Then I thought perhaps I'd send some brownies instead, but as I was trying to decide between double chocolate and salted caramel, Owen walked up to my desk and stood there, stirring his coffee.

'Shame about Wednesday,' he said.

'Oh,' I said, eyes on my screen. 'Yeah. I'm sorry about that.'

'Can you do the Thursday?'

'Sorry?' I said, looking up.

'Instead of Wednesday. To meet up with Carys.'

'No,' I said. I gave him an apologetic smile.

'Friday the week after?'

'Can't do that either. I'm sorry.' I looked back at my screen, not really seeing anything, hoping he'd take the hint.

Owen frowned. He crouched down next to me and asked, 'Is everything all right? Are you annoyed with me?'

'I'm fine. It's just not a good time, OK?'

Owen stood up, eyebrows raised. 'Sorry I asked,' he said.

We didn't speak for the rest of the day.

I didn't buy the brownies. I was about to, but then I Googled *geriatric heart failure diet* and read a lot of articles about how sick elderly people are supposed to avoid foods that are high in fat and sugar and eat lots of fruit and vegetables. I'll just write back to him, I thought.

I Googled Eric when I got home that night. There were hundreds of results; I guess when you're one of the last people that can remember the war, everyone wants to talk to you. There was an interview with the *Telegraph*: Warrant Officer Eric Beecham DFC smiled up at me from my computer screen, grey hair, brown eyes, hands folded over the arm of his chair like he was posing for a school photograph ninety years too late. There was a video of him on the *Argus* website, talking a reporter through his log book – lovely handwriting he had – and articles about a fundraising campaign he'd run, to raise money for a memorial to the men of Bomber Command. There were articles in support from the *Daily Mail* and *The Times*, and others criticizing the 'jingoism' of the memorial in the *Guardian* and the *Independent*.

I decided to tell him about Sam. I hadn't had the chance to come out to Granddad – which might have been for the best, as he'd once told me to watch out for short-haired women in case they got their 'claws into me' – but I decided it was worth taking the risk with Eric.

I went to my room and found a dusty sheet of writing paper and a matching envelope, left over from a set I'd loved as a teenager. I found a fountain pen, too – I thought Eric deserved a fountain pen – and I sat at the dining table and started to write.

I told him how sorry I was about his dicky heart valve, and that the war was playing on his mind, and I told him I thought he was unimaginably brave. I told him that everyone at Stepping Out loved his music recommendations, and added: *We're an LGBT swing-dance group — did I ever tell you that?* even though I knew I hadn't.

And then I wrote:

You once asked me whether I had a fellow, and I never replied. Well, I don't have a fellow, but I do have a girlfriend. Her name is Sam, and she has beautiful brown eyes. I hope that you get to meet her one day.

I would love to come and visit you next weekend, if I'm still welcome. Maybe on Sunday, if that's a good day for you? Soup on the seafront sounds wonderful.

Your friend,
Julia

I was about to go to the post box when I got a text from Sam: *Babes, how about a night in at yours tonight? Takeaway? I'm leaving work in five mins.* So I went upstairs to have a shower and left the letter on the table.

39. A TERRIBLE HUMBLEBRAG

The sex Sam and I had that night was so good that Alice and Dave broke up over it. That sounds like a really terrible humblebrag, I realize. I'm honestly not bragging at all. It was horrible.

We were woken the next morning at eight by raised voices.

'We *do* have sex.' That was Dave.

'I've had to come on to you every time in the last few weeks.'

'I'm just tired!'

Sam rubbed her eyes and pushed herself up on her elbow. She checked the time on her phone and rolled over onto her side again, pulling the pillow over her ear.

'Sam's never tired, is she?' said Alice, in an extremely audible 'whisper'. 'Julia's never tired.'

Sam gave up any idea of going back to sleep.

'Fine, then, dump me and find yourself a nice lesbian to fuck.'

'I don't want to fuck a lesbian. I want to *be* fucked.'

'By a lesbian?'

'No! By you! It's like you don't fancy me any more!'

'Alice, love. You haven't looked me in the eye during sex for years. Years! You're the one that doesn't fancy me!'

A beat. And then Alice said, 'So why are we getting married?'

Sam and I looked at each other. We were sitting so still that I felt they must sense our attention, the way you can feel someone staring at you even when your eyes are closed.

'I knew it,' Dave said.

'Wait, Dave—'

'I knew you didn't want to marry me.'

'I never said that—'

'You've been pulling away from me ever since I proposed. I can't fucking believe this.'

'Dave—'

'Don't bother.'

We heard heavy footsteps, the slam of the flat door. The thud-thud-thud as Dave ran down the stairs.

And Alice's sobs.

I started to push myself up off the mattress but Sam reached out a hand to stop me.

I looked at her. I whispered, 'She needs me.'

'Stay here. She needs some space.'

I sank back into the pillows. And then I changed my mind and pushed myself up again, grabbing a pair of pants from the floor and pulling them on. 'She's my friend.'

'She'll still be your friend in half an hour.' Sam pushed me onto my back and pushed her hand down my pants.

'No,' I said. 'Not now.'

Sam sighed heavily and sat back on her heels. 'Alice has too much of a hold on you.'

I looked at her. 'She's literally crying next door and she knows I'm here. She's going to think I'm a total dick if I don't go in there.'

'Because you run around after her all the time.'

Alice was quiet now. Maybe she'd gone back to sleep. Was that too much to hope?

Sam saw me hesitating.

'Stay with me. Ten minutes?'

I thought about what would happen if I didn't do as she suggested. I wondered how long it would be before she spoke to me again. And then she kissed me, and I didn't want to leave the room after all.

'Ten minutes,' I said.

Sam held her hand over my mouth as she fucked me. Afterwards, she slept with an arm around me. Her breath felt too hot against my neck. When I was sure she was asleep I eased out of the bed, put on my dressing gown and went to see Alice.

Alice was sitting in her bed surrounded by balled tissues. They looked like oversized confetti, which was horribly ironic.

'Why did he have to propose to me?' Alice said, through her tears.

'Just call him. Tell him you didn't mean it.'

'I did mean it, though.'

'But you don't want to break up with him altogether!'

'Don't tell me what I want.'

'Sorry,' I said.

Alice had never spoken to me like that before. Maybe Sam was right, I thought. Maybe Alice did need space. I stood up to leave the room.

But Alice reached out her hand and said, 'Don't go.'

'Sam's here,' I said. Sam was probably awake by now. She was probably aware I'd gone against her advice.

'So?'

'Let me just tell her where I am.'

'She'll know where you are.'

'I can't just leave her there on her own.'

Alice let go of my hand and lay down, her back to me.

'Want me to set up your laptop so you can watch TV?' I said.

'I want you to stay with me.'

'Let me just go and see Sam,' I said. 'I'll come back.'

*　　*　　*

Sam was sitting up in bed waiting for me. She raised her eyebrows as I entered the room and I felt a jolt of guilt.

'Alice and Dave have broken up,' I said, sitting on the end of the bed, trying to keep the apology out of my voice and failing.

'Shit,' Sam said. She held my hand and gave me a sad sort of half-smile. 'We're so lucky to have each other.'

I thought about what it would be like not to have her. I leaned over to kiss her. 'What are you doing today?' I asked.

'Whatever you're doing.' Which wasn't the answer I'd been hoping for. Now I longed for the 'I need some space' Sam, the 'I need to go and paint naked women who aren't you' Sam, even the 'I'm off to France for some kinky sex with an older woman' Sam.

'Why don't I meet you at yours later? I think I've got to be with Alice for a bit.'

Sam's smile disappeared. 'Alice is a big girl.'

'I know, but she's been with Dave for, like, six years, and she's a bit of a mess.'

'I think you need to learn to say no to her.'

'Please, Sam,' I said. 'I just want to hang out with her for a few hours.'

Sam's face changed. 'Why are you saying "please"? Do whatever you want. I'm not stopping you, babes.'

Alice and I watched old sitcoms on Netflix for a few hours, the canned laughter emphasizing the silence between us. I couldn't stop checking my watch and the phone, wondering how long I should be away from Sam. At about four, Alice said, 'I think I'm going to sleep for a bit.' I kissed her forehead and rushed out of the house, calling Sam as I ran to the Overground. She didn't pick up.

She didn't kiss me hello when she opened the door, either.

'I'm sorry about today,' I said.

'That's OK,' she said, but in the way that I say 'Next round's on me!' whenever I accept a drink from someone at the pub, i.e. she didn't mean it.

She was pretty sulky with me all evening, and that night, for the first time, she went to bed without trying to fuck me.

I lay awake for hours, worrying that she'd worked out what had happened with Jane, telling myself not to be paranoid, reminding myself that she loved me. And she did. She woke me up with pancakes the next morning – blueberry ones, with maple syrup. She even dusted them with icing sugar. You'd only do that if you really cared about someone. Everything was back to normal.

40. LEMON DRIZZLE v BLUEBERRY TART

I didn't see much of Alice over the next couple of weeks. She either stayed in her room, only leaving to forage for food and go to the toilet, as all animals must, or went out after work and came back hammered, eating all the food in the fridge before falling into bed. She often woke up crying at 3 a.m., and I'd go into her room and stroke her hair until she fell asleep again. Neither of us would mention it the next morning. I probably could have been there for her more. I should have sat her down and got her to talk to me about what was going on.

I texted Dave to check if he was OK. He said he was, and that he was staying with his brother and sister-in-law in Walthamstow until he and Alice had 'sorted things out'. I was glad he was optimistic, and that he was still paying the rent on our flat, but Alice had taken down all the photos of Dave from the noticeboard in the kitchen and given away his six-pack of IPA, so I didn't feel quite so positive about the future of their relationship.

Cat was back in London – she had left me a voicemail saying, 'Mate! When are we meeting up? We meant to be looking at flats together, or what?' but I hadn't returned her call. Just hearing her voice reminded me of having sex on Jane's grotty bed to a soundtrack of bagpipe music, reminded me of what a shitty person I'd become.

Besides, I didn't want to give away any of my free time. I was saving it for Sam.

Things were still a bit stilted with Owen, too. I'd apologized for snapping at him about arranging a drink with Carys, but I didn't want to explain why I'd done so; I didn't need him to worry about me. Things with Sam were fine now, and I wanted them to stay that way. Anyway, Owen had been for his second interview and was waiting to find out if he'd got the job, and I was finding it hard to pretend I wasn't bitter.

The day that Tom finally resigned was the same day that Owen heard he'd got the Senior Account Manager job. No one in the team knew how to react. We had to look shell-shocked and devastated whenever Tom sidled up to us, delighted whenever Owen walked past.

Owen couldn't believe it, when he got the call.

'It might be a mistake,' he said. 'They might have called the wrong person.'

'Of course they didn't,' I said. If I pretended to be happy for him, maybe that would translate into some sort of genuine emotion, an emotion other than envy.

Smriti called Uzo and me into her office one at a time to tell us the news that we already knew.

'Because Owen's leaving, we're going to give Uzo the Correspondence Officer job,' she told me. 'It would be different if you were on a permanent contract.'

I nodded. I didn't want to cry in her office. I hated crying in other people's offices.

'But we'd like to extend your contract to the end of the year, so there'll be a nice long transition period.'

I nodded again. Four months to find a job. I was sure I could figure something out.

'I've been meaning to talk to you, though, because I think you're really talented.'

I looked up. Maybe I'd misheard. 'Sorry?'

'I've been reviewing your correspondence log, and you have fantastic communication skills.'

'I – what? Right! Thanks!' I said, as if to prove how many one-syllable words I knew.

'The Fast Stream applications are opening next month, and I think you should go for it. I was a Fast Streamer and the opportunities you get are totally incredible.'

'Incredible! Yeah!' I said. My communication skills were getting more fantastic by the minute.

'I'd be happy to coach you some time? Give you some pointers?'

'Yes, please,' I said. And then: 'Fast Streamers are the future, aren't they?' because I'd read that in a briefing document from the Cabinet Office.

We all went for a drink after work to celebrate/commiserate, to a pub across the river that smelled of sweat. Tom sat in a corner with his friends, leaning on a table made out of an old barrel, muttering darkly. They looked like the gunpowder plotters would have looked if they had shopped in T. M. Lewin. Apparently Tom had got the job at the Home Office. Another Grade Seven job, so no promotion, hence the muttering.

'Want to get some food?' Owen asked me, after we had finished our pints.

'Better not,' I said. I had promised Sam I would go to hers, and I didn't want to let her down. Owen didn't bother trying to persuade me.

Sam and I were into each other the way you only are at the beginning of a relationship or after a huge fight, i.e. we had lots of excellent sex and hugged each other for the entire length of Bastille songs. I was beginning to relax into the routine of our relationship; it was so much easier to love her now that Nicky wasn't sowing doubt in my mind every week, and the knowledge that Sam would, at some point, want to shag other women – and the fact that I'd already shagged another woman without telling her – stopped niggling at me all the time and sort of sat there at the back of my mind in the place reserved for things I really ought to address but don't want to think about, like checking my bank balance or replying to text messages from my mother.

But routine is exactly the opposite of what Sam wanted in her sex life.

One Saturday in early October, we were standing at the cake stall in Broadway Market when she said, 'I think we should take our relationship up a notch.' And then, before I had a chance to answer, 'Don't get the lemon drizzle. We can make that at home. Go for the blueberry tart.'

'What do you mean?' I asked.

'It's just much harder to make – it has frangipane in it. Plus blueberries are more expensive than lemons.'

'No, I meant the relationship,' I said, as the poor woman at the cake stall hovered in front of us uncertainly.

'Two pieces of blueberry tart, please,' Sam said, not looking at me. She handed over the money and led me by the hand to one of the vintage clothes stalls. 'I think it's time we tried out some SM.'

'Just the two of us?' I said.

'For now, yes,' she said. She tried on a tasselled leather jacket. 'What do you think?'

'It's a bit country and western.'

'But I think I could pull that off.'

'Then go for it,' I said. 'Can we go back to the SM for a minute?'

'Of course, babes.'

'How will we do that?'

'I have a few ideas,' she said, handing over £30 for the jacket. 'I'll surprise you with it. You'll feel totally worshipped, I promise. You are up for it, aren't you?'

'I think so,' I said.

Sam pulled me towards her. The leather jacket smelled like the trip to Morocco I'd taken with Alice in the summer of our second year at uni; I was a little too aware it used to be a living creature. 'You're delicious,' Sam said. 'You're going to make such a sexy submissive. Isn't it your birthday the Saturday after next?'

'Yes, but Alice said she'd cook dinner for everyone at ours.'

'Not any more, she's not. Keep the whole weekend free, OK?'

My parents were a bit put out that they couldn't see me on my actual birthday. They like to come to London every year for my 'birthday treat', which usually involves dragging me along to something I definitely don't want to go to – a Royal Society lecture about cell structure, maybe, or one of Dad's friends' book launches. ('It'll be fascinating, Julia. Dr Susan Grey from Oriel will be there. She is *the* living expert on ekphrasis.') I invited them down the weekend before instead, and we went for dinner at one of those trendy Indian restaurants you have to queue outside for so long that they bring you tea to keep you warm while you're waiting. By the time we got inside, we were so hungry that we ordered three times as much food as we needed and by the end of the meal I never wanted to see a bhaji again, onion or otherwise.

I felt jittery all evening, the way I often did when I wasn't with Sam. I kept sneaking my phone onto my lap to look at it. At one point, Mum paused in the middle of telling me how idiotic it was of the neighbours to remove the chimney breasts – 'The chimneys could crash through the roof and kill them at any moment!' – and said, 'Put your phone away, darling. It's no good to be too reliant on someone.'

'I'm not,' I said.

308

'We've come all the way to London to take you out to dinner. I'd be grateful if you could give us your full attention.'

I grunted under my breath. Dad was fiddling with his phone too, and she wasn't telling him off.

'Look!' he said, passing it to me.

'Very nice,' I said. 'I have the same one.'

'No,' he said, 'the video.' He unlocked the screen and started it.

It was a YouTube video of my father, sitting in his study, arms waving, spittle flying, ranting and raving about *Songs of Innocence and Experience*. 'People forget that William Blake was a radical. These are not poems for children. These are subversive political texts. The chimney sweeper in *Songs of Innocence* addresses the reader directly: *your chimneys I sweep. You* are complicit in this child's abuse,' Dad said, jabbing his finger at the camera.

'Just an introduction to the poem for first year undergraduates,' Dad said, with a modest smile.

'I feel quite attacked,' I said.

'Good,' said Dad.

'Harry next door helped your father set up his channel,' Mum said, tucking into a samosa.

'I have two subscribers,' Dad said. 'One of them is Geoff. Keeping an eye on the competition, I suppose.'

As we said goodbye, Mum hugged me and said, 'Don't be a stranger, darling. I've hardly heard from you the last few months.'

'I've been busy,' I said.

'I can tell.'

'What's that supposed to mean?'

'Nothing. You've just been a bit distant since you've been with Sam.'

'I thought you liked her,' I said. 'I thought you were delighted that I was a lesbian.'

'I do!' she said. 'I am! You just don't seem like your usual self.'

*　　*　　*

I stayed in on Friday night, just in case the sex was going to start then – I'd never done SM before, so I had no idea how long it would take. Polly had told me about a time Jasper and their friend Tina had burst into her house in the middle of the night, wearing balaclavas, and had tied her up, bundled her into a van and taken her to a warehouse for a kidnap 'scene'. I expected Sam would break me in gently, but it's fair to say I felt pretty apprehensive about it, so I had a couple of glasses of wine in front of the TV to calm my nerves, and then I thought I might as well finish the bottle.

So I wasn't feeling entirely fresh when I was woken at nine the next morning by a text from Sam. *Happy birthday, babes. Tonight's the night. Wear a dress with something sexy underneath it.* I had been hoping we'd spend the day together, but Sam said she needed the time to get ready for our night out, so Alice took me out for brunch. I was too nervous to eat much, though.

'What do you think she's going to do? Whip you?' she asked.

'I don't know,' I said, cutting up my avocado toast.

'Tie you up? Do you think she'll use fire or anything?'

'I hope not,' I said. 'Can we talk about something else?'

Alice took a sip of coffee. 'Dave came round to get his stuff on Thursday night.'

'How was that?'

'He's going to stop paying rent.'

'OK,' I said. 'We'll just have to start buying the economy pasta.'

'He cried.'

'Of course he did.'

'I cried, too.' And she was tearing up now, though she was opening her eyes as wide as possible, trying to stop herself.

'Did you talk?'

'Not really. I still don't want to get married.'

I passed her my napkin, and she wiped her eyes.

'I miss him, though.'

310

'I know you do.'

Alice straightened her knife and fork on the plate. 'Have amazing sex for both of us.'

'I will.'

'Was that a weird thing to say?'

'A bit.'

41. EL JEFE

Sam asked me to get to hers at eight, but I was ten minutes late. I could hear Nicky's voice in my head: 'You'd have arrived on time if this was something you really wanted to do. Are you sure she's not pressuring you into this? You can still turn around and go home . . . have dinner with Alice instead . . .' But I shut it down.

Sam looked amazing; she'd just had her hair cut so it was shaved at the side and curling into her eyes at the front. But she wasn't smiling.

'You're late.'

'I'm sorry . . .'

'Don't worry. I just missed you.' She pulled me inside, pushed me up against the wall and kissed me really slowly. 'I am going to make you come more times than you ever have in your life tonight, birthday girl,' she said.

'That's nice,' I said. My dirty talk still definitely needed work.

'But first I'm taking you for a drink,' she said. 'Somewhere special.'

I sat on the sofa while she went to get something from her wardrobe. I looked around, trying to reassure myself that I was in a completely normal relationship with a completely normal person who happened to have an exciting sex life. She had an IKEA kitchen. Totally normal. There was a yucca plant next to the sofa that looked like it needed watering. Loads of people had yucca plants they never watered. Normal normal normal. The paintings of naked women all over the room weren't completely normal, maybe, but she was an artist, and they were her work, so of course her flat was filled with them, like mine was filled with pens and notebooks I'd stolen from the stationery cupboard.

'Sam?' I called.

'Sorry, I won't be a minute, babes.'

'Can I model for you soon?'

'What?' She appeared from behind the bookcase that separated the bedroom area from the sitting room.

'Can I model for you? Will you paint me?'

'OK,' she said. 'It's just that most of my paintings are associated with a really extreme emotion.'

'You don't have strong emotions about me?' Yes, I was fishing. I'm not proud.

'You make me feel . . . content. And great art doesn't come from a place of contentment.'

'Oh,' I said.

She crouched down in front of me and took my hands. 'That's a compliment, by the way.'

'It's not,' I said, trying to smile. 'Contentment isn't sexy. It's the emotional equivalent of flannel pyjamas.'

'Exactly.' She kissed the back of my hand. 'The sort of thing you want to wear every day.'

'But I want to be exciting. Like a corset.'

'You *are* exciting. But in a lovely comfortable way. You're like sexy silk pyjamas.' She disappeared back behind the bookcase.

I noticed a new painting next to the stove, of a woman with red lips and an impressive cleavage.

'Right,' said Sam, pulling her jacket on. 'Ready?'

*   *   *

In the car, she flicked through radio stations, searching for a suitable soundtrack. She chose some deep, pulsing dance music.

'Where are we going?' I asked.

'You'll see,' she said, and I began to feel nervous again.

'Aren't you drinking tonight?'

'Of course I am.'

'But you're driving.'

'Stop stressing. All part of the plan. I'm going to look after you really well. This is your birthday present! OK?'

'OK,' I said.

'Just remember – it won't be me doing any of the things I do, all right? I'll be playing a character. We'll be acting out a scene together.'

'I'm not a very good actor,' I warned her.

'Don't worry,' she said. 'I'll do most of the talking. And if there's anything you're not comfortable with, you can just ask me to stop.'

'OK.'

'But you can't just say "no" or "stop", because you'll probably be saying that loads as part of the scene.'

'Right,' I said.

'So we'll use a safe word. When you say it, I'll know you want me to completely stop.'

'What should the safe word be?'

'Anything you want,' she said.

'Help?' I suggested.

'No, you might say that anyway. It has to be completely unrelated to sex or danger.'

'Like biscuit?' I asked.

'Yes, that's perfect,' she said.

'That is not perfect,' I said. 'I do not want to be thinking about custard creams during sex.'

'Let's just have "safe word" as our safe word,' she suggested.

'All right,' I said.

*   *   *

We passed through the city and soon we were driving into the very skyline of London itself. The Gherkin bulged above me phallically. The Cheesegrater leaned towards me suggestively. We parked near London Bridge, and as Sam took my hand and led me down the street I looked around for the Shard – my favourite of London's oddly shaped skyscrapers – and realized we were heading straight for it.

Sam led me into the vast, empty reception area. 'Think of all the social housing you could build in here,' I said, as my footsteps echoed on the polished floor.

'Shh,' said Sam. 'Tonight's about luxury. And fantasy. OK?'

And then we were in the lift, hurtling so fast towards the top of the building that my ears popped, and then we were in the bar, being led to a table by a woman with a red dress slashed to the thigh and stilettos that can't have been good for her back. I found myself wondering whether it was legal for employers to require their staff to wear such impractical footwear and then I shook myself mentally and told myself, tonight is about luxury. And fantasy.

But when we reached our table I forgot my principles and was silenced by the view from the floor-to-ceiling windows, by the beauty and scale of the city I loved. From this height, London looked like a place dreamed up by science-fiction writers, too perfect to be real. Everything looks perfect from 400 metres, I realized. If you saw Sam and me from 400 metres, you'd probably think, look at that gorgeous couple, living the dream. Which I suppose we were. I just wasn't sure it was my dream we were living.

'I'll get the drinks in,' Sam said. I nodded, still gazing down at the people going about their evenings in the streets below. The sun began to set, turning the skyscrapers from grey to rose gold, putting on a show for those of us rich enough to afford the view. I was so absorbed that I didn't realize how long Sam had been gone, till my phone buzzed with a text from her:

Room 173.

She wasn't at the bar at all. She had booked a room in the hotel.

I walked down the corridor, feeling increasingly apprehensive as the numbers on the doors ticked up: *170. 171. 172.*

173.

I could barely bring myself to knock on the door. But the alternative was standing Sam up, which wasn't an option, so I did knock, three times, as steadily as I could.

I waited.

No answer.

I checked my phone again – perhaps I'd got the 7 and the 3 mixed up? I hadn't.

I knocked again.

And that's when the door swung open and a hand grabbed the hair on the back of my head and forced me face down so that my nose was crushed into the carpet. I couldn't see anything except the thick beige pile, and moments later I couldn't even see that, because something cool and black and leathery was tied around my eyes. I tried to slow my breathing. I wasn't sure I could go through with it. I considered saying 'safe word'. But we'd only just started, and I didn't want to let Sam down.

I lay there, as still as I could, until I felt something cool, hard and sharp against my neck. A knife. Stopping the scene might be more dangerous than going through with it, now that there was a knife. The knife was pressing into my throat, pulling me upwards, and I scrambled to my feet. I could barely breathe I was so terrified. But as I stood there, knife to my throat, wondering what would happen to me next, my heart started beating wildly and I felt a rush like I'd never felt before, and I realized I was so terrified that I was turned on, incredibly turned on and excited, and I finally got what the fuss was about. I didn't want to say the safe word any more.

That feeling lasted for about another ten seconds.

A hand pushed on my back and I stumbled forward so I was kneeling in front of the bed.

The knife moved from my throat and I felt the tip trail over my body.

I let out an involuntary moan.

And that's when Sam said, 'You like this, eh, *puta*?' In a deep, extremely unrealistic, Mexican accent.

The whole thing was a lot less sexy and scary after that.

Sam began to cut my dress off with her knife. 'You're mixed up in things you don't understand, *no es cierto?*'

'Yes,' I said, because that was definitely true.

'*Mentiras!*' she shouted. 'Don't play innocent with me.'

'Er—'

'I pay you to carry drugs for me, you think you can take some for yourself. You think you can trick *El Jefe*? No one tricks *El Jefe*.'

I wanted to say something – I wanted to tell her to shut up, so that I could enjoy myself again, but I got the impression that I wasn't really supposed to speak until I was spoken to. So I tried to use my imagination. Fine, she was a Mexican drug lord. She was wild and hot and dangerous. She wasn't a fake Mariachi singer at a dodgy taco restaurant, even though that's exactly what she sounded like.

I was naked now, lying on the bed with the knife still at my throat.

'And now you get what's coming to you, *puta*. Beg me to fuck you.'

'Please fuck me,' I said, trying to keep the wobble out of my voice.

'*Pobrecita. Tienes miedo?*' she said.

'*Sí*,' I said, very grateful for my Spanish GCSE. She couldn't be serious. I kept waiting for her to yell 'Joke!' (or, indeed, *'Broma!'*), but that, sadly, was not on the cards.

'I know what *chicas* like you need. You want discipline, *no es cierto?'*

I guessed the correct answer was 'Yes', so that's what I said.

'Say *"Sí, Jefe,"* or I'll slap you one,' she said. (Maybe her Spanish phrasebook didn't have a 'useful phrases for kidnap role play' section.)

'*Sí, Jefe,*' I said.

'You've got some *cojones*, answering me in that tone. I'll show you who's boss. Turn over.'

I rolled over onto my stomach, but got caught up in the bed sheets. There was a bit of a pause while Sam helped me disentangle myself.

'Now. I'm going to hit you. And you're going to count the spanks for me. And every time I spank you, you're going to say, *"Gracias, Jefe."* OK?'

'OK.'

'OK *Jefe*,' she said. 'Start counting.'

'One,' I said.

'*En español!*'

'*Uno.*'

Her palm slammed into my bare right buttock. I felt nothing at first, and then I felt the pain and heat spreading across my arse and a sudden, unexpected rage spreading inside me. I did not like being hit, it turned out. I said, *'Gracias, Jefe.'*

I can do this, I told myself. This happened to children all the time in the old days.

'What comes after *"uno"*, *puta?*'

'*Dos.*'

She hit me again, and she laughed as I flinched.

'*Gracias, Jefe,*' I said.

This is fine, I thought. I'll just pretend I'm in an Almodóvar film. I've always loved Almodóvar.

'*Tres.*' I felt my eyes fill with tears of frustration and pain and pure anger as she hit me again, but I said, '*Gracias, Jefe.*'

I'll pretend Sam is Gael García Bernal. I used to fancy him, before I was a lesbian.

'*Cuatro,*' I said, as her hand slammed down again. '*Gracias, Jefe.*'

Except Gael García Bernal probably wouldn't be this much of a method actor.

'*Cinco.*'

'*Bueno.*' I felt Sam step away from me. 'I hope you've learned your lesson.' Her accent slipped when she said that last bit.

We had sex after that, and it was hot. She used a strap-on, and she held the knife to my throat as she fucked me, and crucially she didn't say anything during the actual banging. The spanking had made me very angry, and the sex was a good way of releasing that. By the time we were finished, I felt both sexually fulfilled and revolted at myself for being sexually fulfilled. I also felt a little less in love with Sam. She got a kick out of insulting me and scaring me and causing me physical pain. I knew it was all role play, but why did she want to role-play that? And the stinging I still felt on my buttocks wasn't pretend.

'How do you feel?' she asked when she had untied the leather blindfold.

I shook my head and began to cry.

'Hey,' she said, pulling me to her. 'Come and lie down and let me look after you.'

'I think I need a shower first,' I said.

I washed with the expensive shower products, looking down at Tower Bridge straddling the Thames – or was it the Thames penetrating Tower Bridge? Everything looked sordid to me. I stayed in the shower till Sam called me back to bed. I didn't want to be near her, but I knew I couldn't put it off forever.

'You were wonderful,' said Sam, as I slid carefully between the sheets.

I didn't say anything. I was turned away from her, looking at the scraps of red material that lay scattered all over the floor. It looked, appropriately, like the aftermath of a bullfight. That had been a perfectly good dress. I'd only bought it a couple of months ago.

'You allowed yourself to be really vulnerable.'

'I didn't like you calling me a whore,' I said. 'I didn't like you hitting me.'

'I didn't call you a whore.'

'I know what *"puta"* means.'

'But I told you, it wasn't really me calling you that. And you found it exciting, didn't you? I know you did.'

'It turned me on, but I still didn't like it.'

'I understand, babes,' she said, kissing my neck. 'It takes some getting used to. But it wasn't real.'

But it had felt pretty real when she'd hit me, and I'd cried real tears, and she'd done it anyway. And I'd let her.

I dreamed of being kidnapped that night. I dreamed I was wearing a fur coat and a diamond necklace and I was held up at gunpoint. I woke up shaking and sweaty with Sam's arm pinning me to the bed, and for a moment I had no idea where I was. Then I remembered. I went to the bathroom and looked at myself for a long time in the mirror. I'd always thought I was strong. Maybe being able to have sex like that was strong. Maybe I was owning my sexuality for the first time in my life, fuck social conventions, fuck political correctness.

I turned around and looked at my buttocks. The right one was still pink and tender to the touch, like a steak, ready for pan-frying. I carefully rubbed it with body lotion. 'I'm sorry,' I said to it.

I didn't think I could get back to sleep, so I pulled on one of the duvet-like dressing gowns and locked myself in the toilet. I sat there, staring down out of the window, watching London wake up. I could leave. I could walk home through the city and start again with someone new, or I could move to Berlin or Rome or

Copenhagen and have sex in a different language. As long as it wasn't Spanish.

Far below, I could just make out the window of a bakery. I was hungry, I realized. We hadn't got around to eating the night before. I'd start there, I decided. I'd go out and buy myself a coffee and pain au chocolat.

I walked back into the bedroom to find something to wear. I looked over at Sam; she looked so sweet and young lying there, her dark head floating on the white pillow, smiling in her sleep. I couldn't reconcile this vulnerable-looking, beautiful woman with the person who had held a knife to my throat just a few hours ago. I couldn't see the knife anywhere, either. I might have thought I'd imagined the whole thing, if it wasn't for my stinging right buttock.

I tugged on the door of the wardrobe on her side of the bed and it opened with a pop. Sam turned over in bed, but didn't wake up. There, on the floor of the wardrobe, golden in the morning light, was the knife. Straight on one side, curved on the other, with a wooden handle. I touched the tip. Not that sharp. I felt calmer, seeing it lying there. Like Sam, it seemed less threatening in the daylight.

I found my bra tangled up at the bottom of the bed and unzipped Sam's rucksack to find the change of clothes she had brought for me. I picked up my wallet and opened the door to the room – but as I did, light swept across the bed like a search beam, and then I heard Sam say in a measured voice, 'Where do you think you're going?'

I stopped and took a breath. 'You frightened me,' I said, as I turned around to smile at her. 'I saw a bakery down the road, so I thought I'd get some pastries.'

'Come here,' Sam said, reaching out her arm.

I walked over and sat on the bed, and she took my hand in hers, rubbing my palm with her knuckles.

'Silly Julia,' she said. 'The breakfast here is famous.' She began to stroke my cheek, and the hairs on my arm stood up in response.

Sam suggested we get room service, but I was beginning to feel trapped, despite the floor-to-ceiling windows. 'There might be a different view from the restaurant,' I pointed out, and she decided to indulge me.

Sam hung the *Do Not Disturb* sign on the door as we left: 'The cleaners might get a fright if they see the cock.'

'A cock shock,' I said.

Sam laughed, and I felt pleased with myself. I'd sounded almost normal.

A few minutes later, a waiter was flourishing a white napkin onto my lap and I was trying to decide between the eggs Benedict and the eggs Florentine.

'You're very quiet this morning,' Sam said. 'Aren't you having a good time?'

'I am,' I said. 'It's just a bit overwhelming, that's all.'

She nodded. 'You'll get used to it. I promise.'

Instead of answering, I turned to look out of the window. The view was less flashy from here, and I liked that. We were looking out over the less spectacular side of the city, past nondescript office buildings to the hills and detached houses and electricity pylons of Kent. I imagined moving there.

'Can you see yourself ever leaving London?' I asked Sam.

'Maybe,' she said. 'I'll probably get sick of the London scene eventually and buy a big farmhouse – convert a barn to use as a studio and paint, and host big sex parties, something like that. You up for it?'

'I don't know,' I said. 'I'm not sure what I'd do with myself in the country.'

'You could help with the sex parties.'

'I don't think I'd be good at that.'

'I could train you up to be a dominatrix.'

Sam was busy detailing what my work as a dominatrix would

involve when the waiter approached. He stood nearby, gazing over our heads politely, while Sam talked about the benefits of wide hairbrushes for spanking, and the amounts of money businessmen would pay to be forced to dress up in school uniform and hit with rulers.

'Good morning,' he said, as soon as he could get a word in. 'Have you decided yet?'

'The full English,' said Sam.

'Of course,' said the waiter.

'I'll have the eggs Benedict,' I said.

'Are you sure?' Sam said. 'The TripAdvisor reviews said the hollandaise was a bit cold.'

'I'm sure,' I said, a bit too forcefully.

'What's wrong?' she asked.

'Any drinks?' asked the waiter.

'A latte for me, please,' I said.

'Tell me what the matter is,' Sam said.

'And for you, madam? Any coffee or tea?' asked the waiter.

Sam didn't answer, so I said, 'An English breakfast tea would be lovely, thank you,' and the waiter went away, relieved.

Sam was staring at me. 'Don't make decisions on my behalf,' she said, which was so hypocritical I assumed she was joking and laughed out loud. But she wasn't joking. And she really, really didn't like being laughed at, it turned out.

'You're humiliating me,' she said.

'I'm not!'

'I will not allow you to speak to me like that.'

'I'm sorry—'

'You're obviously upset with me. The adult thing to do would be to say what the matter is so that we can have a mature conversation about it.'

'OK,' I said. I took a deep breath. 'I just found last night a bit difficult.'

Sam was still looking at me. 'If you really didn't enjoy it, you could have said the safe word.'

'I know, I did enjoy it. It's just that was a new dress—'

'I'll get you another one.'

'I don't want another one.'

'I've spent a lot of money making this weekend perfect for you.'

'And I'm grateful—'

The waiter came back with our food as we sat there in silence.

Sam was right. The hollandaise was cold. I ate it anyway, but Sam didn't touch hers. She stared down at the table, hands knotted in front of her.

'Virginie loves me for who I am,' she said.

I looked up, hoping I'd misheard.

'I gave her up for you. I take you to the best hotel in London, treat you like a queen—'

'Like a rape victim, actually—'

'That was a fantasy!'

'It was your fantasy!'

Not the right thing to say. Not the right thing at all.

'Now it comes out,' said Sam, tossing her napkin on the table. 'What else don't you like about me? I know you don't like my paintings.'

'I never said that—'

'You're not denying it!'

'I think they're beautiful! They're amazing!'

'But you hate that I've hung them in my flat.'

I looked at her. I took a breath. A couple to the left of us, who were having a much less shouty breakfast, asked for more marmalade.

'I just—'

'Go on.'

I said, 'I'm just really aware that they're mostly paintings of people you've had sex with.'

Sam let out a short little laugh. She reddened. She straightened herself and crossed her arms. 'You're seriously that jealous? You're policing my past now?'

'No!' I said, reaching across the table as she pulled away.

She shook her head. 'I've changed myself to be with you. I've ended a relationship. And now you want to tell me I can't display my own paintings in my own flat? How dare you!'

'But that's not what I said—'

'I've done nothing but go out of my way for you, to make you feel comfortable in my home. And it's *my* flat, not yours! You didn't want to move in with me, remember?'

'Fuck you,' I said, my voice wobbly with rage.

I regretted it as soon as I said it.

She pushed her chair back and stood up.

'Wait,' I said, reaching out for her.

'Don't touch me,' she said, and she walked, self-righteously, out of the restaurant.

I didn't follow her straight away. I was too angry. But my anger didn't last long, and I knew that if I didn't stop her it would be the end of our relationship. I ran out of the restaurant, hoping they would add the tab to our room bill and not expect me to pay; I didn't think my overdraft would be able to take it. I saw Sam step into a lift at the other end of the corridor.

'Wait!' I shouted, but she didn't, so I ran down the stairs to our room. By the time I got there, she'd gone.

I felt too keyed up to go home and face Alice. I needed to calm down, to walk the anonymous streets of London and lose myself the way I'd longed to that morning, to remind myself that everything I was doing in my life was a choice and that I could begin again if I had to. I started out in the direction of the bakery I'd seen from the window.

As I stepped off the kerb to cross the street, a car swerved to a stop in front of me.

Sam's car.

She wound down the window, but she didn't look at me. 'Are you getting in?' she asked, though it was more of an order than a question.

I did as I was told.

Sam drove too fast, staring at the road ahead. 'What you said was abusive,' she said, without looking at me.

'What?'

'You said, "Fuck you." That was abusive. I want you to apologize.'

I would have laughed if I hadn't felt so desperate. She had won. She had completely won.

'I'm sorry,' I said, and she smiled. I turned to look out of the window so she couldn't see my face, my tears blurring the view of the skyline as we crossed the river.

And then, without turning round – without really thinking – I said, 'I can't do this any more.'

'Can't do what?' Sam said. And then, more coldly, 'Can't do *what*? Are you trying to *break up* with me?'

I stayed very still.

'You can't break up with me,' she said. 'Because I've already broken up with *you*.'

She sped up.

'Slow down,' I said.

She ignored me.

'Please?' I said.

She let out a nasty laugh and drove straight through a red light.

'Stop it,' I said.

'I'm not doing anything,' she said. She was still driving, towards her flat.

'Just drop me here,' I said, as we passed Monument station.

'If you want to go home, I'll take you,' she said.

'You don't need to—' I said, but the more I spoke, the faster she seemed to drive, so I shut up, and closed my eyes, and I thought about happier times. Like the time we'd walked through Broadway Market and she'd told me why I was more delicious than every cake on sale, and the time she'd come to dinner at our flat and Alice had told me she was the most charming woman she'd ever met, and just the night before, when she'd looked into my eyes like she really knew me and told me she'd never felt so much for anyone before. And I had felt the same.

She gave me the most aggressive lift home in history, probably, and when she stopped I opened the car door and ran up to the house as quickly as possible while her tyres screamed on the road and she disappeared.

My key didn't seem to fit in the front door. I didn't realize I was holding it upside down for at least a minute. When I finally got the door open I sat down with my back against the wall, not thinking anything, until Alice came out to see whether we were being burgled.

42. NO WEDDINGS AND A FUNERAL

'What's wrong?' Alice asked when she saw it was me. She had her arms crossed tight around her dressing gown.

I didn't get up from the floor. My heart was still racing. 'Me and Sam broke up,' I said.

Alice slid down the wall to sit next to me. She put her arm around me. 'Do you want some coffee?'

'Tea,' I said. 'Too anxious for coffee.'

We sat on the sofa and I told Alice all about what had happened. The whole argument seemed a lot more ridiculous and unnecessary now that I'd spoken about it out loud. The sex stuff was quite funny, actually, the way I told it. Alice had to go to the bathroom when I got to the bit about the Mexican accent and the '*Sí, Jefe*' situation, because she thought she was literally going to piss herself laughing.

'So glad we got to talk,' she said afterwards, putting her head on my shoulder.

'Will you think I'm weak if I get back together with her?'

'No!' Alice said. 'No, no, no. You aren't weak *at all*. You are so strong.'

'But you still think we shouldn't be together.'

She didn't answer straight away. 'I think – you've always said you wanted an equal relationship. But do you really think you're in one?'

'No, but—'

'But what?' asked Alice. 'But she's a woman, so it doesn't count?'

'But I love her,' I said, and I heard the wheedling tone in my voice, and I suddenly remembered a night a few years before: I'd been walking through Kentish Town at two in the morning, a bit drunk, when a man grabbed his girlfriend's hair and threw her to the ground, right there on the pavement in front of me. I'd stood there, wondering what to say, weighing up whether I should risk intervening, when four police officers jumped out of a van that had been waiting nearby, handcuffed the man and pushed him up against the wall. I was telling one of the officers what I'd seen when the woman came up to us, crying hysterically.

'Don't take him away,' she'd said. 'He didn't mean it.'

The policeman said that, from where he was standing, the guy had definitely meant it.

I pointed out to the woman that she had a black eye and a bleeding nose.

'But I love him,' she'd said.

Alice made soothing noises while I cried into my hands.

'I'm going to miss her so much,' I said.

'I know,' said Alice.

'Can we stop talking about this now?' I asked.

'OK,' said Alice. She thought for a moment, and then she said, 'How's your lovely Bomber Command friend doing?'

'Oh God,' I said, closing my eyes, 'I wrote him a letter and I still haven't posted it.'

'Want to walk to the post box now? We could get a Double Caramel Magnum on the way back.'

So we walked, hand in hand, to the post box. I felt better for the fresh air, and the Double Caramel Magnum was very comforting.

'Ice cream makes everything better,' I said to Alice, as we walked home through Clissold Park.

'Except type two diabetes,' she said.

I like to think I'm good in a crisis. I seem to come alive; when my grandfather died I remember the strange adrenaline rush that came along with the grief, the feeling that normal service had been suspended and it was suddenly acceptable to eat crisps for breakfast.

I felt a similar adrenaline rush after Sam and I broke up. Admittedly I was a bit of a mess – I was sent home from work for crying in a meeting about handover notes, and I got drunk every night for a week, falling asleep on the toilet floor and waking to throw up, my vomit black with red wine – but I felt completely, tinglingly alive.

I didn't go back to see Nicky, though. I wasn't ready for that. I thought I'd give myself some time to wallow, to cry in front of Meryl Streep films, to eat halloumi cheese straight from the packet. I wanted to have forgotten how much more exciting my life had been with Sam in it and how amazing it had felt to lie pressed up against her in the mornings before I listened to Nicky say, 'I told you so.' I didn't want anyone to tell me my time with Sam had been wasted, or that she'd been bad for me, or any of that. I missed her.

Dad called me as I was watching TV, alone, greasy-haired, a couple of days after our break-up.

'Hello, Julia. It's me.'

'I know,' I said.

'I just wanted to give you a YouTube update. I have over a hundred subscribers!'

'That's great,' I said, trying to sound enthusiastic.

'I have fans in New Zealand now!'

I could hear Mum in the background, practically rolling around the floor at the idea of Dad having fans.

'I went next door last night and Harry played my channel on the widescreen TV downstairs, in their new entertainment centre. My face was the size of a small car!'

'God help us,' Mum said. 'Your face is quite large enough.'

'Now,' said Dad, 'your mother and I have started to think about Christmas.'

'All right,' I said.

'I was wondering whether we ought to try something new this year. Have a sort of theme. Come as your favourite literary character, something like that.'

'I'll come as Anna Karenina,' I said, because that was the sort of mood I was in. 'You could come as Portnoy from *Portnoy's Complaint*.'

'I don't think that would be a good idea,' said Dad. 'He spends a lot of that novel— well.'

'Wanking in a toilet.'

'Precisely.'

'I know, Dad,' I said. 'I was joking.'

'Oh,' he said. 'Anyway. We were wondering.' He cleared his throat, as though he was about to say something difficult. 'Would your girlfriend like to join us?'

Girlfriend. Now that Sam and I had broken up, Dad had finally managed to call her my girlfriend. I burst into tears.

Dad didn't know how to deal with that, so he passed the phone to Mum.

'Thank fuck for that,' she said. 'Pardon my French, darling. But she was *awful*.'

I was even worse at my job than usual in those first few weeks; I couldn't concentrate. I'd be researching a reply to an email about treatment options or alcohol misuse, and then I'd be sucked into a Wikipedia loop, reading about the history of Alcoholics Anonymous, watching videos about how vodka is made, learning useless fact after useless fact, the hours disappearing the way candyfloss does, so you'd never know they'd existed, apart from the sickly guilt I felt. The

Wednesday after our break-up I watched a particularly nasty video, a film shot in 1913 showing a man leaping from the Eiffel Tower to his death. It wasn't a suicide attempt; he'd made himself a suit with wings, and he thought he'd be able to fly. As a spectator it was obvious to me that he wouldn't. But things are always more obvious to spectators, aren't they?

I watched him flap the 'wings' of his suit, which looked like a sleeping bag caught on a clotheshorse, and I found myself laughing.

Owen's eyes appeared over the divider between our desks, grateful for a distraction. 'What?' he said.

'Nothing,' I said, still laughing. Minimizing my screen.

'No, what?' he said.

So I told him.

'That's what you were laughing at?'

'I know,' I said. 'What's happened to me?'

'Well. I mean. You have just broken up with someone.'

I laughed again, and then I felt myself begin to cry.

'Julia,' Owen said, in his quiet monotone. 'Julia.'

I pretended I hadn't heard.

He stood up, and said 'Julia,' slightly louder, so that a few other people looked up, too.

'I'm fine,' I said.

'OK,' Owen said, and he sat down again, but I could feel him still looking at me, and a few minutes later he came over and crouched by my desk. 'Want to come and get some tea?'

I nodded damply.

'Have you heard from her?' he asked me, putting tea bags in our mugs.

I shook my head.

'Good,' he said. 'She wasn't very nice to you.'

'She was, actually,' I said, letting myself cry again. 'Sometimes.'

'No,' Owen said. 'Don't think about the good times. Think about the bad things about her.'

'I don't want to,' I said.

'When Carys got dumped she said there wasn't anything bad about Sarah—'

'Carys got dumped?'

Owen nodded. 'But then I reminded her that Sarah was always taking selfies and pouting in mirrors.'

'When did they break up?'

'Couple of weeks ago. So, tell me the bad things about Sam.'

'She thought she was a stud. She wore a Barbour jacket like that was an original thing to do.'

'There you go.'

'She got angry with me if I didn't pick up the phone when she called. And she did take me to Lyon and spent a lot of time having sex with another woman.'

Owen nodded, at a loss for words, I think.

'She was good in bed, though.'

'That's very hard to give up. Very hard.' He gave me a strange sort of half-hug. 'You can do this, Julia,' he said.

'Thanks Owen,' I said, and I made a resolution to put at least £10 into his leaving collection.

But I missed her – I missed her beauty, her edges, her dangerousness, the spiciness of her. Without her, everything was bland, like the ratatouille my mother makes to use up the old vegetables in the fridge.

Cat and Alice were brilliant. They took me out and bought me drinks and told me I could do much better than Sam, which I needed to hear, because I was still in the 'I'm going to die alone surrounded by crocheted tea cosies' stage of grief.

'She's a fucking psycho,' Cat said.

'You can't say that,' said Alice. 'She doesn't have a diagnosis. But it's fair to say she doesn't seem very happy.'

'She needs to do a fuckload of work on her own problems before she so much as kisses another woman.'

'She probably could do with a bit of CBT,' said Alice.

Alice and I were hanging out lots more now that we were both single; it was like the good old days, before I knew what enema kits were.

She persuaded me to come to the world's most expensive spinning class with her one day after work; she had replaced sex with staring at attractive personal trainers. 'You can pretend that they fancy you, as long as you don't look in the mirror afterwards and remember how red you go after cardio,' she told me, as we took our very uncomfortable seats on the spinning bikes.

'Take a moment to remember why you came here today,' shouted the instructor, as we climbed a hill to a Jay-Z song. Because I've broken up with a woman who likes to have problematic sex in skyscrapers, and I miss her, I thought.

'You're all heroes!' shouted the instructor, which was a bit of an exaggeration. I allowed myself to admire her arm muscles and her midriff. I'd have plenty of time to work on my arm muscles, now that I was single.

My swing dance friends were brilliant, too. Ella hosted a sleepover at her flat – two bedrooms, in an ex-local authority building near the Barbican, completely amazing – and we practised jumps and swingouts in her living room until her downstairs neighbour banged on the door and asked us to keep it down. And then, like teenagers, we played spin the bottle. My bottle landed on Ella, and that was all the confirmation I needed that I didn't fancy her – it felt all wrong, like kissing your sister, or a puppy. But then Ella's bottle landed on Zhu and it went on for ages. Bo, Rebecca and I actually got up to make ourselves another drink and left them to it on the sofa.

We didn't go to sleep till about three in the morning. Bo and Rebecca took the spare bedroom and Zhu and I laid out sleeping bags on the living room floor.

'Auditions for the Friends of Dorothy are coming up again,' Zhu said, after we'd turned the lights out.

'Night Zhu,' I said.

'Please try out?' she said. 'If you do, I'll buy you a pair of sequinned hot pants . . .'

'Gold?'

'Yes.'

I didn't reply.

'Please?'

'I'll think about it,' I said. I hadn't tried out before because I had been scared of not getting in – but I didn't feel scared any more. And now there was no Sam to resent me for the time I would spend going to rehearsals and shows. She had padded out my days and nights and thoughts, like polystyrene, and I was rattling around without her. I needed to fill my life up again.

One Saturday when Alice was out at yoga, I arranged to meet Dave for a secret walk in the Walthamstow Wetlands. We wandered around the marshes, scarves pulled tight around us, occasionally pointing out grebes to each other.

His beard looked limp, like a forgotten lettuce, and he seemed to have lost his ability to make dirty jokes. 'I'm rubbish without her,' he said, scuffing a rotten leaf. 'I haven't been eating much. I'm basically made of beer now.'

So I took him to a café and bought him a pork pie.

'How's Alice?' he asked between mouthfuls.

Glowing was the correct answer. Oddly fond of group exercise. But I said, 'She misses you.' Which was also true.

'I shouldn't have proposed,' he said. 'We were fine as we were.'

'She could have just said no,' I pointed out.

He nodded. 'Shall I call her?'

'I think so,' I said.

'Could you put in a good word for me?'

'I'll give it a go,' I said. I'd have to pick a good moment. She had a tendency to snap when I brought Dave up in conversation. 'You have crumbs in your beard, by the way,' I told him.

Dave brushed them away, embarrassed. 'I'll have to start washing again,' he said. I didn't disagree. He smelled a bit like a dog basket. 'Sorry,' he said. 'I haven't even asked how you are.'

I told him I'd broken up with Sam.

Dave puffed out his cheeks, which I think was supposed to indicate shock, maybe, or sympathy, but I could tell he thought it was good news.

I didn't like that everyone was happy about our break-up. They just saw the headlines of the relationship – that Sam was controlling, jealous, a bit too fond of having sex with strangers – but I saw the grey areas. I understood why she was afraid of monogamy. I got it, that her life felt out of control after her mum died, and that SM seemed like a way of being in charge of something. I could see why she was so scared of losing me that she'd ended up pushing me away. And they didn't get to see the good things about Sam – the way she'd always bring me tea in bed in the morning, the adventures she took me on, the way she made me feel like I could do anything. As long as I was doing it with her.

I got home to find Alice lying on the sofa, watching *Beaches* and eating a wheel of goat's cheese as if it were an apple.

She looked up at me, eyes red and swollen with crying. 'Hillary dies!' she said.

'I know,' I said, sitting down next to her.

'And CC's really going to miss her!' She shook her head.

'Of course she is,' I said, putting an arm around her.

'I don't know what I'd do if you died!'

'I like the fact that you've cast yourself as the world-famous singer and me as the pathetic dead one.'

'Hillary wasn't pathetic!' Alice said. 'She was the wind beneath CC's wings!' Outside in the street, a car alarm started to wail. 'Sorry,' said Alice. She cleared her throat and reached for a tissue.

'You don't need to be sorry for crying,' I said. 'Get it out. You've barely even cried about Dave.'

'I'm not crying about Dave,' she said, crying harder.

'He misses you,' I said.

She looked up. 'How do you know?'

'I'm sure he does,' I said, smooth as anything. 'There's some cava in the fridge. Want some?'

I was half an hour late to work the next morning; I managed to get myself out of the house on time, somehow, but the jolting of the Tube and the crush of hot human bodies had made me feel dangerously sick, and I had to get out at Green Park to avoid vomiting into someone's handbag. I was just going to keep my head down and get through the day.

'Hungover?' said Owen, as I slowly lowered myself onto my desk chair.

I nodded. 'Very.'

'Me too,' he said. 'Went on a Tinder date. She was really boring, so I drank a lot of whisky.'

'Sensible move.'

'I thought we'd get on. She was a gamer. We had a good chat about Final Fantasy XV. But then she wanted to talk about cats, and I don't like cats.'

I nodded; I suddenly felt very sick again and didn't trust myself to speak. I tried to focus on work. I had an inbox full of correspondence to reply to. I opened up the first email. A man in Ipswich, angry that a new arthritis drug wasn't available on the NHS. The next one down was from a woman named Lizzie Beecham. Beecham was Eric's surname.

I knew what the email would say before I opened it.

Dear Julia,

Your letter to my father arrived this morning. I hope you don't mind me emailing — I'm very sorry to be writing to tell you that my dad (Eric Beecham) died in hospital on Saturday night. He was 96, a very good age, which is some consolation.

My dad often talked about the letters he got from you. Your correspondence brought him a lot of comfort this past year and really kept him going. He loved writing and telling you about his life (he'd talk about the war to anyone who would listen). I'm sorry you never got to meet him — he was so looking forward to your visit, and he was full of plans for places to take you.

We're holding a funeral for him in Brighton on Friday at 10 a.m., reception in the community centre afterwards (where he used to play bridge). It would mean a lot to us all if you could come but I am sure you are very busy.

Yours sincerely,
Lizzie Beecham

I put my head in my hands and cried.

Owen rushed over and crouched beside my desk. 'What happened?' he said.

'Eric died,' I said. I closed my eyes. 'I said I'd visit him and I never did.'

'You've had a lot going on.'

'I've been selfish,' I said. 'Horrible and selfish.'

Owen reached out and clutched my shoulder, arm rigid, as though he knew he should touch me but wasn't sure how to. And then he went and muttered something to Uzo, who came over with a cup of peppermint tea.

'I know how you feel,' said Uzo, sitting in the chair next to mine. 'My old lady, the one I visit on a Thursday night, died a few months ago. We had an argument the last time I saw her about who was a greater man: Gandhi or Nelson Mandela. I felt bad for weeks.'

I nodded. Uzo pulled a wrinkled hankie out of her sleeve and handed it to me. I blew my nose and sipped my peppermint tea.

'There you go, my dear,' said Uzo. 'Everything is going to be just fine. OK?'

'OK,' I said.

Smriti was really good about the funeral. She gave me a day off to go and said not to worry about making the time up. I got up early that Friday morning and caught the train to Brighton, along with exhausted-looking parents with screaming children – 'My biscuit is broken! Fix my biscuit!' – and dopey couples off on long weekend breaks. I looked up from the condolence card I was writing and glared at two teenagers who were kissing noisily. I didn't mind people being happy as long as they did it behind closed doors where they couldn't hurt anybody.

I had brought Eric's letters with me in case Lizzie wanted to see them. I took one out and read his familiar phrases: 'Mustn't grumble!' and 'That was donkey's years ago,' and 'I ask you!' I ran my fingers over the imprint his biro had left in the paper.

I'm not a huge fan of funerals; I always feel awkward showing grief in front of people I don't know, and when I see a stranger crying, I tend to come over all English and start making conversation about parking meters. I don't suppose many people are massive fans of funerals, though, except maybe funeral directors, for financial reasons. The point is, I was feeling quite anxious as I got off the train and followed Google Maps uphill, past cafés and vintage shops and Victorian terraced houses, until I reached the crematorium. I stood outside for a while, admiring the manicured flowerbeds, breathing in the thick, salty air and thinking about chips. If you stood on your tiptoes, you could just about see the sea. Eric would have liked that.

A crowd of grey-haired women in dark coats bustled past me towards the chapel of rest. I followed them. At the door, a teenager in a grown man's suit handed me an order of service. One of Eric's great-grandchildren, maybe. I sat at the back of the chapel – I didn't want to take up a family seat by accident. I looked down at the photograph of Eric as a young man, looking so proud in his RAF uniform, probably only a bit older than the suit-wearing teenager. Goodbye Eric, I thought. I'm so sorry I didn't get to dance with you.

We sang 'All Things Bright and Beautiful' and 'Jerusalem' (Dad wouldn't have approved) and then the vicar said a few words about Eric's war record and what a loving father and husband he was, how much he enjoyed getting down to the beach at the weekend for a bowl of soup and half a pint of shandy. I tried to ignore the squeaking sound as the coffin trundled through the municipal purple curtains.

As we filed out, heads bowed, 'We'll Meet Again' played over the loud speaker. I thought about Eric and Eve, and I hoped they were together again, even though I didn't believe in heaven. I couldn't hold it together any more. An old lady with a stick patted my back and said lovely old-fashioned things like, 'There, there,' and 'Get it all out,' that reminded me of my granddad.

'How did you know Eric?' she asked.

'He was sort of my pen pal,' I told her.

She shook my arm. 'Ooh!' she said. 'The girl from the government! Is that you?'

'Yes!'

'You know how to jitterbug, I hear,' she said. 'We'll have to see what you've got, at the wake.'

'I don't know if it's appropriate to jitterbug at a funeral,' I said.

'Oh, Eric would have loved it.' She smiled up at me. 'He was so fond of you. Just the other day he was telling me all the things you were going to do together in Brighton when you came to see him.'

* * *

The lady's name was Irene. She'd been Eric's neighbour at the care home – the one he used to dance with. We walked (very slowly) to the community centre together for the wake. There were balloons taped to the walls, left over from a child's birthday party, and urns of tea and plates of sandwiches. Irene introduced me to Eric's daughter Lizzie, who must have been in her seventies. She was shiny eyed but composed, much more composed than I was. 'I've got something for you,' Lizzie said, and she jogged away and came back with a Sainsbury's bag, full of records – Billy Cotton and His Band and Al Bowlly and George Gershwin.

'What's this?' I asked.

'Dad wanted you to have them,' she said.

I covered my face with my hands.

Lizzie put an arm around me. 'Do you need a cup of tea?'

'This is all wrong,' I said snottily. 'I should be comforting you!'

'I'm bored of crying,' she said. 'I've been doing it all week. Don't think there's any water left inside me.'

We didn't jitterbug in the end (no record player), but I met Eric's other friends from the home, who were a lively lot. At one point, two 90-year-old women raced around the community centre in their mobility scooters.

'Do you think some of your friends would be interested in swing dance lessons?' I asked Irene. 'If I came up to teach sometimes?'

'Ooh, yes!' said Irene. 'They say that dancing's very good for osteoporosis.' And she called the manager of the care home over, to introduce me.

After I'd eaten my fill of tuna sandwiches and said my goodbyes, I walked back down the hill to the station, clutching my bag of records to my chest. I caught the 16.18 to London; the train was pretty quiet, so I had a table to myself. I ordered a cup of tea from the refreshment trolley and took Eric's records out of the Sainsbury's bag. A letter fell out, too. It was addressed to me, in Eric's handwriting.

Dear Julia,

These records have brought me so much pleasure over the years. I hope they bring pleasure to you, too. I think my favourite might be 'You Are My Sunshine'. Eve and I danced to that at our wedding; it was one of the hot tunes of the day during the war. I want you to know that you have been my sunshine over these past few months.

PS — Life is short! Go out and grab it with both hands!

PPS — I hope you find a dancing partner who deserves you!

Your friend,

Eric

That afternoon, when I got home, I called Zhu and told her that I'd love to start teaching beginners' swing classes. I went to the Stepping Out website and registered for the Friends of Dorothy auditions. And then I forced myself to sit down and fill out the Fast Stream application form.

'What are you doing?' Alice asked, when she got in from work.

'Just a bit of life grabbing,' I told her.

43. A COUPLE OF PIROUETTES

The rest of October passed in a blur of pumpkin bread and Halloween parties. My favourite was the Halloween swing dance social at the Rivoli Ballroom, a ridiculously beautiful Art-Deco dance hall, all red velvet and wood panelling and chandeliers. I got extremely drunk on cheap red wine, and danced until my feet hurt and I could barely breathe. The Big Band played 'Ain't Misbehavin'', and the trumpeter's eyes closed with bliss as he blared out the top notes. I knew how he felt. I wished Eric could have been there with me.

And then it was November, and the correspondence team gathered around Owen's desk for his leaving presentation. We bought him a bottle of Welsh whisky and an Xbox gift card, and he made a wobbly-voiced speech about how every member of the team had a different superpower, like the Avengers.

Owen invited his sister along to his leaving drinks. For some reason, I'd thought she would be femme and blonde, but she wasn't – she was butch and stocky, with a swaggery way of walking and lovely green eyes. She was wearing what can only be described as a gilet, but I still thought she was quite attractive. She worked, it turned out, as a TV writer.

'That is so exciting and glamorous,' I said. I was quite drunk at this point. I may have been draping myself over her arm a bit.

'It's not as glamorous as you think,' she said, in a deep voice that made me think of log cabins and crackling fires. 'We spend a lot of time in hotel rooms in Birmingham. And the show I'm writing is called *Cheer Up!* It's aimed at seven-year-olds, and it's about cheerleaders. I hate cheerleaders. I pitched them a show about a girls' rugby team, but they weren't interested.'

'Conforming to gender norms. Disgusting,' I said happily.

'But what I really like to do in my spare time,' she said, smiling at me, 'is host supper clubs. I love cooking for other people.'

She showed me her supper club Instagram account. At the most recent event, she'd made mayonnaise from scratch.

I asked for her number right there and then.

Two weeks later, I arrived at the pub in Clerkenwell for the Friends of Dorothy auditions. None of my friends from class were trying out, though Zhu was one of the judges. She was sitting at a table at the front of the room, next to a man in a three-piece suit, making notes and sipping bottled water. I caught her eye and she waved at me. I waved back. I thought about the promise of sequinned hot pants. I could do this.

Being there gave me horrible flashbacks to every open audition I'd been to over the years: the Formica judges' table, the overconfident dancers doing unnecessary splits during the warm-up, the sound of heavy breathing every time the music stopped. We were tested on our solo jazz technique and our partnered lindy hop, and then, at the end, there was a freestyle section. I knew it was cheating – a bit like cooking a green curry during a French cooking competition – but I pulled off a couple of pirouettes. The other dancers cheered resentfully.

As I was leaving, Zhu called me back.

'You're in,' she said, and she hugged me.

I hadn't felt so good since the night I discovered fisting.

I walked home from the Tube on a high, smiling at strangers. I could handle a boring day job, now that I was going to be a dancer by night. Everything looked full of beauty to me all of a sudden. The sky was cloudless and blue. The grey pavement was flecked with little yellow leaves. Sure, there was an abandoned mattress lying on the pavement, and a little puddle of vomit in the gutter, but that's London for you, isn't it? Without the grittiness, we wouldn't appreciate the good things, like the dome of St Paul's and the delicious flat whites, and the fact that two women can walk down the street holding hands without someone shouting 'Lezzers!' at them.

I was just walking past the new organic grocery store when Carys texted me, asking if I wanted to meet up. I did a little dance in the street – everything was going my way! – and I texted her straight back: *My friends told me about a new lesbian night in Whitechapel on Saturday. Do you fancy going?*

My phone pinged pretty much instantly with a reply.

OK, it said.

But it wasn't from Carys. It was from my mother. My actual 58-year-old mother.

I was a bit put out. I had accidentally invited my mother lesbian clubbing with me, and she was half-hearted about it?

I texted her back: *That message wasn't meant for you, Mum.*

Oh, she replied. *I was looking forward to it.*

I felt a bit sorry for Mum. My dad was obviously spending too much time recording YouTube videos in his bedroom like a teenage boy to accompany her to the theatre/restaurants/other evening activities that are appropriate for people who are almost old enough to collect their state pension.

I was about to text Carys for real this time, when the phone rang.

I looked at the number.

It was Sam.

I picked up. Of course I did.

'Hello?' I said, as stern as I could manage.

'Hello?'

'Sam?'

I heard her let out a breath. 'Babes,' she said. 'I miss you so much.'

I didn't say anything.

'I'm so sorry about how we left things. I should never have spoken to you like that.'

'No,' I said. 'You shouldn't have.'

'Please give me another chance,' she said, voice small. 'Please? I'm not the same without you. I can't live without you.'

'Yes, you can.' Stay strong, I told myself. You are strong.

'I can't. I can't.' Her voice was creeping up the octave, pleading. 'I won't have anything if you leave me.'

'I thought you were the one who broke up with me.'

'What? That's not what happened! That's not what happened at all! Please, babes. Don't you miss me?'

'You called me abusive.' A couple who'd just walked out of Homebase turned to look at me.

After a moment, she said, 'You *did* use abusive language.'

'Look,' I said. 'I don't need this—'

'Just come over so we can talk?' Sam said. 'Please? And if you still want it to be over I'll respect your decision.'

I could feel the acid bubble of anxiety in my stomach. But I had to see her again, just like I have to bite my fingers till I bleed when I'm anxious.

'Fine,' I said. 'I'll come over.'

'Thank you,' Sam said pathetically. 'Thank you, babes. Tonight?'

'Not tonight,' I said. 'I can come over tomorrow if you like.'

'Yes, please,' Sam said. 'You won't regret it. I promise.'

I knew Alice wouldn't be pleased about me going to see Sam, so I bought a nice bottle of red and some Kettle Chips at the corner shop to soften the news. The fact I was nervous about telling my best friend I might be getting back together with the woman that I loved should have given me a clue that the whole thing was a terrible plan. I can't trust my own instincts when it comes to relationships, I've learned – or rather I can, but I can argue my way around them so that I blame my debilitating dread on a rainy day, or the fact that I'm never going to be able to afford to buy a house in London, or whatever. But I have always trusted Alice's judgement. If anything, she's a bit too generous about people. But she wasn't generous about Sam at all.

Kettle Chips under my arm, red wine in front of me like a weapon, I climbed the stairs to our flat and opened the door.

'Julia?' Alice called. 'Come in! I've made roast veg! We're not talking about Dave tonight. Or Sam.'

I walked into the kitchen and put the wine down on the kitchen counter. 'Actually,' I said, opening the Kettle Chips, 'I have some news about Sam.'

Alice straightened up. 'You're not getting back together with her.'

'I'm going to her house to talk.'

There was an unpleasant silence.

I crunched a Kettle Chip.

'Why, though?'

'We're just going to talk.'

'I've seen you crying so many times because of her—'

'I have to, OK?' I said, quite snappily. 'I don't want to regret breaking up with her.'

'You won't,' Alice said, pity in her eyes, which was the last thing I wanted. 'I don't regret breaking up with Dave, do I?'

'Well,' I said. 'You do. A bit.'

Alice's eyes went cold. 'No, I don't. Don't make this about me.'

'You miss him, and he misses you.'

'Have you been talking to him?'

I reached for another crisp and didn't answer.

'You're my friend first! Not his!'

'I'm not taking sides! We are not twelve years old!' And in that moment I felt horribly vindictive, and I said, 'You still love him, and now you want me to be single, because you don't want to see me happy when you're feeling lonely and miserable.'

Alice took a step backwards, as though I'd pushed her, and said, 'Fuck you.' And then she slammed out of the kitchen.

It's incredible the power a swear word can have in the mouth of someone who doesn't usually use them.

I could hear Alice crying in her bedroom. I felt sick with myself. Alice was my best friend. She was just looking out for me. I'd go to Sam's tomorrow, but I'd end it, for sure.

44. LOVE, ACTUALLY?

I kept my head low as I walked to my desk the next morning – I'd agreed to go for a drink with Smriti after work, for my first Fast Stream coaching session. It was too late to come up with a decent excuse for bailing on her – a sick grandmother or a family dinner – so the only possible way of getting out of the situation was to feign illness. I started giving some half-hearted coughs, and I made myself an ostentatious Lemsip. I walked slowly to the loo, past Smriti's office, and collected some tissues so I could blow my nose loudly at my desk.

At five o'clock I looked up to see Smriti hovering by my desk. 'You ready?' she said.

'I'm sorry,' I said. 'I'm really not feeling good. Can we do this next week instead?'

'Of course! You poor thing!' she said. 'Stay home tomorrow if you're still sick!'

Uzo rolled her eyes at me from across the desk divide.

I tried to calm myself down on the bus to Homerton by naming things I could see out of the window: cyclists. Rain. Falling leaves. Wellington boots. Happy couples, sharing umbrellas. Two friends eating KFC.

And then my phone rang and made me jump. It was my mother.

'Julia. It's your mother. Hi.'

'Hi, Mum.'

'What are you doing, darling?'

'I'm on a bus. About to get off.' I tucked my phone under my chin and shouldered my bag, making my way down the stairs.

'Homerton station,' said the treacherous automated voice over the Tannoy.

'Isn't that where Sam lives?' Mum asked.

'I broke up with Sam,' I said. The bus stopped, and I stepped out into the rain.

'Alice told me you were thinking of getting back together with her.'

I stopped still on the pavement. 'What?'

'She's worried about you, darling. You haven't been yourself since you've been with Sam.'

'I don't need to hear this—'

'I know what I'm talking about,' Mum said. 'I was in an abusive relationship before I met your father—'

'I am not in an abusive relationship!'

'She's controlling you!'

'She's not!'

'So come home. Come home now, don't go to her house. I've made a Victoria sponge. And Dad's trying to grow a moustache! That'll give you a good laugh.'

'I can't,' I said.

She didn't answer.

'Look, I'm not coming all the way to Oxford to admire Dad's facial hair. I'm right outside Sam's house—'

'Do not get back together with that woman!'

'Just— fuck off, Mum,' I said.

She didn't say anything. I had never told her to fuck off before. I felt shaky and wired and out of control. 'Sorry, Mum,' I said. 'But it's none of your business.' I hung up and took a breath and

350

walked on to Sam's, purpose in my footsteps. How dare she tell me what to do? How dare Alice?

Sam's lights were on. I could hear some sort of low murmuring – she was listening to the radio. I rang the doorbell and waited.

She opened the door halfway, as though she wasn't sure who it would be, and when she saw it was me, she caught me in a hug so tight that I could hardly move – a hug that reminded me of the one women's rugby practice I went to at university, which resulted in me not being able to move my head for a week.

'I'm so glad you came,' Sam said. 'I wasn't sure you would.' And she kissed me.

It's funny how things can curdle. Like milk – delicious on your Weetabix one day, the next day like drinking a disgusting vinegar/cheese hybrid. Just a few weeks previously, Sam's kisses had made me pulse with desire for her. But when she kissed me that evening, it felt too hot, too wet.

Sam led me into the flat. There was something different about it – I wasn't sure what, at first. It felt lighter. Much bigger, too, and emptier.

I walked into the living room and looked around. The paintings were missing. The naked women, the parade of past sexual conquests, were gone. Rectangles of dust and unfaded paint marked the places where they had been.

'You didn't have to do this,' I said.

She smiled and took my hand, and said, 'Wait, you haven't seen the best bit,' and led me over to her bed.

The wall above the bed was covered with a painting – a bigger-than-life-size painting of my naked body. Sam usually used fluorescent colours, an exaggerated palette, but this painting was muted, naturalistic, exact. It was beautiful – somehow she'd caught the way I carried myself, the texture of my skin (slightly spotty), my one grey pubic hair. She mostly worked from life, but I'd definitely have noticed if she'd been feverishly following me around, crosshatching my jawline, so she must have painted this from memory. Which made the accuracy a little disturbing.

I guess I'd finally inspired an intense emotion in Sam.

'Do you like it?' she asked, so proud, like a cat presenting a dead mouse to its owner.

'It's – really good.'

'You don't like it.'

'I do—'

'Really?'

Sam was standing next to me, watching my face for a reaction. When she didn't get one, she said, 'Aren't you pleased? It's the first in a new series. It's going to be called "Every Woman I've Ever Really Loved". But the paintings will all be of you. Do you get it?'

I nodded.

'And there's something else.' She smiled and took my hands. 'I've missed you so much the last couple of weeks. So, so much.' She closed her eyes and shook her head. 'I know it's been hard recently, but we've been together a while now, and I've realized that I want to be with you. Properly with you.'

'Not having sex with other people?'

She shook her head. 'Just me and you.' She smiled, and I was taken aback again by how utterly I was attracted to her.

Walk away, said the voice in my head – the sensible voice that tells me not to get in unlicensed taxis. Get out, it said. You'll be happier without her. But this was what I'd been waiting to hear her say all along.

Yes, what she'd done was creepy, in a way. Slightly stalkerish, you could say. A tiny bit manipulative and controlling, maybe. But it was a grand gesture, too, and aren't lots of grand gestures creepy? Think about Meg Ryan stalking Tom Hanks, a vulnerable widower, in *Sleepless in Seattle*, luring him to the top of a tall building with his young son; think about Andrew Lincoln in *Love Actually*, filming a close-up video of Keira Knightley's face at her wedding to his best friend and watching it over and over on VHS before declaring his love for her with bits of cardboard; and *Phantom of the Opera* – I can't remember the details of the plot but I feel like there's a bit of kidnap involved. Sometimes love and obsession are hard to tell apart, that's all I'm saying.

I told her we could take things one step at a time. And I didn't exactly protest when she led me to the bed and fucked me with her biggest cock, hard, so that I cried out. She put her hand over my mouth to shut me up. I felt such relief, afterwards, such a high, and the only reason I couldn't fall asleep for ages was the thought that Alice would know I was spending the night with Sam and that she'd be angry with me.

Sam walked me to the station the next morning, holding my hand tight. 'I've got an idea,' she said, as we reached the Overground. 'Let's go away next weekend.'

'Not to do any SM or anything.'

'No!' said Sam. 'No, no. Much too soon for that! Let's just rent a cottage somewhere and get away from it all. A cheap one. It'll be gorgeous. What do you say?'

She looked so excited by the idea, so young and adorable, that I didn't have the heart to say no. If I was going to give it another go with her I might as well really give it a go, right? And what was I going to do otherwise? Cook recipes from Delia Smith's *One is Fun!*, do laundry and not speak to Alice?

'All right,' I said.

'Thank you,' Sam said, pulling me in for a hug. 'Thank you. You won't regret it!'

'I know,' I said, smiling apologetically over Sam's shoulder at the commuters trying to edge past us.

'I'll have a look at places when I get to the studio. You don't have to do a thing. I'm in charge. I'll take care of everything.'

45. SHAG PILE VIRGIN

It's almost impressive how little Alice and I saw each other that week. Her alarm would go off before mine, a harsh, insistent, bleating beep, more like a fire alarm than a wake-up call, and I'd hear her stumble to the shower, and the water hissing down on her. I'd run to the kitchen and take my cereal back to my room and watch episode after episode of *The Crown* out of spite, because we'd promised to watch it together.

I still had my swing dance friends, though, who were refreshingly unjudgemental about me giving it another chance with Sam.

'You can't help who you fall for,' said Ella, who had her arm around Zhu.

'As long as this doesn't mean you're going to back out of joining Friends of Dorothy,' said Zhu.

'Of course I won't,' I said, though I saw Bo throw Zhu a sceptical look.

'Have fun in Lyme Regis,' said Rebecca. She smiled nostalgically. 'Text us about the exciting sex.'

'Rebecca!' said Bo, hitting her arm. 'Seriously!'

Sam and I had decided not to see each other till the Friday night of our trip – or rather, I'd decided, and she'd agreed – but she texted me every morning and lunchtime, texts I'd have killed to receive just a few months previously; things like *Good morning babes. I love you so much, forever xxxx* and *You're the only one for me. Do you know that? Xxxx* and *How's your day going? Thinking about your gorgeous cunt and wishing I were going down on you xxxxxx.* But now her messages made me feel twitchy and anxious, as though she was right behind me all the time, as though she was inside my head, reading my thoughts. And sure, there had always been the risk that she might bugger off with another woman, or decide to have a threesome and expect me to accept it, or that she'd want to tie me to a lamppost and pretend to be Jack the Ripper, or whatever – but that was all sex-related stuff, which was sort of exciting. Since we'd agreed to go away I'd been thinking about what Jane had told me about Sam and her ex – about how possessive Sam had been – and now I was nervous more generally.

After Alice left for work that Friday morning I opened the bathroom door and the steam from her shower hit my face, clammy and scented with her mint shower gel. The mirror was smeared with her fingerprints and her wet footprints made the tiles slippery. It reminded me of Denis Severs' House, a strange Georgian townhouse in the City we'd been to on our work Christmas outing the year before, where the rooms are full of half-eaten food and still-smouldering candles so that it feels ghostly, as though someone has just left. 'You'll be fine,' I said to myself out loud, as Alice wasn't there to say it for me. 'You are going to be just fine.'

I left work five minutes late and ran to the station to meet Sam. She had decided not to take the car to Lyme – too exhausting to drive for three-and-a-half hours on a Friday night – and I was glad; I wasn't massively keen on the idea of getting into Sam's car again after our trip home from the Shard. I caught a crowded Tube. I was wearing my winter coat, and by the time we got to Waterloo my hair was stuck to my forehead like strands of limp seaweed on a rock.

My bag was heavy, so I stood on the escalator, and as we reached the top, a woman bashed into me with a tattered weekend bag. She turned to apologize, and I saw that it was Ella, in a very fetching bottle-green suit.

'Hey!' she said.

'Hey!' I said back.

But people were walking up the escalator behind her, so she couldn't stop to talk. She gave me a wave. I looked around for her as I emerged into the mainline station, but she was already lost in the Friday-night crowd.

I'd arranged to meet Sam beneath the announcement boards. I saw her before she saw me and I felt a wave of hope and love as I watched her watching for me, jostled by commuters. I wasn't late yet, but I could tell she was worried I wouldn't turn up. I wondered briefly what would happen if I just turned around and left the station.

But then she saw me, and her whole body relaxed. As I walked towards her, she said, 'I can't believe how beautiful you are.'

A young woman in a duffel coat turned to see who had said such a lovely thing, and blushed when she noticed me notice her.

'I look like a slug,' I said to Sam, shy suddenly. 'You, though. You look amazing.' And she did. She was dressed all in black with new leather boots, shiny ones, not yet scuffed.

'You think so?'

I nodded.

She pulled me to her and held me the way you hold someone when you fear you might be about to lose them, or when you've just lost them and you've got them back, and I held her that way too, and I began to cry, in a nice way.

As we boarded the train, I saw Ella jogging towards a different platform. She saw me and waved. I smiled at her.

'Who was that?' asked Sam, turning to look.

'Just someone from dance.' I didn't want to say Ella's name.

*　　*　　*

We managed to score a table seat on the train, and we'd both come prepared, Sam with Marks & Spencer chocolate-covered raisins, me with cans of gin and tonic. We toasted the weekend ahead with our cans and soon we were definitely drunk, laughing too hard at a cat photograph Jasper had posted on Facebook. Sam read her book and I gazed out of the window at the trees, turning gold to red to brown, fantasizing about getting off at the next station and starting my life all over again in the middle of Devon. I used to listen to *The Archers* on Sundays over breakfast at my parents' house; I reckoned I could make a go of it.

We caught a cab from Axminster station. It twisted through the narrow lanes of central Lyme Regis, coming to a stop halfway up a hill outside a tiny terraced house. Sam fiddled with the lock as I stood on the cobbled street, breathing deep, filling my lungs with the cold sea air.

'There's a wood-burning stove!' I said, as we walked inside. I dropped my bag, rushed over and knelt in front of it, but Sam said, 'Not yet.'

I stood up, obeying her automatically, and then I realized what I'd done and I knelt back down again. 'I want to light it,' I said.

'First things first,' Sam said, kneeling down behind me and kissing me on the neck. 'We have to christen the house.' She undid my bra through my T-shirt and by that time my nipples were already hard – it had been a week, let's face it – and we had sex right there on the thick shag pile rug, Sam fucking me from behind. I was facing the window, and the Venetian blinds weren't twisted shut. A couple of people walked past and I grabbed Sam's wrist to stop her in case they saw us or heard us, but that made the whole thing even hotter.

When I'd come, shuddering to my stomach, Sam lay on top of me and kissed my ear. 'I've always wanted to fuck on a rug like this,' she said.

'You mean that was your first time?'

'Yes. I was a shag pile shag virgin.'

* * *

It's funny the difference a place can make to the way you feel about things. Sam and I seemed to make sense again in Lyme Regis. The things that mattered in London didn't seem to matter here; there was no Alice to make me question my relationship, no Cat to remind me of what I'd done in Edinburgh, and no Jasper and Polly to remind Sam of the exciting sex she was missing. We were both relaxed and happy and excited about each other again. The little house had no Wi-Fi or phone reception, which made me feel claustrophobic at first – I wondered whether Sam had booked this cut-off cottage on purpose, and why – but then I thought about it for a while and realized the only things I'd miss out on were calls from my mother, loudly advising me to break up with Sam while Sam was in earshot, and reading about other people's engagements on Facebook. If I needed to get in touch with someone I just had to walk to the end of the road. I wasn't exactly in prison.

On Saturday morning we walked along the beach, scarves around our necks against the wind. Sam insisted we walk to the very end of the Cobb, Lyme Regis's famous curved stone harbour wall, even though the waves whipped arcs of saltwater across our path. I worried we'd be washed in, but Sam insisted we wouldn't, and she was right.

Afterwards, we browsed in the shops on Broad Street, which were mostly expensive and touristy, except one: a beautiful, ramshackle second-hand bookshop, the sort that only really exists in films set in Hampstead these days. Sam walked straight to the back and started leafing through a biography of Josephine Baker. I stayed in the fiction section, feeling that if I could just find the right book I might become a different person, a person who had intelligent things to say about the Booker Prize shortlist and had never had racist sex in the Shard.

Books spilled out of the shelves as though begging you to choose them, and framed photos of the shop's bestselling authors peered down at us; I felt Virginia Woolf's eyes on me as I picked up a Jilly Cooper. I put it back down and picked up an Angela Carter novel instead.

Sam moved to the art section and approached the white-haired man who worked there. 'I'm looking for a book by Grayson Perry. I think he's written a memoir.'

'*Portrait of the Artist as a Young Girl.*'

'That's the one.'

I felt my phone buzz in my pocket – I had signal again, and three messages had come through at once.

'We had a copy, but someone bought it a few weeks ago,' the white-haired man was saying.

A message from Dad: *Nice documentary about earthquakes on BBC iPlayer if you're interested.*

And another from Ella: *Hellooooo! Good luck with Sam this weekend!!! When are you back?*

A voice behind me said, 'Who's that from?'

I felt my body jolt, as though I had been caught out. I put my phone in my pocket. 'Just Dad,' I said.

'How's his YouTube channel coming along?'

'Disturbingly well. BuzzFeed featured him on a list of seventeen surprisingly hot YouTubers over 50.' Which was, unfortunately, true.

Sam had booked us a table for dinner in the saloon bar of The Volunteer, a trendy pub by Lyme Regis standards, with mismatched vintage furniture and too many antique mirrors on the expensively grey walls. The booking turned out to have been completely unnecessary as we were the only people in there. Occasionally people would push the saloon bar doors open and tumble into the room, stopping short when they saw the two of us eating a *Lady and the Tramp*-style candlelit dinner before retreating to the other side of the pub, away from the intensity of our relationship.

'We should do a toast to second chances,' Sam said, after we'd finished our fish pie. 'I'll order us some fizz.'

No one was serving in the saloon bar, so she pushed through the swing doors to find a barman.

As soon as she'd gone, I pulled my phone from my pocket to text Ella back. *Going OK so far. Will fill you in when I get back xxxxx*

As I was putting my phone away, Sam came back into the room carrying two glasses of prosecco.

'Here you go, babes,' Sam said, passing a glass to me. 'I love you more every day.'

I nodded. 'You too.'

We drank our prosecco and I felt myself warming up from within. We talked about Sam's new gallery, and what my chances were like for the Fast Stream, and whether I should take on any swing dance teaching, for a bit of fun on the side.

'I didn't think you liked having fun on the side,' said Sam, raising her eyebrows.

I laughed – it was a bit of a hollow laugh, but Sam didn't seem to notice.

I went to take a sip of my prosecco and realized I didn't have any left to sip. 'I'll get us a refill,' I said. I picked up my wallet and pushed through the saloon doors.

The main part of the pub was packed with old men in Fair Isle jumpers and women in fleeces sipping at pints of bitter, and the heat and noise made me feel drunker and more excited. I elbowed my way to the bar and ordered us two more glasses of prosecco.

As I sat down at our table again, my phone buzzed in my pocket. I ignored it and handed Sam her glass.

She smiled at me. 'Aren't you going to check who's texting you?'

'I'll check it later.'

'Go on,' she said, her smile a little forced now. 'Check it now.'

'No,' I said, reddening.

'You're hiding something from me,' she said.

'I'm not!' I slid my phone across the table to her. 'You're being paranoid,' I said.

Sam looked at my phone. 'You've been texting Ella.'

'So? She's my friend.'

She scrolled back through my messages.

'You're not going to find anything else in there,' I said, face hot, praying that I was right.

She was still looking through my phone.

'What are you doing?' I said, trying to grab it, but she pulled it back.

'Why are you looking at my Instagram?'

'Why? Don't you want me to?' she asked.

I leaned over to see what she was looking at. She had opened my DMs. And there, near the top, was the message from Jane. It's like she had known it would be there.

'No,' I said, standing up. 'No, no, no, no——'

Sam turned my phone around for me to see, eyes cold, furious. 'What's this?'

Didn't want to text you just in case . . . Last night was hot. Don't worry, I won't tell her. Call if you ever need someone to talk to, and look after yourself.

Why hadn't I deleted that message? Why had I been such a fucking idiot?

Because your girlfriend isn't supposed to look through your social media messages. Your girlfriend is supposed to trust you.

But she had been right not to trust me. I had proved her right, right to be jealous, right to be paranoid.

Maybe I'd meant her to see it.

I desperately wanted to claw back what had happened, what I had done, but I couldn't. 'I was drunk,' I said, pleading. 'It was a terrible mistake, and I wanted to tell you——'

'When?' she asked. She had started to cry.

'In Edinburgh,' I said, crying too. 'Before you said anything about being monogamous. Just one time.'

She looked up at me. She didn't seem angry. Just hurt. 'You could have just asked.'

'I know. I'm sorry,' I said, reaching across to touch her hand.

But she snatched her hand away and her face was getting redder, and her rage was returning, like a wave, bigger, with more momentum. She said, 'Why did you come to Lyme Regis with me if you were fucking someone else?'

'I'm not fucking her,' I said, scared now. 'It was once. I'm so sorry.'

'You asked me to come here with you when you were seeing someone behind my back.'

'I didn't ask you,' I said. 'You asked *me.*'

'Oh, right. So you didn't actually want to come. You were forced to.'

'That's not what I said!'

'I can't believe you're denying that this was your idea.'

'It wasn't! It wasn't, though!' I was unsure of what I thought I knew. I wasn't wrong, was I? Why was she trying to make me wrong?

'Why are you lying about this?' Sam asked. She looked genuinely upset.

'I'm not!'

She looked at me. She shook her head. She dropped my phone onto the table and pushed her chair back. 'I'm going,' she said.

'Sam—'

'No, no.' She was pulling on her coat now. 'You're a fucking liar and a cheater. And you didn't even want to come here, apparently.'

'Wait,' I said to Sam's back. She was already walking out of the pub.

I stood there, staring at the two glasses of prosecco on the table, the bubbles rising to the surface, waiting for a toast that wasn't going to come.

46. A DYKEY FRENCH LIEUTENANT'S WOMAN

I wrapped my coat around me and stumbled out into the cold, dark street. The wind was slapping my hair into my face, as though it was trying to shake some sense into me.

I phoned Sam. She didn't pick up.

I phoned her again.

'What?' she said.

'What's going on?' I asked.

'How long have you and Ella been fucking?'

I stopped walking. 'What are you talking about?'

'Jane wasn't enough for you, was she? Got a taste for it, didn't you?'

'Look, I am so, so sorry about what I did. But I'm not interested in anyone else—'

'Liar!'

'I'm not a liar!'

'You're seeing Ella behind my back!'

'I'm not!'

'Don't insult me!'

'I'm not insulting you! You don't need to be jealous of her! There is nothing between us!' A pair of teenage boys turned to look at me, curious. I realized I was shouting.

'Don't lie.' Her voice was quieter now, though. She wanted to be talked down.

'Baby,' I said. 'Baby. I am so sorry for what I did. I am so sorry I didn't tell you. I am so disgusted with myself.'

'OK,' she said, voice calmer still. 'OK. A hundred per cent honesty now. Promise?'

'Promise.'

'Do you find Ella attractive?'

'No—'

'That's a lie! You want her!' Her voice was creeping up the octave again.

'I don't!'

'You've already been unfaithful to me!'

'You're such a hypocrite!' I shouted, completely desperate with guilt and frustration and fury now. 'You slept with Virginie when we were together!'

A moment of silence.

'That's different,' she said then. 'You knew what was going on. You knew about Virginie from the moment we got together.'

'But nothing's going on with me and Ella! I don't *want* anything to be going on! I just want you!'

'I can't believe you're treating me like this.' She was working herself up now, as if on purpose, like a child, mid-tantrum. 'I've allowed myself to be so vulnerable with you. I told you about my mum dying. I told you about my dad in Dubai—'

'That's it! That's literally it! I know hardly anything about you!' And as I spoke, I realized that was true.

I could hear Sam breathing on the other end of the line.

'This is ridiculous,' I said. 'Where are you?'

'Don't pretend you care. Don't pretend you care what happens to me,' she said, and she hung up. I was standing on a cobbled street, in front of a slate-roofed cottage. Through the window I could see a couple sitting on a sofa watching Saturday-night TV, her arm around his shoulders.

I ran to the house we were staying in, but Sam wasn't there. I stood on the doorstep, panting, thinking. Where would I go if I were Sam? Where would I go if I were hurt, a hypocrite, a massive fucking drama queen?

To the sea. Obviously to the sea.

I ran down the hill till I reached the beach, the wind wailing, encouraging me or warning me, I couldn't tell. The water was silver-black under the moon, the waves roaring and scratching, roaring and scratching.

I ran along the raised paved walkway that curves around the bay, past pastel beach huts, threatening and grey in the moonlight, standing to attention like a useless army.

I knew where she'd be. She'd be where all the drama takes place in Lyme Regis. She'd be on the Cobb.

And yes, there she was, right at the end of the curved wall, like a dykey French lieutenant's woman, silhouetted against the moonlight, gazing out to sea, ignoring the huge waves crashing behind her, her scarf waving in the wind.

'Sam!' I shouted, but she didn't seem to hear me.

Even then, when I felt solid with rage because of her, I couldn't believe how beautiful she was. So angular and tall and noble and perfect. How could she still look perfect to me?

'Sam!' I shouted again. 'Come back!'

But she didn't. I was going to have to go to her.

I'm afraid of the sea. But I ignored the sign warning people not to walk on the Cobb in high winds and I climbed the steps. The stones were slippery with seawater. I walked towards Sam, keeping to the edge of the Cobb nearest the bay, but a wave curved up above me and slammed right into me, bringing me to my knees, leaving me gripping the paving stones and wiping stinging water out of my eyes and wondering how the fuck I'd got to this place.

'Sam!' I screamed again, and she heard me this time.

'Fuck off back to your girlfriend!' she shouted.

'What?' My vision was still blurry from the saltwater. 'Come on.

This is stupid. Come back!' I stood up, arms out to steady myself like a surfer, and took a few faltering steps.

But Sam was storming towards me, collar up, hands in her pockets, scarf streaming behind her.

I reached out to her as she neared me but she turned towards me and spat on the ground in front of me. 'Dirty fucking slut,' she said, and she just kept on walking, jogging down the stone steps as I made my terrified, crab-like way back to the safety of dry land.

'Wait!' I shouted, but she was running again now.

I ran after her but then she swerved to the right and started running over the pebbles towards the water, stumbling as they turned beneath her feet, taking off her jacket, flinging it onto the beach along with her phone.

'What are you doing?' I called, which was a silly question, because it was clear what she was doing: she was running, fully clothed, into the stormy, black October sea.

'Come back!'

She waded further out.

'Stop it!' I screamed. 'Stop it!'

She was up to her knees now, slowing down.

'Come back! Please, Sam! Please!'

She turned towards me, eyes wide with rage and, frankly, madness. 'You made me do this!' she screamed. 'You made me do this!' And she launched herself into the sea and started swimming as hard as she could.

So I tore off my coat and ran in after her. I'm a strong swimmer, despite my fear of the sea, and I caught up with her easily, but Sam screamed, 'Fuck off!' and pushed me away.

I tried to put my arms around her but I was out of my depth and I could feel myself sinking, and every time I got a grip on Sam's waist she lashed out at me.

And then we were inside a wave, being slammed against the stones on the seabed, and then our heads were above water and we were spluttering for air, and I took my opportunity and dragged her by the arm until we were on the beach, our chests heaving.

And I looked at her, and her hair, her face, her clothes were shining in the moonlight, and she looked at me, and then she was on top of me, pulling at my clothes and kissing me, and I kissed her back and bit her lip, hard, and she cried out and touched her lip, because I had drawn blood, and then she pinned my arms to the pebbles above my head, which hurt, and she started undoing my jeans, which was difficult because they were heavy with seawater, and then finally, finally, I thought to myself, What the fuck am I doing? And I pushed her away so that she fell back on the stones. And I sat there next to her, panting, out of breath. She reached for the jacket that she'd left on the beach, pulled a packet of cigarettes out of the pocket and lit one. And I stood up, shaky, wondering whether to walk away.

She looked at me and started crying.

I started crying, too.

She shook her head and said, 'Why can't we make this work?'

'I don't know,' I said. 'I'm sorry.' And I ached with how much I still wanted her, despite everything, and how much I'd hurt her. It was all such a mess.

'Maybe we can move on from this,' she said, wiping her eyes with the back of her hand. 'Maybe, if we have some new rules, and you put our relationship first—'

But then I thought about how she'd called me a dirty fucking slut, and I thought about Virginie, and the way Sam had stopped me comforting Alice after her break-up, and the fact that she was jealous of everyone in my life, and how she didn't like it when I went swing dancing, and everything, everything else; and I thought about how I had behaved – how I had demanded that she change, how I had cheated on her, how I had laughed about her lifestyle with my friends, how I had become the worst version of myself – and the idea of starting again with new rules made me feel sick.

I shook my head and I said, 'I don't think we can. I don't think we can do it.'

'Don't say that,' she said. She was still crying. She held her arms out to me.

And I can't tell you how much I wanted to go to her and take back what I'd said, how much I wanted to go back in time to the night we met, when everything was new and exciting, unspoiled. It took so much willpower to shake my head instead, to take a step backwards.

Which was when she let out a roar of anger and love and frustration, and she lunged at me, and I was sure she was going to burn me with her cigarette, and I managed to step out of the way – and she stared at me, eyes wide, shaking her head, and said, 'I wasn't going to do that. I would never have done that,' but she looked scared, as though she didn't believe what she was saying herself.

And I turned, and I ran, faster than I knew I could, the sea crashing behind me like a ticking clock.

It took me a while to open the door to the cottage; my fingers were fumbling the key in my hurry to get away. I got in at last and grabbed my suitcase, so grateful we hadn't bothered unpacking. The rug in front of the fire was still rucked up from where we'd had sex earlier. I was shivering and soaking, but I didn't want to waste time changing. I left the keys on the coffee table and shut the door behind me.

My suitcase rattled on the cobblestones like a bell on a cat's collar, letting Sam know where I was, so I picked it up and limped up the hill towards a bus stop. There were no more buses to Axminster that night so I called a local minicab company and waited at the top of Silver Street for the taxi to collect me. I could feel my phone buzzing against my thigh. I ignored it. 'Come on,' I whispered. 'Come on.' And at last the cab arrived, and as the driver loaded my suitcase into the boot, I said, 'Thank you,' the words so loaded with gratitude that he seemed taken aback.

'What's happened to you, love?' said the driver, as I dripped onto his seat. 'Midnight swim, was it? In this weather? You'll catch your death!'

By the time the taxi pulled away, I had six missed calls from Sam, five texts and one voicemail: 'Julia, come back. I forgive you. I can't live without you, babes. If you don't come back, I'm going to do something stupid, I'm warning you. I think I'm going to hurt myself.'

I pressed the button at the top of my phone and as the screen turned black I closed my eyes. She didn't know where I was. Nobody knew where I was. I was free.

47. BACK

That feeling of freedom lasted for exactly as long as the train ride back to London. As we pulled into Waterloo, my heart sped up. I could see Sam everywhere.

Every station I passed on the Tube gave me a stab of sadness. Green Park reminded me of the time Sam and I had walked up Albemarle Street, looking at art in gallery windows and making snide comments about how much people were willing to pay for abstract sculpture. Leicester Square made me think of lazy Sundays in Chinatown: dim sum and hangovers and browsing in the bookshops on Charing Cross Road. We'd had sex in that dingy club in Kings Cross, and Jasper lived on Holloway Road, and by the time I got off at Manor House I was crying openly.

As I walked home I found myself hurrying towards the safety of the hazy orange pools cast by the streetlights. In the dark patches in between, I pictured Sam jumping out at me, carrying the knife she'd had in the Shard, and I allowed myself to imagine the smell of her Barbour jacket and the sound of her voice and the way her breath would feel on my skin as she wrestled me into her car, because that seemed the best defence against it actually happening.

And then I was home, and safe, and as I turned the key in the lock I forced myself to focus on reality: the smell of Turkish food, the sounds of cars and aeroplanes and Saturday night shouts in the street, the silence of the flat once I'd shut the door behind me.

The flat was empty. And I was alone. I turned on my phone. Eight more voicemails from Sam, increasingly high-pitched and desperate.

'I'm sorry! OK? Please, babes. Call me, OK?'

'You fucking bitch. I can't believe how fucking selfish you are.'

'I'm going to do it. I have pills. I'm going to do it.'

'I miss you so much, babes, already. I can't live without you.'

And on. And on. I couldn't bear to listen to them all.

So I texted her. An angrier message than I'd intended to send: *I'm sorry, but please stop contacting me. I can't deal with this any more.*

And then I deleted her number.

I called Alice next.

'Hello?'

'Alice,' I said, sinking to the floor, my back to the wall. 'Where are you?'

'Julia?'

'I'm so sorry.'

'I'm sorry too.'

'Are you coming home tonight?'

'Yes – are you OK?'

'No. I broke up with Sam,' I said, beginning to cry.

'Good,' she said. And then I heard her turn to someone and say, 'Julia's broken up with Sam.'

And I heard Dave's voice say, 'Thank fuck for that.'

'You're back together,' I said, still crying.

'Yes,' she said. 'Just – hold on. I'm coming home.'

'She knows where I live,' I said.

'She wouldn't dare turn up,' Alice said. 'We're coming right now. Dave's bringing his cricket bat just in case. Just hold on till I get there.'

*　　*　　*

So I sat there, jumping every time a car drove past, its lights sweeping the house like a torch beam. And then Alice was home – and Dave, with his cricket bat – and they made tea and wrapped me in a blanket like I'd been involved in some sort of natural disaster.

'Don't let me get back together with her,' I said, once I was safely on the sofa.

'We won't,' Alice said, putting her arm around me.

'I'm sorry for the way I was,' I said.

'Stop apologizing,' she said.

'Sam's scary,' I said.

'Not as scary as me,' Dave said, hoisting his cricket bat, trying to look macho, which made me laugh.

'I love you both,' I told them as Alice passed me a tissue.

'We love you too,' Alice said. 'We've got you back now, haven't we? We've got Julia back.'

But as I was lying in bed that night my phone lit up with a message. *You don't want to deal with ME any more???? Babes, you're delusional. I'm the one who's had to deal with YOU! You've cheated on me and ruined my life and now you're blaming me? You're a fucking psycho—*

I didn't read to the end. I deleted the message, and this time I blocked her number. But the part of the message I had read seemed to be burned into my retinas, visible when I closed my eyes like I'd stared at the sun too long. I lay awake for most of the night thinking, What if Sam was right?

48. RESIDUE

If Sam were telling this story, it would be about a promising queer artist, non-monogamous and proud, who fell hard for a girl she met in a club, even though the girl had only recently come out and everyone knows new lesbians are bad news. You'd hear how her prudish, uptight new girlfriend shamed her for her kinkiness, forced her to give up her lover and lifestyle. How the artist was willing to change everything to make her new girlfriend happy – even her art – and that in the end she hardly knew who she was any more. Her identity as a kinky, queer, poly artist was virtually erased and she was left with rock-bottom self-esteem. And then, despite everything, her girlfriend cheated on her and dumped her. It's not surprising she was driven almost to suicide.

Sam believes that narrative. So do her friends, I'm sure. But I prefer to focus on the opinions of the people I know and love. Alice and Dave. Owen, who gave me a high five and said, 'Can you please go out with my sister now?'

My mother, too. I went home to Oxford to tell her about the break-up, and to apologize for how awful I'd been over the previous few months.

She stood on the doorstep and didn't smile when she saw me.

'I'm so sorry,' I said.

She stood aside to let me in without saying anything.

We sat in my parents' kitchen, where everything is solid and unchanging – the old, scarred wooden table; the noticeboard, heavy with cards pinned up after every birthday and never taken down – and I made a pot of tea. I told her that I had broken up with Sam, and I apologized again, and I cried, and Mum softened at that, and said, 'Never speak to me like that again.'

'I won't,' I said.

She took my hand. 'Well done,' she said. 'It's very hard to end a controlling relationship.'

'It wasn't a controlling relationship—'

'It was, darling. I know what I'm talking about.' She told me about the man she'd been with before she met my father, a banker called Stuart, who had bought her coats and paid for cabs and told her what she could and couldn't wear. And who had stolen two grand from her account and then blamed it on her, shouting at her for being so bad with money.

'Sam wasn't *that* bad,' I said.

'Wasn't she?' Mum said. 'You were together for less than a year. You don't know what would have happened if you'd stayed longer. She was already making you doubt yourself, wasn't she?'

My mother, as usual, was right.

We were drinking our second cup of tea when the door opened. Dad walked in, followed by a thin teenage boy with purple hair.

'Oh! Julia!' said Dad, blustering into the kitchen and dumping a pile of books in front of me. 'This is Harry, from next door.'

'I'll put the kettle on,' said Mum.

Harry and I shook hands. He had a lovely gap between his front teeth. 'I've heard loads about you,' he said.

'And I've watched your channel,' I told him. 'I always do a smoky eye your way, now.'

He seemed very flattered.

'Harry's helping me film a new video for my channel!' said Dad.

'All about queer readings of Romantic fiction! I'm going to talk about the masturbating girl in Jane Austen, and whether there was something going on between Coleridge and Wordsworth.'

'Was there?' I asked.

'Probably not,' he admitted.

I gave him a hug.

'What's this for?' he said gruffly, patting me on the back.

I hung around for the filming, during which Dad referred to his 'lesbian daughter' several times on camera. Afterwards, Harry offered to screen the video for us in his family's entertainment centre, and we followed him up his newly tiled front path.

Mum gasped as Harry opened his front door. Almost all of the rooms in the house had been knocked through. 'It's so big,' she said.

'That's the idea,' said Dad. 'Nice, isn't it?'

Mum didn't reply, but when Harry tried to lead us downstairs, she veered off towards the kitchen. 'I just want a quick look at your bifold doors,' she said.

We found her gazing up at the cloudy sky through the glass panels of the side return. 'There's so much light!' She turned to Harry and said, 'Now tell me – do you know the name of your parents' builder?'

I never heard from Sam again, though a few times, in the weeks following the break-up, I picked up my work phone to silence on the other end, my heart racing as I said, 'Hello? Hello?' into the receiver, like the woman who dies at the beginning of horror movies. I knew she was doing OK, though. Polly told me – she texted to tell me I'd done the right thing breaking up with Sam. I cried as I read that message and I saved it to read again in case I ever felt weak.

Then there was the exhibition. I found out about it by accident

– I picked up a creased *Time Out* on the Tube one morning, and there, staring out at me from the art pages, looking sullen but successful, was Sam, at the private view of a group show at her new gallery. To the left of her head was the painting of her fist – and to the right was a painting of my naked body, in pinks and purples, my mouth open, my eyes afraid. The caption underneath read *Sam King with two of her paintings:* Identity *(left) and* Residue.

It hadn't occurred to me that she'd paint me again, now that we'd officially broken up. I'm not sure why – she'd painted everyone else she had ever shagged. And it hadn't occurred to me that her knowledge of my body would be a weapon she could use against me.

Alice and Dave made me feel better about the whole thing when I showed them the article that night.

'She's so fucking pretentious with her stupid bright colours and her wanky, obvious titles,' said Dave, pouring me a large glass of red wine.

'Yeah,' I said. 'Totally wanky and obvious.'

Alice took the copy of *Time Out* and peered at the photograph. 'That's quite a nice painting of you, actually,' she said. 'I've always been envious of your breasts.'

'Alice!' I said.

'What?' she said. 'They're very perky. Mine look like eyes, staring in opposite directions.'

'They don't. They're lovely,' I said.

'Oi,' said Dave. 'Since when have you two been intimately acquainted with each other's breasts?'

'Skinny dipping,' I said.

But I still see Sam in my dreams. Sometimes she's angry, her face a knot of rage. She shouts at me, and I wake with a jolt, as though I've been thrown forward suddenly. Sometimes she's kind to me, though; she's forgiven me for what I did, and we hug and make peace and wish each other well. Those are the worst dreams, the ones I wake from with an aching sense of loss, my face wet with tears.

It's hard to accept that you're the villain of someone else's story.

49. WOW

'Told you,' said Nicky, as soon as I arrived for my session.

'I really don't think therapists are supposed to say "I told you so,"' I said.

'I did, though, didn't I?' She opened her notebook and flicked back through the pages. 'Here,' she said, stopping on an entry and tapping it with her pen. '*Seventeenth of March. Advised Julia against entering into an open relationship with Sam.*'

'Well. Good for you.'

Nicky took that as a compliment and smiled. 'So,' she said. 'How do you feel now?'

'A bit empty.'

Nicky nodded again. 'She made you feel like you had a purpose, didn't she? But that was all an illusion, wasn't it?'

I nodded.

She reached for the tissues hopefully.

I shook my head.

She drew her hand away, disappointed.

'So,' she said, turning to a clean page in her notebook, 'what else is going on in your life, then?'

'I'm through to the assessment centre for the Fast Stream.'

'Interesting,' said Nicky, in a voice that suggested it wasn't.

'And Alice and Dave are engaged again.'

'I'm surprised he risked proposing a second time,' said Nicky.

'She proposed to him,' I said. 'They were eating calamari and she slipped one of them onto his finger.'

'That's disgusting,' said Nicky. She narrowed her eyes. 'There's something you're not telling me.'

'I got into the swing dance troupe—'

'No. You're seeing someone. Is it a man?'

'No!' I said.

'Oh, good,' said Nicky. 'Who is it, then? Ella?'

'No.'

'Don't tell me it's Jane.'

'If you'd just stop guessing, I'd be able to tell you. It's Owen's sister. We're meeting up next week.'

'Are you nervous?'

I thought about it. 'I am now,' I said.

Nicky shook her head. 'You were already nervous. I've just helped you realize it.'

'Well. Thank you very much.'

'You're welcome,' said Nicky. 'Where are you going for your first date?'

'Ice skating.'

She tutted. 'Such a cliché.'

Carys suggested meeting outside Broadgate ice rink (smaller and less touristy than Somerset House – a promising choice). She was wrapped up in a tartan scarf and one of those sheepskin-lined denim jackets that men with long hair used to wear in the Nineties. I felt silly and shy as I walked up to her, and we had a bit of an awkward 'One kiss on the cheek, or two?' moment, but once we got over that, things were easier. She spoke really quickly, and she had a throaty laugh, and she said, 'Wow,' whenever I told her something about myself, which made me feel like a much more interesting person than I actually am. She told me all about herself straight away – about her supper club (successful) and her relationship with her ex-girlfriend (not so successful) and her love of improv comedy. 'It's based on the philosophy that you should say yes to everything your improv partner suggests,' she told me. I loved that idea. I wanted to say yes to everything. Yes to moving on from Sam. Yes to having a job that didn't make me want to contract tonsillitis to get a week off work. Yes to dancing. Yes to Carys. Yes yes yes yes yes.

The good thing about skating is that there are lots of opportunities for hand-holding and falling on top of each other romantically. The bad thing about it is everything else. We spent a couple of hours clinging to the rail at the edge of the ice, watching 13-year-olds show off their triple axels in the middle, and when we couldn't take the crowds and the tinny Christmas music any more, we went to Shoreditch to find some food.

'What kind of food do you fancy?' I asked her as we walked down Brushfield Street, trying to adjust to our skate-free feet.

'You choose,' she said.

'OK,' I said, feeling an exciting sense of responsibility and power. 'There's a really good Sichuan restaurant down here.'

'Lead the way,' she said, so I did, walking on the traffic side of the street.

Carys and I were still seeing each other a couple of weeks later, so I asked her if she'd consider catering for Alice's anti-patriarchy-themed hen party. She said yes, and she came up with an entire menu inspired by the suffragette colours: beetroot carpaccio to start, mint and pea risotto for the main and panna cotta for dessert.

'You're so clever, Carys!' Alice said as we sat around Carys's dining table, studying the menu. 'But you know the suffragettes were actually quite problematic? I know intersectionality wasn't a thing in the Edwardian era, but they didn't campaign at all for working-class women, or women of colour—'

'Alice, mate,' called Cat from across the table, 'can you stop trying to be woke, for one night? Let's forget about politics and get trashed!'

Everyone cheered, 'Yeah!'

Alice leaned towards me and said, 'Did you hear that? Cat called me "woke"!'

Cat opened the bottle of champagne she'd brought and poured everyone a glass. She was obviously feeling more flush than usual – probably because she had just found out that *Menstruation: the Musical* was transferring to Soho Theatre for a month-long run. She took a sip of champagne through her willy straw, and asked, 'What's your wedding dress like?'

'Black,' Alice said happily.

Samira, Alice's best friend from school, said, 'I'm guessing your dad isn't walking you down the aisle then?' Samira was a bit more traditional than the rest of us – she was responsible for the willy straws.

'No. Julia's walking me,' said Alice, quite proudly, I thought. 'And Dave's walking down with his brother.'

'And you're not taking his name,' said Samira.

'He's thinking of taking mine,' said Alice.

'That's so romantic!' said Carys.

'Dave's surname is Pratt, though,' I pointed out, 'so he has a bit of an ulterior motive.'

The champagne didn't last long – we moved on to prosecco, then red wine, and we were pretty wasted by the time we'd finished eating. Once we had cleared the table, Samira handed everyone a lump of Plasticine, and we had a penis-making competition. Alice judged our entries. There were a real variety of sizes and shapes. Cat's won first prize – it was horribly lifelike, complete with veins and foreskin. Carys's was the biggest, but also the least realistic.

'I hate to say this,' Alice said, examining it, 'but I think this one comes in last place.'

Carys looked quite disappointed. 'It's too smooth, isn't it?'

Alice nodded. 'And there are no balls.'

'Carys is a gold-star lesbian, though,' I said, putting my arm around her. 'So she's at a bit of a disadvantage.'

I stayed behind after everyone had left to help Carys clear up.

'So,' I said, as soon as we were alone.

'So,' she said back.

'Shall we leave the washing-up till the morning?' I said.

'Good idea,' she said.

And I pushed her back onto the sofa.

Our teeth clashed the first time we kissed, but we laughed and kept kissing anyway. 'Let's go to the bedroom,' she said.

I undressed her first. I'm proud of that. And then she pushed me back on the bed and undressed me.

'What do you want me to do?' she asked me.

'Fuck me,' I said.

'Fingers?'

'Lots of them.'

I was worried she wouldn't be as good as Sam – that my run of good lesbian sex couldn't last forever, and that she'd be half-hearted and a bit too fond of licking. But she wasn't. She fucked me slowly, deeply, and the fairy lights around her walls danced as the bed moved, and I closed my eyes as I came, and she laughed as she looked down at me, and I said, 'What?' and she said, 'You're just really fit' – and then we tried to 69, but neither of us could reach properly, so I fucked her from behind, and she shouted, 'Wow!' as she came, and we both laughed again and collapsed in a heap on the mattress.

'I've never really had funny sex before,' I told her afterwards, as we made ourselves toast in the kitchen. 'Good funny, I mean.'

'What's the point of sex if you can't laugh about it?' Carys said, passing me the butter. 'Here. I'm going to put cinnamon and sugar on mine. Want some?'

'Definitely,' I said.

We closed our eyes as we ate it.

'This tastes like New York City,' I said, crunching my toast. 'I'm pretending I'm eating cinnamon toast for breakfast in my Brooklyn brownstone.'

'I'm not,' she said, and she smiled. 'I don't want to pretend I'm anywhere else when I'm with you.'

50. CHRISTMAS SPECTACULAR

I was so busy in December, I didn't have time to watch one straight-to-Netflix Christmas movie. I didn't even have time to feel maudlin when I heard Tchaikovsky's *Nutcracker* playing over the speakers in John Lewis, even though it usually reminds me of the end of my dance career and sends me into a weeping, doughnut-eating self-pity spiral. When I wasn't at work, I was either preparing for the Fast Stream assessment centre, or teaching the beginners' swing dance class, or – best of all – rehearsing for the Friends of Dorothy Christmas Spectacular, which was running for three nights at the Leicester Square theatre. Except that wasn't really best of all, because on Saturday nights and Sunday mornings, Carys and I would hang out and eat delicious croissants and have excellent sex.

Carys and Cat came along to the first night of the Christmas Spectacular. We performed a penguin-inspired Charleston to 'Happy Feet', followed by a tricky routine to 'Singin' in the Rain', which required us to twirl red-and-green umbrellas. My umbrella wouldn't open properly, but I was standing near the back, so it probably didn't matter. After the final number, 'I Saw Daddy Kissing Santa Claus', the audience gave us a standing ovation. I stood there, bowing and blinking in the stage lights, smiling and smiling. I caught sight of Cat in the audience, and she was crying, and I cried too, until Zhu whispered to me to pull myself together.

Once we were back in the dressing room – it was so exciting to have a dressing room, with lights around the mirrors – Zhu slipped me a £50 note.

'What's this for?' I asked.

'Your share of the ticket sales,' she said.

I held the note tight. I had done it. I was a professional dancer again.

I moved in with Cat just before Christmas, to a two-bedroom house (an actual house, with our own front door) in Highams Park. We persuaded our friends to come round for a pre-Christmas dinner, despite the terrible transport links. Everyone brought a bottle of wine and we drank them all, which was probably why Bo ended up running naked around the block at two in the morning, screaming 'Gender is a construct!'

After we'd pulled the crackers and eaten the turkey, we all gathered around the television for the soon-to-be-traditional screening of Cat's German supermarket commercial. Lush strings played as she carried a plate of food to the table.

'Bit phallic,' Ella said, as on-screen Cat closed her eyes and bit into a bratwurst.

'Kind of sexy, actually,' said Zhu, and she reached out for Ella's hand.

On screen Cat smiled at everyone Germanly while a deep-voiced woman said something we couldn't understand, probably about what good value the sausages were.

Everyone cheered.

On actual Christmas Day, I arrived home to find my mother in the kitchen, dressed as Lizzy Bennet, looking over some sort of blueprint with Dad (Frankenstein's monster). I could hear my aunts and uncles in the living room, arguing about which of my cousins made the most convincing Hermione Granger.

I put my bag down and hung the empty picture frame I was carrying around my neck to complete my costume (Griet from *Girl with a Pearl Earring*). 'What's going on?' I asked.

'Just looking at plans for the building work,' she said.

I stared at her, amazed. 'You're not,' I said.

'We are,' said Dad. 'She's come to her senses.'

'I have *not* come to my senses,' Mum said. 'We are *not* having an entertainment centre. We're having a tasteful kitchen extension, that's all. With French windows. And underfloor heating. And maybe a side return. And while we're at it, we might as well see about getting the loft done.' She smiled. 'We're going to give the neighbours a taste of their own medicine.' She picked up a bowl full of crisps from the table and held it out to me. 'They're champagne and prosciutto flavour. Revolting, but moreish!'

51. IT'LL PASS

One Sunday morning in February, Cat told Carys and me that she hadn't had sex for six months. She didn't so much tell us as shout it, really – it came somewhere in the middle of a monologue about how we had to stop having loud sex at three in the morning. We were eating bagels at the time, and I almost choked on a piece of smoked salmon.

'You literally woke me up,' she said. 'Right in the middle of a sexy dream.'

'Who were you dreaming about?' Carys asked.

'I don't fucking know,' Cat said. 'I have sexy dreams about fucking everyone at the moment, I'm fucking desperate!' Which is when she told us, about the six months.

'Wow,' said Carys.

'Don't worry,' I said. 'It's just a dry patch. It'll pass.'

'Don't be so fucking patronizing,' said Cat. She'd accused me of being patronizing several times since I'd got into the Fast Stream, which wasn't really fair, as I hadn't actually been that smug about it. I was going to be an HEO (D) (The D stands for Development!) in the Department for Digital, Culture, Media and Sport. I hadn't even started yet and she was already lobbying me about arts funding for regional theatres.

Carys and I thought it might be a good idea to get out of London for the day. I was teaching swing dance at Eric's old care home that morning anyway, and there was a queer arts festival on in Brighton, so Carys came up to join me for the afternoon.

She went to a life-drawing class while I was teaching, and at lunchtime we watched a drag-king improv team perform a twenty-minute set inspired by the word 'cabbage'. We considered going to a poetry jam after that, but Carys said she wouldn't be able to watch performance poetry with a straight face, so I took her to visit Eric's spot at the garden of remembrance instead.

I put a bunch of tulips on the grass in front of his rose bush, and introduced Carys to him, but silently, so she wouldn't think I was mad. 'This is my new dance partner,' I said, in my head. The sun came out from behind a cloud after that, so maybe he was listening.

As the sun set, we walked arm in arm along the seafront, towards the burned-out West Pier, looking for the hotel where Oscar Wilde had once stayed with Bosie. We were talking about what to have for dinner – sausages, maybe, or chilli con carne – when I noticed someone walking towards us, pushing a bike. Someone tall, and dark-haired, and golden skinned.

She wasn't as beautiful as I remembered. Maybe that's because she had such an ugly look of hate in her eyes. She called after me, 'Fucking hypocrite!' and Carys turned to challenge her, but I said, 'Just leave it,' and we walked on, past the crouching, spidery remains of the old pier.

'I can really see what you saw in her,' Carys said.

'She wasn't quite that sweary when we were together,' I said. I liked that I could joke about it; I didn't want Carys to think I still cared about Sam. But of course I did – less than six months ago she and I had been the ones in love, walking arm in arm along a beach, full of hope and fish and chips. I wanted to call out to her, to tell her how sorry I was, and for her to apologize to me. But I knew there was nothing I could say to make things better.

So we kept walking along the seafront — but I still felt dirty and guilty and full of adrenaline, and I wanted to do something stupid, so I stopped in the middle of the concrete walkway and said, 'Let's go in the sea!'

'No,' said Carys.

But I don't like people telling me what I can and can't do these days, so I started rolling up my jeans.

'It's the middle of winter,' said Carys.

'The sea's warmer in winter,' I said. 'I'm not going to swim. I just want to get my feet wet.'

'You should keep your shoes on till the last minute,' said Carys, but I didn't listen, and I ran towards the water saying, 'Ow, ow, ow,' as the pebbles bit into my feet.

I stopped at the water's edge and turned to see if Carys was behind me. And she was, pelting down the beach towards the sea.

I yelped — I didn't want her to beat me to it — and ran into the water, up to my ankles.

The sea was freezing and exhilarating, and it stopped me thinking about Sam, and we kissed and laughed and splashed each other. And then we ran back up the beach, because we couldn't feel our toes any more.

We dried our feet with our socks and pulled our shoes back on, our skin sticky with saltwater. And then we turned away from the sea and walked to the butcher to buy sausages — two extra for Cat, to make up for the loud sex — as if it were an ordinary day.

Acknowledgements

I've been writing this novel for a very long time, so please excuse this Oscars-acceptance-speech-style acknowledgements page.

Thank you first of all to Judith Murray, the very best of agents and women. I am so very grateful to you for everything. Here's to a future full of cocktails, salty rimmed and otherwise. Thank you also to Kate Rizzo for finding such excellent publishers in other countries, and to the rest of the team at Greene & Heaton, especially Eleanor Teasdale, Rose Coyle, Holly Faulks, Alisa Ahmed and Imogen Morrell. Thank you to Sally Wofford-Girand for finding *In at the Deep End* the perfect home across the Atlantic, and to Emily Hickman, my brilliant film and TV agent.

Thank you to the amazing Suzie Dooré for believing in this book and for being funnier than me and a delightful person as well as a brilliant editor. Thanks to everyone else at The Borough Press, particularly Ore Agbaje-Williams, Micaela Alcaino, Emilie Chambeyron and Fleur Clarke.

Thank you to the wonderful Lauren Wein for being such an insightful editor and the best champion I could have hoped for in the States. Thanks to Pilar Garcia-Brown, Liz Anderson, Larry Cooper, Hannah Harlow, Christopher Moisan, Taryn Roeder and everyone else at Houghton Mifflin Harcourt.

Thank you so much to my other editors, Jasmin Duering, Erika Degard, Jacqueline Smit and Iina Tikanoja.

Lots of people gave me notes on my book and advice of all kinds. Thank you to Linas Alsenas, Grant Foster, Nina Gold, Annalie Grainger, Rachel Hewitt, Hanna Johnson, Eishar Kaur, Laura Macdougall, Jack Noel, Helen Thomas, Piers Torday and Jo Wickham.

Thank you to Marcia Williams and Rufus Williams for all the inspirational weekends in Lyme Regis.

Thanks to all the people who have written with me over the years, especially Michael Bedo, Katie Cotton, Ellie Farrell, Mo Oldham, Alice Sanders and the Walker Books Write Club.

Thanks to the Black Dog in Vauxhall (great coffee), the Breakout Café on Caledonian Road (amazing porridge), the Southbank Centre members' bar, the British Library, the London Library and the Arvon Clockhouse retreat. Thank you to Karen McLeod's creative writing course at The Bookseller Crow, Ways into Screenwriting and Stand-up Comedy at City Lit, Chris Head's sitcom writing class, Monkey Toast and Free Association improv classes and the Alphabetties.

Thanks to my friends, especially Naomi Baars, Laura Barnicoat, Michelle Erodotou, Flo Bullough, Jamie Gabbarelli, Steffi Hunt, Cath Hunter, Rachel Jones, Nic Knight, Alexia Korberg, Rachel Korberg, Kirsty Malone, Luke Massey, Aurelie Marion, Marina McIntyre, Charlie Moyler, Anna Nagy, Hannah O'Sullivan, Albi Owen, Lynton Pepper, Amy Perkins, David Perry, Jenny Prytherch, Nick Sharp, Debbie So, Ying Staton, Will Tosh, Louie Stowell and Zoe Vanderwolk.

Thank you to my family and the Campbell and Fitzpatrick families. Sorry about all the sex scenes.

Thanks most of all to Sarah Courtauld and Zanna Davidson, fellow members of the embarrassingly named Sacred Circle. I wouldn't be a writer without you. We vow.

And thank you to my incredible wife Victoria, who always believed I could write, even though she had no proof because I refused to show her my work for years. This book is for you.